VOID FORGED

VOID FORGED

VICTOR OF TUCSON ✢ BOOK TEN

PLUM PARROT

Podium

Published in 2026 by Podium Publishing
www.podiumentertainment.com

Podium

VOID FORGED

1

ONWARD TO BANDIA

When Victor stepped through the portal into the palace at Gloria, a dozen soldiers lowered polearms in his direction, though when their captain saw it was Victor, he quickly barked, "Stand at ease!"

Victor nodded to the man, tugging at the lapels on the brocaded uniform jacket he'd put on for the visit. It was part of his official attire as Gloria's champion, and he never wore it when he was at Iron Mountain. Since the queen had returned to her palace, though, she'd been more of a stickler about formality.

This was his third visit since she'd moved back into the renovated capital, and nearly a month had passed since the previous one. Victor had an idea about why he'd been summoned; Bryn had come to him just the day before with rumors that Kynna had finally cornered Queen Madge Hajarnen of Bandia into accepting a duel—the first Victor would have to fight since defeating Trinnie Ro almost four months ago.

As he walked, nodding to the guards and royal staff he passed by, Victor couldn't help feeling a little dread at the thought of another duel. It wasn't that he was afraid. No, it was more the opposite; Victor didn't want to be pitted against someone he could easily dominate. The three kingdoms between Gloria's expanding borders and Bandia had all bent the knee to Kynna, folding after only a little pressure—a result of Victor's hard-fought triumph over Trinnie Ro. They simply didn't have a champion in Victor's league.

The same could be said about Bandia, from what Victor had learned in his intelligence dossiers, but Kynna wouldn't *allow* Bandia to bend the knee, not without death for their queen and banishment for the royal family. Kynna had come to believe in her accusation that Madge had been behind Thorn's betrayal, and she wouldn't let her rival walk away from the situation with her life. Of course, that put Victor in the position of having to fight whatever champion Madge could come up with.

When he arrived at the queen's study, the two Queen's Guards stationed there saluted sharply, and one of them opened the door wide, announcing, "Your Majesty, I present His Grace, the Duke of Iron Mountain."

Victor nodded to the woman—a familiar face, but he'd never learned her name—and stepped through the door. Kynna sat, regal as always, behind her enormous polished desk, the cherry-colored wood luminescent in the light streaming through the blue-and-white stained glass windows. Kynna's crystal crown reflected that light and seemed to gather it, creating a sparkling halo effect between its tall peaks. Her lips smiled when she looked at Victor, but her blazing, fiery eyes were intense, and no humor marred the angle of her brow. "Thank you for coming right away. Please sit."

"Your Majesty." Victor bowed and then did as she'd asked, sitting in one of the high-backed chairs before her desk. Things had been more stilted between them lately. He figured it had started when he'd implicitly rejected her advances after his win with Trinnie Ro. It didn't help that the queen felt some guilt about that duel—she'd received very favorable terms for not contesting Lovania's sudden acquisition of a steel seeker champion from the eastern continent. In her mind, she'd put Victor's life at unnecessary risk, though he'd assured her that he was up for it.

"Let's dispense with formalities for the moment, shall we? How are things at Iron Mountain, Victor?"

"Things are . . . *peaceful*, I guess, is the best way to put it. The Haveshi clan do most of my job for me, so I'm left to my own devices."

Kynna smiled and nodded. "It was wise of you to employ them in the management of your duchy."

Victor snorted, shaking his head. "You were the wise one. I just followed your lead."

"You're kind to mention it. So, tell me about them, these 'devices' of yours. What have you done with the months since you were last called to do battle?"

"I'm pretty sure you know. You hired half the personnel in my palace."

Kynna's smile faltered a little, maybe turning a bit more toward chagrined, and she tapped her nails on the desk as she admitted, "More than half, I'd wager."

Victor smirked, mimicking her by drumming his fingers on the arms of his chair. "So, wouldn't it be easier if you just asked me what you want to know?"

"Hmm." She leaned back in her chair, the leather squeaking slightly as it compressed. "Tell me about the project you have the Artificer Trobban occupied with. My people tell me he's taken over the western ballroom of your palace and that no one is allowed in and out."

"You don't know any more than that?"

"Only that you have guards watching over him around the clock, and rumor has it that he's working with materials valuable enough to warrant new magical wards being engraved on every wall and even the ceiling."

Victor didn't want to lie to Kynna, but he also wanted to protect Arona's secrets. If he were honest, he'd admit that he thought Kynna knew more than she was letting on, that there was no way Trobban's activities could have been thoroughly hidden. That being the case, he knew honesty would be the best road forward. "I hired Trobban to create a new vessel for a friend of mine, one who had her body destroyed in a dungeon."

"Her spirit is intact?"

"Yeah. She had a phylactery."

"Ah." Kynna frowned, distaste clear on her face. "A Death Caster. I hope you haven't—"

"She *was* a Death Caster. That's going to change when her new vessel is complete."

"Ah! A change of affinity? Yes, the materials your Artificer is working with must be potent, indeed. So." Once again, her nails drummed on her desk. "Need I worry that this 'friend' of yours will distract you when your project is finished?"

"I'm not sure what you're suggesting," Victor sighed, "but no. If anything, I'll be able to focus on my duties more easily, knowing I have an ally close at hand."

"Very well. You'll tell me nothing more about her?"

"What more can I tell you? She's a friend, and she needs a new vessel. It was a project I took on before coming here, so I felt duty-bound to complete it. She's not going to cause any trouble for you."

"Isn't that what you said about your *other* ally? The one who mysteriously appeared at Iron Mountain without using the teleportation network?"

"Kynna, what are you fishing for? I introduced you to Tes the day after her arrival. She's been at Iron Mountain the entire time since, and she's been nothing but helpful. She's *training* me. You should be grateful to her, not suspicious."

The queen folded her arms over her chest, causing the pearl-studded embroidery on her sleeves to shine and glitter in the sunlight that shone through her high windows. "You certainly have a way of surrounding yourself with interesting, potent women."

Victor's mouth partially opened, but he stopped short of asking her if she was jealous. He was beginning to think that was *exactly* what the issue was, and he didn't want to upset her by calling her out, not directly—that wasn't how things were done on Ruhn. Instead, he tried to placate her. "Kynna, your words are true, and no, I don't know why, but I've always had more female friends than male. I'm lucky to have you and Bryn—strong women I can confide in—but I'm reasonably good friends with Draj and Feist and Florent.

I've spent many long hours with Trobban as he worked on his project, learning from him as he went."

"And Tes? She's not steering you away from my ancestor's plan?"

"What? No, Kynna! She's just being a good friend, trying to help me prepare for the champions I'll face when we start challenging the great houses. She's smart, and her advice is objective—she doesn't have a dog in this fight."

"A dog in—"

Victor waved his hand, shaking his head. "Never mind. That's a saying from my homeworld and one I've never used before—no idea where I dredged it up from. All I'm saying is that she's not part of the political machinations on Ruhn; it's been good for my mental state to have her to talk to. She's simply a friend." He shrugged, deciding not to elaborate further—better to let Kynna fill in the blanks.

"Thank you, Victor, for being willing to share that with me. I'm your queen here on Ruhn, but I know better than to consider you a simple subject. I know, especially with a friend like Tes, who seems able to travel between worlds without using the System Stones, that you could leave me and all my problems behind. I suppose it's simple insecurity that has me making such personal inquiries."

"I made you a promise, and before that, I made one to your ancestor. I'm not someone who would back out of obligations like that."

Kynna inclined her head, the light glittering in her crown dazzling Victor as it reflected on the walls of her study. "Understood. Shall we speak about why I called you here? Shall I confess yet another reason for you to hate me?"

"What? Kynna, I don't hate you!"

She smiled wryly, the right side of her mouth higher than the left as she shook her head and clicked her tongue. "Perhaps you don't, but you've reason to. I'm not proud of the negotiations I made before your duel with Trinnie Ro. Now, I have an opportunity to advance our cause, but it, once again, comes at your expense. Will you hear it?"

"Have you agreed to it yet?"

"No." She shook her head. "Nor will I, should you refuse."

"Then there's nothing for me to be upset about. Stop being so hard on yourself. Kynna, you're a queen. Your people are your main priority. I don't think the deal you made before my last duel was unfair. Didn't I tell you that I could win that fight?"

"It's not a matter of whether I was *right*, Victor. No, the issue is with how I *felt* when I made those negotiations. I *knew* what the great houses were doing. I knew why Trinnie Ro was suddenly willing to fight for an insignificant kingdom thousands of miles from the center of the empire. Trinnie Ro was manipulated,

I was manipulated, and in turn, I manipulated you. I *knew* you would agree to the fight! Have you ever backed down from one?"

"Um . . ." Victor couldn't remember doing so.

"So, I used you. Whether I was right to do so matters not to me. Victor, as a queen, I've had to study philosophy and ethics. Most rulers follow a simple dictum: What benefits the most people in their care is the correct choice. My father ruled differently. He believed that every individual was inviolable. Do you know what that means?"

Victor frowned. "That he wouldn't use a person for something."

"Precisely. In his mind—and he credited the philosopher Surnass for this— no man or woman should be used for a purpose that wouldn't align with their own free will. Most rulers would say, 'One man to save a thousand is a good trade.' My father believed in absolutes, however, and he believed that there was no situation in which even a single person should be used as a tool, no matter the benefit to the nation."

"Sounds like he was a man I'd like to follow, but it also sounds like it would be hard to stick by those words when push came to shove—as a king, I mean."

"I learned that lesson very pointedly when I chose to allow you to fight Trinnie Ro with no preparation and without *trying* to void her placement as Lovania's champion. I fully expected you to die, and regardless of your assurances, I cannot allow myself to accept what I did lightly."

"Fair enough, Kynna, but just so you know, I'm not holding a grudge about it." Victor shrugged. He thought her father's philosophy was admirable, but he also understood perfectly well the pressures Kynna had felt.

"Thank you, Victor. However, that brings me to our current situation."

"Which is?"

Kynna stood from her chair and approached her tall, multi-paned windows. The panes in the center weren't stained glass and provided a clear view of her rebuilt palace gardens. Victor stayed in his seat, watching her, and after a few moments, she began to speak. "This situation has much to do with Trinnie Ro, so it's appropriate that we began this discussion with a reminder of what I did prior to that duel."

"Yeah?"

She turned to face him. "Yes. You see, the reason you haven't had to fight since that duel is because Trinnie Ro obviously outclassed the champions on the western continent—all of them. When you beat her, it sent a message to our neighbors: to stand against Gloria is to court death. So, we've annexed three more kingdoms, and now we surround and harass Bandia, the seat of Thorn's cousin, Madge."

"I'm aware." Victor folded his arms, waiting for the other shoe to drop.

"She's tried to sue for peace already, but she knows I won't let her remain in power, so she stops short of offering a full surrender. Now I have her surrounded on all sides save one: the east, where her country has two hundred miles of coastline. You know Gloria was besieged by Xan and Frostmarch, but we still held out for nearly six years."

"So you're saying it could be a while before Bandia is suffering enough that the people force the duel?"

"Exactly. Of course, I'd try to speed things along with statecraft and other pressures—buying the loyalty of her nobles and the like—but yes, she could hold out for years, perhaps decades."

"*But . . .*" Victor was still waiting for her to get to the point.

"But she's come to me with an offer. She'll accept a duel on two conditions: I must agree to allow banishment for her and her kin, and she insists that no champion in her stable can stand against you, so she offers a choice."

Victor sighed, unfolding his arms. "Are you going to make me beg to hear it?"

"She will agree to the duel if you don't participate—I can choose another champion from my stable—or if we allow her to field *two* champions against you." Maybe Victor didn't react as she'd expected, because her eyes narrowed in consternation when he simply nodded, frowning thoughtfully. "Have you nothing to say?"

"Is that allowed? I mean, will the veil walkers let me fight two champions at once?"

"*Unbelievable!*" Kynna clicked her tongue again and turned back to the window. "I should have guessed you wouldn't back down, and here I am again—some part of me knew you wouldn't. So, do I use your foolish pride to get my way, or do I refuse, regardless of your willingness?"

"Is it allowed?" Victor asked again.

"There is precedent, yes. Similar accommodations have been offered on more than one occasion to coax a lesser kingdom into accepting a challenge."

"And any idea the ranks of Bandia's champions? Do I need to worry about the great houses sending more ringers down here?"

"I inquired with the Council of Oversight and received assurances from Grand Judicator Lohanse that no changes have been made to Bandia's roster. He also indicated that if it happens after we agree to the two versus one duel, he would invalidate the agreement and force new negotiations."

Victor smiled and stood up. "So, any idea who I'll be facing?"

"Two iron rankers, Victor. Should I infer that you are willing, then?"

"I'm willing. I don't want to wait decades, Kynna. We need to keep this ball rolling."

"Well." Victor saw resignation in her eyes—resignation and guilt. He didn't know how else to reassure her, and he didn't think anything he said would matter. She was struggling with her inner demons and the expectations of a father who was no longer there to temper his past words. She'd weigh whatever Victor said against her father's tutelage, and Victor was pretty sure his words would come up lacking. After a long moment, she nodded. "I will have my people send dossiers to Bryn."

"Was there anything else?" Victor wasn't trying to be rude, but he also wasn't enjoying the queen's stuffy, formal behavior or her constant attempts to make him see her behavior as a betrayal when he didn't think it was.

"I've had reports that the great houses are increasingly suspicious of me. After we take Bandia, assuming you win, I will no longer have an excuse for expansion. Already, Gloria holds the largest economy on the western continent. By land, we're the third largest, and with your display against Trinnie Ro, you're ranked as the top champion. We've begun to look like a threat to the great houses. Once I declare a challenge against one of the eastern kingdoms, I won't be able to disguise my intention to start a war of succession."

"Which will mean what? More assassination attempts?"

"Yes, from the great houses. They'll attempt to put us down before we can engage them in a challenge. We have eight nations to get through before challenging the closest great house, Voth. That said, I'll want you close if we win our fight against Bandia."

Victor nodded. "Makes sense. Should I move back here?"

Kynna reached up to tap her crown, and it rang like a chime as a shield of blue Energy surrounded them. "My study is warded, of course, but a little extra caution makes me feel more at ease." She stepped closer to him, and Victor noticed her fingers nervously worrying at the fabric of her wide cuffs. "I think Iron Mountain is more secure than this palace. I have too many cousins whom I don't trust living here. I will make the move, but I won't announce it. We can coordinate the first strike against the eastern continent from your palace."

"Will they accept the duel? It seems like it would be hard to put pressure on a kingdom across an ocean."

"We'll have to choose a strong kingdom—a ruler with great hubris and a likewise-minded champion. We'll seek a king or queen who will be confident enough to take the risk in order to snatch up all that we've built. You can rest assured that they'll be aided by the great houses, so the champion you face after Bandia will be deadly."

"I figured." Victor shrugged.

Kynna's eyes narrowed in consternation, but she didn't object. She gestured to the door, and though the flick of her fingers was dismissive, her tone was almost mournful as she said, "I've nothing more for you at this time, then. I can find no fault with your willingness to fight, Champion."

Victor wanted to comfort her—to try to make sense of the impossible standard she was holding herself to, but on the other hand, he thought it was good that they had some professional distance between them. Victor liked Kynna. He liked that she seemed to care so much that she tormented herself over decisions that would have been a snap judgment for most rulers. On the other hand, her moral philosophy was so strict that she seemed to be causing herself pain by simply making good, solid decisions for her nation.

All that said, when Victor's first impulse was to reach out and comfort her further, he stopped himself because he didn't want to send the wrong message. He wasn't sure he was the right person for anyone at that time in his life, let alone a queen with a guilty conscience. So he saluted sharply, snapping his heels together and pounding his fist against his chest. Then he bowed and turned to the door. Before he stepped through, he turned to face the queen, and, unable to ignore the pained look in her eyes, he said, "I'll be ready, Your Majesty. Honestly, I usually fight better against more than one enemy."

"I hope you're ready for the hero worship coming your way if you pull this off."

Victor stepped closer, putting himself back into the dome of her secrecy spell. "Do you mean the duel or the toppling of an empire?"

Kynna sighed, and Victor could see her fighting and losing the battle against the corners of her mouth as they turned upward in a small smile. "Both, you impossible braggart. Both."

2

VENTING

Victor flipped through the tome he'd come to think of as his "elder magic book," amazed at the progress he'd made in the last few months. Azforath's spell patterns and notes took up the first few pages, but the next nearly two hundred were filled with his notes from the texts Dar had given him and then his own patterns, pieces of patterns, and further notes on what he'd learned in his experiments and lessons with Tes. He only wrote something into his elder magic book when it was perfected after hundreds or thousands of iterations on loose pages that Victor was careful to destroy as he made improvements.

"Quite a lot of good work you've done. Yet . . ." Tes trailed off, letting Victor fill in the rest of the sentence—probably something like, "Yet you've not put any of those spells into practice." It was a regular discussion between them. Tes was certain the veil walkers overseeing Ruhn would take note if he started working elder magic, because the System would step in and issue a bunch of warnings, just as it had when he'd altered his spell for summoning his totems.

There wasn't anything *wrong* with doing so, not unless you worshipped the System as a deity, and that didn't appear to be prevalent on Ruhn and certainly not among the veil walkers. No, the concern was that the veil walkers who had hidden allegiances to the great houses might spy from a distance and report what they learned about Victor's talents to potential enemies. For the same reason, Victor refused to use abilities he'd yet to display in the arena when practicing. As much as it pained him, he'd even refused to try out his Flight of the Lava King.

"Yet secrecy is paramount, and you refuse to shield us from prying eyes." Victor cocked an eyebrow at Tes, wondering if she'd argue.

"I wouldn't be welcome on this world if they knew who I was, Victor. I can mask our conversations, but to block out the use of elder magic would be to tip my hand. Such a shielding would, in itself, be as much of a signal as if you employed your new spell patterns."

Victor snorted, closing his book with a *thud*. "Just making sure you remember why these are untested, because it felt an awful lot like you were judging me."

"I'm not! I'm simply . . . *complaining*. Can a woman not vent?"

"Nah, I get it. I'm frustrated, too. I almost hope I'm forced to use one of my new spells when I fight Bandia's champions. Then the cat will be out of the bag, and I can start practicing all of these." Again, he held the book up.

"Well, *that's* why I was teasing you ever so slightly. I feel as though experimenting with new spells in the middle of a fight has the potential for disaster. Better to practice now and let the cards fall where they may, if you ask me."

Victor sighed. This was what he'd been hoping to head off by reminding her why he was being cautious. They went round and round in circles like this every time the topic came up. The thing that worried him was that Tes didn't *always* take that side of the argument. Often, she'd be the one pressing for caution. Victor decided to give her a taste of her own medicine. "Yeah, you know what? You're right. I'm going to go ahead and try some of these new patterns out. Might as well get used to them."

"Victor—" Tes started but stopped, narrowing her eyes at him as he stood and walked toward the balcony.

"Yeah. Figure I'll test out these damn wings while I'm at it." Stepping out through the open door, he employed the strange, comfortable pathway that pulled Energy out of his Breath Core and into his feat—Flight of the Lava King. It was so natural and easy that Victor could almost believe he'd had the ability his entire life. He honestly couldn't remember what it had been like to *not* be able to do it. Such was the way with abilities his titanic bloodline allowed him to absorb; it was a part of him now.

As fire erupted from between his shoulder blades, Tes groaned, and he felt her magical veil spread to encompass the balcony, hiding his fiery, magma-dripping wings from prying eyes. Victor turned, careful not to burn the furniture on the balcony, and arched an eyebrow. "What?"

"I notice you called my bluff with an ability that won't draw the System's ire or signal the veil walkers."

Victor shrugged, pulling his Energy back and causing his wings to flicker and fade. The little pools of lava he'd created sizzled and popped, rapidly cooling on the cold marble tiles. He stepped back inside. "I just wish . . ." He trailed off, folding his arms over his chest, tired of rehashing the same frustrations over and over.

"You could be yourself? Free? Unfettered?" Tes stepped closer to him. She wore one of her breezy flowing knee-length dresses, this one layered in shades of pale pink and lavender. Like Victor, she didn't seem bothered by cold weather.

When she rested one of her slender pale hands on his wrist, an electric tingle ran through Victor, and he had to use every ounce of his prodigious will to keep his face neutral. "I play devil's advocate, but you know what I really think, don't you?"

"Yeah, of course. You agree with Dar and pretty much any military strategist ever: Keeping my capabilities obscured is better for my long-term survival."

"Yes. Now, regarding the upcoming challenge—do you really think you'll need one of the newer spell revisions we've been working on?"

"To beat a couple of iron rankers? I doubt it. I might need to play one of my other cards, though."

Tes squeezed his wrist and gave a quick, almost imperceptible nod. "And how are you feeling about all that? You haven't told me much about your conversation with the queen."

Victor sighed, shaking his head. "I'm fine. I'd rather fight two versus one than beat the shit out of one poor guy."

"That hubris is going to get you in trouble someday. Not all iron rankers, as the people in these parts call them, are created equal."

Victor nodded. "Yeah, I didn't mean it that way. I just don't like fighting people weaker than myself, and it sounds like that's going to happen."

Mischief entered Tes's eyes. "Would you like me to bind part of your potential?"

"Huh?"

"Just as your Energy and potential are reduced when you use the Alter Self spell to make yourself smaller, there are other ways to tie up that power. You can cancel your Alter Self, but if you allowed me to bind your power away, you'd be forced to make do with what you had." She slid her fingers away from his wrist to the meat of his forearm and firmly squeezed the muscle there. "Would you enjoy that?"

Victor looked into her eyes, sky blue in the current lighting, and narrowed his eyes. "Are you being serious?"

"Not really. I'd be beside myself with grief if you died trying to prove some kind of point—trying to hold yourself to a standard no one else adheres to."

"Yeah. I guess it would be dumb to risk everything just so I could feel less guilty about winning."

Tes's eyes glittered with amusement. "I've missed your brand of vernacular, though I feel you've improved your vocabulary significantly since Coloss."

Victor shifted, pulling away from Tes's touch. He was annoyed by both her teasing tone and her flirtation; she'd been clear on more than one occasion over the last few months that she wasn't there for romance. "What was funny about what I just said?"

"Oh, just the use of 'dumb' where anyone else I know would have said 'foolish.' There's a difference in connotation, you know?"

"Sure. You got my point, though, right?" Without waiting for an answer, Victor turned and walked back outside, leaning on the balcony as he looked out at the colorful forest carpeting the slopes of Iron Mountain. Fall had come to the duchy, and it was beautiful—broad swaths of red, orange, and yellow intermixed with the deep shades of the evergreens.

Tes came to stand beside him. "You're awfully broody."

"Just frustration, Tes. And no, I can't put it all into words. I think part of it boils down to irritation that people like the veil walkers of this world"—Victor waved a hand toward the gray sky as though the people he spoke of were floating around up there, literally watching over Ruhn—"have so much goddamn say in what I do or how I act. No matter how much I improve, how strong I get, there always seem to be more people like that, ready to exert some sort of control."

"And you feel I'm being just as bad?"

"No!" Victor turned to glower down at her. "I mean, yes, but not in the same way. I'm frustrated that you don't take me seriously." There—he'd said it. He *was* tired of Tes treating him like a kid brother.

"Oh, Victor," she sighed. "I take you seriously. I just care about you too much to let you think you're ready to stand against 'veil walkers' and their rules or their cheating schemes. I know I've yet to meet any of those looking over Ruhn, but I fail to believe that none have ties with the great houses. I *refuse* to believe it. Where people exist, you will find corruption."

"You always do that—say 'steel seeker' or 'veil walker' as though you're putting quotes around the terms. What do they call people like that on your world?"

"Aradnue or Luminaris?"

"Aradnue is the name of your homeworld, right? Where dragons live?"

"Yes, and Luminaris is the world where my order, the Celestial Envoys, make their home. Well, no need to choose, I can answer for both places. On Aradnue, we speak of dragons in their various stages of power in terms of maturity. A young or juvenile dragon would be equivalent to an 'iron ranker.' Because we don't accept the System on Aradnue, advancing requires knowledge and practice and the ability to harness Energy in the appropriate quantity. It would be rare for a juvenile dragon to climb into ranks that would be equivalent to that of a 'steel seeker,' so I would equate such with an adult dragon."

"And veil walkers?"

"Hmm. The ranges of power among adult dragons are vast. I'm considered an adult, but on this world or Sojourn, I could easily pass for a 'veil walker.' I'd say it's more a matter of learning at that point. Yes. On Aradnue, a 'veil walker' would be something like an adult dragon who had completed many years of journeyman studies and could be called a master of at least one art."

"Are there any higher ranks for dragons?"

Tes snorted, shaking her head in amusement. "Of course! Just as there is a great range in power among adult dragons, the elder or ancient dragons have a power structure of their own. Among the many thousands of such dragons on Aradnue, each would know where he or she stood in relation to the others. There's a hierarchy."

"Sounds a lot more complicated." Victor shrugged. "I mean, in a way, it's simpler, but there aren't any neat labels for people."

"And how well have labels served the people who sought to kill you?" Tes chuckled. "No, Victor, putting great numbers of people with disparate bloodlines, histories, training, minds, and imaginations into broad categories is a fool's errand."

"What about the other world—Luminaris?"

"You'd feel more at home there. It's not unlike Sojourn, though the world is larger and older and houses a hundred cities as great as the capital where your master lives."

"Don't call him—" Victor sighed, shaking his head. What was the use? Ranish Dar, for all intents and purposes, was his master. Wasn't he stuck on this world, frustrated and irritated, because of Ranish Dar's demands?

"I'm sorry. I won't do that." Again, Tes gripped his forearm, and Victor felt the tension melting out of his muscles. He could feel her touch resonating through his entire body, like an electric charge running through him, and though he loved it, he felt further frustration building. Even so, he didn't pull away again, and rather than snapping at her, he cleared his throat and tried to steer the conversation back to something interesting.

"Well? What do they call iron rankers there?"

"Knowledge is revered above all else on Luminaris. You can imagine, then, that their labels revolve around learning. When someone gains their first class on Luminaris, they become 'initiates.' As they advance to Tier Two, they become 'adepts,' at Tier Five, they earn the title of 'scholar,' and at Level Seventy-Five, they become 'sages.' When someone on Luminaris reaches Level One Hundred and begins to work on their custom class, they are known as 'architects.' Finally, their equivalent of 'veil walkers' are 'lore masters.' Clear enough?"

"The System is there? On Luminaris, I mean?"

"Yes, though many of the worlds in that part of the universe, like Aradnue, refuse the System access."

Since he had Tes in such a talkative mood, Victor decided to press his luck. "And? After 'lore master,' what is there?"

Tes grinned and squeezed his arm again, threatening to turn Victor's bones to jelly. "You're silly, you know that?"

"Come *on*, Tes! Just tell me this much—if I ever make it to steel seeker and then figure all that shit out and become a veil walker, am I going to learn that a whole other class of powerful *pendejos* is out there, waiting to remind me that I'm just a small fry again?"

Tes giggled and leaned against his shoulder. "I love it when you speak that way. I'll tell you this much—there aren't any veil walkers I know who could push around the titan sleeping under yonder mountain."

"So . . ." Victor frowned, feeling a trickle of rage seeping into his pathways. "So there *are* stages beyond veil walker!"

"Come, Victor! You've met more than one." Again, she nodded to the mountain, but then she surprised him. "And the pretty insect queen you met? What did you name her? Crystal?"

"When did you hear—"

"My first night here, silly! You should be careful when a dragon comes bearing alcohol."

Vague memories flashed through Victor's mind—Tes, red-faced and laughing; he bemoaning the state of his heart and his frustrating, recurring desire to drop everything and find Valla; and a hundred other, frankly, embarrassing moments. "Ah, yeah. Right."

"So," Tes said, sliding her hand down his forearm so she could entwine her fingers with his. "You've done a good job avoiding my earlier question."

"About?" Victor knew but wanted to make her ask.

"Your meeting with the queen. How are things there? She's awfully suspicious of me, or at least that was the impression I got at our one and only meeting."

Victor knew what she was fishing for; he'd *definitely* confessed his frustrations with Kynna's advances and his rather surly response to her. He'd been worried that the queen was angry with him, and he'd made the mistake of telling all of that to Tes—damn her potent liquor! "She's still a little cool with me, if that's what you mean. I'm pretty sure she thinks I've got something going with you or Bryn or even Arona."

Tes squeezed his hand. "So many options."

"My *friends* aren't options, Tes, they're people."

She let go of his hand and turned to face him, leaning sideways against the railing. "Oof! So serious! Should I leave you to brood?"

"Nah, I'll try to lighten up. I've got five days before the duel. I'm going to try not to think about it."

"Is that the right strategy?"

"Probably not, but I can't cast any of the new spells or refinements you and I have worked out—not without pissing off the System and getting a bunch of nosy veil walkers around here, so—"

Tes held up a hand, laughing. "Please! Let's not rehash that conversation. No, I might have another idea for you, though."

"What's that?"

"Well, it might get me into some trouble with the Celestial Envoys, but what if we took a small trip? What if I opened a gateway to that little world where you conquered the, um, what was it? Untamed—"

"You can *do* that?" Victor turned and grabbed her shoulders, eliciting a laugh from her.

"I *can*! I have a powerful artifact on loan from my order, but we have to ensure I'm not interfering in any worldly affairs by using it. It's just a visit, understood? We'll not steal away any rulers of Ruhn, and you'll return before your obligations to your queen, and when we go to Fanwath, you *mustn't* get involved in any politics. In fact, we shouldn't announce your arrival to your more . . . *influential* friends."

"Like Rellia?"

"Precisely. Let's go to your homestead and visit some of your loved ones and, while we're there—"

Victor snapped his fingers. "I can try out some of the elder magic we came up with!"

Tes's face was bright with pleasure, and Victor could see his excitement was making her happy. It reminded him that she didn't *owe* him anything, and he ought to act a little more grateful to her. "I'm sorry, Tes!" he blurted. "I'm sorry I've been venting to you. You know you're the only person here that I really trust, right?"

"How could I not? You've told me as much in a dozen different ways. Well? Shall we? You should arrange things with your people here and ensure you have a shared Far Scribe with—"

"I have one with Bryn and also Kynna."

"Go, then! Speak with Draj and Bryn; I'll gather my things." Tes had taken guest quarters beneath Victor's in the same tower, and she'd made herself at home, changing out the furnishings and decorating with her own art, knickknacks, and curios. Unlike Victor, she enjoyed seeing all of her jewelry and clothing, which meant her belongings were all over her suite and not neatly stored away in a container like most of Victor's. He only knew as much because Tes liked to cook and insisted he visit her quarters for lessons and meals several times a week.

Victor started for the door, suddenly full of purpose and excitement. "I'll talk to Arona, too. She'll want to stay with Trobban."

"We'll return the day before your duel, so we'll only be gone for four days. I doubt anyone will even notice."

"Yeah, but, as you said, we don't want people to worry."

"Wisely said, Your Grace," she teased, following him toward the door. "Come to my quarters when you're ready. I'll prepare the portal diagram."

3

HOME AGAIN

Victor found Bryn on the southern parade grounds outside his palace. Since Tes had arrived at Iron Mountain, he'd given his loyal guardian more free time—no need for anyone to stand watch at his tower when a dragon was nearby at all hours of the day. Of course, he hadn't said as much to Bryn and her squire, Feist. He'd described Tes as an old friend, a formidable ally, and a tutor in the magic arts. And though Bryn had been reluctant, Victor was the duke—what could she do? When he walked onto the practice field, Bryn, in the midst of combat drills with Feist, threw her squire to the ground and jogged over to him. "Is all well?"

Victor chuckled, shaking his head as he watched Feist struggle to a sitting position and then, upon seeing Victor, flop back onto the hard, yellowing grass, no doubt capitalizing on the extra rest period. "Everything's fine. I'm going to need you to stay on top of things for me around here for a few days, however."

"You're going somewhere?"

"Yes. Tes and I are leaving to conduct some training where we won't have to worry about prying eyes."

"You have a duel in just—"

"Five days. I know." Victor smiled and clapped her on the shoulder. "Can you keep things running smoothly around here for me? Send me a note every day with an update? I'll reply so you know I haven't disappeared or died or something worse."

"Something worse?"

Victor laughed, folding his arms as he inhaled deeply, looking farther out on the field where some of his household guards were working on team drills. He didn't know any of them very well, but he'd come to learn many of their names. "I'm just messing around."

"What about Lord Draj?"

"He's aware. He'll manage the day-to-day business, as usual, but I need you to keep an eye on things. I trust you more, understand?"

Bryn straightened up, her spine stiffening as she nodded. "I understand."

"How's your work with the glaive going?"

"Excellently! It's a wonderful weapon, Your Grace! I can't begin to thank—"

Victor waved a hand. "No more of that, Bryn! You've earned it. Will you keep an eye on Trobban for me, too?"

She nodded. "As always."

"All right. I'm off, then. Look for my first message tonight; I'll let you know we've arrived safely."

As he began to turn back to the palace, she asked, "Does anyone know where you're going?"

"No." He turned back toward her and sighed heavily. "I'd tell you, Bryn, but I feel like I'm always being watched. You know how veil walkers can be."

"They're bound by oaths to remain neutral in all matters—"

"Right. Yeah, I know, but let's just call me paranoid and leave it at that. I'll message you in a few hours."

Bryn saluted before he could turn, so Victor felt compelled to salute her back. With a final nod, he returned to the palace and made his way back to his tower. Inside his little magical elevator, he selected the floor beneath his suite and waited as it hummed its way upward. He yearned for the day when he could openly fly with his fiery wings. He could have soared up to Tes's balcony instead of walking through the tower and suffering through the elevator's relatively sedate pace.

Finally, it halted, and the brass doors parted to reveal the little antechamber before Tes's rooms. He walked to her door, slightly ajar, and pushed it open. "Tes?"

"I'm here. Come in." Victor stepped into her chambers, chuckling softly at the disarray—dozens of dresses covered one sofa, hat boxes obscured her dining table, and other clothes were liberally slung from chairs, lamps, and end tables. Adding to the disarray, Tes had moved the furniture away from the center of her little sitting room and was setting some glowing silver objects that looked almost like dominoes into a complicated pattern on the floor. "I'm preparing our gateway."

"I was going to ask you about all that. Remember back on Zaafor when you had to find us a, um, acolyte of Boaegh's to open a gateway back to Fanwath?"

"Yes, I remember. I didn't have this artifact then."

"But with all your power, can't you travel between worlds?"

Tes paused where she knelt, adjusting one of the little glowing rectangles, and looked up at him. "I can travel between worlds, yes, but my method creates a violent, Energy-filled rip in reality that would kill most beings should they enter it. You'd probably survive, hearty as you are, but I promise you this: our departure would not go unnoticed, and you can be certain the veil walkers of this world would be watching for my return."

"And this artifact?"

"Is subtle and sophisticated, designed to allow one of my kind to enter a world with powerful Energy users undetected."

"That's cool." Victor gestured to the clothes scattered around the suite. "Um, are you still packing?"

"Oh, I was just going through my wardrobe, choosing some outfits. Don't worry, I'm ready."

Victor rubbed his chin, nodding slowly. "Ah, I see." He stepped a little closer. "And what are you doing there? How does this thing work?"

"I can try to explain it sometime, but it's not as easy as it may look. I have to arrange these nodes in the proper pattern to reach Fanwath. Luckily, when I left Zaafor, I did some research into your surrogate homeworld, and I believe I've created the proper pattern."

Victor nodded again, stopping at the edge of her circle of tiny silvery rectangles and trying to take in the pattern as a whole. It *was* complicated, with many little offshoots, swirls, and sub-patterns within the greater one. "And if you make a mistake?"

"In that case, we can *hope* that the pattern won't work, and I'll know I need to make adjustments. On the other hand, it may, in a worst-case scenario, open a doorway into the void of space." She laughed at Victor's widened eyes. "Don't worry. If that happened, I could freely use my ability to open a much surer gateway—no veil walkers of Ruhn would be watching."

Victor nodded. He supposed it made sense; with an epic-tier bloodline and the power of regeneration, he could probably float around in space for a while before dying. "Anything I can do to help?"

"Almost done, love," she said, clearly concentrating on the placement of one of her "nodes." Of course, her term of endearment had more of an effect on him than she probably intended, and Victor found himself frowning, wondering about that. Tes wasn't some young woman unaware of the impact her attentions had on him. When she held his hand or hugged him, when she called him "love" and "dear" and other pet names, she had to know what she was doing. What was her game? She'd overtly rebuffed his advancements, ensuring he knew she wasn't there for "romance."

Something crept into his spine—a bit of iron fueled by his Quinametzin pride, no doubt—and he said what was on his mind. "You shouldn't tease me like that if you don't want to pursue a relationship with me."

For a long moment, Tes didn't reply, but then she set her final node into place with a click, and the entire pattern pulsed with silvery light three times. She stood, smiling and cocking her head sideways as she stepped closer to him. "I'm sorry about that, Victor. I like to tease, and I *do* care about you. You know that, right?"

"Yeah, I know it."

"I'll tell you this as plainly as I can so we can clear the air and enjoy our visit to your home on Fanwath. I am very intrigued and excited by you. You're the most interesting person I've met in a long, long time. The growth you've exhibited over the last couple of years is nothing short of heroic and amazing and—" Victor started to laugh nervously, embarrassed by the praise, and Tes stopped short, staring into his eyes until he became serious again. "The point is that, yes, I would like to explore more with you, but the time isn't right."

"Because . . ." Victor frowned and folded his arms.

"Because your heart is still wounded from your break with Valla, whom I also care about. Need I remind you of that?"

"No, but is that all—"

"And I refuse to be the one you use to mend those sores on your heart. I refuse because, in a year or five or ten, you might ask yourself if I took advantage. If you didn't, I *would.* Let's spend time together, grow closer to each other, and see what fate brings us. I won't rush anything with you because I care about you too much. Still,"—she reached out and gripped his forearms where they rested against his chest—"I don't see what's wrong with a little affection. You *are* very dear to me."

Victor, being a young man with a heart full of passion, had fixated on a simple point. "So, if you don't want to be the one I 'mend my heart' with, then you're cool with me getting together with someone else? Don't you feel jealousy?"

Tes moved her hands to Victor's shoulders, stood on her tiptoes, and gently, delicately nuzzled her cheek against his neck, holding herself close. She tilted her head so she could whisper right into his ear. "If I must compete with another woman when I feel the time is right, then compete I shall."

As tingles raced down the nape of his neck, and figuring he'd already laid bare his intentions, Victor took advantage of her closeness and wrapped his arms around her, pulling her even tighter. She allowed it for the briefest of moments, but then Tes pushed him out to arm's length, her strength irresistible—her hands against his chest unyielding bulwarks. Victor grimaced as he tried to resist her briefly, but after just a moment, he laughed and dropped his arms. "Okay, I get your point."

Tes smiled impishly, brushing some golden curls away from her face. "So? Shall we enjoy our time together, have some fun, and just let fate run its course?

Regardless of anything I say, Victor, I'm a person. I'm a woman with feelings, and sometimes, despite my better judgment, my emotions get the better of me, just as they do to you."

"There you go again," he sighed, "baiting your hook with hope."

"I am what I am!" Tes laughed and turned to her pattern. "Ready?"

Victor tried to frown at her for several long seconds. He wasn't remotely satisfied with their little discussion, but he supposed he'd have to let it go if he wanted to enjoy his time with Tes. They'd already had similar talks at least twice since she'd arrived in Iron Mountain, though this had been the first time she brought up Valla. He supposed he couldn't hold that against her.

It was a valid concern; if Tes cared about Valla, he could see why she wouldn't want to reconnect with her—possibly very soon—and announce that she was with Victor now. The implication that she'd been lying in wait, knowing that Victor and Valla would fail together, would be too difficult to deny. He also knew that his acting like a petulant, lovesick boy wasn't going to impress any woman, let alone a dragon with Tes's beauty, grace, power, and clever mind. No, he'd have to do better than that.

"I'm ready." He smiled and shrugged. "I was ready the minute you made the suggestion."

Tes returned his smile, her eyes bright as she held out a hand. "Join me in the center of the circle, then." When Victor stepped close, careful not to step on any of the silvery nodes, she took his hand. "Picture your home in your mind. It will help me fine-tune the pattern so we arrive where we want to be."

Victor nodded and closed his eyes, fixing the garden of his "hermitage" in his mind. He remembered the fountain vividly and the colorful flowers that lined the little patio where Cora, Chala, and Deyni had been playing with one of the girls' little pets. He remembered the narrow, winding pathway that led down from the garden to the beach. He could almost smell the flowers and the salt air. He could hear the gulls in the distance and the trill of a songbird in the trees nearby. Victor snapped his eyes open and laughed when he saw that he and Tes stood in the very place he'd been picturing.

"Talk about *smooth*!"

"I told you it was a sophisticated artifact!" Tes grinned and stooped to gather up the little domino-shaped, silvery nodes. Victor couldn't help watching her for a moment—she'd worn one of her more formal-looking dresses. It was silvery and white, with a section of pale blue in the middle. Like all of her dresses, it seemed multi-layered but effortlessly comfortable. She moved gracefully as she snatched up the little silvery tiles, and as her skirts swished around her feet, he saw she wore silvery, crystalline slippers that somehow flexed with the movements of her delicate-seeming ankles and feet.

"You look really nice, Tes."

She picked up the last node, tucked it into some hidden storage container, and then stood to beam at him, curtsying. "Why, thank you, milord. I love this garden, by the way. Its understated beauty and calming atmosphere are perfect. I can hear the waves crashing nearby. Is that the Silver Sea you mentioned?"

"Yeah. You'll be able to see it from inside the house." Victor gestured to the glass doors leading from the patio into the solarium. "Shall we?"

Tes stepped closer and took his elbow. "By all means! I'm eager to meet your friends."

It turned out that the only person home to meet Tes was Gorro ap'Dommic, his governor. The man was startled beyond words when Victor strode through the dimly lit house and found him sitting at his little desk, reviewing one of his ledgers. The man stammered and sputtered his apologies, thinking he'd forgotten about a scheduled visit, but Victor reassured him that it was a surprise. Gorro's eyes flew wide as though he'd just remembered a roast cooking in the oven. He hurried around his desk and stood before Victor, wringing his hands. Victor narrowed his eyes and said, "What is it, Gorro?"

"I'm afraid your charge isn't home! She and her governess have gone to the Shadeni village to celebrate the hunters' return. They're not due back for several days!"

Victor smiled and squeezed the man's narrow bony shoulder. "Don't worry about it, Gorro. I'm here for a few days and wouldn't mind visiting the Shadeni. I'll go there tomorrow."

"Excellent, milord. I will call the house staff to duty and see that rooms are made up for your guest." For the second time, Gorro let his gaze drift in Tes's direction, and then, with wide-eyed awe, he jerked his face away as though he'd just witnessed the birth of a star.

Victor chuckled. "That's great. Please do that. We'll take a walk through the village and down to the beach."

"Supper will be waiting when you return, milord." Gorro turned to Tes, quickly lowered his gaze, and stammered, "V-very nice to meet you, milady."

"And you, dear Gorro. Victor has told me so much about your talented stewardship of his properties."

Gorro struggled to respond and ended up simply clearing his throat and nodding nervously. Victor clapped his shoulder again, then led Tes out into the courtyard. "He's smitten with you," he remarked once the big front door clicked shut.

"Poor man. Has he no wife? He seems quite sad, sitting there in his dim little study, reviewing the import lists from the various towns and villages of the Free Marches."

Victor chuckled, leading the way to his gate. "Is that what was on the ledger? You're so observant! Anyway, yeah, Gorro's a private guy, and he seems to thrive by doing his job. It's what he loves. I tried to tell him it would be fine to keep the house 'awake,' as he puts it, but he insists on keeping things shuttered and dark when no one else is home. I'm sure the place is more lively when Cora and Efanie are home."

"Are you upset that they weren't here to greet you?" Tes followed him out the gate and onto the cobbled lane that would take them down the hill and into the little village.

Victor paused and turned to face Tes. "I'm not upset, no. Honestly, I'm relieved. I told you about how I came to be responsible for Cora, and yeah, she seems to have forgiven me, even accepted me as a . . . well, a person responsible for her, but I still get nervous when I think about talking to her."

"I'm sure it will be fine, Victor. As you said, life can be cruel, but you were just as much forced into that duel as she was forced into your care—circumstances of fate."

Victor smiled, pleased, as always, to have Tes on his side. "We should make ourselves a little smaller. If you didn't notice from the doorways in my house, a big person on Fanwath is six feet or so."

Tes nodded, and before Victor could blink, she'd reduced herself to the point that she looked like a child beside him. Victor shook his head, unable to fathom how quickly and easily she could cast a complicated spell like Alter Self. He formed the spell pattern, and several seconds later, he, too, was more reasonably sized for Fanwath. He took a step down the path, but Tes reached out and grasped his arm, turning him back to her.

"Of course I'm interested in seeing your village and meeting some of your people, Victor, but, you know, we're on *Fanwath*—no veil walkers are watching you." Suddenly, delicate blue wings sprouted from Tes's back, stretching wider and wider until she stood before him with human-sized dragon wings. He could see the bones in the thin, pale blue membrane as she flexed them, beaming at his reaction. "How about a flight?"

Victor grinned and nodded, sending Energy into the pathway for his wings. He heard the rush of fire as they erupted into being, dripping hot lava onto the cobbles. "Race you," he cried, looking toward the sky and *willing* his wings to work. When he launched off the cobbles, leaving behind a spiral of smoky, hot air, he couldn't stop laughing, especially when he saw Tes surging after him, each stroke of her wings pulling her closer and closer. Victor looked down at his village and, beyond it, to the sea, and with another surge of magma-attuned Energy, he ripped through the air toward the water like a fiery projectile, forcing Tes to contend with a black plume of smoke in his wake.

4

OLD ACQUAINTANCES

Victor pulled another driftwood log onto the makeshift bonfire he and Tes had put together. It was damp and didn't combust right away, but the fire was already roaring, and the log began to steam immediately; soon it would burn. "That ought to last a while."

"You're well-loved around here, Victor," Tes remarked, watching the couple who'd just stopped by walk back toward the town. Their flight had garnered some attention, and many of the former members of the Ninth had come by to greet Victor and meet Tes as they'd strolled along the beach, enjoying the sound of the waves crashing and the generally charming atmosphere.

"Well, we fought a war together." He nodded toward the departing couple. "What did you think of Nia?"

"Very intriguing. Her story makes me think the Death Casters who fled Earth for their new world must have been formidable."

"Is that unusual? For human-like people to reach levels of power like that without the System?"

"Unusual, but not unheard of, and humans have a high natural affinity. My research indicates that there were many great cultivators on Earth before the Energy stopped flowing, and they weren't all members of elder species like our ancestors."

"So the undead lords on Dark Ember could be as strong as veil walkers?"

Tes moved a little away from the fire and sat down on the sand as she answered. "I'd say it's not only possible but likely. To flee through the veil to another world, especially as Energy ebbed—that would require sophisticated magic."

Victor nodded, turning to face the fire, watching the orange tongues of flame licking the sides of the big damp log he'd thrown on. He glanced at the sky; they'd just watched the sunset, and now the light was fading entirely from the western horizon, and the stars were beginning to emerge. "Are you hungry?"

"Not particularly. Why don't you try one of your new spell patterns? It's why we came here, after all."

Victor turned to look at her, sitting on the sand, her bare feet curled underneath the skirts of her dress. The fabric shimmered in the firelight, and flames danced in Tes's eyes—reflections of the fire. He wanted to tell her she was beautiful, but he'd learned that such direct flattery wouldn't get him far, especially if he constantly lavished it on her. "Which one should I start with?"

"I think the Energy Charge revision. You'll face opponents with similar abilities—some System-based classes are awarded them in the high 'iron ranks,' as you've already seen; only your incredibly sturdy nature saw you through those battles."

Victor nodded. They'd had the discussion before. One of these days— perhaps soon—he would face someone who could move faster than his senses could perceive and who also had the ability to do enough damage to him to overcome his sturdy body and regeneration. Such a combination would be difficult, if not impossible, for him to counter. So Tes had helped him figure out how to take his System-granted Energy Charge spell and alter it. The new elder-magic variant would, theoretically, allow him to maintain the speed of his Energy Charge while moving and fighting for as long as he wanted to expend the Energy required.

More than that, Tes had helped him expand the spell's effects to include his mind. While he moved under its influence, he would no longer feel like a passenger, hanging on for dear life. His mind would speed up commensurate with his body, and he'd—again, theoretically—be in complete control of his movements. The most critical side effect of the revision would be that his enhanced cognition would allow him to perceive *other* fast-moving people and things.

Victor nodded and sat down, summoning his elder magic book from his storage ring. He flipped to the page where he'd transcribed the final iteration of the revised spell pattern and carefully studied it. At the time, when he'd first copied it into the book, he'd pretty much had it memorized. Since then, though, he'd done the same with half a dozen other spells and, though he could probably write a significant portion of it from memory, parts of the complicated, multi-page pattern were less than clear in his mind's eye.

Tes watched him, shifting so she leaned on one hand in the sand. "It's good that we came here to try this. If you found you needed one of these new spells in your duel, you would have struggled to build the pattern from memory."

"Yeah. I was just thinking the same thing." Victor ran through the pattern twice, then closed his eyes and turned his gaze inward, drawing a strand of inspiration-attuned Energy into his pathways. He could use any attunement for the spell; it wasn't particular. He liked using inspiration when he was learning, though—he felt that it influenced his success rate, even with something like casting a new spell. Of course, he had no factual basis for the belief; it was just an instinct and perhaps superstition, but he'd come to trust his instincts, especially since his vision where Tenecoalt had instructed him to do so.

He had to glance back at his notes several times, but soon, the pattern was nearly finished—just a few more loops and a connection of the final thread remained. Victor stood, then looked at Tes. "Here goes."

"Luck!" She smiled impishly, remaining seated.

Victor swallowed, bracing himself, and then finished the pattern. As the final thread fell into place, the entire pattern flashed with white-gold Energy, but before the spell could engage the Energy in his Core, Victor felt things freeze, and a System message flashed before his eyes:

*****Warning! The spell being cast incorporates and alters another System-granted spell. If you complete this casting, your System-granted spell will be removed.*****

*****Warning! The spell being cast does not follow System-designed iterations and may be too powerful for you. Proceed at your own risk.*****

*****Warning! Non-System spell pattern detected! You will only receive this warning one time. Do you wish to halt this process? YES/NO.*****

Victor had learned his lesson about antagonizing the System with questions and a mocking tone. This time, he simply said, "No."

A tremendous wave of Energy flowed out of his Core, fueling his completed spell. Victor felt his muscles come alive with boiling power and urgency, and the world turned bright, his eyes blazing with the light of inspiration. He glanced at the fire, and his jaw dropped—it rippled in blinding glory, though the flames' liquid dance was slow, each flicker unfolding in what felt like seconds, each ember drifting off as if it were caught in air thick as molasses.

Victor turned to Tes, and she winked at him, but her eyelid moved too slowly to be natural, her cheek rising and her brow descending over the course of several breaths. Victor was aware that a river of Energy was feeding the spell while he looked around, so he decided to try moving before he spent every drop in his Core. He jogged around the fire toward the ocean and saw the waves coming into shore at a snail's pace. His movements felt normal, his thoughts felt unaltered, but looking down at the white-gold Energy limning his body, it was clear that he was moving at a charged rate.

He darted toward the water and kicked one of the near-frozen waves as it descended in slow motion. Water erupted from his foot's impact, but it flew away as if it were fighting against an invisible force—a spray of slowly separating, misting droplets. Grinning, Victor turned and ran back to Tes, and then, with a flick of his will, he stopped the flow of Energy into his pathways.

"Bravo!" she cheered, just as System messages scrolled across Victor's field of view:

*****You have discovered a new spell: Velocity Mantle, Epic.*****

*****Your new spell renders a System-granted spell obsolete. Removing.*****

*****You have lost the spell: Energy Charge, Basic.*****

*****Velocity Mantle, Epic: You have mastered the intricate art of merging body and mind into a state of heightened synchronicity, pushing the boundaries of speed and perception. Activating this spell drastically accelerates your physical and cognitive functions, allowing you to move, react, and think at rates far beyond normal capacity. This effect enhances your awareness, enabling you to perceive and counter high-speed movements, and grants unparalleled precision in battle or flight. The duration of the spell is determined by the Energy you invest. Energy Cost: Variable.*****

*****Warning! This spell is not System-designed! Use it with caution—there are no safeguards in place. This is the only time you will receive this warning!*****

"It worked—epic!" Victor laughed, mildly amused by the System's passive-aggressive language and behavior; it hadn't *needed* to remove Energy Charge from him; the two spells were different enough that he could still find the shielded charge of his old spell valuable. Still, he was pleased enough with the upgrade.

"I told you it was a good pattern. You did an outstanding job with it, Victor. Was it costly?"

"Oh, good question." Victor called up his Energy level to see how much he'd spent:

Energy: 37099/43812

"Yeah." He nodded. "It's costly but not *terrible*. As I continue to gain intelligence with my Warlord class, I think it will become more and more usable."

Tes nodded. "Naturally. I could barely see you move; that's going to be quite the fun card to pull out when the time comes, don't you think?"

"Hell yes!" Victor laughed, stooping to pick up his book, eager to try out another one of his new patterns. Tes leaned back on her elbows, staring up at the stars. Victor was about to ask her what spell she thought he should try next when a disturbingly familiar feminine voice called out from near the shoreline.

"Oh, it *was* the one we suspected! I thought it was a familiar sound, Fox! It's the tasty morsel we heard crashing about the spirit plane once upon a time!"

"It's still so young, though, Three," came a rumbling basso voice, rolling his tongue as he said, "Three."

"Oh, shit," Victor sighed, glancing at Tes. Her eyes narrowed with consternation, and she stood smoothly, moving to stand beside him.

"Step into the light, hunters," she snarled, her voice suddenly harsh.

"Hunters? We?" Three asked, her smooth, almost purring voice coming from the shadows to Victor's left. The odd thing about that was that he could see quite well in the dark, especially with the bonfire throwing light in a fifty-yard radius. Still, he couldn't see either of the strange individuals he'd met so long ago on the spirit plane.

"This one's different," Fox rumbled from the other side of the fire. "It's not meant to be here—perhaps more of a morsel than we care to bite."

Tes growled, and then she *surged*, expanding suddenly to what Victor *hoped* was her actual size—a blue-scaled, four-limbed, winged reptilian terror the size of a city bus. She pounced into the darkness, and as her claws swept out, a sharp clang resounded, and suddenly Victor could see Fox—the giant man clung to a saber that gleamed with red-black light that seemed to cut his mind as he glimpsed it, forcing him to look away. The fellow looked much like Victor remembered—dressed like a pirate, ten feet tall or so, and with the girth of several similarly sized men rolled into one.

"Ho ho! Ease your rage, dragon! We're simply here to investigate!" He chuckled as Tes swiped again and rebuffed her mighty claw with his horrible saber. "It's angry, Three!"

"Aye," came the orange tabby woman's sibilant reply, directly beside Victor. He lurched to the side, whirling to face her, but she just winked one of her big emerald eyes and grinned sideways, exposing her feline fangs. Tes also whirled to the voice, slashing her tail at Fox, who somehow ran ahead of it, circling the fire to stand a bit behind Three. When he sheathed his terrible red-black sword, Tes growled deeply but suddenly stood in her human form again, stepping toward Victor.

She moved to stand before him, folding her bare arms over her chest, her silver-and-white dress flickering with orange and red from the fire. "You made your point. I cannot defend him from both of you, but I swear to you this much: Harm him now, and I'll kill one of you and hunt the other to the ends of the universe for my vengeance."

"So," Three said as she made a show of licking the fur on her left wrist, "our morsel has a protector. Hmm. Why do you stand for the disruptor? Don't you think it'll bring you trouble down the line?"

"Disruptor!" Tes barked a laugh and shook her head. "Come to Aradnue and meet a world full of *us*. Your System might have gotten its hooks into him, but that doesn't mean he's sworn any oaths. He's not causing any trouble. He's not sharing what he learns. He's not recruiting for a cause—simply learning to fashion Energy on his own, without crutches."

"Ah." Three looked at Fox and sighed. "*That* old canard."

The big man nodded, his jowly neck jiggling with the motion. "I feared as much, Three."

Three looked at Tes, reaching one pointed nail up to her teeth as though to wriggle something out from behind her right canine. After a moment, she said, "And who started this tasty morsel on this road? Perhaps *you're* the disruptor, hmm?"

Victor stepped forward, well aware that Tes had, indeed, given him his first taste of elder magic. Still, she wasn't the only one. "Perhaps you're under the impression that elder magic doesn't run in my blood," he growled, severing the thread of Energy sustaining his Alter Self spell. As he surged in size and let his aura flow freely, he said, "I'm a titan, and if I wish to work the magic of my ancestors, I'll do so."

Of course, his aura might be impressive to other iron rankers, even steel seekers, but the two before him hardly blinked as it washed over them. They did seem to take his words into consideration, however. Three seemed amused, and she chuckled softly as Fox backed up a step, forced to look up to meet Victor's gaze. "So it is, so it is! And this one? She didn't teach you to work the elder runes? She didn't *disrupt* your progress with the System?"

Tes opened her mouth, but Victor spoke first. "She cautioned me off it—warned me not to talk to others about it. If you're trying to keep people from learning how to make spells outside the System, you ought to thank her." Victor had a feeling the two could smell a lie, so he didn't tell one. Every word he said was true—Tes had been reluctant to share her elder magic with him. She'd given him a pattern to learn, but she hadn't hand-fed it to him. In fact, the thing had been nearly indecipherable to him when she first gave it over. And she'd absolutely cautioned him about it and asked him never to reveal her as the source.

Three licked her claw, arching an eyebrow over her big emerald eye. "And now? We've witnessed you work three non-System spells, morsel. She doesn't aid you?"

"Enough," Tes barked, stepping forward. "What I do with my time is none of your business, you pair of opportunistic, sycophantic System-slaves. I've provided my testimony—Victor is *not* a disruptor; he keeps his learning to himself. My actions are my own, and if you care to judge me, then by all means, do so. You haven't a leg to stand on."

"We'll see about that, *Celestial Envoy Tesia'liveen'ashalah*," Three hissed.

"Oh, bravo! You've managed to suss out my identity. Not that I didn't *show* you my true form. Are there many mature blue dragons wandering this part of the universe? Go ahead, visit Luminaris, make an appointment with the Grand Envoys, and ask if I have permission to be with Victor. Ask if I've made a case for my involvement in his progression. I'll save you the six-month wait—I *do*, and I *have*. Now, unless you'd like me to track down *your* employer, I suggest you leave us to our own devices. You've seen what the noise was about; Victor is trying some new spells that *he* devised and has no intention of doing any *disrupting*."

Three never stopped smiling slyly as Tes spoke, but she looked at Fox and shrugged. "What do you say, Fox? Shall we leave this angry dragon to its business?"

Fox yawned, scratching his belly where it hung out over his pantaloons. "I'm bored, Three. Let's find another morsel. We can check up on this youngster another time—you know how they go."

Three's smile widened as she looked back at Victor. "Aye, I do. Maybe it's not disrupting yet, but I can see it in those eyes. It's going to be a handful. I think we'll get our taste eventually." With that, she put a furry, razor-clawed hand on Fox's shoulder, and the two turned to walk up the beach. Victor watched them go, counting seven steps before they shimmered like a mirage and disappeared.

"Victor, I think you neglected to tell me something." Tes flopped down onto the sand with a heavy sigh.

Victor sat beside her, his mind racing through all the implications of that strange encounter. Had he understood correctly? They were agents of the System? When he cast a non-System spell, it had thrown up some kind of red flag, and they'd come sniffing around? Why hadn't it happened when he cast Alter Self? He'd always assumed they found him on the spirit plane because he'd made such a . . . *bang* when he first cast Wild Totem.

"Victor?" Tes prompted.

"Oh." He looked at her and shrugged. "Yeah. Um, when I revised my totem spell, they found me on the spirit plane. I didn't realize they worked for the System. What the hell?"

"They don't work *for* the System. They collect System bounties. Disruptors are worth a great deal, but they have no evidence that you are one. That's likely why they left you alive the first time they found you. They're *hoping* you won't keep your knowledge of elder magic to yourself. They're hoping you'll start actively working against the System. If they can provide even the tiniest bit of proof, the System will award them tremendously for killing you."

"Did I get you in trouble?"

Tes smiled and leaned her cheek against his shoulder. "No trouble that I didn't already have, sweet boy."

"Man," Victor grunted, eliciting a giggle out of Tes. "I can't believe that dude stood up to your attack!"

"Ha! That wasn't an attack! That was a reminder that he probably didn't want to tussle with me."

"Well, I'm glad you were here."

"As am I." She straightened and turned to smile at him. "All the more reason for you to learn more spells. Someday, you might have to defend yourself from the likes of those fiends. Come, they know you're not here teaching your forbidden arts. Go ahead and cast another."

With a grin, Victor hopped to his feet and took out his elder magic book again, flipping through the spell patterns. "Let's see here, what will I cast next . . ."

5

DOMAIN

I think I want to try the one from the dungeon book." Victor and Tes had spent several days deciphering the strange elder magic book he'd gotten in the Iron Prison. At first, it seemed to have bits of patterns without a greater purpose—Energy direction nodes, Energy density weaves, Energy gateways, feedback loops, containment matrices, reversal nodes, conversion threads, and dozens of other pattern components. When Victor began to understand the pages and pages of spell components, he thought he'd gotten some sort of ancient primer on elder magic.

In a way, he was right; it was a primer, but Tes had shown him how the first few seemingly disparate components could be put together to form the skeleton of a spell pattern. From there, Victor had diligently added the other pieces of the puzzle to the whole. It wasn't a primer on Elder magic in general; it was a guidebook that deconstructed a highly complex pattern, one that filled an entire—albeit small—book.

Tes leaned back on her elbows, her eyes fixed on the bonfire. There were more embers than flames now, but its heat was comfortable in the cool, night-time sea breeze. "I'm not sure you're ready for that one."

"What's going to happen to me if I'm not?" The question was rhetorical. Victor was pretty sure all that would happen was that he'd fail to cast it.

"It might completely drain your Core, and then you'll feel sick for a little while."

Victor nodded, flipping through his elder magic book to the nearly thirty pages dedicated to the dungeon book's spell pattern. "That's all right. I'll be ready for a break after this, anyway."

Tes yawned and then stood up, nodding. "I'm going to walk along the beach for a while. Maybe I'll go for a swim. It'll take you a long time to build that pattern."

"You'll come back before I cast it, though, yeah?"

"Of course! I wouldn't miss it."

Victor smiled, watching her walk lithely over the sand to the gentle, moonlit waves. He sat down and put the book in his lap, and when he glanced up at Tes again, she was gone, but he swore he caught a glimpse of a great blue-scaled tail slipping into the silvery water. "Shit," he chuckled, "wouldn't want to be a fish around here right now." He watched the water for another minute or two, but when Tes didn't surface and he saw no sign of her, he turned back to his book and began reviewing the long, complicated, multifaceted spell pattern.

Copying a complex pattern into his Energy pathways was one of Victor's fortes. The ability to hold Energy where he wanted it was tied to his will attribute, and with that being his primary focus for most of his career as an Energy user, the spell didn't start getting difficult for him until he'd made it about halfway into the pattern. Pulling his inner eye back, seeing what he'd built as a whole—all three dimensions of the elder magic pattern—he found it hard to believe he was only halfway through it. It was like a hollow cone, with both ends open to Energy strands, filled with loops, whorls, angles, shapes, and intricate weaves.

Of course, he'd chosen inspiration-attuned Energy to build the spell the first time. Part of the pattern was an Energy differentiation matrix, and Tes had taught Victor how it would take the Energy input and *format* it for the spell's purposes. It was a spell designed to use the caster's Energy to their advantage, so, unlike many of his spells, it really *mattered* what Energy he cast it with. That being the case, Victor didn't want his first attempt to be with fear or rage.

In addition to inspiration being his most "positive" affinity, it seemed to respond better to his mental nudges, which made it ideal for forming a spell pattern for the first time. Even so, as Victor turned the page in his book and began adding in more and more complexity, he found himself beginning to sweat with the strain of keeping those thousands of Energy lines steady. "Come on, *pinché* son of a bitch," he growled, gently, delicately tweaking his line of Energy into a bowl-shaped pattern against which a star-shaped cascade of other lines would reflect.

He was vaguely aware of soft footsteps behind him, but he couldn't spare a glance to see if Tes had returned. He knew it was her, though; he could smell the saltwater mixed with her jasmine and citrus perfume. She sat behind him, and when her cool hands pressed against the sides of his neck, Victor felt some of his tension bleed away. "You're doing very well, Victor. I'm quite impressed you've gotten this far; this is a pattern a so-called steel seeker would struggle with."

He didn't respond, but as she gently kneaded the tension out of his knotted neck muscles, he redoubled his efforts, continuing his work. He pushed away the excitement her touch elicited in him, and a tiny part of his mind wondered if she was helping or hindering his progress, but the proof was in the doing: He worked through two more pages in record time, adding their components to the pattern in his pathway.

He was inserting new twists, glyphs, angles, and functions on the interior of the cone now, so he had to strain his inner eye to either see *past* the outer layers of the pattern, or he had to rotate his perspective and push his perception into the bottom of the cone. He chose the latter because it gave him a proper view of the spell's complexity, and he could glance at the whole from the inside to ensure he wasn't breaking anything with the new components.

Slowly but surely, he worked his way through the pages, and all the while, Tes's fingers worked magic, draining away his tension and helping him focus. When he reached the final page, he was sure he was drenched in sweat, but he was no longer aware of his body; his entire being existed in that pathway outside his Core. If someone had asked Victor to make an analogy about the effort of will it took to hold those thousands of delicate lines of Energy in place, he would have said it was like balancing a skyscraper atop his palms while participating in a log-rolling competition—absurd, but it made the point.

As he connected the final hexagonal prism of Energy lines to the dangling thread of Energy at the top of the cone's interior, the entire pattern flashed, and Victor felt his Core drain as a flood of Energy populated the completed spell. Just as before, though, everything seemed to freeze in place, and the System sent him an unwelcome warning:

*****Warning! The spell being cast does not follow System-designed iterations and may be too powerful for you. Proceed at your own risk.*****

*****Warning! Non-System spell pattern detected! You will only receive this warning one time. Do you wish to halt this process? YES/NO.*****

Unlike with the spell pattern that he and Tes had modified, Victor looked at the first warning and gave it serious consideration. This spell was from a book he'd found in a prison dungeon for iron rankers. It didn't belong. Was it a trap? Was it a boon? He didn't know, but even Tes thought it might be too much for him. Would she let him cast something that could seriously harm him, though? Now that the spell was formed—and frozen in time—he sought some reassurance. "Seriously, what's the worst that can happen if this spell is too powerful for me?"

When she didn't answer, and he realized her hands weren't moving on his neck any longer, Victor looked over his shoulder to see she, too, seemed frozen in time. Was that it? Was the System stopping time, or had it moved Victor *outside* of time? He had a feeling his awareness had sped up or been pulled away from the normal flow of time as he understood it. After all, affecting him ought to be a whole lot easier than affecting the entire world or universe. Whatever it was doing, the System didn't seem to like doing it long. It flashed the question again, this time with larger, red-tinted letters:

*****Do you wish to halt this process? YES/NO.*****

Gathering his courage, Victor mentally pressed the "NO" option. Again, he felt the draw on his Core, like a vortex siphoning the Energy out, and Victor watched as the world around him *changed*. A wall of shimmering white-gold Energy expanded away from him, forming an enormous dome, something like two hundred yards in diameter. Inside that brightly lit space, the ground shimmered in rainbow-tinted reflections as a bed of gravel appeared, consisting of millions of tiny, prism-like crystals. The fire's orange flames and embers became blue and purple, and the ocean's waves tinkled like crystalline wind chimes as they crashed at half their normal speed.

Victor stood, his eyes wide with wonder as the clarity of inspiration filled his senses. He whirled to see Tes also on her feet, looking about, her hands covering her mouth as her big sapphire eyes filled with unshed tears. "It's beautiful!" she cried, walking in a slow circle, the crystalline gravel tinkling with each step. "My mind is so *clear*! Victor, you have to talk to Valla!"

The comment, out of nowhere, was puzzling at first, but as Victor thought about it, he understood Tes's point of view. He owed it to Valla to tell her he was home. She deserved to know Tes was there. It was important to clear the air. "I will."

"If this . . . *environment* has this effect on us, what will it do to your enemies?" Tes wondered, reaching out to run her fingers through a slowly flickering purple flame.

"I don't know, but I can't hold it long. My Core's draining like someone opened a valve into a black hole." Victor took one more long look around, his eyes mesmerized by the dancing motes of white-gold light that seemed to float about the space like fireflies. "God, everything's so clear!"

"It's a wondrous spell. You've created an environment attuned to inspiration!"

Victor looked at the crystalline waves and then at the strangely beautiful fire, smiling almost sadly as he severed the thick ribbon of Energy connecting his nearly empty Core to the spell. When the mundane world came crashing back, dark, chilly, and clad in the usual colors of nature, he stumbled and fell backward onto the sand, catching himself on his palms. "Damn," he laughed, "not so pretty out here anymore, is it?"

"Of course it is!" Tes laughed, skipping around the fire, her eyes bright, her smile glowing with pride and happiness. "It'll just take a moment for the magic of your spell's effects to fade a little, and then you can appreciate this lovely world again. I can't *wait* until you're strong enough to keep that spell going longer. Imagine what we could accomplish in an environment like that!"

Victor nodded absently, having realized he had more System messages waiting:

*****You have discovered a new spell: Core Domain, Epic.*****

*****Core Domain, Epic: You have learned to impose your will upon reality, shaping the environment into a reflection of your Core's affinity. By channeling your Energy, you create a localized domain where your chosen affinity manifests in both form and function, altering the environment to empower yourself, support allies, and suppress enemies. Each affinity dictates the domain's effects, making it a versatile but demanding tool. The domain persists for as long as your Energy sustains it, and its influence grows with the strength of your will. Energy Cost: Variable. The greater the Energy invested, the larger and more potent the domain. Prolonged use risks feedback effects, including exhaustion, emotional strain, or destabilization of your Core.*****

*****Warning! This spell is not System-designed! Use it with caution—there are no safeguards in place. This is the only time you will receive this warning!*****

Victor read the description twice, then, grinning, read it to Tes. He finished with a question: "Be honest; did you know what the spell would do?"

She shook her head, looking down at her feet where her toes wriggled in the sand. A moment later, she sat beside him and sighed deeply. "I knew it was a spell that would affect the environment, and I could tell it was sophisticated with many different effects based on the Energy being poured into it. Other than that, though, I wasn't sure. I *think* I could have studied each component in relation to those around it and come up with a better estimation, but I thought it would be safe to try with a positive Energy source like your inspiration."

Victor's eyes widened. "Shit, man, I didn't think about that! What's it going to be like when I cast it with fear or rage?"

"Or justice or courage or glory? You know, those other Energy weaves you started might provide even more potent alternatives. You should work on finishing them."

Victor nodded idly, drawing his fingers through the sand as the fire popped. He'd begun the work of trying to weave glory and fear into some of his other Energies, but it was complicated stuff, and he'd been met with failure so many times that he'd put it on a back burner. Tes was right, though; he was probably missing out on some serious potential.

Another topic was on the tip of his tongue, however. "Why do you think the System still gives me a spell description and adds the new spell to my status sheet? If it doesn't like people stepping outside its influence, you'd think it would ignore the new spell and make me figure out what it does and keep track of it."

"The System isn't foolish. It wants to keep you a part of it for as long as possible. By acknowledging your success, despite its efforts to dissuade you, it reminds you of its utility and, I suppose, helps smooth over any animosity its warnings might have engendered."

"So, it knows I'm doing my own thing, but it wants to keep some hooks in me."

"You're doing your 'own thing' to a degree. You're still gaining levels and earning new skills and spells under the System's care. Things will change a little when you build your own Class, but even then, the System will take part in your milestones. Unless you break from it, that is." Tes spoke softly, mimicking his behavior by idly drawing stars and circles in the sand while she spoke.

"Do you think I should do that?"

She shook her head and then leaned her cheek against Victor's shoulder. "I wouldn't. Not until you've gained all you can from it. Not until you're ready to stand on your own against the System zealots out there like your two friends who paid us a visit earlier."

Victor was quiet for a while, thinking about Fox and Three, wondering when they'd next come calling. It felt as though they followed some kind of unspoken code. Would they leave him alone as long as he didn't spread his use of non-System magic to others? As long as he didn't "disrupt"? He didn't want to dwell on it at the moment because he had another question for Tes, one he was a little reluctant to bring up but couldn't keep from popping back into his mind. "When I created my inspiration domain, the first thing you said was that I should talk to Valla. Is that because it's been on your mind?"

Tes sighed again and sat up straight, shifting to look more directly at him. "It has been, yes. I'm sure you realized the wisdom of the words while you were in your domain. Didn't you? You agreed immediately."

"Yes." Victor nodded, smiling crookedly. "It was good for me to break contact with her for a while, but I owe it to her to write. She should know I'm home. She should know you returned. I should be *interested* in what she's been doing. Valla's never been anything but good and kind and supportive to me. Well, until she decided we needed a break, that is." He chuckled ruefully, and Tes playfully punched his knee.

"You have such *big* emotions. It must have been so hard for her to talk to you about that! She must have been terrified."

"What? *Terrified?* Of me?"

"Of how you would take it. She loves you, and I'm sure she was worried about you flying off in a rage or becoming self-destructive or—"

"I get it, I get it." Victor waved a hand, then lay back in the sand, staring up at the brilliant expanse of stars. "You were right."

"About?" Tes, too, lay back in the sand, cushioning her head with an arm.

"About the world becoming beautiful again after the spell faded a bit."

"That's not the world!" She chased the words with trilling laughter, and Victor groaned.

"You know what I mean."

"I do. So? Are you done with new spells for the night? Shall we return to your home and see what dear Governor ap'Dommic has had the staff prepare?"

"Um, yeah, I suppose. We can do some more in the morning before we fly over to the Shadeni encampment."

"Encampment? Don't they build permanent structures?" Tes hopped to her feet and held out a hand. Victor took it, and she grunted, hoisting him up. "You're like a sack of lead bones!"

"Oh, please! You could throw me halfway across that sea if you wanted. As for the Shadeni, that's a good point. They used to be nomadic, but, yeah, I bet they've built up quite a little town by now."

"Shall we fly back to the house?" Tes arched an eyebrow.

"Let's walk through town. I want to see what's been built and maybe say hi to a few more folks. That okay?"

"It's perfect!" Tes took his elbow and leaned against him as they strolled up from the beach, and Victor did his best to simply enjoy the moment without fixating on his desires for the future. Things were going well, and one thing he knew about life and people was that if you gave it or them an excuse, things could go from good to shit in the blink of an eye. So he savored Tes's closeness, the beautiful weather, and the breathtaking field of stars overhead. With a warm heart and a smile, he waved at the people lingering around the front deck of the tavern on the edge of the village—The Ninth's Rest.

6

LETTERS, LIGHT, AND FLIGHT

Victor sat alone in his suite on a couch he was acutely aware Valla had chosen, purchased, and placed there. Tes had gone to bed, seemingly quite satisfied with the meal they'd been served, but Victor, despite his busy day, couldn't muster enough sleepiness to force a yawn. His mind was alive with a thousand different thoughts, but most of all, he kept thinking about the revelation he and Tes had experienced under the influence of his inspiration domain. That was why he was sitting on the couch, staring at a painting of a forest at sunset that Valla had hung. That was why the Far Scribe book he shared with her was on his lap.

With trepidatious fingers, he pulled back the leather-bound cover and leafed through the pages until he came to the last entry he'd read. Before he let his eyes drift past it, he reviewed the meat of what she'd written:

. . . I'm leaving for a new world tomorrow—an ocean world populated by aquatic people who live on islands and swim and breathe freely under the water. It's called Crydagh, and there are rumored to be creatures living in those waters that rival dragons! Fantastic beasts called booraghi roam the oceans, unafraid of anything—even your mentor, Ranish Dar, would think twice about crossing one of them. If treated with respect, they're peaceful, though, and will sometimes speak to lesser beings who visit them. I'm going to seek one out; rumors have it that they'll grant boons to visitors they take a fancy to. Even if they refuse to speak to me, which I'm told happens often, I believe the trip will be worthwhile. Wouldn't seeing such a creature be a reward in itself?

He wondered if she'd seen the great sea creatures that had so intrigued her. He supposed that was a good place to start, assuming she hadn't already written to him about her experience—he hadn't looked. The thought brought his mind around to the words he'd used in the last letter he'd written. He scanned over them, groaning as he read.

. . . I don't know if I'll ever get over you and the missing piece of my heart that you took with you, but I'm going to try. I'm going to try to remember that no matter

what, I love you, and I don't want you to be gone from my life. So, yeah, I'll try to be better about writing, but I can't do it every day, every week, or even every month. I have to give myself room to breathe, to experience life without you, 'cause that's what you wanted, and it's too hard to let you go if I'm constantly reminding myself about how much I miss you . . .

He hadn't written to her since, and it had been a lot longer than a month—closer to six. With something like dread in his heart, he turned the page to see if she'd written any sort of response. His feelings were a mixture of relief and guilt when he saw two new letters from her. One was short and quick to read:

Victor,

I'm so sorry for the pain I've caused you. I hope you know that my heart is heavy, too, but as you said, it will be good for you to find room to breathe. There's so much in the many worlds available to us; I want you to experience the peaks that I'm not ready to climb. Don't you see that it was a burden on me, too, when I saw you being held back? Don't you see that I, too, must "find room to breathe"? I love you, and I will write again. I look forward to hearing from you when you're ready.

Love always,

Valla

Victor couldn't help a smile from creeping onto his lips as he read. It was *just* like Valla to use his words against him. She was right, he supposed; if anyone in their relationship had made it hard for the other to "breathe," it was Victor. He let his eyes drift down to the next, lengthier message:

Victor! I have amazing, wonderful news! My journey to Crydagh has proven fruitful beyond my wildest dreams. Oh, I have so much to tell you, but I doubt you want to read a book-long entry, and besides, I don't want to use up all of our pages, not until we can meet again and exchange a new Far Scribe journal. Let me just say that this world is truly a wonder.

As I told you, the natives breathe freely in air or water, and the chamber where the System Stone deposited me was like a great inverted fishbowl at the bottom of a shallow sea. I stood in wonder, watching the colorful fish, beautiful people, and strange, moving plants for hours before seeking out a guide.

I'll get to the good part: I joined an expedition to seek out the booraghi, and we found one of their caravans—that's what the people here call their nomadic family groups. They're simply breathtaking creatures! Bigger than a house—no, half as big as one of the crystal spires at the center of Sojourn! They're not scaled like a fish but have beautiful, colorful flesh—yellow, orange, pink, blue, and purple. And their many fins flow through the water like colorful wings, though I dare say they aren't feathered. Rather, they're like gigantic, elegant fronds—almost plantlike.

I'd purchased an apparatus to allow me to breathe underwater, and with the rest of my tour group, I swam out with the desperate hope that one of the creatures would speak to me; they don't use words, but project a surprisingly beautiful song. To most, it sounds like meaningless music, but if they direct it at an individual, it can be understood. So, as the water filled with the trilling music, everyone grew hopeful. I waited and listened, swimming desperately to keep up with the tremendous leisurely creatures, and then, to my delight, one of them spoke to me.

His name is Oomah, but he tells me it's much longer and more beautiful in song form. To make a very long conversation short, he saw something in me, Victor. A potential he described as "remarkable." He's offered to take me on as a student, something so rare that only a handful of such cases have been recorded in all of the Crydaghians' history. To my great wonder and delight, he invited me to join his clan on their migration—to perch upon his enormous back as a passenger. You wouldn't believe the envy of the others in the tour group!

When we arrived in the booraghi's summer waters, Oomah taught me how to create a dwelling for myself, though there are other structures here; it's apparent that I am not the first or only land-born person to live among them here. Still, for now, Oomah keeps me apart from any others, aside from the booraghi; he's teaching me a new way of living and thinking, and it's been a truly inspirational few months for me.

I catch my own fish and cook it with spices and herbs I've harvested from the sea bed. Oh, goodness! You wouldn't believe the many elaborate steps I went through to come up with something that tasted like pepper. I'm getting lost in anecdotes again! I'll end up writing a novel after all, if I'm not careful.

The point I'm working up to, Victor, is that Oomah has an interesting way of teaching and philosophies about life that I've never seen before. He's not entirely selfless, either; his tutelage comes with strings attached. There are worlds where the booraghi cannot easily travel, and he has . . . quests for me in such places. He says they'll all contribute to my development, but I can't help but be reminded of Ranish Dar and his strange way of "teaching" you. I hope things are going well in that regard, by the way.

Victor, I know you're taking a break from the Far Scribe journal, and I will respect that. Still, Oomah doesn't mind me communicating with you, and though I have many new booraghi friends here, sometimes I feel a little lonely. They're all so vast, and they send their words to me from distances that sometimes make it hard even to see to whom I'm speaking. So, when you feel up to it, please send me a note to let me know how you're doing.

Missing you,

Valla

The whole while Victor read the letter, his smile strained the muscles in his cheeks, and he found himself picturing Valla in a beautiful, colorful, underwater landscape, living in a bubble and swimming in the shadows of colossal creatures that—in his head—looked like gigantic whales. He was proud of her for earning the attention of one of them and being singled out to be a student, though he had to admit some worry entered his mind. Regardless, he was no one to talk; his current circumstances on Ruhn were tenuous at best. Still smiling, he picked up his pen and wrote a response:

Valla,

I can't tell you how happy I was to open this book and find such a wondrous tale to read. I'm so proud of you! The booraghi sound like amazing creatures, and I hope your new mentor has a lot to teach you. I got a strange feeling, though, when you said he's teaching you a new way to think; don't let him change you too much, okay? There's a reason people love you. There's a reason you stood out to Oomah; don't ever lose the things that make you . . . Valla. Yeah, yeah, I know: Who am I to give advice like that?

Anyway, I'm happy for you. I wish I were there to see what they look like. On my homeworld, there are creatures called whales that live in the oceans, and they, too, communicate with strange songs. That's kind of what I picture when you describe the booraghi.

As for me, I think I'm over my sulking. The sting of our parting has begun to fade, though I won't lie; I think about you all the time. That's part of the reason I'm writing. I had a chance to take a small break, and I'm currently visiting Fanwath. Everywhere I look in my—our—rooms, I see your touch. It makes me a little melancholy and sharpens feelings that had grown dull, but it's also nice to see these reminders of you. I know we're very far apart right now, but as you and so many others have said, a lot can change in the course of years and decades and centuries.

Do you note a difference in my writing? I've taken the Warlord class, and while I've only gained a single level in it, I swear it's been affecting my thinking. It doesn't hurt that I've made some bloodline advancements and gained some new feats, either. I suppose being forced to deal with some politics has affected me more than anything. Using that less-than-elegant segue, I'll just say that things are progressing well on Ruhn. They could be worse, but an unexpected visitor and her tutelage are, in my opinion, turning the tide in my favor.

Speaking of inartful segues—Tes is the unexpected visitor. She came to see me on Ruhn because of some . . . waves I stirred up. She's very worried about you, and I know she'll be delighted to hear about your experiences on Crydagh. I don't suppose Oomah will allow you to visit Fanwath? I'll be here three more days. I don't even know how long it'll take for my message in this book to find its way to yours.

Victor paused, wondering how much he should say about Tes. Should he reassure Valla that nothing had happened between them? He felt like broaching the topic unprompted would be crass. He and Valla were just coming to terms with their new status; why should he bring up romance involving anyone else, even if it were simply to deny it was happening? More than that, a denial felt dishonest; he might not have made anything happen with Tes, but he *wanted* to. Clicking his tongue with faint frustration, he finished his letter:

I'm going to let Tes read your last message as I think it'll make her very happy, and I hope you don't mind, but I'll give her the opportunity to write a note to you in this book. In the meantime, please write again whenever you like; I'll be checking this book far more frequently.

Love always,

Victor

Victor closed the book and leaned back with a sigh. He felt lighter, as though he'd shed a burden he hadn't known he was carrying. It was good to have all that off his chest. It was good to know Valla was doing well. A sudden yawn gripped him, and he arched his back, wringing forth several pops. Grinning, he got ready for bed and climbed into the soft sheets, letting the enchanted feather mattress engulf him. In moments, he was asleep, his chest rising and falling with slow, steady breaths as his untroubled mind drifted into oblivion.

When Victor woke and went downstairs to find some breakfast, he found Tes in the kitchen, teaching the cook, an elderly Ardeni woman named Grissa, how to make what she claimed was the "flakiest, tastiest tart crust in seven universes." Victor was no tart expert, but when the timer dinged and the little pastries came out of the oven, he couldn't stop eating until he'd consumed seven sweet fruit tarts and three savory sausage ones.

When Grissa tried to hand him another, he laughed and shook his head. "I could eat twenty, but save some for the rest of the household."

"But, milord, they're all away!"

"No, Grissa, I meant you and the others working today. Enjoy yourselves!" As she blushed, curtsied, and thanked him, Victor turned to Tes. "Care to join me outside? I figure I'll try another one of our patterns before we fly off to visit the Shadeni."

"T'would be my pleasure." She stood, smiling in that confounding "I know something no one else does" way of hers, and followed him to the gardens, where they strolled down the trail to the beach. After they'd put a bit of distance between the garden wall and themselves, she looked up at him. "You seem different this morning. Lighter. What happened?"

"Seriously?" Victor looked at her, shaking his head. "Is that a dragon thing or a Tes thing?"

"What? Being able to read someone close to me?"

"Yeah."

"Hmm, maybe a bit of both. So? Out with it!"

"I read Valla's latest letter and wrote back to her." He smiled, nudging Tes with his elbow. "I'll show you if you like. I told her I would."

"I'd like that! Nothing too personal?"

"Nah, nothing you don't already know." They were both quiet for the rest of the walk to the beach, but when they arrived, Victor looked at Tes, clasping his hands behind his back. "You pick the spell I do this morning."

"I was hoping you'd ask! Let's see how your new light spell works."

Victor smiled and nodded; he was eager to try it, also. If it worked the way they hoped, his new spell would replace several others: Enraging Orb, Globe of Insight, Dauntless Radiance, and Harsh Light of Justice—all his light spells. They all had almost identical patterns, only slightly altered by the System when Victor channeled different Energy affinities into his Globe of Insight pattern. This new spell took that pattern, added to it, perfected it, and, just like his new Core Domain spell, contained a matrix for altering and modifying the spell based on what Energy Victor channeled into it.

In other words, if things went right, the new pattern would be a more powerful utility spell that would work with any Energy type; he wouldn't have to build four subtly different patterns to effect different outcomes. Those thoughts idly passed through Victor's mind as he reviewed the spell's pattern. Despite only being a "light" spell, it wasn't exactly simple, consisting of three pages of densely packed designs. "No, that's not right . . ."

"Hmm? Found a mistake?"

"No, a mistake in my thinking. It's not just a light spell anymore."

"No, each of your affinities should provide different benefits. Will you start with inspiration?"

"Yeah, I actually really like my Globe of Insight spell, so I'm nervous about losing it. I'll feel better when I see the new one isn't any worse."

Tes chuckled and plopped down on the sand. "It won't be."

Victor knew she was right—in theory. They'd built the pattern together, after all. He knew the matrix would take the spell's attuned Energy and run it through a refinement algorithm—a construct in some elder spell patterns that would alter the spell's final effects to maximize the potential of the Energy running through it. "Here," he said as he summoned the Far Scribe journal he shared with Valla and handed it to Tes. "Write her a note if you want."

Tes took it, her eyes bright, and suddenly, a fancy, sapphire-studded onyx calligraphy pen appeared between her fingers. Victor turned back to his pattern, slowly building it in his pathway as he worked his way through it. It wasn't easy, but not nearly as hard as the Core Domain spell. The funny thing was that it was a similar spell—just a much cheaper, watered-down version. Like the domain spell, this light spell would affect him, his allies, and his enemies, though the effects would be less significant and wouldn't affect the environment beyond the obvious—light.

When he stood, Tes looked up from her writing and watched as Victor finished the last flourish of the pattern in his pathway. The spell flashed, began to fill with Energy, and then, to no one's surprise, the System stepped in:

*****Warning! The spell being cast incorporates and alters other System-granted spells. If you complete this casting, your System-granted spells will be removed.*****

*****Warning! The spell being cast does not follow System-designed iterations and may be too powerful for you. Proceed at your own risk.*****

*****Warning! Non-System spell pattern detected! You will only receive this warning one time. Do you wish to halt this process? YES/NO.*****

With a resigned sigh, Victor quickly selected "NO." The spell finished populating with Energy, and then, to his delight, a blazing orb of white-gold light appeared in the air before him. It almost looked like the old iteration of Globe of Insight when he overcharged it with Energy. He noticed a difference in the effects, however. As always, the world seemed brighter, and everything he focused on was sharper and more detailed, somehow made bigger and clearer without actually *being* any bigger.

He turned in a slow circle, staring at the waves as they crashed, wondering what it would take to build a pier. Could he do it himself? He started imagining where he'd put the piles and what type of wood or stone he'd use, and then he thought about how he'd place the beams and joists. "Man, some teak planks would go nicely for decking. Imagine! We could walk out there and fish; how relaxing would that be?"

"Hmm?" Tes asked, her voice a little dreamy.

"I was thinking about building a fishing pier out there."

"Funny, I was just thinking about your armor. We've put off evaluating your new pieces too long. You have to fight soon! Old gods! When was the last time you checked on Lifedrinker?"

"Ha! Not long ago. She's almost done, I think. We can both look in on her after our visit to the Shadeni. How's that sound?" Lifedrinker had taken a *lot* longer to consume her latest bit of magical metal—the second of the two he'd gotten in the Iron Mountain dungeon. Tes thought it was mostly Victor's fault; the axe had barely finished incorporating the silvenite when he'd given her the ferrithium to process. Tes had been annoyed to hear about it, saying he should have spent some time with her, learning what had changed with the silvenite, but the damage had been done; he couldn't interrupt the process halfway.

"It sounds good—Victor! This light is quite impressive; I've felt your old orb, and this one is certainly a great deal stronger as far as the inspiration influence goes. Was the System pleased with your work?"

Victor chuckled and looked at the messages awaiting him:

*****You have discovered a new spell: Prismatic Illumination, Epic.*****
*****Your new spell renders System-granted spells obsolete. Removing.*****
*****You have lost the spell: Harsh Light of Justice, Improved.*****
*****You have lost the spell: Dauntless Radiance, Basic.*****
*****You have lost the spell: Globe of Insight, Improved.*****
*****You have lost the spell: Enraging Orb, Basic.*****

*****Prismatic Illumination, Epic: You wield the power of light itself. This spell will conjure a multifaceted aura of illumination, capable of banishing darkness, revealing hidden truths and insights, or striking fear or blind rage into the hearts of foes. Depending on the Energy channeled, the light shifts in nature, offering a spectrum of boons to allies and banes to enemies. Whether bolstering resilience, confounding senses, or unleashing destructive brilliance, Prismatic Illumination adapts to the given affinity. Its intensity and duration scale with the Energy invested. Energy Cost: Variable.*****

*****Warning! This spell is not System-designed! Use it with caution—there are no safeguards in place. This is the only time you will receive this warning!*****

Victor read the spell description to Tes, and she clapped her hands. "As we anticipated! Well done, Victor! Your second epic-tier design!" She wasn't counting Core Domain, as it was complete in the book he'd found.

"Well, I had your help." She didn't reply, and he added, "I'm interested to see how the new Alter Self works." She'd helped him make nearly a hundred adjustments to his first elder magic spell. When he'd created the pattern so long ago, struggling simply to comprehend the notes Tes had given him, he'd made a few mistakes, and Tes had admitted that she'd left out a few components to simplify it.

"Now? Let's *fly*! You can do it later! You've only three more spells to try out, and we still have three days of vacation!"

"Vacation? Is that what this is?"

"For me, yes! You wouldn't *believe* the nonsense I've been putting up with since Coloss."

Victor folded his arms over his chest. "I might believe it, you know, if you *told* me about it."

Tes nodded, sighing as she reached out to rest a hand on his folded forearms. "Fair. I'll try to communicate better. But, seriously, can we please *fly?*" Victor answered by summoning his fiery wings, but Tes grabbed his wrist, narrowing her eyes at him. "Don't make me take my natural form to show you what *true* speed is! Let's make it a fun flight, not a race! I want to see some of the sights."

Victor nodded, gently extracting himself from her grip. He turned his gaze to the north along the beach. "Want to see where I killed Karl the Crimson?"

7

GIFTS

As they descended toward the Shadeni settlement, Victor had to make some mental adjustments; his expectations and memory of the nomadic tribe had him looking for something far less permanent. He saw cobbled roads, tall, artful stone structures, and even a park near what had to be a market square. He saw roladii and carts in great numbers, indicating a bustling, thriving local economy.

As he and Tes swooped in from the northwest, he steered toward the park, sure they were drawing a lot of attention thanks to his flaming wings; they were hard to miss, even in the bright sunlit sky. As he'd suspected, when they made their final descent, Victor's wings crackling in the wind and Tes gliding far more gracefully, a crowd of Shadeni were already running toward the park.

Victor extinguished his wings as his feet neared the ground. He'd already dropped some magma into the grass, creating little blackened circles, and he didn't want to do any further damage. His feet thudded down, and he ran a dozen steps or so to kill his momentum. Tes, meanwhile, landed smoothly, her wings fading away as she lightly touched down.

Well aware that he no doubt looked like a threat soaring into the settlement on fiery wings, Victor lifted a hand and waved toward the approaching Shadeni. He could see Tellen among them, so he called out his name, "Tellen!"

He heard several whoops and Tellen laugh as his jog broke into a run. "Victor!"

As they closed the distance with each other, Victor spread his arms, and Tellen charged into him, whooping as he squeezed him around the ribs and lifted him off the ground—Victor had reduced his size significantly—laughing as Victor pounded him on the back. "Brother! You can fly?"

"I can!" Victor laughed. "Now, put me down before I start squeezing you back." He hadn't seen Thayla or the girls among the welcoming party, but Victor recognized many of the Shadeni hunters. He waved and grasped hands with any who reached out to him, and then he took a step back and pointed to Tes.

"This is my friend, Tes. I've known her a while, and she was eager to see what our home was like." He pointed to Tellen. "This is Tellen, the Ban-tok of the Shadeni tribe living here."

Tes, of course, curtsied elegantly, her smile bright enough to endear even indifferent strangers to her. "Ban-tok, I am honored."

"You will call me Tellen, as most do!" He laughed. "It is *my* honor; any friend of Victor's is welcome, indeed." He turned to Victor. "Shall I give you a tour, or would you rather look in on Thayla and the children? I'm sure they noticed your arrival, though they may be waiting for my hunters to announce the all-clear."

"They're all together?"

"Yes! Thayla's teaching some advanced tracking techniques." He turned toward the hills to the south, shading his eyes with his hand. "They'll be up that holbyis track in the meadow just past the first hill."

Victor looked at Tes. "Shall we?"

"Oh yes! I'm eager to meet your charge and also Deyni." She turned to Tellen. "When I first met Victor, he couldn't stop talking about Thayla and Deyni."

"Ha! A more beloved 'uncle' you'll be hard-pressed to find." Tellen thumped Victor on the shoulder. "You'll be staying for dinner, yes?"

"For dinner? *Hell* yes—wouldn't miss it."

"Come on, then. I'll guide you to her. Let's walk through the park and pass through the market; you can see at least part of the settlement and the hard work we've put into Brighthome."

"Brighthome? Is that the name of your town, then?" Victor felt a little stupid asking the question before so many witnesses; shouldn't he know the names of the towns and villages springing up on his lands and borders?

"It is, Victor, and it's with thanks to you that we have such a bright, hopeful future. Some of the veterans from the war wanted to name the village after you—"

"Yes!" one of the burlier nearby Shadeni shouted. "Victorhome!"

Victor laughed, shaking his head. "I'm glad you chose Brighthome, Tellen."

"Well, come on, then." Tellen walked back toward the street on the park's edge, and Victor and Tes followed. The rest of the crowd did, too, though Victor thought most would go back to whatever had occupied them before he and Tes had fallen from the sky. As they walked, Tellen looked at Victor, grinning as he asked, "Was I supposed to know you were coming today? Thayla doesn't always tell me everything."

"No." Victor shook his head and glanced at Tes. "It was a spur-of-the-moment decision. I only have a few days before we have to leave."

Tellen nodded, glancing at Tes, who happened to be looking about and taking in the scenery. Victor could tell he wanted to ask why she was with him, but the Shadeni leader just nodded and moved past it. "Last I heard, you were on another world—not Sojourn. Hmm, something like helping a queen to regain her throne?"

"Not exactly. She still has her throne, but we're trying to, uh, conquer the world now." Victor chuckled. "That's one of the reasons Tes is with me. She's sort of . . . training me."

"Ah, I see, I see. Well, that's certainly ambitious, though nothing I'd put past you." His nearly wincing expression said he knew he was pushing his luck when he asked, "Any word from Valla?" Of course, Tellen knew they weren't together; Victor had written to Thayla about it. Even so, he nodded, smiling to reassure his old friend.

"Yeah. She's on some world that's covered in water. There are powerful creatures there, and one of them took her on as a student."

"Ah! That's exciting. I'll have to ask Rellia for more detail next time I visit the capital."

Victor grunted in assent, glad that he wouldn't keep pressing the subject. "I like the style of your buildings; they're graceful." It was true; the shops and homes near the square were tall and slender with rounded corners, and the bricks or stones they'd used to construct them were covered with pale mortar-like stuff that reminded Victor of stucco. He especially liked the windows, which had a hand-blown look with bubbles in the glass that sparkled in the sunlight.

"This is a traditional Shadeni building type. You'll find some neighborhoods in cities like Persi Gables with this sort of construction, but not many entire towns any longer; the Ardeni prefer right angles, and the Ghelli use more living material. Don't get me started about the Bogoli and Cadwalli." He chuckled, shaking his head. "I prefer doors I don't have to crawl through."

"Ha, right." Victor gripped Tellen's shoulder, jostling him. "It's so good to see you, old friend. It's strange to think of the time we've spent apart now that I stand beside you; it feels like only a few days."

"That's what friendship does, Victor. You'll always be comfortable in my presence, and I yours, because we know we can be ourselves among friends." He looked past Victor to Tes, and when he caught her eye, he said, "I hope you know that I've heard your name in a tale or ten, Tes. Victor spoke highly of you."

"Well, he'd better!"

They all laughed and spent the rest of the walk making small talk. Tellen pointed out features in the town as they went by—shops and their wares, a well, a watchtower and barracks, and then, as they passed it, a holbyis farm. The sheep-like animals were far from the track, bunched together, busily munching on the blue-green grass. When the trio crested the hill, Victor immediately saw Thayla in the distance.

She was kneeling in the grass, pointing something out to her five young students. Before they moved closer, Tellen slowed and said, "I'll let you say hello. If you don't mind, I'll go finish a bit of clan business so I can meet you back at the house without any burdensome thoughts on my mind."

"Yeah, of course, that's fine." Victor smiled and shook Tellen's proffered hand, smiling broadly. "See you soon, right?"

"Yes, just an hour or so." With a smile and nod at Tes, the Ban-tok turned and retraced their steps.

Victor looked at Tes. "Ready?"

"Of course! I wasn't lying when I said I was eager to meet these people."

Looking into her eyes, Victor could see she meant it. He gave a quick nod, then started toward Thayla. Her back was to them, but the children saw them approach, and, of course, Deyni immediately shrieked, "Victor!" She charged toward him, leaving the others behind, her turquoise braids bouncing off her back with each stride. Victor laughed, squatted, and held out his arms. When she slammed into him, he grunted and stood tall, squeezing her to his chest.

"You're getting big! Sheesh! I think you grew a foot since I was last home!"

"Really?" She leaned back, her big teal eyes wide.

"Yep." Victor squeezed her tight; he wasn't exaggerating; Deyni had hit a growth spurt. Over her shoulder, he saw Thayla and the other children approaching, including his ward, Cora. Her thick brown curls were also pulled back into braids, giving her a very different look than when he'd left. On top of that, she was dressed like a Shadeni hunter—as were all the children—in leathers and furs. As they approached, Victor set Deyni down, surprised yet again by her size compared to Cora, who was a few years older.

He was smiling, about to call out a greeting to the orphaned girl, but Chala charged forward and grabbed him in a hug. "Victor! You're smaller than last time!" She laughed.

He grunted, surprised by the strength in the girl's wiry arms. "Someday, maybe I'll teach you how to do that."

Thayla stepped close and took ahold of Chala's arm. "Let him loose, Chala. He hasn't even said hello to his ward."

"Okay, but don't go away, Victor! We have a new pet for you to meet!"

"I wouldn't miss it." Victor looked at Cora, flanked by two older boys whom he'd never met, or, if he had, he couldn't recall their faces or names. "Hello, Cora. I've read many reports from Thayla and Efanie—" He paused, frowning, and looked at Thayla. "Where's Efanie?"

"She's back at our home; it's her turn to feed these brats lunch, so she's working on that."

"*Brats?*" Chala howled, whirling on Thayla. Deyni, too, was outraged by the label, and they both expressed their displeasure while Victor squatted before Cora, speaking more softly now that the attention was off the two of them.

"I've heard good things. It seems you're making lots of friends. Are you well?"

She nodded, a tiny dimple forming on her right cheek as she smiled tentatively. "Yes, milord." She folded her hands in front of her, nervously entwining her fingers.

"You'll have to do better than that! What's your favorite thing to do these days?"

"Swim!" Deyni answered for her. "We swim near your house all the time when Miss Efanie is teaching us."

"Oh?" Victor knew the girls often spent time at his home with Efanie, but not the details of their every activity. "Is that right, Cora?"

She nodded, her dimple deepening as her smile reached her brown eyes. "Yes! I love the sea!"

While she spoke, Thayla took the two boys aside, and Victor heard her say, "Sorry, lads, we'll cut the lesson short today. Don't worry; I'll pick up where I left off tomorrow. Run along now, and tell your mother that we're spending time with visiting family." As their footsteps thumped away on the grass, Victor felt his heartbeat quicken and his eyes fill with moisture. Could he really be so emotional at just the idea that Thayla thought of him as family?

Blinking rapidly and clearing his throat, he stood and pointed to Tes. "I want you all to meet a dear friend. This is Tes, and she's saved my life more than once."

"Tes!" Thayla exclaimed. "I never thought we'd meet you, but I've heard so much! Valla and Victor both sang your praises when they returned from . . ." She trailed off, wrinkling her nose.

"Zaafor," Victor finished for her.

"Well, I've heard no end of good things about you, Lady Thayla." Tes put her hands on her knees, leaning closer to Deyni and the other two girls. "And very much about all three of you. I even brought you gifts!"

"*Gifts?*" Chala repeated, eyes flying wide. "For me, too?"

"Of course, Chala, sister of Chandri, fierce huntress of the Shadeni. How could I leave you out, especially when you've helped so much with these other two?" Tes smiled brightly as she nodded toward Deyni and Cora. "In fact, I'll present you with your gift first."

Victor cleared his throat, feeling a little uneasy. Why hadn't he thought of that? Kids *loved* getting little presents, and he didn't see them very often. He should bring them something every time he came home! Now Tes was rescuing him once again. He almost laughed at the silliness of the thought but only smiled, shaking his head ruefully. Thayla caught his eye, and her arched eyebrow said she knew what he was thinking.

"Now, as I understand it," Tes said, glancing at Thayla, "Chala is allowed to hunt on her own. Is that right?"

Thayla nodded. "She is."

"Would it be appropriate, Lady Thayla, for me to gift her a weapon?"

"A *weapon*!" Chala howled.

Thayla only smiled and nodded, once again displaying her trust in Victor; he'd told her Tes was a friend, and she knew how much she'd helped him and Valla. "If you think it's appropriate for a young huntress, I'll trust your judgment, Lady Tes."

Tes's face grew solemn as she held out her hands. A moment later, she held a sleek, silvery bow with a golden bowstring that reminded Victor of a piano wire. It was short—woefully undersized for someone like him—but in Chala's hands, it would be perfect. "This was a weapon I used to hunt for food when I made a pilgrimage through the forests of Wan'lo—a world where my mother's ancestors lived for many millennia. It served me well, but I've since found other ways I prefer to hunt. Will you put it to good use, Chala?"

"It's beautiful," Thayla said as Chala nodded vigorously.

"I will! This is perfect! I've been using the spear, but my bow skill is close to improved; I'm sure of it!"

"Practice with this a while, and you'll be improved in no time; if your skill hasn't ranked up to advanced by next summer, I'll be shocked." Tes handed the bow to Chala, and the Shadeni girl practically wept with excitement as she stepped back, her eyes tracing every line and curve of the elegant weapon. Tes turned to Cora and smiled, a gesture immediately mirrored on the young girl's face. "I'm very pleased to hear you enjoy swimming."

"You are?"

"Yes! It means the gift I chose is just right." She held out her hand, and a silvery bracelet dangling with polished seashells appeared on her palm. "This is a magical bracelet. If you wear it in the sun until the shells begin to glow, it will allow you to breathe underwater for as many minutes as there are shells." She held it up, and Victor watched Cora count the shells. There were twelve.

"I can swim underwater for twelve minutes?"

"Yes! When you come up for air, just hold the bracelet in the sunlight until it starts to glow again. It only takes a minute or so—look!" She twisted the dangling bracelet so everyone could see how the shells were beginning to glow with a faint silvery light. "It's working already."

Thayla cleared her throat, a note of worry in her voice as she asked, "And if she's deep underwater when the magic wears off?"

Tes nodded knowingly. "Let me see your wrist, Cora." Cora held out her arm, and Tes secured the bracelet around it. As soon as she fastened the latch, it shrank to fit perfectly around her narrow bones. "This enchantment is twofold, Lady Thayla. As soon as the magic fades, it will become incredibly buoyant. If Cora is deep underwater, the bracelet will rapidly pull her to the surface."

"Ah . . ." Thayla sighed, nodding.

Tes looked up at her and winked. "She'll be safer than ever."

Cora was staring at her wrist in wonder, and Thayla, reminding Victor of his failings as a steward, nudged her. "What do you say, sweet girl?"

Cora's fingers trembled with hesitant excitement as she gently touched the bracelet. At Thayla's prompting, her eyes jumped to Tes, and she blurted, "I love it! How can I thank you, Lady Tes?"

Tes grabbed her into a hug, pulling her tight. "Oh dear. It's nothing! Just a plaything from a different world. I hope you enjoy it." When Tes released her, Cora's eyes were moist, but she looked happy, and that's all Victor wanted for her. Thayla looked at him, and her eyes said the same thing—it was good to see the girl openly happy.

"Isn't it too much?" she asked, again glancing at Chala and her beautiful bow. Victor knew she meant the value of the two gifts. Before he could answer, Tes did.

"Nonsense. These are trinkets, nothing more. I've gathered many such treasures over the years, and it gives me far more joy to see them used well than stored away forever in my storage containers!" She looked at Deyni. "Now, you, young lady, are something of a beast tamer, is that right?"

"Well, we all are!" Deyni pointed to Cora and Chala.

Chala shook her head and poked her smaller stepsister. "We all have many *pets*, but Deyni makes bonds with them. She can feel their thoughts!"

Tes smiled and reached out to grip Deyni's wrist, turning her hand so her palm was facing up. Deyni's skin was deep purple-red, but her palm was different— a pale shade of violet. Victor had noticed that before, but the stark contrast caught his eye. When she opened her fingers, it was almost like a flower unfolding, revealing softer, more delicate petals. "I have a gift for you that might be something very special or might just be a lot of work ending in some heartache and frustration. Do you want a challenge, or should I find something simpler?"

"I want a challenge!" Deyni answered immediately.

Tes grinned. "I thought you might say that." She still gripped Deyni's wrist, but now she held out her other hand, and a small gray egg, speckled with yellow dots, appeared there. It was a little larger than a chicken's egg. "This is a spire drake's egg. It's dormant and will never hatch in its current state. Spire drakes are special creatures from my homeland. They're friends to my people and very intelligent, though they're still beasts."

Deyni stared at the egg, eyes wide with wonder. In fact, everyone had gotten silent, leaning closer to the two, trying to see the egg more clearly. Chala asked, "It won't ever hatch?"

Tes shook her head. "Not if left alone like this. In order for it to hatch, the little drake inside has to feel a bond with someone outside. In nature, that would be its mother. Now that it's been taken from its home, it will have to be someone else."

Deyni caught her breath, and the look of hopeful excitement she gave Tes brought tears to Victor's eyes again. He blinked them away, smiling as she asked, "Could I do that?"

"That's what I'm hoping, Deyni. If you can keep this egg nice and warm and spend lots of time with it—talking to it, singing to it, rolling it very gently in your palms, the little seed of a drake in there might feel the connection with you and start to grow. It will take a long time, and it might be very frustrating. Are you sure you want this, or would you rather I gave you something you could use right away, like Chala's and Cora's gifts?"

"N-no! I want the egg, Lady Tes, please!"

"Okay then, young tamer Deyni. I pass this responsibility on to you. I hope you have luck." She placed the egg in Deyni's hand, and the girl gently cupped her fingers around it, pulling it close to her chest. "It's warm!"

"Just a little. That's from my touch. You should make a bed of coals for it each night. Don't worry about burning the unborn drake; it would take something like a smithy's forge to hurt it." Tes straightened up, smiling, and then she produced a small blue scale. Victor immediately recognized it as one of hers. She held it out to Thayla. "Lady Thayla, should Deyni succeed in getting this egg to hatch, please channel some Energy into this scale. I will feel it and visit as quickly as possible to help Deyni get started training her newborn companion."

Thayla took the scale delicately, smiling and chuckling as she nearly dropped it. "It's heavier than I expected." She tucked it into a small beaded pouch on her belt and then looked up. "Thank you, Lady Tes. Now, if you're done spoiling these rascals, would you like to see our home?"

Victor laughed and stepped forward, grabbing Thayla into a hug. "Not before I collect a proper hello from you!" He squeezed her and buried his face into the crook of her neck.

Thayla laughed at first, but then she began to kick her feet. "Your whiskers are scratching me! Oof! Too *tight*!"

Victor put her down, smiling ear to ear, then he whistled for show and summoned Guapo in a swirl of glittering, golden, glory-attuned Energy. The stallion, massive compared to a roladii—the most commonly used mounts on Fanwath—reared and whinnied. When he settled, Victor laughed and grabbed Deyni, hoisting her up. Then he reached for Cora. "Deyni, hold his mane; Cora, hold Deyni, and—" Victor laughed as Chala leaped atop the enormous stallion, vaulting onto her belly behind Cora and sliding a leg over. "Good! He'll take you three ahead. Hold on tight!"

8

GOOD THINGS

Victor and Tes spent the night and the next day with the Shadeni tribe. At night, they ate and drank and laughed, and during the day, Victor spent time with the children. He showed off his spirit companions, and, of course, Guapo stole the show. He used his new Core Domain ability, dazzling the children and adults alike with his inspiration domain. The children showed him their many semi-tame animals, and, all the while, Deyni clutched her drake egg close to her chest, held there in a soft leather sling Tellen had immediately crafted her.

The busy night and day rejuvenated something in Victor's spirit, and when he woke the day before their departure, he sought out Thayla before the sun came up and asked her if she'd like to take a walk. Looking up from stirring a pot of stewed grains, nuts, and dried fruit, she smiled and nodded. "I'd love to, Victor. I promised the kids we could get back to their training today, though. Will we be back before they finish breakfast?"

Before Victor could respond, Tes spoke up from the hallway, surprising them both. "I'd love to spend the morning with the children. Do you mind if I teach them a few old tricks I learned for making snares in the wild?"

Thayla set her wooden spoon on the counter and turned toward her. "Really? You don't mind?"

"Not at all. I think it'll do you and Victor some good to have a moment of peace! The children are wonderful, but they're demanding. I can see why you and Efanie split the duties."

"They're not bad." Thayla smiled softly and looked at Victor. "They just want to be involved in everything because he's here."

Victor shrugged. "What can I say? I'm famous."

Thayla grabbed a dish towel and snapped it at him. "Well, come on, then. It's been a while since I stretched my legs into a proper hike."

"Victor, while you're out there, why don't you try one of your spells? The rescue one shouldn't be dangerous."

Victor nodded. "Yeah. That's probably a good idea." He waved, snatched a blue apple-like fruit from the counter, and then stepped out the back door onto the expansive wooden deck Tellen had crafted. Thayla followed him out and then led the way down some steps and out the back gate onto a trail that Victor could see meandered up the hillside into the woods on the distant slopes.

Thayla looked over her shoulder at him. "She's very nice, Victor."

"Yeah, I know. When I first met her, it made me suspicious of her. It didn't make sense that someone so powerful was being so damn nice to me." He frowned. "Well, she helped Valla a lot, too, so not just me."

When Victor caught up to her, and they walked side by side, she arched an eyebrow at him. "I was surprised you wanted separate rooms. I thought you were bringing a new love here for my approval."

"Ah," Victor chuckled, shaking his head. "Nah, we're friends, despite any intentions I might have."

"Maybe she's just being careful with you. I get the feeling she's not exactly . . . *inexperienced*."

"Hey." Victor jostled her with his elbow. "I hope you're not saying—"

"No, I mean in love, Victor. In life. Maybe she's just forcing you to take things slowly. After all, you don't want another situation like—" She stopped abruptly and grabbed his hand. "I'm sorry. My foot keeps finding my mouth. Are you still hurting from Valla?"

"My heart's not gushing blood anymore," he said with a chuckle, "only a little sore." Desperate to change the subject, he asked, "And Tellen? Are things still good? It seems like it."

"Things are wonderful!" She laughed, slapping his shoulder. "I'm sorry to push you into sensitive topics. What did your *friend* mean by new spells?"

"Oh, well, like I've said—she's spending time with me to help me prepare for some difficult duels, and part of that is helping me develop some new spells. It's the main reason we came home, other than my desire to see you all, of course."

"Why'd you have to come home for that?"

Victor clicked his tongue and kicked a rock off the trail. "There are some nosy *pendejos* on Ruhn. They're veil walkers who—"

"Like your mentor, Dar?"

"Right. So, anyway, they're very powerful, and one thing I've learned about people with that kind of power is that they can snoop on us little people pretty easily. They're supposed to be neutral, but even Tes agrees with me that they're probably not. The 'great houses' on Ruhn have been in power for a long, long time, and I think it would be foolish to think none of the veil walkers are related to them one way or another."

"So you don't want them to see you working your new magic?"

"Basically, yeah." He looked at her sideways. "Hey, speaking of magic, how are things going for you? How's your Core coming along?"

"Do you fear I've let your gift go to waste? Fear not! Old Mother taught me a thing or two about cultivating my courage-attuned Energy before she passed, and I've been diligent. The band of moonlight-hued Energy that circles my death-attuned Energy has grown thick and vibrant, compressing that cold blue center into a smaller, denser heart. It's there but never leaks out unless I call upon it. Meanwhile, the courage you gifted me is a boon to all the Shadeni I care for."

Victor smiled, his heart warmed by the success. He put his arm over her shoulders and squeezed her tight to his side. "I'm happy about that, Thayla. Do you Spirit Walk often?"

"Oh, yes. I have duties as the mother of this clan that require it." She tugged him to the side, and they left the main track on a narrow game trail, weaving between tall, mature trees up into the hills. They walked quietly for a while, and then Thayla stopped, turning to look back the way they'd come, sighing happily at the vista.

The sun was turning the eastern horizon yellow and orange, and the thin, wispy clouds were painted with the same shades. "I haven't watched a sunrise from this spot yet. Thank you for getting me out so early, Victor."

"It's beautiful, isn't it—this land we took from the undead?" He moved to a flat spot on the ridge and summoned a chair from his storage ring, setting it down for Thayla and then pulling forth another for himself.

Thayla sat, but her face had gotten serious, her smile fading. "It is beautiful, but we paid dearly."

Victor nodded. "Yeah, and not just to the undead—to the Ridonne on the way here. Your people paid more than most."

Thayla shook her head. "Not as much as the Naghelli or the people from Nia's world."

"Dark Ember," Victor growled, the words coming from his lips like a curse. "I want to go there. I want to help the people there, but Tes thinks the 'great vampire lords' are probably veil walkers—steel seekers, at least."

Thayla nodded, watching him sit beside her. "And you've many other commitments. Is it up to you to save everyone?"

"No, not everyone," Victor sighed, summoning a small camp stove and setting it up before his chair. "I feel like I ought to help those I know about, though. Of course, I promised I'd help the giants of Zaafor deal with Warlord Thoargh, too. I'm actually looking forward to seeing his *pinché* smug face again."

Thayla laughed. "Glad you're still the same old Victor in there underneath all those layers of power."

"Layers of power? Do I seem different?"

"I can feel your Spirit Core. It's like being a little too close to a campfire."

"Oh, shit." Victor looked inward and ensured he was holding his aura well in check; he was. "Is it uncomfortable?"

"No!" Thayla laughed and smiled at him, her eyes crinkling at the corners. "It's not like that; it's more, well, it's more that I can tell you're holding back—like a compressed spring. It's different with Tes. If I didn't know better, I'd think she was just a normal Tier Two or Tier Three cultivator. Why is that?"

Victor shrugged. "I think it has to do with her being past the iron ranks. Like, she's as strong as a veil walker, but she doesn't use that terminology. I think once you reach that kind of power, it's easier to hide it somehow. Dar seems perfectly harmless half the time, too—other than his size and pissed-off expressions." Victor laughed. He leaned forward and summoned a little kettle, setting it on the stove to heat up.

"What are you making?"

"Some coffee. I bought it in Sojourn." While he spoke, he summoned a little table and set it beside the stove. Then he brought out his coffeepot, strainer, two cups, a bowl of sugar, and a carafe of cream. He loaded some fresh coffee grounds into the metallic strainer and placed it atop the pot. "I think there are better ways to make it, but I never really learned before leaving home. My *abuela* always made it in an old electric coffeepot."

"I'm eager to try it!"

"Well, while that's heating up, wanna help me try out one of my new spells?"

"Of course I do."

Victor stood and held out a hand, pulling Thayla to her feet. Then he pointed to a spot a bit farther away, near a large fallen tree. "Stand over there by that tree and pretend a bunch of monsters are surrounding you, getting ready to kill you."

Thayla laughed, shaking her head as she walked over to the tree. "How am I to pretend that?"

"I don't know. Hold up your hands and cower."

"Ha! I wouldn't! I'd die with spear in hand!"

"Okay, fine—do that!" Victor watched as she summoned her spear and began jabbing it at imaginary enemies, then he pulled out his elder magic book, flipping to the spell he had in mind. "Perfect! Keep that up for a few minutes while I review this pattern."

"What? A few minutes?"

Victor chuckled, nodding as he examined the pattern. It was one of the easier of his new spells, only filling a couple of pages. He started building the pattern in his pathway, using, per usual, his inspiration-attuned Energy. Two minutes later, he turned the page and continued, delicately weaving multiple threads of Energy in and out of the intricate pattern. In the end, it had two complex sections—one that was very familiar to him and part of a System-granted spell meant for shielding, and another that was totally new to him, something Tes had guided his hand on.

When the pattern flashed and solidified in his pathway, the System brought forth its now-familiar complaints:

*****Warning! The spell being cast incorporates and alters another System-granted spell. If you complete this casting, your System-granted spell will be removed.*****

*****Warning! The spell being cast does not follow System-designed iterations and may be too powerful for you. Proceed at your own risk.*****

*****Warning! Non-System spell pattern detected! You will only receive this warning one time. Do you wish to halt this process? YES/NO.*****

He glanced at Thayla and saw her seemingly frozen in place, fighting her imaginary enemies. "Okay, let's see how this works." Victor mentally indicated he wanted to proceed with the spell, and then Energy poured out of his Core, empowering the magic. With a flash like a bomb going off, a brilliant, white-gold ball of Energy enveloped Thayla. At the same time, with a dizzying surge of power, Victor's stomach fell away as he was ripped through the fabric of reality and, in the space of a single heartbeat, brought back exactly where Thayla had been standing. Meanwhile, she had gone to his previous location, her golden shield still intact.

"What—*ack!*" Sounds of retching emerged from the shield of inspiration-attuned Energy surrounding Thayla, and Victor understood why; he was dizzy, and his stomach was churning from the sudden relocation. He leaned forward, hands on knees, as the sensation faded. Blinking away watery eyes, he read the System messages:

*****You have discovered a new spell: Guardian's Rescue, Epic.*****

*****Your new spell renders a System-granted spell obsolete. Removing.*****

*****You have lost the spell: Guard Ally, Basic.*****

*****Guardian's Rescue, Epic: You have mastered the art of tactical intervention. When cast, Guardian's Rescue encases your chosen ally in a cocoon of Energy. This protective cocoon absorbs incoming damage and rebuffs attackers with damage based on the attunement used to cast it. Simultaneously, the spell triggers a teleportation effect, instantly swapping your position with that of your ally, provided they are within your line of sight. Whether to pull an ally from danger or place yourself at the heart of the fray, Guardian's Rescue grants unparalleled control over battlefield positioning, offering a lifeline in critical moments. Energy Cost: 10,000.*****

*****Warning! This spell is not System-designed! Use it with caution—there are no safeguards in place. This is the only time you will receive this warning!*****

"Not bad!" Victor laughed, straightening up. "Are you okay?"

"I'm fine," Thayla called from within the blazing shell of Energy, though she sounded a bit put out. "How long will this persist?"

"I don't know. Hang on." Victor summoned the fancy broadsword he'd gotten inside the Iron Prison. It was a heavy, wonderfully crafted weapon with a faintly luminescent silver-flecked dark-metal blade that was, if Victor remembered correctly, crafted from sableglow steel. It felt comfortable in his hand, and the balance made him want to swing it, almost as if it had its own inertia. He stepped closer to Thayla, and then, careful that his blow would hit the shell of magical Energy but not her, he swung the sword at it.

His blade impacted the barrier and penetrated it, though barely. Meanwhile, a wave of doubt and discouragement washed over Victor, and he gasped, "Shit! Are you okay?"

"Fine." Thayla narrowed her eyes at him through the haze of Energy. "Why? That sword didn't even come close to me."

Victor stepped back, his hand shaking, his mind clouded by confusion. After a minute, he started to laugh. "Holy shit! That's what my own Energy did to me! It basically did the opposite of inspiration." He stepped close again. "Hold still." With a grunt, he lifted the sword and brought it down even harder on the shell. This time, the barrier shattered, but Victor fell back, his mind racing for answers to questions he couldn't grasp. He stumbled and fell onto his butt, pawing at the ground with his hands as he crab-walked away from Thayla.

She looked at him as if he were mad, laughing as she asked, "What are you doing?"

It took a good twenty or thirty seconds before Victor could form a coherent thought and piece together what was happening. "I just blasted myself with confusion or doubt or something. Holy shit, that's cool."

"You teleported me *and* shielded me! If I hadn't gotten sick, I'd congratulate you." She stepped close and held out a hand. Victor smiled and took her hand in his, laughing as she grunted and failed to pull him to his feet. "Help me a little, you oaf!"

"All right, all right." When she tugged again, Victor surged to his feet and smiled. "Sorry about the upset stomach; I didn't know it would do that."

"That spell is amazing, Victor. Do you think I could learn it?"

Victor frowned, turning to walk over to the kettle. It was bubbling, so he slowly drizzled its contents onto the coffee grounds, watching as the darkened water dripped into the pot. "I think you *could*, eventually, but, for starters, it takes ten thousand Energy to cast. Also, the System doesn't like it."

"What does that mean?" Thayla moved to sit in her camp chair.

"It's not a System-granted spell. It's built using a kind of magic that I'm nervous even mentioning to you because I don't want you to gain some new enemies—the kind of enemies that can appear out of nowhere and kill you with a snap of their fingers." He illustrated by holding his hand in front of her eyes and snapping.

She slapped his hand away. "They'd kill me?"

"Well, they might not kill you for *learning*, but they'd certainly put me on a to-be-killed list for teaching you. I don't think we're ready to face that risk yet. Let me get more powerful, and you need to gain some strength, too." He paused his pouring and looked at her. "Do you think you want to do that? I mean, keep gaining levels? Now that you know what's out there?"

"I think so, but I'm in no hurry, Victor. I'll content myself with this quiet life for a decade or two—I'd like to see the children grow up and start their lives. Then maybe I'll visit one of the worlds you've discovered. Maybe you can give me a suggestion."

Victor grinned. "Hell yes, I can."

After a while, when Victor finished the coffee and poured them each a cup, she held it close, savoring the aroma as she looked out over the hillside. "Are they more beautiful?"

Victor poured some cream into his cup and narrowed his eyes. "Who?"

"Not people. I mean those other worlds you've seen. Are they more beautiful?"

"Than this?" Victor looked out over the countryside, taking in the blue-green treetops and the great fields of shimmering grass reflecting the morning's bright rays. "Not a chance, Thayla. Some of the worlds I've been to were godawful—wastelands filled with poisonous air or deserts with hardly a thing growing in them. Sojourn is pretty in a way; you can see the stars all day and night like you're practically in space, and the city is wondrous. Ruhn is pretty, too, but no more than Fanwath, though Iron Mountain is something awesome. You've got to see it to know what I mean."

Thayla smiled at that and took a tiny sip of her coffee. "Oh," she said, holding it out to peer at the dark liquid. "It smells better than it tastes."

Victor laughed and took her cup. "You might like it more with some sugar and cream. It takes a little getting used to."

She smiled at him and squeezed his shoulder. "Like many good things." He knew what she meant: she hadn't exactly been fond of him when they'd first met.

He nodded, grinning as he scooped a tablespoon of sugar into her cup. "Yeah, Thayla. Like many good things."

9

GLACIAL WRATH

Victor and Tes spent their last night on Fanwath back at his estate. He hadn't wanted to say goodbye to Thayla, Tellen, and the girls, but he was thankful for the pleasant visit, and he thought it had been good for Cora and Deyni, in particular. They'd gotten to see that he still thought of Fanwath as home and meant it when he said he'd be back to visit whenever possible. He wasn't under any sort of delusion that Cora loved and missed him, but he felt as though she thought of him as responsible for her, and some consistency was important in that regard.

In the morning, considering their travel time home would be instantaneous, he and Tes decided to go down to the beach again so he could practice his last couple of elder magic spells. One of the remaining spells was a modification of a System-granted spell, like the one he'd cast with Thayla, but the other was something else: the spell Azforath had gifted him—Glacial Wrath.

He'd spent a long time studying the complicated pattern—several days. That was nothing, however, compared to the weeks Tes had helped him puzzle out how to apply the elder magic modification that Azforath had written for him separately. It was a component that would allow him to remain conscious and free-willed while the deep rage of the glacier simmered under the surface. Of course, he'd done other things in those weeks; Victor's mind could only focus on the twisting, multifaceted spell pattern and its intricate lines for so long.

In the end, they'd succeeded, but only with the Glacial Wrath spell. He'd tried to apply what he'd learned to Volcanic Fury, but there was something about the folds of rage-attuned Energy in Glacial Wrath that fit more easily into the modification. Tes theorized that the rage was different, that the anger of a glacier had a different quality than the fury of a volcano. Victor thought she might be right, but it didn't matter to him; he was happy with the success and would continue to work on Volcanic Fury as his skill with elder magic progressed.

As they walked down the path toward the beach, Tes skipped ahead but slowed after only a few steps, turning to walk backward, graceful as always. "You had a nice day with Thayla?" Her eyes were bright, her smile impish.

"What does that mean?"

"I mean, you were much renewed after your time hiking in the hills. It was nice, was it not?"

Victor shrugged. "Yeah, it was nice. I trust Thayla, so it's easy to talk to her."

"Mmhmm. That's good, Victor. It's not so common to meet people who'd put your interests above their own. I think Thayla would do that for you." She laughed, a light trilling sound, then added, "You know, there are quite a few folks you've told me about who might do that for you. Maybe I should say it hasn't been easy for *me* to cultivate such friendship."

"I'd do anything to help you, Tes. Valla would, too."

"Yes, but I think you'd struggle to name someone you wouldn't aid—"

Victor started holding up his fingers. "The Sojourn Council, Warlord Thoargh, any kind of *pinché* Death Caster—"

Tes laughed and darted forward to poke him in the chest. "You can't just list off enemies. We're not talking about those. Besides, half of that is bluster; you're spending a fortune to help a Death Caster who happens to be waiting in your palace back at Iron Mountain!"

Before he got dragged into a frankly bizarre tangent, Victor asked, "How was your time with the kids? I know you told Thayla and Efanie it was a lot of fun, but was it really?"

"It *was*! Those girls are something special, Victor. I can feel karmic ties forming between them. They'll be hard to separate. Already, Deyni talks about seeking out her stepsister across the sea, and, of course, the other girls want to join in the adventure."

Victor frowned. "Yeah? Well, according to Thayla, Chandri plans to return before winter. She's found dungeons, mines, ancient ruins—all manner of resources—and charted them all. Thayla thinks Chandri will try to sell her maps to me, Rellia, and Lam."

"A reasonable thing to do, don't you think? She risks much adventuring into unknown lands."

"Yeah, definitely. I'll have Gorro check them out to see if he thinks any would be a good investment for me. As for the girls, I won't approve of them running off with Chandri until they've reached Tier Two. Don't you think that's also reasonable?"

"Well, Victor, Chala's nearly a woman grown, but as Cora's guardian, you have the right to keep her home. As for Deyni . . . I'm sure Thayla would listen to your opinion, but you should respect the fact that you aren't that girl's father."

"Yeah." Victor sighed and roughly rubbed his fingers through his hair. "I spoke before thinking. I know I don't control them. I just—"

"Relax, Victor!" Tes laughed. "It'll be years before Thayla and Tellen think Deyni should go off exploring. You have time to adjust to these sorts of ideas."

Victor nodded, laughing. "Right."

"What spell will you try first? The Glacial—"

"The other one. Let's save the big one for last."

"Well, you should step into the surf a ways before you cast it. If it works as we hoped, it might make a mess of the beach."

"Yeah, all right." Victor reached into his pathways and severed the Energy threads that maintained his Alter Self spell. As he surged to his normal size, he strode across the sandy portion of the beach into the rougher rocky area closer to the water, and then he waded out nearly a hundred yards until the water was up to his chest. He shivered a little; one thing the Silver Sea wasn't was warm.

When he turned, he saw that Tes had waited on the beach, watching him, the ocean breeze flapping her yellow skirts around her knees. Her hair, woven with matching ribbons, streamed behind her, and Victor stared for a while, admiring her beauty.

"Well?" she called, her voice muffled by the crashing waves and wind.

He lifted a hand to wave, and then he summoned his elder magic book, glad for its many enchantments; he could drop it in the ocean, and not a molecule of water would cling to its pages. He turned the page to the spell he wanted to cast, and then, after carefully studying the entire pattern, he began to craft it in his pathways.

This spell didn't have a matrix that would differentiate Energy types and provide varied results. It would behave the same way no matter what Energy he fed into it. Even knowing that, Victor chose to craft the pattern for the first time using inspiration-attuned Energy. He wondered if his preference for working with that Energy type was due to its nature; was it more willing to go where he wanted it to? Was it the Energy that guided him, or was he guiding the Energy? He chuckled at the thought, then flipped the page to finish the second half of the spell.

Ten minutes later, the pattern flared with Energy—another success—and the System froze the world around him, blaring its usual warnings:

Warning! The spell being cast incorporates and alters another System-granted spell. If you complete this casting, your System-granted spell will be removed.

Warning! The spell being cast does not follow System-designed iterations and may be too powerful for you. Proceed at your own risk.

Warning! Non-System spell pattern detected! You will only receive this warning one time. Do you wish to halt this process? YES/NO.

Victor watched the waves around him, fascinated by how they seemed to hang in place, even the frothy bubbles refusing to burst in the System's iron grip. Before he received a scolding demand to make a decision, he looked at the question and selected "NO." The world moved again, and Energy rushed out of his Core to fill the pattern.

The waves that had been jostling him suddenly stopped having any sort of effect. They broke on his back, and he didn't move even a millimeter. A second later, the world exploded in steam as geysers of lava burst out of the ocean floor. They sprayed in fanlike eruptions in every direction around him, sizzling and popping as they instantly cooled in the endless supply of salt water. As soon as the eruption started, it was over, and Victor once again felt the push and pull of the waves as the enormous cloud of steam slowly wafted away in the breeze.

*****You have discovered a new spell: Roots of the Angry Mountain, Advanced.*****

*****Your new spell renders a System-granted spell obsolete. Removing.*****

*****You have lost the spell: Roots of the Mountain, Basic.*****

*****Roots of the Angry Mountain, Advanced: You have harnessed primal Energy to anchor yourself to the very fabric of the world. When activated, the spell will render you immovable, making you as unyielding as the mountain itself for several seconds. Any force—physical, elemental, or magical—will struggle to shift your position during this time. The spell will call forth the mountain's roiling blood, causing it to erupt violently from the ground in an explosion centered on you. This explosive release will not discern between friend and foe. Energy Cost: 7,000.*****

*****Warning! This spell is not System-designed! Use it with caution—there are no safeguards in place. This is the only time you will receive this warning!*****

When the steam cleared and he'd wiped away the System messages, Victor looked to the shore to see Tes clapping her hands and whooping. Victor grinned and jogged toward her, easily pushing his legs through the chilly water. "That was spectacular!" Tes cheered. "Imagine your foes surrounding you, thinking you overwhelmed—what a bitter pill you'll make them swallow!"

"That was pretty cool in the water, wasn't it? Like a bomb going off. It wasn't epic, though. Just advanced."

Tes laughed, repeating his words, "*Pretty cool.* Don't complain about an advanced spell. A bit of tweaking or maybe adding in additional functionality, and you can make it epic."

Victor smiled at her teasing tone and looked past her, down the shore and to the east, where some of the village buildings were visible in the gray morning light. "You sure it's safe for me to try the spell from . . . you-know-who?"

"Your titan friend? Yes! His design was flawless, and I'm quite certain we integrated the modification he gave you properly. Besides, if you lose your mind and threaten innocents, I'll pick you up and carry you into the ocean!" She winked at him, and Victor shook his head, narrowing his eyes at her.

"Could you pick me up like that, or would you have to take your true form?"

"Oh, we'll have to see how large this spell makes you, but I fear there might be some villagers who would witness their first dragon."

"All right, well, here's hoping that won't be necessary." Victor pulled out his elder magic book again, but he only had to study the spell for a few seconds before he began crafting it in his pathways. He'd grown intimately familiar with this pattern over the last few months. Even though it was more complicated, he found it easier to weave than some of the other spells simply because he was working with two types of Energy. He drew a thread of blue ice out of his Breath Core and, of course, rage from his Spirit Core. With those two threads in hand, he focused his will and got to work.

Tes watched him, her eyes glowing faintly, and he wondered if she could see what he was doing with the Energy in his pathways. As he worked, he asked, "Can all veil walkers do that? See into a person's Core or their pathways?"

"No. People who reach that level of power are as varied as iron rankers. They—we—vary in power, too. For instance, I'm much stronger than most veil walkers you might find in Sojourn. And, as you no doubt have guessed, there are stages beyond. Remember our talk about your titan kin and the ivid queen?"

"Yeah."

"So, focus on your task at hand. There's an ocean between you and the need to worry about what a veil walker can do."

Victor smirked; he wasn't so sure it was as wide an ocean as she implied. He could feel the power he was awakening with each of these epic spells. He was determined to reach Level One Hundred and begin his "steel-seeking" journey as soon as possible. The veil walkers of Ruhn constantly watching, judging, and controlling him felt like a collar around his neck, and Victor didn't like collars.

As part of his mind went down those prideful paths, most of his concentration remained on the spell he was building in his pathways. He thought it was beautiful. The pattern was a delicate, multi-pronged galaxy of bright blue and smoldering red suns interlocked with a weave of glittering, contrasting ribbons of Energy. When he finished the final loop, sweeping the rage through the control structure Azforath had designed for him, the spell flared brilliantly, and Victor felt a rush of accomplishment as the System slowed his perception of the world.

*****Warning! The spell being cast does not follow System-designed iterations and may be too powerful for you. Proceed at your own risk.*****

*****Warning! Non-System spell pattern detected! You will only receive this warning one time. Do you wish to halt this process? YES/NO.*****

"No," Victor said, his voice like thunder in the silence the System had wrought. Instantly, the world continued its usual course, and Energy siphoned out of his Cores, feeding the hungry, powerful, elder magic transformation. Victor arched his back and roared as ancient might swelled his body. His muscles and bones, his organs and flesh—all exploded with rapid growth as sulking, malevolent cold radiated off of him, steaming like dry ice.

Victor was only partly aware of his body's transformation. His mind had become focused on the many things that nagged at the corners of his awareness—things that angered him, that deserved a thoughtful, calculated destruction. He thought of how it chafed, knowing he was beholden to Dar for simply wanting his friend's spirit returned from the undead scum who had stolen it. He contemplated the veil walkers who controlled his every move on Ruhn. He thought of the Warlord of Zaafor and his betrayal. His fists clenched, and white fog rolled out of his nostrils.

He thought of Valla and how she'd decided life apart in the hopes of coming together again was better than grasping every moment together. Visions of opponents, people he'd fought, rushed across his mind. Images of friends he'd lost danced through his thoughts—Yrella, broken and pitiful; Sarl, torn to shreds by ghouls; Oynalla—Old Mother—gone, abandoning him to seek a new life; and hundreds of other faces, from slaves in the mines to soldiers on the battlefield to fellow iron rankers forced to fight him to the death.

Victor stomped toward the ocean and bellowed his fury, but he didn't lose himself. No, though his rage was monumental, and he practically vibrated with the need to destroy, he managed to whirl and narrow his eyes—pale blue-white like windows onto a glacier's slopes—at Tes. "I don't like this feeling," he growled, his voice echoing strangely off the icy ground. Had his presence frozen the moisture in the sand?

"Push the fury aside, Victor. Tell yourself you'll brood about it later. Instead, savor the power that flows through you. Do you feel your strength? Do you comprehend the destructive potential and resilience?"

Victor nodded. He did. He knew his sulking rage was ready to explode if he needed it to, but he could keep it back. He could bide his time. He was a glacier incarnate. His progress was inevitable. He would grind away whatever opposed him. His mighty form was built for destruction; like the glacier, any scars his foes piled upon him would smooth out as the inevitability of his nature froze the very air, filling the gaping chasms of destruction on his slopes.

Tes, shielding her eyes and looking up at him, called out, "You're enormous! Look beyond me. How far can you see?"

Victor let his frozen gaze travel up the sloping hill toward the village, and there, he could see dozens of buildings all the way to his home. People stood about, some of them gaping and pointing his way. His frigid vision turned things cold and lifeless. Colors were bland, and people looked frightened. Victor didn't like it. Without another thought, he reached into his pathway and yanked the threads of Energy away from the spell pattern, shattering the magic and ending the transformation.

As his Cores reclaimed their Energies, Victor fell to his knees, his body rapidly decreasing in size. He cradled his face in his hands, shaking his head. "So much," he groaned.

"So much?" Tes hurried to his side, gently cradling the back of his neck.

"So much that I'm pissed off about—things I never think about." He looked up at Tes—she must have increased her size to match his unmodified bulk. "The blue ice is different from magma. Magma has hot, passionate fury, but the blue ice is more brooding, calculating, and cold. It had me thinking about all the little things that have upset me over the years: insults, lost friends, lost loves, enemies—everything!"

"But you were in control . . ." Tes trailed off, gently kneading his neck. "I know what you mean, however. It wasn't a pleasant state of mind."

Victor inhaled a deep breath and then blew it out shakily. "Right. It worked, though, Tes. Oh, shit—" Victor turned his eyes to the System messages in the corner of his vision:

*****You have discovered a new spell: Glacial Wrath, Epic.*****

*****Glacial Wrath, Epic: Prerequisites: 1. An affinity for rage, fury or hatred. 2. An affinity for blue ice. You channel the cold, patient anger of the glacier. While affected by this transformation, you are immune to fire-based or cold-based attacks. While the spell persists, abilities that make use of your blue ice attunement double in effectiveness, and you benefit from modified Berserk effects: double strength, massively increased resilience, and powerful regenerative capabilities. Be cautious, for while your mastery affords you control over this deep anger, it may take a toll on your psyche. Energy Cost: 5,000, scalable. Cooldown: Long.*****

*****Warning! This spell is not System-designed! Use it with caution—there are no safeguards in place. This is the only time you will receive this warning!*****

Victor read the description to Tes, and she nodded sagely, continuing to rub his neck. "Save this for a last resort, Victor. As you continue to strengthen your will, it will grow easier and easier to control how that cold anger affects you."

"Agreed." He sighed and stood, taking another cleansing breath of the sea air. "Thank you, Tes."

"For?"

"For being here." He gestured down the beach toward the trail that would lead them up to his home. "Let's go get a bite to eat and say goodbye to Gorro.

I'm ready to get back to work." Smiling, trying to put the raw emotions behind him, he led the way back home. As they walked, he took a moment to look over his spells, enjoying the warm glow of satisfaction as he saw all the new entries:

Spells:	
Iron Berserk	Epic
Inspiration of the Quinametzin	Epic
Channel Spirit	Improved
Prismatic Illumination	Epic
Project Spirit	Improved
Heroic Heart	Basic
Spirit Walk	Advanced
Tether Spirit	Basic
The Inevitable Huntsman	Improved
Aspect of Terror	Advanced
Imbue Spirit	Improved
Honor the Spirits	Improved
Alter Self	Improved
Velocity Mantle	Epic
Banner of the Champion	Basic
Wild Totem	Advanced
Impart Nightmare	Improved
Guardian's Rescue	Epic
Volcanic Fury	Improved
Wake the Earth	Basic
Roots of the Angry Mountain	Advanced
Greater Spirit Binding	Advanced
Voice of the Angry Mountain	Basic
Locate Ally	Basic
Core Domain	Epic
Glacial Wrath	Epic

10

LET DOUBT ENTER THEIR HEARTS

Despite an underlying feeling of dread, almost as if he'd done something wrong, Victor's return to Ruhn was uneventful and on schedule. In fact, it almost felt as though nobody noticed his absence. He supposed it helped that he'd prepared Bryn and Draj Haveshi, putting them in charge of his affairs. However, it still felt sort of anticlimactic when Tes's magical artifact deposited them back in his chambers, and nothing was the matter. The palace was peaceful; there weren't any panicked missives from Queen Kynna, and he still had a day and a half before he had to report for his duel.

"We never got around to looking in on Lifedrinker or going over the equipment you pulled from that strangely generous dungeon, Victor," Tes reminded him after he'd suggested they go down to meet with Trobban to review his progress on Arona's new "vessel."

"Yeah, shit. I wonder how she's done with that ore." Victor pulled the vault and key from around his neck and set it in the space he'd cleared in the study. He twisted the key until the marble-sized vault began to vibrate and heat up, then put it on the floor and took a few steps back. "She must be done by now, don't you think?"

"I'm not sure. Generally, yes. As you've seen before, it usually only takes a few days or, at most, a couple of weeks for a conscious weapon to process a new metal or Energy source, but as I said, I fear you rushed things, giving her so much potent ore in such a short amount of time."

Victor nodded. He'd been nervous about Lifedrinker ever since Tes had first admonished him for feeding her two different ores back-to-back. He wondered if his "forgetting" to look in on her was because of the faint sense of dread that he'd done something that might harm the axe. "Denial," he muttered, shaking his head. Tes looked at him sideways, a slight frown on her lips, but didn't respond.

Back when Lifedrinker had finished processing the silvenite ore, she'd seemed excited, eager to explore the new capabilities of the magical, silvery metal. Victor had noticed a different quality to her dark, depthless black sheen—an underlying luster that seemed to reflect light differently, but otherwise, she'd looked almost the same. He'd lifted her, and she'd definitely gained some heft from the new ore, but otherwise, her shape had remained constant—an axe too enormous for a normal human to begin to pick up, let alone wield. That lack of change had prompted him to give her the incredibly dense ferrithium rather than explore its other uses.

Before he could continue obsessing over his decision and how it had worried Tes and then, of course, him, that Lifedrinker was taking so long to process the second ore, the vault finished expanding, and he couldn't justify any further procrastination. Victor stepped forward and finished turning the key. The door opened with a hiss of escaping vapors, and when he pulled it wide, he felt a surge of relief and also confusion.

When he'd last looked in on Lifedrinker, she'd had a thin vein of the red ferrithium running a few inches into her massive blade from the brick of ore. Now, however, the vein was gone, and the ore was still there, unchanged in size from when he'd first given it to her. Tes voiced a possible explanation: "I think she rejected it, Victor. It's for the best, in my opinion. Ask her!"

Victor nodded and stepped into the vault, still illuminated in the strange magenta glow of the dungeon Core that hovered at its center. He reached down to grasp ahold of Lifedrinker's haft, smiling at the familiar feel of her. "Hey, *chica*. Sorry, it's been a little while."

"War-mate! I've dreamed away the hours, remembering our battles and imagining new ones. I yearn for the open air, the crunch of armor, and the taste of blood and Energy!"

"I know you do." Victor chuckled. "I know. How are you, though? You didn't like the metal I left with you?"

"I tried to like it, battle-heart, but it won't bend to my desires! It won't follow the plan I have for myself. In truth, though it pains me to ask it of you, I dream of more of the last kind of metal you gave me—the one that shines like silver and molds like clay, dense with a primal desire to hold Energy."

"The silvenite? I think it's rare, but I'll get you more if that's what you want, beautiful." Victor smiled as the axe vibrated faintly, and pulses of satisfaction and blatant adoration flowed out of her and into his hands. Chuckling, he hoisted her onto his shoulder and turned to Tes. He'd expected a little teasing, but she wasn't even listening to his half of the conversation with the axe; she was standing in the doorway to his vault, her eyes trained on the satchel where he'd stowed the ivid royal jelly.

He didn't like the look in her eyes; he'd never seen the expression on her before—longing? Jealousy? Self-doubt? Something like that, but he couldn't put his finger on it. "You good?"

She shook her head and jerked her gaze toward him, licking her lips and visibly swallowing as she held up her hands. She turned and practically fled the vault. Victor followed her out, but not before whispering to Lifedrinker, "I'm going to put you into your container for now, okay?"

"Please, not for long, War-king!"

"No, not for long. We'll fight again soon." With that, Victor sent her into his high-quality ring, then stepped out to find Tes standing in the doorway to the study, arms folded over her chest, her pale blonde brows pulled together in a sharp V.

"Please close that vault."

"Let me get the armor out of it first."

"Do so, then, but hurry."

Victor's scowl deepened. Even though he thought he knew the answer, he asked, "What's wrong?"

"Later. Get the equipment you want me to look at and close that vault!" Without awaiting a response, she turned and strode across his parlor to the sitting room. He watched as she pulled open the balcony doors and stepped outside. Sighing heavily, worried that he knew exactly what was bothering her, he went into the vault and began carrying out the equipment he'd won from the Crucible of Fire.

The Aegis of Charyssor was the heaviest piece, but Victor was pleased to find it quite a lot easier to manage than when he'd stowed it there. He supposed gaining more than a hundred points of strength would make anything feel lighter. After he set it on the study floor, frowning as it split and bowed the hardwood planks, he retrieved the Crown of the Dark Colossus, the Terror-Scale Boots, and the Gauntlets of the Mountain's Might.

That done, he pushed the vault closed and twisted the key until it began to shrink down to its compact form. He hung the key over his head and then made his way out to the balcony. Tes was leaning against the railing, her gaze fixed on the distant, majestic slopes of Iron Mountain. "I guess you could feel the royal jelly." Victor had, of course, told her about the gift from the ivid queen, but it was one thing to hear about it and another to witness it.

"I'm very glad it was shrouded in something. I only felt the barest hint of its power, and still, I was almost driven to snatch it up and flee. Of course, I wouldn't do that to you, Victor, but you must never let someone more powerful than yourself get wind of what you have there."

"It's that good, huh?"

"I could feel the promise of breakthroughs in the complexity of its Energy signature. It must be quite potent if it promises so much when so many natural treasures would be wasted on me. Even my bloodline hungered for it, and I thought I'd reached something of a pinnacle." She shook her head, clicking her tongue. "That may not be true. Your System would call my bloodline 'epic,' and I know for certain there are ancient dragons who stand apart from those of us who've reached this stage."

"You said 'even my bloodline,' but is there something more?"

"Oh, yes. The Energy I tasted held all manner of promised breakthroughs and insights—to my Core, my understanding of magic, my innate abilities or, as you call them, 'feats.' I don't think . . ." She trailed off and shifted her gaze to him, slowly shaking her head. "I don't think it would be wise for you to consume that potent brew. Not yet. Perhaps when you're a steel seeker, though, should you drink it *before* you construct your archetype?" Again, she shook her head, sighing. "You may have the shortest career as a steel seeker in the history of the System."

"Crystal, the, uh, ivid queen, warned me to wait until I was far sturdier. She also said she wasn't sure it would be wise *ever* to consume it. I guess the ivid use it to make a normal larvae into a queen, and, yeah, there was a pretty damn big difference between Crystal and the other ivid."

"She feared it would change you too much?"

"She didn't say that, but that's the feeling I got—change me too much or destroy me." Victor chuckled, leaning on the banister and inhaling deeply. The air had a much different quality from that of Fanwath, at least near his home. There was no hint of the sea, and it was cooler, with more of a scent of pine and earth. He hadn't realized it before, but he could feel the change in Energy density, too. It was thicker here, though Fanwath was certainly not deprived for such a relatively young world.

"I saw your dungeon Core in there, too. What will you do with it?"

Glad for the change in topic, Victor shrugged. "Any ideas?"

Tes nodded, moving to stand closer to him. "I'd make a deal with it."

"With Du? What kind of deal?"

"He's a powerful Core, capable of providing challenges even to someone like yourself. He doesn't have to do so, however. He can provide challenges up to and including his maximum level. I'd offer to give him a new home, but I'd make him promise to tailor the difficulty of his encounters to the entrants. It would prove invaluable for those with access. They wouldn't have to seek out appropriately lev-eled dungeons. Of course, access would have to be managed, which would require dedicated personnel." She looked at him, an eyebrow arched, and Victor had the feeling she was waiting for him to connect some dots. It wasn't difficult.

"You think I should bring it to Fanwath—to my land."

"Wouldn't it be wonderful to give your people the means to advance in power right on their doorstep? In fact, I'd not advertise its whereabouts to any but those closest to you. Otherwise, it may become something people will fight over, and you can't always be there to discourage aggressors."

Victor slowly nodded. He liked the idea until he started imagining Deyni or Cora in the dungeon, facing wave after wave of deadly monsters. Still, he couldn't shelter them forever; they'd no doubt find their own danger further afield. "I'll think it over. Maybe next time I visit, I'll bring it up with Tellen and the others. Kethelket would have an opinion."

"Indeed. I'm sorry I didn't meet him."

"Maybe next time."

Tes smiled, but Victor could see it wasn't reflected in her eyes. Even so, she nodded. "Maybe so. Shall we look at that armor of yours?" She walked back inside, but Victor hesitated, ruminating on the fact that he was getting damn tired of nobody ever speaking plainly. He cared about Tes; he figured he probably loved her to some degree, but he hated how she acted as though she couldn't be straight with him. There were secrets on secrets brewing in her mind, and despite her insistence that he'd grown tremendously, he still felt she regarded him in some respects as a child.

The most frustrating thing about it was that he couldn't argue. To a dragon who'd lived god-knows-how-long, how could he, a guy who might be twenty-one— Victor wasn't sure—ever claim to be more? Naturally, he'd thought about it long and hard, and he tried to tell himself that there were other ways to show maturity besides age. He could prove himself with deeds. Hadn't he already done more than most men could ever claim? He'd led armies; he'd *fought* armies—alone. He'd killed powerful, evil enemies and discovered things that would make even a dragon envious. His most recent conversation with Tes was evidence of that!

The frustration was almost enough to counterbalance his infatuation with her, but not quite. Despite it all, he was smitten, and the unrequited nature of that attraction was beginning to wear on him. It would be one thing if Tes flatly said, "No. It's not going to happen," but she didn't do that. It was clear that she was attracted to him, but there were things that held her back. And so, his frustration came full circle; once again, he was met with the wall of mysteries Tes kept between herself and him.

"Are you coming?"

Victor stared at Iron Mountain for another long couple of seconds, then turned and nodded. "Yeah. On my way."

"So," she said, smiling, as he walked with her back to the study, "you're reluctant to wear this new armor because you don't want to be bereft of the scale armor I lovingly crafted you?"

Victor clicked his tongue and sighed, nudging her with his elbow. "The thought crossed my mind, but I didn't think I was strong enough for the new stuff anyway, at least the aegis." He nodded to the ornate, lustrous armor—more than just a breastplate; it featured pauldrons and a high neck guard on the left side and hinged flaps that would cover his thighs. The material, apparently carved from the natural shell of a sea creature called Charyssor, was black overall, but a sheen of blue luster seemed to lurk just beneath the surface, ready to come forth when touched by direct light.

"It's beautiful, Victor!" Tes said softly, reaching down to lift the enormously heavy thing. Victor gawped at her, again reminded of how much power lurked in the delicate-seeming figure she seemed to favor. "Very dense, naturally capable of resizing, self-mending, and, if I'm not wrong, deflecting incredible amounts of Energy. You should be wearing this." She set it down and rested a soft, warm hand on his forearm. "Put the armor I made you somewhere safe and look upon it from time to time to remind you of when we first met."

"It's so damn heavy, though—"

"It won't be so bad once you've put it on. Besides, these other pieces will add to your strength, will they not?" She leaned over to pick up the crown. "This, for instance . . ." Her eyes narrowed as she turned the depthless black metal in her fingers, the black opals on each point winking in the glow lamps. "This metal was tempered with dragon's blood, and a piece of the dragon's spirit lurks within. He'll try to influence you, but it's just an echo, easily silenced by someone with a formidable will. You'll be fine." She held it out to him. "Try it."

Victor took the heavy crown, frowning at the dark metal. "Really? I almost didn't want to show you this one because I thought you might get angry."

"Because a dragon gave a piece of himself in its crafting? It's ancient, Victor—I've no idea who that dragon was or whether he did so willingly or not. The echo of its spirit doesn't make much sense to me." She put her hands under his, nudging the crown upward. "Try it! You'll see what I mean."

Victor tilted the crown left and right, watching the lamplight play in the beautiful black gemstones. Finally, he shrugged. He trusted Tes, didn't he? He lifted the crown to his head, and the supple black leather lining cradled his skull as if it were made for him. He felt Energy flow down from it, fortifying his spine, shoulders, and arms. It felt terrific—potent and invigorating. He was just about to call up his status page to see the effect when a sibilant hiss sounded in his left ear:

"Fetching lass, our horde's delight, to taste her lips for only a night."

"What the . . ."

"Silken flesh, spun gold hair, a fitting bride to grace our lair."

Tes tilted her head to the side. "What's he saying? He whispered to me about flying, a rusted portcullis, and cooking eggs, of all things."

"It's, um, I think he's complimenting you?" Victor scratched the rough stubble on his jawline.

Tes laughed and pulled his hand away from his face. "You do that when you're nervous or unsure. Did you know that?"

"*Touch electric; a heart beats wild. With haste! Get her with child!*"

"*Chingado!*" Victor hissed, reaching up to take the crown off.

"No!" Tes grabbed his wrist. "Use your will, Victor—silence him."

"How?"

"Like you'd focus your aura on someone! Just put this ancient spirit fragment in his place."

Victor turned his gaze inward, looking at his Core space. He shifted his gaze outward with that "inner eye," and sure enough, he saw the wisps of a foreign spirit lurking nearby, somehow vaguely "above" him. He gathered his will and reached out to where his aura hung, surrounding him like a fiery, furious wall of black shadows and flames. With a mighty surge of will, he gathered it up and drove it toward the fragmented spirit, pushing it down and into its vessel—the crown. "You will stay there and be silent unless I call on you!"

"*Cruel master, heartless beast! A sad fate awaits you—a dragon's feast!*"

"Be still!" Victor growled and, to his relief, felt the presence recede, and no further rhymes were whispered in his ear.

"Easily done, wasn't it?" Tes clapped him on the shoulder.

"Yeah." Victor shrugged. "I guess so."

"How much stronger did it make you?"

"Just a moment." Victor pulled up his status page, focusing on his strength attribute:

Strength:	680 (780)

"Shit," he muttered. "It's giving me a hundred strength!"

"Truly? That's a significant boon for anyone, Victor! It's quite fetching, too. You look regal but not in a foppish princeling sort of way. It will serve as excellent armor, too. I imagine it will be difficult to pry from your head if you don't want it off."

She reached down to pick up the impossibly heavy gauntlets, smiling as she weighed them in her hands. "Another strength boon, though not a direct boost; you won't see this reflected on your System's status sheet. These gauntlets will make it easier for you to lift, strike, and deflect. They'll boost you beyond your natural means and would do so for anyone, though a person without a suitably robust skeletal structure would likely find themselves crippled by their power."

"But I'm good? I already put them on once, and it seemed fine, but I wasn't sure I wanted to wear them instead of my Sojourn gauntlet."

"Oh, yes. An epic-tier titan bloodline? You'll be fine. As to your other concern, yes, these are far more potent than that lava whip of yours." She handed the gauntlets to him, and Victor shrugged, stuffing his hands into them. As with the crown, he felt Energy infuse the bones of his hands and arms, flowing warmly through his shoulders and down his spine. The gauntlets hummed with power, the dark metal plates practically begging to be smashed into something.

Grinning, flexing his hands into fists and relaxing them, he nodded. "The leather under the plates is damn comfortable."

"See how difficult it is to lift that aegis now!" Tes gestured to the heavy armor, and Victor obliged, reaching down to almost effortlessly hoist it up.

"Ha!"

"It has a seam in the back; it's designed to be easy to equip. Put your arms through here." She showed him how the armor could be pulled apart on invisible hinges, and when he slid his arms through and pushed it closed around his torso, the seams magically disappeared, and the armor made itself snug to him; it felt amazing.

"I feel like a walking tank."

"A tank?" She narrowed her eyes.

Victor tried to shrug, but the armor wouldn't convey the gesture. "A heavy, armored piece of war equipment."

"And the boots?" Tes asked, reaching down to pick up the black-scaled footwear. "Oh!" she gasped softly. "That dungeon Core was trying to make a friend of you! These boots are designed for Spirit or Death Casters. You should have an easier time spirit walking with them. Victor, you may be able to travel between worlds like your mentor!"

"Well, I'll definitely give 'em a try, but I don't think I want to risk getting lost right before my duel." Victor was half joking, but he had some serious concerns about trying to find his way between worlds, especially for the first time. He thought it might be wise to have Dar along until he properly understood how to find those pathways.

"Even so, you should wear them. They're excellent armor, and your Sojourn set is a bust now that you have these other pieces. Perhaps you could gift it to one of your comrades."

Victor nodded, taking the boots and walking through his chambers to his bedroom, where he could look into a full-length mirror. "You think I should wear this armor in my upcoming duel?" Staring at himself, he had to admit the set was badass. Everything was primarily black with different sorts of highlights, and the crown and aegis made him look more formidable and . . . *solid* was maybe the right word. He looked as if he could shrug off an avalanche.

The various enchantments did more than make him *look* tough, too. He felt the potential and strength buzzing through his bones and muscles. If he were a heavyweight before, he'd suddenly become a juggernaut. Tes hadn't answered him right away, but she nodded as she came to stand beside him, looking into the mirror with him. "I would wear this armor in your future duels. It's time to stop hiding what you are. It's time to give the champions of the great houses something to think about. Let doubt enter their hearts and fester there."

11

A YELLOW ROSE

Victor stood in his ready room, stewing. His mind was troubled because he wasn't eager to slaughter a couple of iron rankers whose only crime against him was a desire to defend their queen and their homeland. He knew he was being prideful with such thoughts; any decent advisor—and he had more than a few—would tell him that he was saving thousands of lives by having this fight, that champions paid the price to keep armies from dying. It still didn't feel right.

"*Chica*," he said, twisting his gauntlet-clad hands on Lifedrinker's haft, "Am I being a cocky asshole when I say I don't think these poor *pendejos* will be able to touch me?"

"*You speak honestly and with a heart that bleeds for the foes you slay. You're right to warn fools away; how can a pack grow strong if every challenger is torn to bits? Still, if fools from other packs will challenge your might, you must set an example. Let us shower their blood far and wide so others will learn caution.*"

"You sound . . . like Tes." Wasn't Lifedrinker saying essentially the same thing? Was it time to instill some doubt in the minds of the champions of the empire? Would a decisive victory now save on bloodshed later?

"*The dragon woman is wise and beautiful. My wisdom has a sharper edge, Battle-heart. I will guide you to victory with my blade. I will part the flesh and bones of your foes, and I will curse the souls of any who wrong you.*"

Lifedrinker rested on the ground before him, and he was leaning on her long haft, the polished, not-wood, not-metal material resting on his cheek. When she spoke, he felt the conviction in her words and understood them more clearly through the emotion she sent his way. She was loyal and loving and growing more and more eloquent with her speech. Even so, this was the first time she'd ever spoken of cursing or souls, and Victor wondered if all of her advancements were broadening her concept and understanding of life.

"Thank you, *chica*, but—"

The door latch clicked, and the sound of hard-soled heels interrupted him. Victor turned to see Kynna approaching, two of her Queen's Guard standing just outside the door. When he turned, straightening from his slouch, Kynna froze in place and looked him up and down. She'd never seen him armored the way he was now: his crown, his aegis, his gauntlets, and boots. The only part of his equipment that wasn't some sort of powerful artifact were his pants— he'd opted for simple leather ones, stained black to match the overall theme. "Victor . . ."

"My Queen." He performed a short bow, the aegis more accommodating than it had any right to be.

She turned and pushed the door closed. "You've donned armor. No more bare-chested battles, then? A crown, too, I see—is that appropriate?"

Victor reached up to touch the offending object. The bottom of the crown rested about half an inch above his brows and ears, and the dense, dark metal covered most of the top of his head. The seven ridges weren't particularly high; they barely rose above his short, stiff hair, and it certainly wasn't gaudy. The black opals, dense with Energy, were muted; even in direct light, they gleamed more than sparkled. He cracked a cocky smile. "I made sure it was shorter than yours."

Kynna's answering smile changed her completely—she was a beautiful woman, but her usual serious, almost dour tone muted that beauty. The playful smile she showed him was the equivalent of turning on the lights in a chandelier. With eyes twinkling with amusement, she reached up to adjust the tall, crystal crown in question. "That was a wise decision." She stepped a little closer. "Worry not; I jest. You're a ruler in another world and a powerful duke in my kingdom. You're entitled to wear what you please."

"Well, to be honest, I didn't choose this because it's a crown. I'm wearing it for its value as an artifact."

Kynna nodded, entwining her fingers before her as she looked him up and down. "That armor looks formidable." Her gaze drifted down to Lifedrinker's enormous, depthless black blade. "Have you decided to alter your usual strategy?"

Victor barked a short laugh. By "usual strategy," he knew she meant getting beat to a pulp before finishing his fight. "I guess you could say that the time for playing the fool is over."

"Is that so? Well, in that case, I'll need to adjust my strategy for finding you duels."

"That was bound to happen, wasn't it?"

She nodded, glancing at the clock. Victor's duel was scheduled to start in only six minutes. "That's true. I told you we'd need to find a prideful kingdom to challenge next—a ruler and champion whose hubris won't allow them to back down. It'll be someone like Trinnie Ro, perhaps worse."

Victor nodded. "I'll be ready."

Her smile fell away, and her face grew solemn again. "I know you will, Victor. Would you do me a small favor today?"

"Yeah, of course." Sometimes, Victor wanted to cut his damned tongue out; couldn't he have thought about it or heard the favor before agreeing? Hastily, he added, "If I can ask for one in return."

"Hmm." Kynna touched a finger to her chin, her polished silver nail gently tapping a small dimple there. "I was merely going to ask if you might wear something of mine for the battle. A token—nothing more."

Victor wasn't stupid. Tes would be in Kynna's box to watch the battle, and he had a feeling Kynna was making some sort of move here—marking her territory, so to speak. Did he care? As a slow smile crept over his lips, Victor realized he did not. In fact, he thought it might be amusing to see how Tes reacted. Was he playing with fire? He certainly was, but he'd done so before; he was a titan, was he not? "Yeah, sure, I can do that."

Kynna's smile was bright as she summoned something into her palm—a delicate-looking, metallic yellow rose. The stem and petals were crafted from something with a luster like white gold, and the petals were crafted from the same material but set with gorgeously cut, many-faceted yellow gemstones. "The yellow rose represents Gloria, as you know. These gemstones are yellow sapphires." She held it out to his chest, and it clicked as it secured itself to his armor on his left breastplate. "It's enchanted to hold fast, don't worry."

"It seems delicate . . ." Victor shifted Lifedrinker closer to the two of them, illustrating the kinds of destructive implements the little rose might encounter.

Kynna was undaunted. "Yes. Keep it safe for me, will you not?" Victor sighed heavily, and she added, "Now, your favor?"

"I'd like to offer Queen Madge a final chance to accept banishment— without the duel."

"She won't. With banishment waiting as the only consequence for a loss, she'll take the chance that her champions might win."

"Still, I'd like to present the offer. It'll make me feel better about the fight."

Kynna looked into his eyes for a long moment, and Victor watched the white flames dancing behind their crystalline surface. They were beautiful in a way, different from Dar's in that they didn't constantly look angry and ready to flare with violent heat. She nodded gently, hardly moving the crown atop her head. "Very well. I won't object."

Victor looked at the clock and saw he had only three minutes. "Better get to your seat then."

"Keep my rose safe, Champion." Without awaiting a response, she turned and exited; somehow, her Queen's Guard knew to open the door ahead of her.

Victor reached down and adjusted the beautiful little rose on his armor. "*Pinché* son of a bitch," he grumbled. When the announcement to proceed to the arena came, he shouldered Lifedrinker and marched through the tunnel onto the red and black sands. The crowd had been noisy when he fought Trinnie Ro, but this time, they were thunderous in their adulation and derision. Victor didn't care that some people were booing, hissing, and making rude gesticulations. He didn't even look at them. He simply turned in a slow circle, basking in the attention.

The glory-attuned Energy in his Core flared and surged, and, holding Lifedrinker steady with his left hand, he lifted his right in a fist, grinning madly as the crowd's roar intensified. He paced in a small circle, biding his time as he slowly made his way toward the center of the arena—the demarcation line between red and black. When he was nearly there, he paused, lowered his fist, and, for the first time, set his eyes on his waiting opponents.

Hunt Kreeze stood to his left, a tall, powerfully built man in heavy, gleaming, silvery armor. He wore a massive shield, and in his right hand, he clutched a war hammer that vibrated with sonic Energy. To his right was Vo Brahn, another bruiser in dark metal plates adorned with spikes, some of which were nearly a foot long. He fought with spiked gauntlets, and thus, his enormous metal-clad fists were empty of other weapons. Victor briefly let his gaze drift over them, then looked up toward Kynna's box.

Just as he'd expected, Kynna was there with her attendants, but so were Bryn, Tes, and, for the first time, Florent, the spatial mage who'd been spending time at Iron Mountain in Victor's service. Victor saluted briskly, careful not to smash his fist into Kynna's rose, and then he turned his gaze upward, seeking out Grand Judicator Lohanse. He didn't have to look far; the veil walker was gliding down on his crystalline flying disc, descending rapidly toward the center of the arena.

Lohanse performed his usual spiel. "Citizens! I am Grand Judicator Lohanse, and I am here to ensure all rules of law are abided by, that the agreed-upon terms are upheld, and that no outside interference mars the sanctity of this most venerated ritual of succession. Do any dare challenge my authority in this place?"

His booming voice brought silence to the arena; even drunken, rowdy revelers knew better than to insult one of the veil walkers who enforced the empire's laws. When no one objected, Lohanse glided closer to Kynna's section of boxed-off seats. "Queen Kynna Dar of Gloria, I have read the terms of this duel of succession. Do you agree to abide by them?"

Kynna tilted her crystal crown forward and back. "I do!"

Lohanse whirled around, his disc carrying him across the arena to hover before the entourage from Bandia. "Queen Madge Hajarnen of Bandia, do you agree to abide by the terms of this duel?"

The queen, a bulky woman with massive shoulders, wearing ceremonial, gilded armor, slammed a gauntleted fist to her breastplate and shouted, "I swear it!"

Lohanse nodded and glided in a wide loop, running his eyes over Victor and his two opponents. "Champions! You will not be permitted to access storage devices or use potions, tinctures, salves, or other consumable aids during this duel. Are you all equipped to your satisfaction?" He drifted closer to Hunt and Vo Brahn, letting his gaze linger on them momentarily before prompting, "Champions of Bandia?"

"I am ready!" Hunt replied, his voice deep and booming.

"Ready," Vo Brahn growled, slamming his gauntleted fists together.

Lohanse whirled in the air, gliding toward Victor. When he drew near, he spoke, and Victor could tell his voice wasn't amplified, for it didn't echo off the arena walls as it usually did. "I see you've deigned to wear your armor? Was the last duel a bit too close for your comfort?"

Victor smiled. "It wasn't a good time."

Lohanse nodded, and then his voice boomed, "Are you ready, Champion of Gloria?"

"May I address the Queen of Bandia, Grand Judicator?"

Lohanse reached up, flung his long, spun-silver hair over his shoulder, and then regarded Victor for a long moment. His eyes, always aglow, shifted through various colors from magenta to crimson, then to yellow, and back to silvery white. "I see you're sincere. You may speak."

"Thank you, sir." Victor walked along the line of sand where it shifted from black to red, careful not to cross over. His opponents stalked along in the red sand, watching him, growling, grimacing, and doing everything they could to look intimidating. Victor ignored them, and when he stood directly beneath the Queen of Bandia, he looked up and shouted, "Good Queen of Bandia, before this duel begins, I ask that you save the lives of these loyal champions. Accept Queen Kynna's generous offer to allow you to leave Ruhn. There's no need for—"

"Ha!" the queen barked, her voice surprisingly deep and powerful. "This one has lost his nerve. What's the matter? Don't want to lose that pretty crown your queenie put on your head? Didn't know she'd pit you against two devil-blooded war-hounds? Too late to save the embarrassment, but at least die like a man." The crowd couldn't resist a reaction to the drama; murmurs, laughter, and even jeers began to break out. Only Lohanse, flying a fast circle around the arena, glaring down at the thousands of spectators, brought back the silence.

Of course, her words and the crowd's reaction triggered the heat of Victor's rage-attuned Energy, and he had to concentrate for a moment to push it back before he spoke again. He glared up at the queen, trying to see her eyes beneath the ridiculous beak of her slotted helmet visor. "As you wish. These deaths are on your hands." With that, he dropped Lifedrinker off his shoulder and held her ready in two hands. As Queen Madge chortled, he looked at Lohanse and nodded. "I am ready."

Victor hadn't been sure how he wanted to handle this fight. Should he go "all out"? How much should he hold back? Should he draw things out? The queen's response to his words had settled the debate in his mind. These two men were brave and full of pride, but they didn't realize how badly they were outclassed. Victor had read dossiers on them. Or, more honestly, he'd had Bryn read the dossiers and give him a summary. They were both bruisers—powerful men who could take a pounding and dish one out, too.

Hunt could create Energy barriers and perform an action similar to Victor's new Guardian's Rescue spell. He had a dozen deadly abilities he could employ through his war hammer, and according to some rumors, he could regenerate his health to some degree. Vo Brahn, on the other hand, was a berserker.

He had a Spirit Core entirely focused on hatred, which was a rage-related attunement but rooted in deep, simmering resentment or malice. Where Victor's rage was explosive and passionate, a berserker with hate-attuned Energy driving their madness was, according to Tes, more cunning and remorseless. A man without any balance for such an affinity wasn't likely to be a pleasant individual.

None of it mattered. Queen Madge had sealed these men's fates. Victor twisted his hands on Lifedrinker's haft and built a spell pattern in his pathways, waiting for the judicator's signal. He watched the two men, one with beady black eyes, the other with luminous green orbs beneath his helmet's visor. They looked ready. Their stances were low, their posture forward, and Victor could feel the Energy building in their pathways. When Lohanse shouted, "Fight!" all three exploded into action.

Tes watched the challengers down below. They fidgeted idly while the crowd's clamor made their quiet conversation impossible to hear. She could cast a spell to listen to their words, but she didn't need to. A delicate probe, just a tiny tendril of her aura, was all she needed to pierce their veils and see that Victor would prevail in the fight to come. Their equipment was fine—sturdy, Energy-rich materials with potent enchantments, but their armor wouldn't stop Lifedrinker. The axe had grown hungry, and she had the teeth to feed herself.

A noise behind her and Bryn murmuring "Stand up straight" to her squire told Tes that the queen had finally arrived. She turned to observe the regal woman and perform a delicate curtsy before returning to her seat. The gesture never failed to lower a person's guard. Kynna wore a slight smile, a knowing twinkle in her eye, and Tes wondered what she and Victor had discussed. She could have listened in, of course; hiding from the likes of these folks wasn't beyond her, but it would have been risky with veil walkers lurking nearby. It didn't matter in any case; she wouldn't do that to Victor.

"Hello, Lady Tes," the queen said as she sat down. "I missed you at the Rannisday celebration. I'd hoped Victor would bring you."

"My apologies, Your Majesty, but I thought I'd be intruding and didn't want Victor to feel burdened by me, him being my only acquaintance in this world." In truth, Tes hadn't wanted to perform a dance like this one, especially when, at the time, she'd only been on the planet for a month.

"We'll have to remedy that." Kynna nodded toward the arena. "Here comes our champion."

Tes turned to see Victor striding in, clad in his ornate blue-black armor. A glint of something shiny on his chest drew her eye as he lifted a fist and turned to bask in the crowd's adulation. She peered more closely, using her peerless dragon senses to study the lovely little rose broach. It was the signet of Gloria, so she supposed it made sense that he'd wear it as their champion. Still, it was awfully gaudy for a bloody brawl in an arena.

Thinking about it and Kynna's knowing smile, she put it together rather quickly. "Lovely sapphires. It's rare to find such bright yellow ones."

Kynna beamed at her. "Why, thank you! It belonged to an ancestor: Ranish Dar's first daughter."

Tes nodded, smiling delicately at the queen. "An heirloom? I'm sure Victor will keep it safe." As if he didn't have enough to worry about! She wanted to scold the queen but knew the game too well to fall into that trap.

"I'm sure he will."

Tes nodded, resting her chin on her fist as she leaned on the arm of her seat. Was Kynna making a statement? Was she marking her "territory"? Tes almost frowned, but she was too disciplined for that. Let the queen have her fun; Tes knew where Victor's heart lay, even if she couldn't do anything about it yet. Of course, the thought reminded her of her obligations and her conflicting principles, and *that* nearly brought a frown to her face. The judicator, a veil walker of middling strength, was giving his spiel, and Tes tuned him out, focusing on Victor.

He stood easy—relaxed. He knew he was more than a match for these two men. One was a hateful brute, the other a . . . more durable brute. No, "brute" was the wrong word for the man in the silver armor. He wasn't particularly clever, but he wasn't an animal. She could find pity in her heart for him. When Kynna signaled her intention to follow the rules, and the other queen did as well, Tes felt the tension increase in the box. Not everyone was so sure Victor would win. She looked at Bryn—a woman she'd grown to like a great deal—and said, "He'll be fine."

Bryn looked at her and smiled nervously, nodding. "I hope so. At least he's wearing armor this time. You missed some bloody fights, Lady Tes."

The queen nodded, clearly wanting to be included in the conversation. "Fear not, Bryn. He's assured me that he's done playing about."

Tes smiled, careful not to show her face to the queen. On the sands below, Victor was walking toward the far side. When he shouted, offering the Queen of Bandia a final chance to forfeit the duel, Tes clicked her tongue and sighed. "He's so idealistic." When the Queen of Bandia made a mockery of his gesture, she saw the heat of his Core and watched as he pushed *most* of the rage back into it. He clung to some threads, though; he was angry.

"I told him she wouldn't accept the offer." Kynna sighed.

Tes looked at her. "He asked you about this?"

"Oh, yes. I could see he didn't want to fight these men, but when I looked into his eyes, I knew it wasn't fear but pity driving him."

Tes narrowed her eyes. Perhaps this woman was cleverer than she thought. "You saw that, did you?"

"I did."

Tes nodded and looked back at Victor. She saw a familiar pattern taking shape in his pathways. "Watch closely, Your Majesty. This will happen quickly."

Before Kynna could reply, the judicator shouted, "Fight!"

Tes sped up her mind, and the world slowed in her perception. She saw the spike-clad warrior, the hateful brute, flare with red, seething Energy as his body expanded with tremendous muscles. She saw the silver-clad giant slam his shield downward as an Energy barrier expanded out of it, protecting his forward arc. But, at the same time, she saw Victor flare with white-gold Energy as he moved. His actions were like lightning, but he was easy to track with her enhanced cognition.

He darted forward, and while the baleful red Energy expanded through the brute, Victor hacked Lifedrinker through his knee, severing it. The man tilted to the side, but Lifedrinker was already up and descending toward his neck. She split his spiked gorget and slipped through the meat of his flesh like a cleaver through a piece of fowl. Even before the berserker's Energy had finished surging through his body, he was dead.

As the brute's corpse hung in the air, blood still erupting out of the wounds Lifedrinker had inflicted, Victor moved in an arc around the silver-clad warrior, and a tremendous *clang* rang out as the axe slammed into his back. *Clang, clang, clang*—Victor lifted and dropped Lifedrinker three more times, pounding the giant forward as the axe bit deeper with each blow. Gasps around her told Tes that the other spectators had finally begun to realize something was happening.

She slowed her mental operations to a normal pace and watched Victor move to stand behind his toppled enemies, Lifedrinker resting on his shoulder. While the Energy and blood fled his foes, Bryn gasped, "What happened?"

Kynna, too, was dumbstruck. "Did—did he hit them? I heard a crash, but I missed . . ." She trailed off as the crowd began to realize what had happened, and gasps and murmurs broke out, giving way to scattered shouts—some outraged and some exuberant.

"He slew them, Queen Kynna, and now you know why Victor's heart was heavy. He's not a butcher; he took no joy in this battle." It was true. Victor was stomping out of the arena, crowned head down, axe on his shoulder, her blade dripping into the sand.

"Is he angry?" Bryn asked.

Tes was trying to think of an answer for her, but then the crowd started to chant—first a small section, but it spread rapidly. Before Victor was out of the arena, the roar of thousands of voices shouting, "Victor, Victor, Victor!" slowed his steps, and he halted. He looked up at the crowd, and though he didn't smile, he lifted Lifedrinker high in both hands and pumped her up and down in time with the chant.

Tes smiled and shook her head. "He's not angry now, but I think the other queen's mockery irritated him. Otherwise, I don't think he would have ended this so quickly. Still, perhaps it's for the best." Tes looked at Kynna. "He kept your flower safe, at least."

12

❧

CRUEL IRONY

When Victor stepped out of the tunnel into his ready room, he expected to see Kynna or someone from her retinue waiting for him. Instead, he felt his ears pop, and then, as though materializing out of the air itself, Grand Judicator Lohanse stood before him, arms crossed, a glower on his face. "We'll speak for a moment. I've sealed this space outside of time."

"Outside of—"

"The magic you employed wasn't something an iron ranker should be capable of. Tell me, Victor, are you somehow hiding your true nature? Are you a steel seeker or . . . *more*? Lie to me now, and you'll face Ruhn's entire Veil Walker Council."

Victor glowered at the man, his Quinametzin pride bristling at the implied insult to his integrity. "I'm Level Eighty-Two, as you no doubt can tell. The spell I cast was crafted by me against the System's wishes. Don't tell me I'm the first iron ranker to learn about elder magic."

"So." Lohanse nodded, and his narrowed brows evened out. "Then you've truly been playing the game well to this point. I sensed something *more* about your ability to alter your size, but I'd assumed it to be a side effect of your advanced titan bloodline. Are you hiding more secrets?"

Victor folded his arms. "What kind of champion would I be if I went around revealing all my cards? I've already said more than I like, thanks to your threats. Is this how you display your impartiality—kidnapping me and demanding to know my secrets?"

Lohanse bared his teeth, white and sharp; his jaw clenched as his eyes grew stormy. He stretched out his hands as though to grab Victor, but he stopped short of touching him. "You dare impugn my honor?"

Victor lowered his arms to his sides, but he stood up even straighter if that were possible, his gaze unwavering from the veil walker's. "I'm only showing you the same courtesy you gave me." In the back of his mind, Victor wondered if this was it. Was he about to have an actual fight with a veil walker? Would he be able to stand up to his aura? Would his new Core Domain spell help in that regard? Would he be able to finish the fight before he burned through his Energy? Just using Core Domain was a drain, let alone trying to cast Velocity Mantle at the same time.

To his relief, Lohanse's glower began to relax and then turned the corner toward a reluctant smile. "Fair enough. You're certainly in a different league than the iron rankers of Ruhn, and you've got a hell of a lot more backbone, to boot. I don't envy you the crucible you must have come through to reach this point at such a young age. Listen, Victor, I'll admit I'm beginning to root for you and your queen. I'll give you a friendly warning: You aren't the only monster in this world, though the others are steel seekers, and they're watching and waiting, biding their time. Don't think all your fights will go like the one you just had."

"Yeah, I fig—" Victor cut short his response when his ears popped, and Lohanse no longer stood before him. "*Pinché*, son of a—" Again, he cut off his words as the door opened, and Kynna stepped through. He smiled at her. "Your Majesty."

"Well done, Champion!" She smiled radiantly and stepped closer, her eyes drifting to his armored chest. "You kept my rose safe."

Victor carefully grabbed the delicate broach and tugged, disengaging its magical grip on his armor, then held it out to her. "Yeah."

Kynna came closer to take it, her fingertips lingering on his palm before pulling it away. "Thank you, Victor. I think it made a point to some of my rivals among the rulers of Ruhn. Many were in attendance today, far more than in your previous duels."

"Oh?" Victor arched an eyebrow. "Was that what you were hoping to accomplish by having me wear that?"

Kynna looked away, her pale, gray-hued flesh darkening over her cheeks. "Of course. Nothing more than a display of your loyalty—your . . . *devotion* to my cause."

"I see." Victor shrugged. He'd teased her enough, and in honesty, he didn't want to be too flirtatious with the queen.

"I saw you didn't claim a trophy from your foes. You weren't interested in their weapons or armor?"

Victor shook his head. "Let their children or loved ones have them."

"And . . ." Kynna looked at him, almost nervously, her eyes only meeting his for the briefest moment. ". . . their hearts?"

Again, Victor's chin moved side to side. "Unworthy." He didn't want to elaborate, but he wasn't lying. He didn't fully understand the ritual that allowed his titan blood to take something from his conquered foes, but he knew his gut told him nothing much would be gained from those two hearts, and he'd grown heedful of such feelings. Besides, even the suspicion that those men's hearts wouldn't grant him a benefit made the thought of eating them unpalatable. His Quinametzin pride wouldn't stoop to it.

"Well, then. I'll have to be sure to award you something worthwhile for your efforts. You've advanced the status of our nation a great deal today." She glanced at the door. "Shall we return? I believe it's time for me to move my operations back to Iron Mountain, and that will take some preparation."

Victor nodded, wishing he had a storage container that could contain his armor. With a bit of experimenting, he'd learned that the container he kept Lifedrinker in was at its limit. It could hold his crown and smaller artifacts without the axe but couldn't manage the aegis, even when empty. As he pulled the door open for the queen, he voiced an idea his thoughts had provoked. "You know, if you were looking for ideas, a high-quality storage ring—something that could contain this armor—would be a worthy reward."

"Oh?" As they stood in the doorway, Kynna's Queen's Guards just a few feet away, she reached out to rest a palm on Victor's aegis. He thought he saw a shudder run through her, but she nodded. "I'll look into it, Victor. I fear it will take the craftsmanship of a great master—someone well beyond their iron ranks."

"If it's too much, don't—"

"No." Kynna moved her hand up, her fingertips lightly brushing his jawline. "Don't undervalue yourself, Victor. If this is something you desire, then I will move mountains to find it."

Victor decided not to argue. Thanks to him, Gloria was the most powerful nation on the continent; she could dig into the treasury, and if she had to shop off-world, he should let her. At least, that's what he told himself as he nodded, and she let her fingers slide away, tickling his recently shaved flesh. "It's settled, then. I'll see you at Iron Mountain in a few days." She walked away with her guards, wearing a parting smile that was almost coy as she averted her gaze.

Victor watched her go until she'd rounded the corner, then, with a heavy sigh, followed slowly behind; he preferred she be gone before he reached the teleportation chamber. "You're getting yourself into trouble, *pendejo*." As he spoke, he rounded the corner and came face-to-face with Tes and Bryn, who were walking briskly toward him.

"We thought we might have missed you!" Bryn said by way of greeting. "That was incredible, Victor!"

Tes was less flattering. "I hope you don't expect the champions of the great houses to—"

Victor waved his hand. "I know, I know." He chuckled at Tes's frown, then added, "Hello to you, too, ladies." He fielded their questions, mainly deflecting or shrugging off concerns, as they walked to the teleportation chamber and then through the portal to Iron Mountain.

"Any orders for me today, Victor?" Bryn asked. He'd given her permission to be informal, even with Tes present.

"Nothing special. I'm going to get changed, then spend some time with Trobban. I think he's getting close to finishing his project. Why? Did you have something you wanted to do?"

Bryn sighed, nodding while she rolled her eyes. "Feist is getting married and has asked that I attend."

"Feist is getting *married?*" Victor stopped in his tracks and turned to stare at her. "Why didn't anyone say something? I should at least get him a gift!"

"Well, it's a rather sudden arrangement." Bryn chuckled, clicking her tongue. "He's going to be a father soon."

Victor couldn't stop himself from barking out a laugh. "Seriously? Well, damn it, where's the wedding?"

"At the bride's parents' home down in the city. He and his lady-love didn't want a big affair, Victor."

Tes grabbed his arm, getting his attention, and Victor looked at her. "You should pay for the food and refreshments."

"Yeah!" Victor nodded, looking at Bryn. "Tell his folks I'll cover all the expenses. I hope you're giving him some time off from his duties?"

"Yes, of course. He and his brothers are building an addition to Treya's parents' home—rooms for them and their child."

"Treya's her name, huh? Well, pass on my congratulations and, like I said, make sure they don't worry about expenses." With a final nod, he clapped her on the shoulder. "Have fun."

Bryn smiled and curtsied, looking up at him cheekily. "Thank you, Your Grace."

"And Bryn," Victor said before she could turn away, "let me know when the kid's about to be born. I'll come up with a birthday present."

"I will do so!" This time, she saluted, and it looked as if she meant it as she spun on her heel and strode down the hallway, her heels ringing out on the marble floor.

"That was nice of you. You haven't known Feist all that long, have you?"

"Nah, but he's a good guy. Kind of hilarious, really." He started walking toward his tower. "Come on, let me go get out of this stuff."

"How did you find it? I saw you moved quite easily with Velocity Mantle— the armor didn't affect you."

"Yeah." Victor reached up and touched the dense, heavy crown on his head. He could almost imagine he wasn't wearing it. "It feels great."

"Why'd you choose that tactic, do you think? Was it because the queen taunted you?"

Victor thought about it as they walked, and when they passed through the hallway leading to his tower, he shook his head, frowning. "No." He pushed the button to summon his elevator. "Well, maybe partially—I *was* trying to make a point. I also didn't want to torture those two guys. I figured the quicker I put an end to things, the better."

When the elevator arrived, its gilded metal doors noiselessly sliding open, Tes stepped inside ahead of him. "I thought so. You didn't enjoy that battle, did you?"

Victor narrowed his eyes at her as the elevator glided smoothly upward, its Energy-driven mechanisms utterly silent. "What are you getting at?"

"Well, I remember you reveling in your battles back on Coloss. Today, you nearly left the arena without acknowledging the crowd's cheers. Even the Energy from your foes didn't lift your mood?"

"Oh, yeah." Victor leaned a shoulder on the gold-inlaid black paneling beside the door. He'd almost forgotten that this was the first time Tes had seen him fight since she'd arrived on Ruhn. It was true about the Energy, too. It hadn't felt like much—not after his battles in the Crucible of Fire. "I didn't like it at all, really. Hopefully, the next—"

Tes darted forward and thumped her fist on his breastplate. "Don't do that!"

"*What?*" Victor's voice rose with indignation.

"Wish for a 'challenge' or whatever you were about to say. You should take your victories where they come and not tempt fate by complaining that they're too easy!"

"C'mon, Tes. You know I can't be happy about beating the shit out of some poor *pendejos* who weren't even close to being ready for me."

Her blonde eyebrows narrowed, and her mouth opened and closed several times as she considered her words. Finally, she snorted and offered a quick nod just as the doors opened. "Fine. You wouldn't be you otherwise, I suppose. Still, I can feel the storm coming. As I've told you several times, I visited some of those 'great houses' before I came here to Iron Mountain. There are some dangerous men and women from other worlds serving as champions."

"Yeah, I know." Victor led the way into his chambers, closing the door. "Can you give us some real privacy?"

Tes nodded, and Victor's ears popped as the air grew still around them. "What is it?"

"Did you know Lohanse confronted me after the fight?"

Tes's eyebrows shot up. "The veil walker?"

"Yeah. He was suspicious after I used elder magic. I think he thought maybe I was a steel seeker or even a veil walker in disguise. Is that possible?"

"Of course! Given the right preparations and rituals, it's quite possible for a person to sequester some of their potency. A close examination, though, by someone with the right set of abilities would bring forth the truth."

"Yeah, I don't know if Lohanse could spot that kind of thing, but I had the feeling he could tell if I was lying. He asked me some . . . *blunt* questions. He also admitted to me that he was kind of rooting for me. He said there were some monsters fighting for the great houses."

Tes sighed and shrugged. "Nothing I haven't already been telling you. I *just* said as much!"

Victor grinned crookedly. "Yeah, but it hit different coming from him. I thought maybe you were just being overprotective."

Tes lifted one of her small, human-shaped fists and glowered at him. "I ought to give you a thrashing for that."

"Now we're talking." Victor took hold of the bottom edge of his aegis on either side and pulled, signaling to the armor that he was ready to take it off. It split down its invisible seam along his back, and he pulled it off, grunting as it grew heavier in his hands.

"If I decide to knock some of that impudence out of you, I promise you won't find it enjoyable!" Tes *sounded* angry, but Victor could see in her eyes that she was having fun, so he just shrugged and carried the armor over to an empty spot near the wall, carefully setting it down so he didn't destroy the floor. "Well," she said, abruptly changing the subject, "what about your other visitor?"

"Who says I had another—"

"Don't be coy. Kynna and her Queen's Guards walked past Bryn and me before we ran into you." She pointed to his armor. "I notice your little rose is gone."

Victor grinned, tugging his gauntlets off. "Yeah, I gave it back to her. She was glad I didn't get it smashed. Why?"

Tes was wearing a dress, as usual, but this one was simpler, with less frill and a plain ivory color instead of her typical pastels. He supposed it was more suitable for attending a duel—more reserved or something like that. She folded her arms over her chest, her wide, bell sleeves hanging from her wrists. "Be careful of that woman, Victor."

Her words caught him a little off guard, and he looked up from tugging his boots off. "Huh? You think she's going to betray—"

"No, not that. I think she's set her sights on you romantically. I can't tell if she wants to conquer you, love you, or maybe just have a child with your bloodline."

Victor snorted, shaking his head as he set his boots beside his gauntlets and aegis. He summoned a pair of much lighter, less imposing boots and stuffed his feet into them as he replied, "Tes, I know an easy way to keep her at bay. All I need is someone else who might—"

"Victor! Be serious!"

Victor had been teasing, but now he felt some genuine frustration as he straightened up, adjusting his shirt where it had pulled free of his trousers. He couldn't stop a bit of emotion entering his voice as he said, "I am being serious, damn it!"

Tes's expression softened, and she came to stand before him, pressing her palm against his chest, over his heart. "I know. I'm sorry about how I sounded. I *do* take you seriously, Victor. So seriously that it hurts. Wouldn't it be easier if I could just dismiss your affections and tell you I don't feel the same? I feel something, though, but that just makes things harder."

"Why, though, Tes? Why is it so damn complicated?"

"Many reasons, as you well know! I'm older than you—a lot! I'm more powerful than you, too, though that gulf is narrowing by the day." She chuckled, shaking her head and sending her carefully curled hair bouncing around her ears. "Still, where I come from, and in most worlds where Energy users live for thousands of years, such a disparity in age and power is seen as problematic. Again, though, things aren't clear. My species matures differently than yours. I'm considered a young adult among my people, much as you would be among yours. And, as for power, I feel some patience would mitigate that objection. Me being here, helping you, guiding you, teaching you before you reach your potential, though—how can I argue that you truly have the freedom to choose to be with me?"

Victor growled and moved away from her, looking toward the balcony windows for want of something to focus on. "I don't give a shit about that stuff."

Tes sighed. "Push your emotions down a little, Victor. Your rage is seeping into your pathways, and you're not being rational. Put yourself in my position; I have mentors and colleagues of my own. Shall I drop everything to run away with my young lover?"

Victor didn't answer right away. Instead, he looked inward, watching his roiling Core and the threads of rage, fear, and even glory seeping out into his pathways. He *was* being emotional, but goddamn it, that was who he was! Rather than rein in his emotions, he let them flow and turned to face her. With a thick, almost hoarse voice, he said, "I don't know, Tes. I'm a passionate person, and I'd throw away a lot for love."

"You *are* passionate. I know. I love that about you!" Moisture gathered in her eyes, and she darted forward, grabbing him around the waist and hugging herself to him. "Don't change that. I'm sorry I suggested it."

Her affection and apparent willingness to bend hit Victor harder than any logical argument would have. He hugged her tightly and gathered his thoughts over several long seconds and a few deep breaths. "Look, Tes. I'm not trying to screw up your life. I get it. You've got your own goals, and you've built relationships with people and organizations like your, um, Celestial Envoys. If hanging around me while I'm so far beneath you is problematic, maybe you shouldn't. Give me some more time to build up my strength—to, uh, reach my potential."

She pushed him back, her hands gripping his biceps as she looked up into his eyes. "Truly? Victor, I think I would . . . I'd give up much to be with you. I'd face the judgment of my peers. If we fled somewhere and let enough time pass—"

"Nah, come on, Tes. I'd never feel right knowing you did that. It means a hell of a lot that you said you would, though." He grinned crookedly, reaching up to gently cup the side of her head while he wiped away a tear with his thumb. "Dragons cry, huh?"

She sniffed. "Is this the first time you've seen me cry?"

"Yeah, I think so. How about kissing? Do dragons do that?" Victor leaned closer to her, and when she didn't pull away but rather continued to stare into his eyes, his heart began to race, and he felt adrenaline as if he was about to fight for his life. Gently and with no intention of taking it further, he pressed his lips to hers. When she kissed him back, he felt as though his heart would burst. He heard a roaring in his ears, and he swore the world began to tilt sideways. Tes tightened her grip on his arms, though, and he grounded himself in that touch, savoring the warm softness of her lips for a second before pulling back with the stupidest grin he'd ever worn.

"We do," she said breathily.

"Shit, Tes. What are we going to do?" Victor was still reeling from the wave of emotion he hadn't expected. Had he built her up so much in his mind that a simple kiss could floor him like that?

"I think you were right. I think I should give you some time. Prove yourself here. Conquer this world. Become a steel seeker. Gather your power and develop an aura that will silence critics. If it takes you a year or a hundred, I'll—"

"No, fuck that, Tes! I'm not going to let you slip away for years and years! Give me a way to contact you. Can we share a Far Scribe book, at least?"

Tes smiled. "I can do better than that. I'll make us a pair of dream crystals; we can meet on the plane of dreams."

Victor grinned. "Seriously?"

"Yes. It won't take me long—a few hours. Go and see your artisan friend and check in on that poor disembodied Death Caster."

"So," Victor growled softly, reaching up to viciously scrub the side of his head, dragging his nails through his hair.

"What, Victor?"

"I kind of wish I'd just let things lie. Why'd I have to get all riled up and . . ." Unable to finish the thought, he jammed his hand into his palm, driving it in until his knuckles popped. "And now you're leaving."

"Hush. You did the right thing. Besides, I'm the one who brought up Kynna's affections. We had to confront this. You need the freedom to become who you are meant to be."

Her words triggered memories of Valla and her reasons for parting with him. He groaned, unable to fight down the feelings those memories evoked. Was he cursed? Was every woman he met going to say it wasn't the right time? Valla wanted to grow beyond his shadow, and now Tes wanted him to grow beyond hers. What twist of fate had brought about this cruel irony? He almost laughed at the absurdity of it all. Couldn't two people who liked each other just *be* together?

Tes sniffed, grabbing his wrist. "Are you well?"

Victor realized he was grimacing again. He wanted to say that he wasn't, but he didn't. Hadn't he just told Tes he didn't want to mess up her life? If he needed to get stronger to stand beside her among her peers, then that's what he'd goddamn do. "I'm good." He forced a smile and nodded. "I'll go see Trobban and Arona later, though. If you're leaving soon, then I'll hang out while you work on the dream crystals."

Her smile was gentle as she nodded. "That would be nice, Victor. We can chat while I work." She nodded toward the table. "How about some wine?"

"Yeah. One of mine, or—"

"I have something I've been saving. It's from a vineyard on my uncle's lands on Aradnue." She tugged his wrist. "Come. I have advice for your upcoming duels. Imagine how guilty I'll feel if you die after I leave?"

13

EVERYONE DIES

Victor withdrew into himself for several days after Tes left. At first, he let his loneliness and frustration get the better of him, and he languished in heavy, emotional doldrums, refusing audiences with Bryn and instructing her—through the door of his suite—to keep others away. That didn't last long, though, because he found another emotional outlet: anger. He was angry at himself for pushing things to a confrontation with Tes. He was angry with her for worrying so much about the conventions of the society she was a part of. Ultimately, though, he railed at fate or God or whatever invisible forces had set his path through life on collision courses with women like Valla and Tes.

Fortunately for Victor and the citizens of Gloria, he'd been through all of this before and had grown resilient to the effects of heartache. After a few days, he began to force himself—a true feat of his prodigious will—to focus on the positives. Wasn't it great that he'd earned the love of such incredible women in his admittedly short life? Shouldn't he be happy to know that Tes wanted things to work out, that she was eager for him to continue to grow and one day, hopefully soon, be able to stand up to the scrutiny of her peers? Hadn't it been amazing to kiss her and hold her and see the matching heat of emotion in her eyes when she left?

So, on the fourth day after her departure, Victor got himself up, took a nice long shower, dressed in fine clothing suitable for a duke and champion of a kingdom, and left his quarters, determined to make the most of the time remaining until his next duel. He'd yet to hear from Kynna, but he knew she'd be arriving with her retinue any day. He also assumed she was already hard at work trying to coax one of the great houses into accepting—or even preemptively issuing—a challenge.

"Are you well?" Bryn asked when he stepped out. Victor hadn't provided much clarity when he'd hollered at her to keep people away, simply growling that he didn't feel well and needed peace.

Victor smiled and nodded, stepping into the elevator. As Bryn followed him in, he said, "I'm good, thanks for asking. How are you? How's Feist doing?"

"I'm well, though I admit to some worry over the last few days. I reasoned you were probably going through some sort of breakthrough—another natural treasure you'd been holding onto. Such thoughts quelled my fears and provided an excellent excuse to keep your administrators at bay."

"You told Draj I'd eaten a natural treasure?"

"Not in so many words. I simply hinted in that direction. Where are we off to?"

"To see Trobban. Any word from him?"

She nodded. "He inquired about your status; he wasn't aware you were back in the palace."

"All right. Oh, and Feist? The wedding went well?"

"It was a very festive affair, and his family was appreciative of your gesture. I've submitted their expenses to the treasury. I hope that's all right."

"Yeah, of course. I was going to pay out of my own pocket, but . . . yeah, let the duchy cover it. Feist may only be a squire, but he's earned some hazard pay after our expedition to Iron Mountain."

Bryn was quiet as they exited the elevator and walked for a while, then she hesitantly asked, "Victor . . . have you heard anything about your next duel?"

He looked at her sharply, her tone making him wonder what *she* had heard. "Are there rumors?"

"Oh, many rumors, but it's said that King Bayle is clamoring for your head. He wants to mount it, along with Queen Kynna's, atop the gates of his palace."

Victor snorted, scratching his chin. "Yeah? What kingdom does he rule again?"

"Alvessia. It's a large kingdom on the southern point of the eastern continent. Those of us who grow up here on Ruhn are taught of that kingdom because it boasts the longest coastline of any kingdom—eleven hundred miles along the Central Sea and thirteen hundred on the other side, facing the Vast Deep."

"Well, I guess that's good. If he's so eager, then Kynna won't have trouble getting me a duel." Victor turned down the long hallway leading to the ballroom that Trobban had taken over. "Do you know anything about his champion?"

Bryn nodded, her heels clicking on the marble floor as she walked beside him. "Yes, but only because of the king's outrageous vitriol. His champion is named Loss Chenasta, and he's an off-worlder, or was until last month. More than that, I can't tell you."

"Loss, huh?" Victor resisted the urge to make a stupid joke, partly because he feared he'd jinx himself.

"Yes, a strange name and rather at odds with your own."

Victor looked at her just in time to see a sly smile on her lips and laughed. "Nice one, Bryn! And the queen? Any word?"

It was her turn to look at him sharply. "I thought that was why you came out today. Her chamberlain came through the portal and announced her imminent arrival. The palace staff is in a frenzy!"

"Ah." Victor shrugged, smiling ruefully. "Maybe I felt her shadow falling over me." By then, his long strides had taken them to the ballroom door, where two guards stood on duty. He nodded to them, and the one on the left pulled the door wide for him.

"Welcome, Your Grace," the man said from within his shiny helm, slamming his right fist into his breastplate.

"Thank you." Victor stepped into the doorway but paused, looking at the guard holding the door and then the other one. "I've heard good things about your work, soldiers. Excellent job keeping this important work safe."

"Milord!" the other guard cried, imitating his colleague's salute. Victor nodded, then stepped into the ballroom. The space still looked like a formal dance or gathering hall; the white marble floor gleamed with fresh polish, and the wainscoting around the perimeter shone with a deep cherry luster in the bright light thrown by the high, crystal chandeliers. At the center of the space, however, was an improvised workshop: a dozen long tables strewn with equipment and materials, sheaves of paper, and stacks of books.

At the center of the loose circle of tables, Trobban leaned over something metallic, wielding a crystalline implement that ticked and buzzed as he did something that required close concentration. Victor nodded to Bryn, who took up a position near the door and walked quietly around the tables until he stood by the Artificer's side. "How goes it?"

"Ah, Victor!" Trobban's voice was pleasant and warm. "Give me just a moment to finish this, and then you'll have my undivided attention."

"No problem." Victor turned and walked over to a table at the center of all the others. It, too, was stacked with books and scribbled notes, but in the middle lay the new "vessel" that Trobban had been building for Arona. Victor hadn't laid eyes on it for a while, and he sucked in his breath at the sight of it. The last time he'd visited, Trobban had been learning how to work with the silvenite—Victor had given him half the ingot before giving the other half to Lifedrinker. Now, though, Arona's new body was clad entirely in the smooth, silvery stuff.

For the first time, Victor could get an idea of the final form—not just the bones and innards in a vaguely humanoid shape. He'd expected Arona to be out, helping Trobban, but when he saw her future body there, he suddenly felt glad she wasn't; the vessel was anatomically correct. Small breasts, complete with areolae and nipples, rose from the chest, and there was a definite cleft between its legs. "*Chingado,*" he hissed, summoning a cloak from his ring and draping it over the vessel, leaving only the arms and head exposed.

Leaning close, he saw delicate lines around the finger joints and even carved nail beds. Victor turned his attention to the head and was stunned by how eerily the monochrome, silvery flesh resembled the Arona he'd come to know back on Sojourn. Even her hair had been sculpted—hundreds of thousands of tiny filaments hung in short, wavy curls around her oval face. The vessel's eyes were open, and within those metalline orbital bones sat two crystalline spheres that glowed with soft, silver-blue light.

"It almost looks alive already, doesn't it?" Trobban asked, stepping close.

"She's going to be silver?"

"No! When we complete the ritual to transfer Arona's spirit into the vessel, the silvenite will take on a fleshlike appearance. It's very malleable and easy to impress. Arona's self-image will imprint. Of course, I've had to sculpt it into an approximation that conforms to the skeletal structure I built, but the details will come from Arona's mind."

Victor nodded, reaching to touch the vessel's small, dimpled chin. To his surprise, the silvery surface yielded to his touch, soft like flesh. "Is it finished?"

Trobban grinned broadly. "Nearly! Your friend rests, gathering her strength, and I'm attuning the Azurite Star to her chosen affinity." He gestured to another table where a spherical, dark metal container hummed, emitting faint pulses of yellow-hued light. "At its current rate, it should be ready within the week."

"What affinity, Trobban?" The last time Victor had spoken to the crafter and Arona, they'd yet to decide. The Azurite Star could, apparently, take on any affinity given enough of an Energy infusion, so Victor gave Arona the five Energy hearts he'd won in the Crucible of Fire to choose from.

Trobban grinned. "She's truly going against her old nature; she's chosen a solar affinity."

Victor grinned. "I like it. It's not exactly the opposite of death, but the undead *pendejos* definitely don't like the sun or its light." He nodded, his mind drifting back to a conversation he'd had with Arona while they'd been in the Iron Prison. She'd spoken about a member of the ruling council, a woman of Fae heritage who was feared and respected by all—Consul Rexa. Arona had dreamed of earning the woman's respect, but the Fae wouldn't abide a Death Caster. How would the consul feel now if Arona showed up in this new vessel with a solar affinity? For Arona's sake, he hoped it would be a happy meeting.

"Honestly, Victor, if all goes well, we'll be ready to perform the ritual this time next week. Do you think you'll attend?"

Victor nodded, still staring at the strangely beautiful glowing eyes in the vessel's serene, smooth face. "I want to, yes. Whether it will align with my schedule, we'll have to wait and see. I'll meet with the queen soon, so I imagine I'll have a better answer for you in the next day or two. Don't do anything until you hear from me!" He nodded to the cloak he'd draped over the vessel. "And keep her covered up, damn it. She might not be in there yet, but have a little respect for her future body."

"Well, Victor, I've had to carve and craft every small detail on this vessel. You could think of me as a physician in that regard—"

"Don't give me that! How many physicians would leave their patient nude on a table in the middle of a ballroom where others might wander by to observe those tiny details?"

"But, Victor . . . you don't let anyone else come in here, and—" He must have seen Victor's glower, and he stopped short, nodding and bowing slightly. "My apologies, Your Grace. I should have had more thought for Arona's, um, future modesty."

"Good." Victor took one more look around the gathered tables and then asked, "Anything else you need before I leave you to it?"

"No, no. You've been so generous. This space will work perfectly for the ritual." Trobban looked around, mimicking Victor's earlier perusal. Victor took a minute to give him a good look. The Artificer looked much the same as when Victor first met him, though he was undoubtedly more disheveled. His beard had grown, his hair was in tangles, and his robes were filthy with ink and other fluid stains. "If something comes up—"

"You're taking care of yourself, right? Sleeping enough? Eating?"

"Oh, certainly!" He smoothed his robes while looking down at himself. "I apologize for my appearance; it's just that this project is the greatest undertaking I've ever attempted. I can't stop thinking about it. I would leave to clean myself up more often, but my mind is constantly gripped by the many little tasks ahead. Even now, I'm working on the inscriptions for the rune tablets that will guide Arona's spirit into the new vessel. We have to attune them perfectly so that the latent Energy in her aura can be properly altered from death to solar attunement. It's a delicate process, and I'm constantly thinking of new ways to tweak the patterns."

"Well, listen. Here's an order from me: Before we go through with the ritual, you're to have two solid days off to think about everything you've done to prepare. Sometimes, you need some distance and a clear mind to see mistakes."

Trobban nodded, his ink-smudged face severe with his conviction. "Very wise. I swear it, Your Grace."

Victor clapped him on the shoulder, nodded, and then turned back to the door where Bryn stood waiting. "See you soon, Trobban."

When he approached Bryn, she smiled. "If you'd hoped to get any peace today, you should prepare for disappointment."

Victor arched an eyebrow. "Why's that?"

"There's a page waiting outside. He wanted to speak to you—a message from the queen. I told him to wait." Bryn's smile turned a bit wicked as she added, "When he insisted his message was urgent, I might have mentioned that if his voice distracted you while you were in this room, I wouldn't be able to save him from the curse you put on this threshold."

Victor chuckled. Bryn had a way of surprising him, and it was clear his influence had rubbed off on her. Hadn't she been straightlaced and by-the-book when they'd first met? He couldn't imagine that Bryn, the one who rarely smiled and kept her helmet on through every waking minute, would have teased a poor page like that. "Well, nothing wrong with a bit of harmless teasing. Come on, let's see what this is all about."

He pulled the door open, nodded to the two guards, and approached the young man wearing a tunic emblazoned with a golden rose. "What have you got for me?" he asked by way of greeting.

"Your Grace! Her Majesty, Queen Kynna Dar, would have you know that she's resumed residence in the eastern wing of your palace and would appreciate a meeting with you as soon as possible."

"Anything urgent?"

"Your Grace, the queen's time is always precious. I pray that you won't keep her waiting."

Victor glowered at the young fellow. It wasn't really his fault that he was enthusiastic. After all, Kynna was the most powerful monarch on the continent; a little hero worship was to be expected. He nodded to the kid, probably only fifteen or so, and, with a grunt, waved him away. "I'll be along shortly. Let her know." The page didn't waste time. He bowed and, before straightening, turned and sprinted down the hallway, his polished black shoes clicking in a staccato rhythm on the hard floors.

"Enthusiastic," Bryn observed.

"Yeah. I haven't seen that one before."

"Gloria has absorbed quite a few new nations recently thanks to the threat of your challenge. I'm sure the queen has had to take on many noble children to serve in one capacity or another."

"Huh. That's a good point, Bryn. Well, lead the way, Baroness—let's see what's in store for me." Queen Kynna had given Bryn official status in House Dar. Bryn smirked in reply, but she did as he asked, taking the lead through the palace, waving away servants, guards, and dozens of nobles, staff, and attendants whom Victor wasn't familiar with. His palace had been serving as a second capital for the queen's burgeoning empire for a while now, and Victor had been quite happy to pass obligations off to the Haveshi clan. Draj and his mother, Tyla, had been hosting dignitaries on a regular basis.

His presence outside the area directly adjacent to his tower, walking through the long, opulent corridors of the central palace, was unusual, and many of the aforementioned folks were eager to try to meet him. They undoubtedly hoped for some favor at court or, at the very least, a story they could barter for influence with their peers. Victor smiled and nodded but was happy to have Bryn take on her role as his escort and personal guard, growling and shouting with a voice from somewhere deep in her belly for people to "Clear the path!" or "Make way for the duke!"

Before long, they entered the eastern wing of his palace, and once they'd passed by a squad of the Queen's Guard, things calmed down, and fewer people crowded their path. Nearly everyone was familiar with him, and they knew better than to slow him on his way to see the queen. The guards directed them to her current location, a study Victor was rather fond of, with tall glass doors that opened onto one of his gardens. Bryn took up a position with the Queen's Guard outside, and he let himself in.

Kynna sat before the garden doors, the sun's rays warm and bright on her silvery blue gown. Her thick hair was pulled up with silver pins, somehow woven between the spires of her crystal crown. When she heard the door close, she turned and regarded him pleasantly. "Thank you for coming right away, Victor. My messenger said that you were in the midst of something important when he found you."

"Just speaking to my Artificer friend. If I'd known you were waiting, I would have hurried, but the guards told your page to wait for me." Victor shrugged, stepping toward the empty chair near hers. "It's my fault, really. They know they're not allowed entry to that room, so of course, they wouldn't allow a page inside."

"Of course. This is the man who's working on your . . . *friend's* new vessel?"

Victor grinned at her tone, taking his seat. "Yeah. He's nearly finished."

"Excellent! I do hope I'll be able to meet your—"

"Her name is Arona, my Queen, and yes, of course, I'll gladly introduce you." Victor leaned back in his chair, enjoying the warmth the cushions had absorbed from the sunlight. In a more informal tone, with a bit of a smile, he asked, "How are you, Kynna?"

"I'm well, Victor, thank you. I'd heard rumors . . . Well, I won't insult your intelligence. I received reports from some of the staff that you've been keeping to yourself in your chambers. Is all well? Is aught wrong with your other companion, Tes?"

"Everything is fine. Tes is gone, however. She was called away to attend . . . other matters." Victor tried to keep his voice even and his face pleasant. The last thing he wanted was for Kynna to get involved in his relationship with Tes.

"I see!" She leaned forward, her hands clasped on her lap. "Will she be returning soon?"

Victor wondered what was running through her mind. Did she think her little gambit with the rose broach had struck gold? Did she believe Tes had given up because of Kynna's implied interest in Victor? He almost chuckled, but he just shook his head and shrugged. "I don't think so, Your Majesty. She has many obligations. I was lucky to have her here as long as I did." Hoping to steer the conversation away from Tes, he added, "I heard there's some king on the eastern continent who might be eager to accept a duel."

Kynna's eyes widened, and the fires inside those crystalline orbs flared brightly. "That's right; it's the reason I called you to me. The fact of the matter is that Rogan Bayle already issued a challenge!"

"Shit, seriously?" Victor wondered if Loss Chenasta was one of the champions Tes had been worried about. She'd seen two with her own eyes and learned their names: a young dragon masquerading as a giant who styled himself Goz and a Death Caster named Osk Graveborn who'd conquered an entire world before answering the call of one of the great houses. She'd heard rumors of other deadly mercenaries coming to serve as champions but hadn't had a chance to set her eyes on them.

"Yes, and Victor, know this: Gloria has too many borders, including a coastal one, for him to force my hand easily. If you wish to stop our forward momentum here and now, I will understand. In fact, I'll be happy. You've already done so much! Why risk everything?" Kynna looked sincere, and she wasn't wrong; Gloria had grown its borders tenfold since he'd arrived. More than that, she'd absorbed some very wealthy nations.

Kynna's legacy was assured. Stopping now wasn't what Victor had agreed to, though. He'd promised Dar to help her conquer this entire world, and, more importantly, he needed to keep challenging himself if he was going to build up his strength—his gravity. The kind of man who might impress a world full of dragons or a city full of equally powerful beings wasn't the kind of man who settled for "good enough." Victor had ambitions, and he had enemies, and an iron ranker who'd won a few duels wasn't going to measure up to either.

"That's not what your ancestor wanted for you. It's not what I promised him I'd do. More importantly, Kynna, this will give us a foothold on the eastern continent, and it does so without you having to declare a succession war. Honestly, you couldn't have asked for anything better. If King Rogan Bayle wants to invite calamity, let us give it to him."

"All true. Those are all wise words. However, King Bayle was at your last duel. He saw you slaughter those two iron rankers. No doubt his champion was also in attendance. He would not issue this challenge if he didn't think he could beat you. So, considering those circumstances, some of the wisdom in your words falls a bit flat. His champion is an unknown. None have seen him fight. He came from off-world only a month ago—*after* you killed Trinnie Ro and the great houses got an inkling of your threat."

"Even so, Kynna, you know what I think, and you know what Ranish Dar will say. If you want to fight your ancestor on this, go ahead, but I'll stand by what I said: We should push on."

"And my *ancestor* will listen to you! Should we risk everything? This champion is a killer for hire, and he can't have come cheaply. Perhaps Rogan won't be able to employ him through a protracted siege. If I can hold out for a decade or three, he might back off, and then—"

"Kynna, I'm sorry, but I've got . . ." Victor thought about his words carefully before continuing, "I've got other obligations to consider. I'll keep at this as long as we're trying, but if we're just stalling, I'm going to have to have a heart-to-heart with Ranish Dar. I can't sit around for decades."

Kynna's eyes grew stormy, and a deep frown marred her expression. It was always amazing to Victor how a mood could alter a person's entire persona. She looked mean and cold now, whereas moments ago, she'd been sunshine incarnate. "You don't leave me much choice, do you? Very well, then, Victor. I'll accept the challenge and put everyone's fates in your hands once again. Do you find such a burden so comfortable? Are you content to risk death?"

Victor stood, his mind fighting with his tongue, trying to keep him from saying something flippant or cruel, something harsh or angry. He considered it a well-fought victory that he managed to say what he considered the simple truth. "Everyone dies." With those words, Victor nodded to the queen, who seemed stunned by his bluntness, and walked briskly out of the room. As he strode past Bryn, she hurried to catch up, saying something, but his mind was too busy to hear her.

He wasn't sure what had upset him. Was he angry that Kynna wanted to grasp peace and content herself with the power she'd gained? Was he angry that she—again—doubted his ability to win? Was he frustrated to realize that now, more than ever, he was the one pushing this conquest? Kynna wanted to stop, and he could probably convince Ranish Dar that they'd accomplished enough. He knew it was more than that, though. He was angry at himself for putting Kynna into that corner. He'd given her the illusion of choice, but she had no control over this situation.

The question he had to ask himself was a simple one: Why? Why was he doing this? Did he simply like killing? Did he like the risk? He hadn't been lying when he indicated a lack of fear. He *wasn't* worried about dying. If he went out fighting, if he did his best, if he made his ancestors proud . . . well, then if he died, he'd be content. His spirit would find its way to the next world, and he'd try harder in his next life. The truth was, none of those motives explained his behavior.

No, the truth of the matter was that Victor hated having a boot on his neck. Ranish Dar might be a pleasant master, but he was a master nonetheless. He'd taken advantage of Victor's need to help Edeya. Just as bad as Dar were all the implied threats made by stronger and stronger people. The veil walkers of Ruhn, the consuls of Sojourn, the Warlord of Zaafor, the ancient masters of Dark Ember—everywhere Victor went, he met more and more people who used their strength to lord over him and others. Above them all, lurking and listening, shaping things through its connection to nearly every living thing, was the System. He was sick of it.

"So," he growled, startling Bryn, "if I'm going to get out from under these boots, I'll need to keep goddamn fighting."

14

A LOVELY DAY

For the next few days, Victor mostly kept to himself. Not entirely, though; one morning, he visited Trobban again and reclaimed the Energy hearts that the Artificer hadn't needed for Arona's ritual. They were all rare attunements—void, healing, mind, and metal—and Victor knew he could trade them for what he sought. He gave the job to Bryn, and it only took her a single day to teleport to the capital city, Gloria, and barter on the auction house to get Victor a heart attuned to blue ice.

He'd given her permission to trade aggressively, wanting to get the job done, so he wasn't surprised or upset to find she'd traded away two hearts for his one new one: healing and mind. When trading for rare Energies, one must be prepared to make sacrifices. So, with his heart of blue ice and the one attuned to magma that Dar had given him, he'd embarked on a new project—a cultivation chamber designed to focus Energy into his Breath Core.

His chambers atop the largest, tallest tower of his palace were extensive, including a workshop and two storage rooms beyond his small library and study. Combined, the three chambers took up a third of the tower's top level, and considering his lack of interest in crafting, he felt it was a bit much; he hadn't set foot in the workshop since he'd first toured the tower. So Victor brought in a palace work crew, and he had them redesign the space.

He walked the crew through his plan: He wanted to add a wall, effectively cutting the workshop in half and leaving one storage room available to it. The wall would be built from sturdy stone blocks, and in its center, the crew would leave a round doorway designed to fit a vault-style door that Victor would commission from an artisan in the city. On the other side of the wall, the crew was to remove the wall that separated the other storage room from the remainder of the workshop space, and then, to the foreman's delight, they would remove most of the ceiling.

Inside that ample, open space, the work crew would build a perfectly round chamber constructed from stone molded and made smooth by an Earth Elementalist employed by Iron Mountain. Because of its curved walls and ceiling that rose above the tower's roofline, some void would be created at the corners, and Victor wanted them filled with stone as well; the chamber had to be sturdy because the interior would be lined with amber ore.

Even to a duke with the wealth of a duchy like Iron Mountain behind him, so much amber ore would have been a prohibitive expense, but Victor had a plan for that. He established a new mining company and gave it the exclusive right to plumb the ore from the enormous wall that the ancient King of Iron Mountain had built to keep interlopers away from the Crucible of Fire. After all, it was no longer needed; the dungeon no longer existed on Ruhn but sat within the vault hanging from Victor's neck.

So, with things in motion and crews hard at work, Victor happened to be strolling through the palace a few days later when a young page found him and asked if he'd make time to visit with the queen. He'd just received a missive from Trobban—the ritual was ready, and he was embarking on Victor's mandated two days of rest. Victor had intended to visit with Arona or, more precisely, to see if she was available for a visit, but he looked at the page and nodded. "I'll go now. Lead the way, young lady."

The page, probably only twelve years old or so, blushed crimson and attempted a smart salute, fumbling the timing of her heel click. She looked mortified, but Victor just smiled and motioned for her to proceed. She turned and double-timed it, her little legs struggling to keep ahead of Victor's relaxed stride. He wondered what conquered noble's child she was. And decided he didn't *have* to wonder. "What's your name, page?"

She looked over her shoulder, moving to the side, attempting to bow and respond while maintaining course. She almost walked into a rack of spears but managed to right herself as she said, "I'm Revannah of House Bordany, Your Grace."

"Bordany? What nation?"

"Bandia, milord. It's just a province now, however. I am a proud citizen of Gloria."

"Ah, Bandia." Victor nodded, rubbing his chin as they walked. He had more questions but feared he might make the girl uncomfortable. For all he knew, she'd lost family members in the transition of power. He hadn't gotten the details from Kynna about which relatives of Bandia's ruling house would be banished. So he pushed his curiosity aside and walked in silence, nodding to the many nobles, retainers, staff, and soldiers they passed along the way.

Kynna was, once again, in the parlor that opened onto the garden, or so her guards assured him. However, when he entered, he found the parlor empty and the garden doors opened wide, letting in a cool breeze. Frowning, wondering if some coup was about to be sprung, Victor summoned Lifedrinker and, with her held ready, stepped outside into the early afternoon sunlight. To his relief, Kynna greeted him with a smile, standing not far away, leaning close to a row of flowering hedges.

"My Queen."

"Victor." Her smile widened, taking in his axe. "Did you fear for my safety?"

"It wouldn't be the first time you were threatened, and as you know, the great houses aren't too happy with you or me."

"No, you're quite correct. My Queen's Guards are stationed nearby, but I feel safer here in Iron Mountain. Your palace is nicely situated outside the city, and we've got the portal chamber well regulated. I didn't expect you to arrive so quickly, or I would have prepared some refreshments."

Victor smiled, sending Lifedrinker back to her container. Kynna's tone had certainly changed in the days since their last meeting. He'd regretted his coldness and abrupt departure, but only a little. He was tired of the queen's doubts and irritated that she'd effectively put the succession war firmly on his shoulders. He'd counted on her ambition and willingness to move forward; with her as a partner, he could allay some guilt, but now . . . now, he had to come to grips with the fact that everything that occurred moving forward was all on him.

"I'm sorry about how things went in our last meeting, Victor. I won't dwell on it, but I just want to say a few words if you will allow it. I'd like you to understand me a little better, and I'd like to show that I understand you. Will you listen?"

Victor moved further into the sunlight, folding his arms over his chest as he regarded her. She was, as always, dressed in a fine gown, though this one was more sheer than usual, and its pale green material was shot through with silver embroidery that reflected the sun's light. Of course, her crown did the same, making her seem almost ethereal as she stood there beside the flowers. "I'm happy to listen, Your Majest—"

"First, will you please stop that? You know I prefer you to be informal when we're alone."

Victor nodded. "Of course, Kynna."

She moved a little closer, and when they were just a yard or so apart, she began to speak. Her voice was soft at first, unsure, but her words picked up steam as she made her points. "I understand ambition. I had an older brother; did you know that?" She didn't wait for Victor to answer. "He was meant to be king, and my father pushed him to be great long before he was ready to give up the throne.

"My brother worked so hard, Victor! He fought in wars on other worlds, traveled to attempt challenges and dungeons, and even served as my father's champion for a short while. He was nearly out of the iron ranks when he died. He was alone on a distant world, consumed by a great behemoth. An ignoble end with nothing left behind for his troubles, not even a body to send home."

She clicked her tongue and looked toward the sun, shielding her eyes as though trying to see something in the clear blue sky. "I was never so ambitious. When the weight of rule fell on me, I depended greatly on Galentine, Tomorran's father. When he left, it wasn't long before I found Gloria surrounded, besieged by Xan and Frostmarch. The truth is, I've never sought great power. I doubted I'd ever become a steel seeker. Why would I when the next step would take me from this world?

"Of course, that didn't mean I wanted to die or lose the kingdom. Ranish Dar wasn't the first person I went to for help. He's not the only member of our family who has left this world for one reason or another. I sent out dozens of pleas for aid. None were answered. How *little* we must mean to those people, I thought. Or, I supposed, perhaps it was only me. I wasn't significant enough to trouble the great members of my kin. It was in desperation that I sent my request to Ranish Dar. I had little hope of a response.

"Are you aware he didn't respond immediately? It was years before, out of the blue, I received his reply and his intention to send a disciple—an iron ranker who would serve as my champion and free Gloria from her troubles." Kynna tentatively stretched out a hand and rested her cool fingers on Victor's crossed forearm. "I could scarcely believe it when I set my eyes on you the first time. I didn't think you could possibly do what Dar sent you to accomplish."

She let her fingers drop, shaking her head and chuckling softly. Victor wanted to say something, but she didn't wait before continuing, "Your victories, one after another, were hard to fathom. When you told me of Dar's desire for our house to rule this world, you know I was reluctant. I was fearful. I still *am*. You saw the trouble Gloria was in when you arrived; I am unfamiliar with the mindset of the truly ambitious. I failed one negotiation after another over the course of years to bring our nation to that lowly state. Of course, the decline had begun long before I was queen, but that doesn't . . ."

When she trailed off, Victor seized the opportunity to get a word in. "Kynna, I know all that. Well, most of it. I don't blame you for—"

"Let me get this out, Victor. Please." She looked up at him again, the fire in her eyes very dim in the sun's bright light. "I fear for myself, my family, the future of our nation. I fear my ancestor and what he'll do if I refuse. I fear *you*.

I fear our enemies and—" She took a deep, shaky inhalation. "I fear what will happen if you die or, more bitingly, what will happen if you win. Victor, I barely believe I can be the queen of a small nation. Now, I'm struggling to believe I am the most powerful ruler on this continent. Here I am, hiding in your palace to avoid the drama and infighting at my court. How can I possibly be an empress? How can I rule an entire planet?"

At first, Victor felt angry at her words. Was she trying another tactic to get him to back down? However, the more he thought about it, the more he began to understand her. She was trying to confess to him that it wasn't doubt in him that was terrifying her anymore; it was her burgeoning belief that he might actually pull the whole thing off. "You doubt yourself?" He unfolded his arms and took hold of her shoulders. "That's fine, Kynna!"

"It's not—"

"No, it's my turn. Listen." Victor took a deep breath, nodding as he gathered his words. "You're not ambitious. You weren't raised to rule. You're fearful." He saw moisture building in her eyes and smiled. "I'm not insulting you, Kynna. I'm describing you. You have virtues, too, chief among them being the love you engender from your people—they're *devoted* to you. You know that, right? So you're not a great conqueror, not in the traditional sense, that doesn't mean you can't be a great ruler. You'll manage a small nation or a great empire the same way—with love, empathy, and a desire for every person in your care to be happy. That's more than most ambitious, cutthroat conquerors can boast.

"Of course, your nature left you open to trouble. You allowed people to take advantage of you, and you would have backed off this campaign and been content with too little. That's why you have to be wise and surround yourself with people you trust, people with the qualities you lack. Right now, that's me. I know about pushing an advantage. I know when to recognize that mercy isn't the right choice. I know you've already shown yourself to be a threat to the great houses, and Kynna, they aren't like you. They won't let a threat fester.

"So, we need to clear the table. We need to put you in charge, and you need to fill this empire with kings and queens who are loyal to you. I'll help you get there, but you're going to have to keep what I earn. You should be spending the time between now and the day you ascend the final throne building up a close inner circle of people you can trust. People with the qualities you lack. Let them help you keep the empire. House Khaliday has been in power how long?"

"Eleven centuries."

"A long time, in my opinion. Do people love the emperor?"

Kynna shook her head, her voice small as she replied, "No."

"Well, they're going to love *you*. I'll write to Ranish Dar and let him know that he needs to find you a strategist—an advisor, someone you can trust and who will help you control the other monarchs. I'm not an expert at diplomacy, but even I know that when you rely on ambitious people, that very ambition can lead to your downfall. You'll need someone crafty to help you keep control. You're the kind heart; someone else must be your iron fist."

Kynna reached up, resting a palm on Victor's knuckles where he gripped her shoulder. "What's wrong with this fist?"

Victor smiled and shook his head. "I'm sorry, Kynna. I think you're wonderful, and I've come to truly care about this world. I have other ambitions, though. I didn't come here with any intent to stay."

She inhaled deeply through her nose and then sighed out the breath. "I know. I know, but I hate it." They stared at each other for a few moments, and then she asked, "Will he listen to you?"

"Ranish Dar?" When she nodded, he answered, "I think so. He has thousands of iron rankers vying for his attention—people dreaming of being his students. I'm sure among them are a few crafty strategists. Let them earn his tutelage by helping you."

She sniffed and let go of Victor's hand. She gently brushed away a small tear that had leaked from the corner of her crystalline eye, and at that moment, Victor wanted very badly to hug her. He knew better, though; the gesture would do too much to encourage her burgeoning affection for him, and he didn't want to lead her on. "I feel better." Again, she sighed heavily. "Much, much better. Thank you for helping to clear the air between us. Thank you for giving me hope that I won't fail as a ruler. I don't want to feel too hopeful, but I find it difficult not to trust your word by now. If you think my ancestor will send me advisors, I will try to believe."

"Thank you for being so open, Kynna—for sharing your fears. There's nothing shameful in that, you know? I've had to battle my fears for my entire life."

Kynna chuckled, shaking her head. "It's hard for me to believe. Thank you for saying so, Victor. There were other reasons I asked you to come here, chief among them being to tell you that I've accepted Rogan Bayle's challenge. We'll discuss terms in three days, and if things go well, you will fight Loss Chenasta the following morning at dawn."

Victor nodded, pressing his lips together. "Four days. All right."

"I also have a gift for you." She reached into the neckline of her dress and lifted out a silver chain, from which dangled a large, ornate, platinum-colored ring. It was made for a much larger finger than Kynna's, and as she pulled the chain over her head, he saw that it was set with a beautiful gemstone that shimmered between amber and ruby hues. "This is a very durable and capacious dimensional storage container. I've been assured that it can hold the equivalent of ninety thousand tons. Moreover, it's been designed to allow Energy to stream in and out; conscious items will not suffer within."

"Wow," Victor said, opening his hand so Kynna could place the ring in his palm. It was heavy and cold. He wore many rings these days, but he had room on his right pointer finger and slid the new ring onto it. "I need to get rid of some of these old rings. I'll confess to being a bit of a hoarder."

Kynna chuckled. "It's easy to do when you don't have to see the contents! When I was a child, my governess would make me sort my storage devices twice a month."

Victor flexed his fist, nodding. "Thank you, Kynna."

"You're welcome. I sent an emissary to Sojourn to buy that at their auction house. We couldn't find a suitable one locally. I'm not complaining; you've more than earned it. In fact, I know I owe you more growth items per our arrangement with Ranish Dar. However, it isn't easy to find items that will appropriately affect you. I don't know your exact level, but growth items for iron rankers near the peak are few and far between. Moreover, I have it on good authority that your bloodline is within the epic tier, and epic-level racial advancements are even harder to come by."

"I trust you, Kynna." Victor smiled and nudged her shoulder. "See what I mean? People believe in you, even me. I know you won't hold out on me. Just let me know when you find something."

"I will, Victor." She nodded toward the garden path. "It's such a beautiful day, and I feel more at peace in my heart than I have for months. Will you walk with me?"

"Yeah." Victor crooked his elbow so she could take it with her hand. "I'd like that. Let's enjoy the day." He'd almost said, "Let's enjoy the calm before the storm," but aside from it being too cliché, he didn't want to throw a dark cloud over Kynna's good mood. So, feeling better about things and glad to know the fate of the world wasn't solely on his shoulders, Victor walked Kynna through the garden, enjoying the scent of the blooming flowers, the trilling tunes of songbirds, and the soul-warming rays of the sun.

15

SOLAR CASTER

For the next two days, Victor spent his time supervising the workers as they made progress on his cultivation chamber. Having access to master artisans, all the materials he could ask for, and Elementalists who could shape and mold stone made for much quicker progress than he'd imagined. The demolition phase was done in the days leading up to his meeting with the queen, and in a single day, the masons employed by the duchy, combined with the efforts of an Earth Elementalist, constructed the new wall and the spherical chamber beyond the round portal—ready for the amber ore once it arrived.

Victor had established his new mining company with Draj's help. His chancellor had all the necessary connections; he was familiar with every major private mining company and even had dossiers on their owners, managers, and supervisors. Victor made it clear that the "amber mine" would be a private endeavor, though he would pay the duchy its taxes like any private miner would, and Draj agreed to find him an available manager and crew. All that had been left was to show them where the ore was, and Victor tapped Bryn's squire, Feist, for that.

Feist, newly married and only recently back to work in the palace, was all too eager for some time on the road. Victor found his enthusiasm funny, but Bryn only shook her head in disgust, promising a renewed focus on weapons training when the squire returned. Victor didn't envy the squire the beating he likely had coming his way. Along with the duty of guiding the company to the amber ore, Victor had charged Feist with the job of securing oaths and contracts with each employee; they weren't to disclose the richness of Victor's stake to anyone on their visits to town.

Draj had been concerned that if word got out about Victor's claim on the amber ore, people would decry the injustice, so he'd suggested Victor personally pay for the mining lease in addition to the taxes he'd pay on his profits. He'd also suggested that the proceeds from the mine's fees be set aside and used for infrastructure improvements around the duchy—let the people see with their own eyes how Victor's good fortune was theirs as well. Victor wholeheartedly agreed because, despite those expenses, he stood to extract an enormous fortune from his "mine." It made him wonder just how wealthy Iron Mountain had been as a kingdom before it had fallen to the empire. He couldn't imagine spending so much to guard a dungeon from competitors.

On the morning of Arona's vessel ritual, Victor summoned Draj to have breakfast with him in his quarters. As they both finished eating, he sipped his coffee and regarded his chancellor over the rim of his cup. "How long do you think it'll be before I see the first shipments of amber ore in the city? I've hired an artisan for the mechanical pieces I'll need, and our metal shaper is standing by; all I need is the metal."

Draj cleared his throat and dabbed his napkin at the corners of his mouth. "Have you had an update from your man? Is the crew in place?"

"Yes, they were setting up their operation yesterday."

"Well, it's my understanding that the primary obstacle is the removal of the warding runes carved into the, um, *ore*." Draj chuckled. "Petallis is one of the best glyphbinders in all of Gloria, and she spoke confidently when I hired her onto the job. However, it may take her days or weeks; I honestly don't know. I'm sorry, Your Grace, but it's outside my expertise. I'm sure she has an idea by now, however. Perhaps your man can wring a commitment out of her."

Victor nodded. "I'll have Bryn message Feist." He pushed his chair back. "Listen, I've got a commitment this morning. Will you walk with me? I have a couple of things to go over with you."

"Of course!"

Victor nodded and led the way out of his quarters, past the waiting kitchen staff who rushed in to clear his table. In the elevator, he said, "Tomorrow, I'm going to join the queen as she negotiates the terms of my next duel. I want to get a look at the champion I'll be facing."

"Understandable, milord." Draj frowned and opened his mouth but closed it before speaking again.

"Go on, Draj. Speak freely."

"Are you concerned? Do you . . ."

"I don't intend to lose. I'm not concerned so much as curious. Nobody knows this guy, and King Bayle is very confident."

"I can see why you'd want to assess your opponent." Draj's tone was carefully neutral, and Victor figured the man was trying not to say something that might shake Victor's confidence. Victor would be lying if he said he hadn't had a few sleepless nights while his mind ran through a million scenarios. There were just too many possibilities for him to build a coherent strategy; he figured he'd have to adapt on the go, and it might be painful, but he'd pull through. It wasn't like Loss Chenasta was in a much better situation; despite his duels up to this point, the people of Ruhn had yet to see the vast majority of Victor's abilities.

"Well, I mentioned it to you because I have another ally who will soon be joining me here at Iron Mountain. In fact, if all goes well, she'll be here today. I was hoping you'd familiarize her with the duchy and show her around. Let her shadow you tomorrow and the next day while I'm busy with the duel."

"Shadow me, sir? Am I to be replaced, then?"

Victor chuckled, clapping him on the shoulder as they stepped out of the elevator. "You wish, Draj! No, you're stuck with this job, I'm afraid. Arona—that's my friend's name—will be advising me and spending most of her time by my side. I think it's important for her to know what sorts of responsibilities I have. You know a lot about the duchy, but you're also familiar with the other nations of Ruhn—the rulers, champions, and all the rumors that go along with them. Get her up to speed for me, will you?"

"Ah!" Draj smiled and nodded emphatically. "I will do so, but if it pleases you, I'll also introduce her to my mother. If I'm a journeyman on court intrigue, she's a grandmaster."

Victor nodded. "Excellent idea. Between you and Tyla, I think Arona will be up to speed in no time." They reached the central junction of major corridors in the palace, and Victor nodded to the right where Trobban and his makeshift workshop awaited. "I'm going this way. Perhaps I'll track you down later today and introduce you to Arona."

"Very good, Your Grace. I'll let you know if I hear any news on your mining endeavor." Draj bowed and departed, walking toward the east wing, and Victor turned the other way. A few minutes later, the guards opened the doors, and he was striding across the ballroom to Trobban. The floor was clear; all the tables and paraphernalia were gone. In their place was an elaborate ritual pattern drawn in liquid metal that shimmered and sparkled in the chandelier lights.

Arona's new vessel lay at the center of the pattern, clad in a spectacular, silken mauve gown embroidered with pale pink gemstones. Other than the gown, the vessel looked exactly as Victor remembered it—silvery flesh and hair, with softly glowing blue crystal eyes. Trobban walked around the pattern, placing the artifacts necessary for the ritual in key locations. Victor saw Arona's phylactery bone and dozens of Energy stones—gems charged with pure, unattuned Energy that would power the transfer ritual.

"How goes it? Will Arona be present?" Victor hadn't spoken to her since he'd come to collect his extra Energy hearts.

"No, Victor. She should be assuming a meditative trance inside her phylactery. This process will be trying for her. As to your first question, it's going well.

I successfully implanted the Azurite Star in the vessel, and it was, as far as my probing could discern, completely attuned to solar Energy."

"And everything else?"

"Everything is in place. The only object that gave me any trouble was the egg of crystalline sentience. Such a delicate, powerful artifact—I toiled for months just to make the runic connections from it to her heart, Core, and nervous system. Still, it sits ready to receive Arona's intellect."

"How can you be sure it's right?"

"I have probing spells, Your Grace. Certain classes grant such abilities. I can test connections and gauge the perfection of my work before committing. This vessel is as perfect as I can make it. Every part of it is at least of epic-tier quality."

"So Arona won't lose any levels?"

"Ah," Trobban chuckled. "I would promise that if she'd maintained her original affinity, but when her spirit goes through the pattern here"—he gestured to the glimmering silver lines and runes—"her accumulated Energy will be transformed so that it can find purchase in her new Core. She may lose a small percentage in the process."

Victor nodded, thinking about Lam and Edeya. This was a very different process than they'd gone through; he'd already had that discussion with Trobban. The main difference was that Arona had been a Death Caster with a phylactery. When her body had died, she'd had a "backup" of sorts in her phylactery—an artificial battery that would hold her Energy, along with her spirit. Ideally, a Death Caster who lost their body but had a phylactery wouldn't be any weaker when they entered a new vessel. If everything went right here, despite her desire to abandon her death-attuned Energy, Arona would still be close to the same power level in her new body.

"Will she be able to gain levels?"

"Of course! The Azurite Star, once it's infused with her Energy and connected to her spirit, will function just as any natural Core. It will expand as she cultivates Energy. Her vessel, likewise, can gain Energy density. Our preparations ensured that she could reach the rank of steel seeker and beyond."

"The 'epic-tier' materials."

"Correct. Of course, academically speaking, there are tiers beyond epic, but nobody I know has reached them."

"That you know of." Victor was more than confident that many veil walkers and probably some steel seekers had reached "legendary" in one or more aspect of their development—skills, spells, bloodline, even classes. People like him and Trobban simply weren't privy to such knowledge. Great masters didn't like to advertise their secrets; if they wrote them into books, they didn't tend to fall into the hands of iron rankers.

"Exactly so, milord."

"Well," Victor asked, looking around the pattern, "what's left to do? Can I help?"

"Not at all. I'm nearly finished. If you'll but stand to the side there, a few feet away from the pattern, so there's no risk of your aura interfering with the process, I'll be ready to begin in five minutes or so."

Victor moved several paces back, folding his arms over his chest as he watched the man move about, tracing his lines and muttering softly. He could only imagine how nerve-racking this process was to him. He'd worked tirelessly for months and months. There were priceless artifacts involved, not to mention Arona's life. Honestly, Trobban had spent more time with Arona now than Victor had. He doubted it could be easy to shoulder so much responsibility.

At the thought, he almost chuckled. He wasn't a stranger to having weight on his shoulders, either. As Trobban worked, another thought came to him, and he asked, "Hey, Trobban. If this works, do you think you'll gain a level?"

"Ha!" the Artificer laughed, shaking his head. "I would say so, milord. More than that, I anticipate several of my harder-to-improve skills will advance. This has been a wonderful opportunity."

"You're not nervous, huh?"

"I'll admit to some anxiety, but I'm more excited than worried. As I said, I've tested everything a hundred times. Barring some calamity, I'm confident things will go as planned." Quietly, Victor took several steps back and knocked his knuckles against the dark wooden wainscoting—no sense in letting Trobban jinx things. "I'm ready, Your Grace!" Trobban announced, moving to the far end of the pattern where a single large Energy gem sat, pulsing with yellow-white light. "Once I initiate the spell, things will happen quickly. Watch her phylactery!"

Victor nodded and focused on the dark, rune-etched bone. He remembered when Arona had given it to him, her scratchy voice coming to him in the dark cave, asking him to bury it for her if she died. He remembered watching Ronkerz's Big One ripping her body apart in his crocodilian jaws and nearly losing himself to his rage.

Clicking his tongue, he watched the bone, hoping everything they'd done wouldn't be for nothing. Trobban began to chant, his words strange and foreign, the System failing or choosing not to interpret them. Victor felt a great rush of Energy, and the gems around the pattern all blazed like thermite flares. With a rush of cold wind, a fountain of dark blue, death-attuned Energy rushed out of the phylactery.

The Energy rose into the air, forming a cloud that exuded frigid darkness, but then it began to seep downward into the pattern, flowing into the metallic lines. In moments, the entire cloud of death-attuned Energy soaked into the pattern, and Victor could see it tracing through, almost like watching water running through a channel. The pattern was enormous and complex, and despite the speed of the Energy, it took a long time to flow through it.

The Energy was still tinted blue in the pattern, but as Victor watched, the leading edge began to shift, paling toward white and then picking up a bright golden hue. "It's working!" Trobban cried. Victor felt some relief at those words, and he continued to watch as the Energy traced through the pattern, first around the perimeter, then spiraling toward the center where Arona's new vessel awaited.

It took nearly five minutes, and by the time the leading edge of Energy hit the thick circle of silver that surrounded Arona's body, it was clear that it had taken on the solar attunement; it blazed white-yellow, almost too bright to stare at. Once the thick silver circle was filled with Energy, it began to fill tiny spiderweb veins that ran directly into the vessel's palms where they lay against the ballroom floor.

"The pattern provides resistance, allowing the Energy to trickle into her safely, lest we overwhelm her pathways!" Trobban yelled.

Victor was a good thirty yards from the pattern's center, but he had good eyes. He squinted, peering at the vessel's hands where the Energy poured into them, and when he saw the first sign that Arona was imprinting, he smiled broadly. Her fingernails had taken on a lifelike hue—opaque but no longer silver. More than that, the flesh beneath them was pink, and while he watched, the fleshy color spread down her fingers, over the backs of her hands, and up her wrists and forearms.

As the Energy gathered in the ring around her body, it grew brighter and brighter, and the glare made it impossible to see Arona's vessel, even for Victor's eyes. He shifted his gaze to Trobban and saw the man pacing near the circle, wringing his hands with nervous energy. At first, Victor thought something was wrong, but when he looked up, Trobban's face told the tale—he was ecstatic, not worried. A flickering pulse from the pattern's center stole his attention, and Victor looked back toward the vessel.

The Energy was dimming, more than half of it having been absorbed, and as Victor watched, the body began to lift off the floor, hovering in the air as the final threads of bright Energy flowed into it. Victor couldn't believe his eyes. Arona's hair hung in black, luxurious curls; her flesh was pale but vibrant, just a hint of rosiness to her cheeks, and as Victor held *his* breath, the vessel's chest began to move—up and down with slow, steady breaths.

When the last of the Energy streaked into her, Arona's aura came alive—warm, vibrant, powerful, washing through the ballroom as she opened her eyes, no longer crystalline, but fully alive, blazing with brilliant Energy behind her pale, sky-blue irises. She arched her back and gasped, and then the ritual ended, and she floated down to the floor, murmuring and writhing weakly.

Victor started toward her, worry warring with excitement as he wondered if everything was all right. He'd only taken a few strides when a *thud* drew his attention to Trobban. The artificer had collapsed, arms and legs spread-eagled as a look of pure ecstasy washed over his face. "What the *hell?*" Victor chuckled and hurried to Arona's side, kneeling beside her. She was human-sized, so he concentrated and threw more Energy into his Alter Self spell, reducing his size to match hers.

"Arona!" he said, taking her hand in his. It was warm and soft. Could it really be made of metallic flesh and crystalline bones?

She blinked her eyes rapidly and then looked at him. At first, she frowned and pulled away, but after a second, she blinked again and smiled. "V-Victor?"

"Did I get uglier?"

Her soft pink lips spread into a smile, revealing regular white teeth; her old sharp teeth were gone. He wondered about that. Was it a decision she'd made when Trobban crafted her skeleton, or had her spirit decided she wouldn't have sharp teeth any longer? She spoke again, proving she still had her trademark scratchy voice. "No, but things are *different* with these eyes—brighter, clearer. I wonder if it's the lack of death's miasma in my pathways. I feel so good!"

She struggled to push herself upright, and Victor pulled on her hand to help her sit. "It *looks* like everything went well."

"I believe it did." She stared into space, her face blank, and Victor thought something was wrong, but then she spoke again. "I lost three levels, but I'm still Tier Nine. Damn it, but that stings—something like eight years of work."

"Was it worth it?"

"To be alive? To be free of Vesavo Bonewhisper? To have a bright, life-loving Energy at my Core? I would have traded far more!" Despite her scratchy voice, it practically bubbled with happiness, and Victor felt a weight disappear, a worry he hadn't realized he'd been clinging to.

"I'm happy for you, Arona. Here, let me help you up." He stood and tugged on her hand, and she lithely sprang to her feet.

She stared into space momentarily, leaning on Victor, but then she straightened and smiled again. "My intelligence attribute has improved! The mind you gave me! Victor, I'll never be able to repay you!"

"Nah, that's not true. Having a friend by my side will be worth more than any artifact. Come on." He gestured at Trobban's prone figure. "Let's see how our friend is doing. When the spell succeeded, he collapsed, no doubt struck dumb by the Energy infusion and skill improvements he reaped."

"Oh!" Arona looked at Trobban's twitching form and giggled. "Are you sure we shouldn't give him some privacy?"

Victor laughed. "Maybe."

Arona stopped and tugged on his arm until he turned to look directly at her. "Thank you, Victor. I'm so happy! You spoke lightly before, but I swear to you—while I live, you will have a loyal ally."

He smiled and nodded. "That's all I can ask for, Arona." He'd never spoken truer words. What more could he want than close friends? If he'd kept all of those treasures, hoarded them away in his vault, what joy would that bring him? The warmth in his heart at seeing Arona break free from her cursed life was worth a hundred Azurite Stars. He tugged her toward Trobban again and yelled, "Get up, Trobban! This isn't a private room!"

16

THE VOID

Victor stood before his ready gate, fists clenched around Lifedrinker's haft, leaning heavily on the mighty axe as he fought to push doubt from his mind and focus on a strategy. At the meeting to discuss terms, he'd been disappointed to find King Rogan Bayle there alone—no Loss Chenasta. So, despite his desire to get a look at the guy, he'd been left gnashing his teeth, staring into space while the monarchs hashed out terms.

He'd groused all night, ruining Arona's celebration of her new vessel; she'd wanted to have a party but had relented, bowing to Victor's stress about the upcoming duel and leaving him in peace, gamely suggesting she had new spell variants to study in any case. Thinking about it, Victor snorted, shaking his head. "*Pendejo*." Even being self-critical, though, he couldn't fault himself for being nervous. Why was King Bayle so eager for this duel? Why was Loss Chenasta such a mystery? He wished Tes were there.

He almost confided to Lifedrinker, but he knew what the axe would say. Imagining her words—something about showering Chenasta's blood over the sands, no doubt—lifted his mood, though, and he was almost grinning when the signal came for him to enter the arena. Like last time, the stands were full of rowdy, vociferous spectators. As Victor made his way across the red sand, he glanced up to see Queen Kynna and her retinue watching him. Her guards and retainers were cheering, and he lifted Lifedrinker's massive blade high in salute.

He was pleased to see Arona sitting close to Bryn. The former Death Caster waved, and Bryn leaned forward, shouting something like, "Fight well, Victor!" He couldn't quite discern her voice among the clamor, but he could almost read her lips. Victor looked toward King Bayle's box. The man was there with a retinue of nobles and guards, much like Kynna's. He was a formidable figure—nearly as large as Victor in his non-berserk state. He carried a massive broadsword and wore gem-studded, flat-gray armor that looked as if it would be difficult to pierce.

The king glowered at Victor from beneath his heavy golden crown but then looked away, dismissing him. Victor almost frowned but kept his face neutral as he finally forced himself to look across the sands to his opponent. His first view of Loss Chenasta didn't exactly impress him, but it did nothing to assuage his doubt. The man was tall for a humanoid, but not giant-sized—maybe seven feet. He wore a black leather vest covered with straps and buckles as though he had to fight the material to stay bound to him. His arms and legs were wound with frayed, black, rope-like rags, and his feet and hands were bare.

Victor frowned at the man, irritated that he couldn't see his face inside the black cowled hood. Darkness met his stare, so Victor looked down, examining the champion's only exposed flesh—his hands and feet. They were longer than a human's, gray-fleshed, and tipped in pointed black claws.

"Huh," Victor grunted, then he realized Grand Judicator Lohanse had already begun his spiel and was asking the monarchs if they were in favor of the terms and whether they'd stand by the results of the duel. Bayle had been so arrogant during the negotiation that he'd allowed Kynna the opportunity for banishment while he'd agreed that he would give his life should his champion die. Victor had difficulty understanding such a risk, which said a lot, considering his own titanic pride.

"Champions! You will not be permitted to access storage devices or use potions, tinctures, salves, or other consumable aids during this duel. Are you each equipped to your satisfaction?"

Victor sighed at the same old warning and watched as Lohanse swooped over to Chenasta. "Champion of Alvessia?"

Victor held his breath, eager to hear the stranger's voice. Chenasta disappointed him again, though, simply inclining his head and shoulders in a bow of acquiescence. Victor ground his teeth as Lohanse swooped toward him.

"Champion of Gloria?"

"I'm ready," he grunted.

Lohanse locked eyes with him momentarily, and Victor remembered his softly spoken warning after his previous battle. Was Loss Chenasta one of the champions he'd thought Victor should fear? Victor knew he was putting words in the judicator's mouth; he hadn't said Victor should be afraid. What had he said? Victor wasn't the only monster in this world? Something like that. Chenasta was a steel seeker. That was enough reason to take him seriously, so Victor flexed his hands on Lifedrinker, put himself into a fighting stance, and primed his Velocity Mantle spell. He wouldn't be caught flat-footed when—

"Fight!" Lohanse screamed, and Victor cast his spell.

Like before, the world grew slow as he darted forward. The crowd's roar became an incoherent wall of white noise, Lohanse swooping upward in a loop, slowed like a feather drifting through thick air. Loss Chenasta lifted one hand and, in slow motion, as Victor advanced, a length of black *nothingness* extended from that hand—a dark void shaped like a sword. Victor was there before he could bring that weird weapon into play, though, and he hacked Lifedrinker in a deadly cleave, one that would surely split the man in two.

Something crackled, and weird sparkles devoid of color or light—the absence of light, perhaps—surrounded Chenasta. Then he was gone, and Lifedrinker split the air and nothing more. Victor spun faster than thought and lifted Lifedrinker again, just in time to parry that flickering sword-shaped void. The impact hissed and sizzled, and Lifedrinker screamed through her connection to him—fury, pain, and a desperate desire for vengeance.

Victor spun away, using his speed to put some distance between himself and Loss. He glanced at Lifedrinker's blade and was relieved to see only a faint discoloration—a streak of dark gray in her depthless black that was rapidly fading. He could feel the Energy pouring out of his Core to keep his Velocity Mantle running, so he canceled it, circling Loss warily. Was he fast, or was it only his ability to teleport that had allowed him to contend with Victor's speed?

He still hadn't seen the other man's face. He hadn't heard him make a sound. He still didn't, as the strange champion began to stride toward him, unhurried, his sword held out to the side. "Can you take it if I get into a fight with that *pendejo, chica?*"

"Fight, Battle-heart! Fight! I will have my vengeance! Every wound I take, every pain I feel, I will deliver back tenfold with your brave, strong hands to guide me!"

Victor nodded, growling, as he lifted her into a high guard, ready to lash out. He built his pattern for Velocity Mantle again but held it ready. He'd test this champion a bit. When the weird warrior approached, Victor used his much greater reach to begin pressing him with attacks. He hacked down, frowning as the swordsman slipped the first blow and swung that black sword toward his hands. Nodding, Victor showed him what an epic-tier master of the axe could do.

He wove Lifedrinker's blade between those flickering, brain-twisting sword feints, pressing Loss into a steady retreat. He cut ever closer, learning the man's patterns and growing accustomed to his uncanny slipperiness. Lifedrinker took several hits from the void-sword but didn't scream again. She let her fury build, and she shared it with Victor, and he felt his Core responding, filling his pathways and lending speed and power to his strikes.

He was beginning to think he might be able to beat the other champion with simple, good, solid axe work, but then the air around the other champion flickered again, and that weird static-like sound of light and air being unmade crackled through Victor's mind. Chenasta was gone, and before Victor could cast his Velocity Mantle, something smashed into his back, sending him stumbling forward.

He completed the spell and, with his enhanced speed, whirled around in time to parry another blow. He'd taken a full-on assault, but he wasn't hurt—his aegis had turned the void-sword, or at least hadn't been destroyed. He couldn't see his back, so he wasn't sure how well it was holding up. Growling, going for broke, Victor kept his Velocity Mantle up and pushed the attack, whipping Lifedrinker's multiton blade faster than most people could see. She ripped the air with cracks that sounded like thunder, and Chenasta fell back, weaving, ducking, and even performing a backflip.

He was fast, but not as fast as Victor, and, to Victor's great pleasure, Lifedrinker caught his shoulder—a glancing blow, but enough to darken her edge with purple-black blood. Victor bared his teeth in a savage grin as Lifedrinker howled her triumph, but then the world came apart around Chenasta again. The air crackled and complained, and Victor, sure he knew what was happening, whirled, hacking Lifedrinker downward in a deathblow—only to smash her into the sand, shaking the ground for a twenty-yard radius.

Chenasta wasn't there, but as soon as Lifedrinker bit deep into the sand and Victor canceled his Velocity Mantle, afraid his Core would be drained, the other champion appeared again and drove his void-blade into his back. This time, Victor heard the enormously dense material of his aegis give way, parted by the anti-material of Chenasta's weapon. As it happened, the breach in his armor pierced the air like a high-powered rifle round, and Victor stumbled, then rolled, barely keeping his grip on Lifedrinker. Despite his armor's damage, he hadn't been cut.

Victor spat, holding Lifedrinker ready, keeping Loss in his sights. He glanced inward, measuring the Energy in his Core. It was doing better than he'd feared despite the hungry Velocity Mantle. He was sitting on more than two-thirds. He sniffed, slowly pacing to the side, watching the other champion. He wasn't as fast as Victor when under his elder magic speed boost, but Loss was fast enough to defend, fast enough to cast his weird teleportation. Victor had to come up with a plan, and he thought he had one; he just needed to be sure his Energy was topped off for it.

He strode toward Chenasta, axe ready, and when he heard the air crackle and his mind bent around the strange sight of a void gobbling Chenasta out of existence, Victor dove forward, rolling. He'd learned that the champion didn't have to appear immediately. He seemed able to lurk wherever he went between one point in space and another, so Victor didn't try to time a strike or parry. He dove again, rolling, and then, just as he gained his feet, he used Titanic

Leap—not wanting to give away his ability to fly—to send himself high into the air.

As he reached the apex of his jump, he scanned the arena, looking for a clue as to where Loss Chenasta might be lurking. The sands were empty, though—no sign of the other man. He braced himself for a landing, ready to dodge again, but the air crackled, and the light bent in weird refractions, and Loss appeared a dozen feet from where Victor would land. "Got you, *pendejo.*" It seemed the man's ability to hide was limited; he couldn't do it forever.

As he smashed into the sand, sending a force wave rippling through it, he charged for the other caster, and this time, Chenasta didn't disappear. Was there a cooldown for his teleport? He barely lifted his sword, and Victor was sure he was about to cleave the little bastard in half, but then a wave of rippling black—no, worse than black; it was the absence of light, of anything—poured outward from Chenasta, and suddenly, Victor was floating in a void.

He tried to breathe, but nothing came into his lungs. He tried to face Chenasta but had nothing to push off from—his movements only sent him spinning in that emptiness. He held his breath, and with no other means to direct his view, he craned his neck, straining to see where his enemy was. His heart hammered, his mind raced, and his face beaded with sweat, but it didn't drip—it crystallized instantly. That's when Victor noticed the cold. The void had no warmth, no Energy—absolute nothingness. It was a place where even time felt frozen.

If he weren't a titan with a Breath Core of blue ice, he wondered if he'd be dead already. If his bloodline weren't epic, would his flesh be dying? He could feel his skin prickling, a numbing chill sinking in like death's blanket. He could hold his breath for a long time—an hour or more—but how long could he survive in a heatless void? Could he outlast the spell? Could he break it? Could he—

Something slapped his chest, and a blinding pain erupted there, right at the center of his sternum, despite his armor. A sibilant, raspy voice whispered, seemingly from everywhere, "Enjoy the Curse of the Void. You're dead already."

Suddenly, the void was gone, and Victor fell to his back, hot sand under his palms and against the back of his head. The crowd was roaring, screaming, and jeering, but Victor couldn't hear them. He couldn't even breathe. All he knew was pain, as something *unmade* him, something in his chest, something under his armor. In a panic, he slapped his hand to his chest, gripping his aegis where the high gorget collar came up around his neck. He pulled, and of course, it did nothing. He was panicking, struggling to think through the blinding, burning, freezing, electric pain that rocked through him.

He tried to send the aegis into his ring, but Lohanse's magic wouldn't allow dimensional containers to work. Finally, something clicked in his brain, and he remembered how to open the seam on the side of the armor. He ran his hand over it, and when the tightness relented, he *pulled* the top half and rolled out of it, screaming as the pain continued in his chest, radiating through him. He heard footsteps as he flopped onto his back, and then he saw Loss Chenasta standing over him, arms folded.

Victor ignored him, scrabbling at the pain in his chest, trying to grab what hurt there and throw it off him. Pain ignited in his hand, and, with another scream, he held his hand up to see his fingers and thumb truncate, the tips simply *gone*! Even as he watched, his regeneration began to regrow them, and, seeing that, he realized what was happening in his chest.

Gasping with pain, he pushed himself up onto an elbow and looked down to see a ball of utter blackness slowly sinking into his chest. His shirt was destroyed. His skin near the void was gone. His sternum was tougher, dissolving more slowly, but the ball of—of *nothing* was slowly growing, slowly eating into him despite his regeneration.

Victor screamed again, panting, desperately looking around. He saw Lohanse floating above, watching, eyes sorrowful, head shaking. He saw his enemy, standing ten feet away, watching him. Why didn't he finish him? Victor knew: He wanted to see him suffer, or maybe he'd been ordered to do it. This was a lesson. This was an example for other upstart kings and queens who might challenge a great house. The crowd's noise, coupled with the pain as the void ball slowly ate him, was too much. Victor blocked them out, squeezing his eyes shut.

He turned his gaze inward, and with every ounce of his prodigious will, he pushed the pain down so he could *think*. An idea immediately came to him: He was healing against the destruction, but too slowly. He had a way to heal faster, though. A way to make his flesh even more durable. If he used it, he'd burn Energy rapidly. Would it be enough for him to finish the fight? No, he needed something more. A refinement to his plan came to him, but it would drain him even more quickly. He'd have to be perfect.

"One shot," he hissed, pulling blue-ice-attuned Energy out of his Breath Core and rage from his Energy Core. He wound them into a perfect pattern, and when he opened his eyes, he cast Glacial Wrath. The void had consumed his sternum. It was eating into his innards, dangerously close to his heart, but then Victor's body exploded with power and size. His bones and flesh reknit, and the pain of the void curse became a minor irritation.

He clambered to his hands and knees, enormous now, towering over Loss Chenasta even in that position. Chenasta didn't stand still. He darted forward, slashing his wicked sword-shaped void at Victor's neck. Victor put an arm in the way and grunted as the blade stung his dense, thick flesh, but nothing more.

He swiped at the Void Caster, but the air crackled and warped, and his enormous hand hit nothing. Victor stood, stepped toward his fallen axe, scooped her up, and then, as cold fury radiated from his bloodshot, icy eyes, he scanned for his foe. He was hiding.

Victor almost didn't care. He had so *much* hate—so many things that deserved his cold, calculated destruction. Still, he supposed the foe at hand should suffer first—time to plan the ruination of his many foes after Loss had been dealt with. With the patient, frozen fury of a glacier, he reviewed his earlier plan and modified it. *This* would be better. He gathered the bright, clever Energy from his Spirit Core and bent it into shape with a tiny flex of his will, casting Core Domain.

In his persistent rage, Victor couldn't appreciate how the arena changed. A wall of shimmering white-gold Energy expanded outward from him, encompassing it from wall to wall. Overhead, the Energy arched into a dome, and within that space, the sand bubbled as tiny crystalline prisms floated up, creating a shimmering rainbow-filled field of pebbles that danced with light and color. More important than its beauty and brightness, the space had become Victor's domain.

As the master of a domain of inspiration, Victor could feel the tiniest change in that space. He could contemplate his options and plans, running through them by the hundred in the time a person might blink. He hefted Lifedrinker, the mighty weapon light in his enormous, thick fist, and as soon as he felt the air change, as soon as the first crackle of Loss Chenasta's void magic tickled the hairs on his eardrums, he whirled and whipped her like a tomahawk—a tomahawk that weighed tens of thousands of pounds.

Chenasta appeared and managed to throw up his arms and take a half step before Lifedrinker smashed into him and then tore through the air like a cruise missile, crashing into the arena wall and reducing Victor's foe to a black and purple smear of paste. The impact sounded like a bomb; the fascia of the magically reinforced wall shattered into rubble, and even the thick stones behind it cracked and crumbled, sending a dangerous quake through the high arena stands.

As stone dust exploded into the air and the concussion of the impact faded, Victor delighted in the sounds of screaming. His cold heart couldn't rejoice, but it could take wicked pleasure at the idea that the amoral spectators who fed on his bloodsport had felt a bit of the danger they so loved to see inflicted on others. He strode toward the ruined wall, Lifedrinker in his sights. He'd need her in hand as his frozen deliberations devised a plan to deliver his wrath.

He took four long strides, but then, to his initial dismay, he felt an aching pull in his Core, and he realized his Energy had run dry. Without the rage from his Spirit Core, his blue ice Energy could no longer sustain his transformation. Victor shrank into himself, even as his glittering domain of inspiration flickered and faded away. When he shook his head and looked around at the chaos he'd unleashed, his lips spread into a stupid grin.

Everywhere was pandemonium—people were streaming away from the damaged portion of the stadium. Others, in the more stable sections, were cheering or howling or cussing—Victor couldn't be sure in the riot of noise. He wondered why Lohanse hadn't restored order, but then his gaze drifted toward a flash of light above and to the right, and he realized the veil walker was caught in a battle with King Bayle and the guards he'd brought to the duel. They were trying to kill the veil walker!

Victor stomped over to his aegis and slapped his hand on it, sending it into his new storage ring, and then he jogged toward Lifedrinker. He intended to aid the veil walker and wanted her in his hands. As he stooped to pull her from the pile of rubble where she'd been buried, though, he felt a twinge of pain at the center of his chest. He slapped his hand to his sternum but quickly pulled it away when he felt the sting transfer to his finger. Looking down, to his horror, he saw a tiny mote of swirling nothingness slowly eating his skin. It didn't go far before he regenerated, but it only started eating again in a cycle that was none too pleasant.

As a cataclysmic bolt of lightning ripped through the bright sky—some spell of Lohanse's, no doubt—Victor groaned. "What the hell, *chica*? How do I get rid of a curse when I already killed the asshole who cast it?"

17

TRIUMPHANT RETURN

As a horrific scream split the air, Victor pushed his curse to the back of his mind and hefted Lifedrinker, looking up to the box where Lohanse struggled against King Bayle and his six remaining defenders. He could see smoldering body parts scattered over the sands and figured they were Bayle's fallen guards. Even so, Lohanse seemed pressed; Bayle and his guardians had to be steel seekers to put up such a fight against the veil walker.

It wasn't lost on Victor that he hadn't received any Energy for killing Loss Chenasta. Did the System consider him a part of the ongoing battle? Was it waiting to see if he'd join in? Victor grinned, ignoring the pain in his chest as he glanced at his Core. It was rapidly recovering—close to ten percent full already. He twisted his hands on Lifedrinker's haft, bunched his legs, and used Titanic Leap to send him into the fray.

As luck would have it, Lohanse was fighting defensively, his back to the stands, moving up, row by row, as the king and his men pushed him. Naturally, this put their backs to Victor, and he took full advantage, coming down like a screaming, axe-wielding comet falling from the heavens. Lifedrinker's edge split one of Bayle's guardians from shoulder to crotch. The man's armor screamed as her edge peeled through it, and he managed a tortured scream before his body fell away in two pieces.

The battle was chaotic, with lightning, blades, fire, and all manner of Energy abilities exploding in the air like a fireworks display set ablaze—another advantage for Victor. The king didn't realize one of his flanks had been exposed by Victor's decisive stroke, and Victor knew how to capitalize on the momentum. He whipped Lifedrinker up, her blade dripping gore and trailing stolen Energy, and brought her around in a terrible sideways cleave, aiming to relieve the rebelling monarch of his lower half.

Lifedrinker's edge hit something in the air, an orange-tinted shield of Energy, and she slowed while Victor strained. His shoulders and arms, his back and legs—every muscle in his body exploded with effort, straining like great, rippling pythons under his flesh as he pushed Lifedrinker forward, inexorably carving a path through Bayle's steel-seeker-level personal protection spell.

"My flank! Guard me!" Bayle shrieked, and then two of his guards broke off from pressing Lohanse to dash toward Victor, one with a halberd and the other wielding a great sword. Victor wouldn't be dissuaded from his goal; he meant to put Lifedrinker's edge into Bayle's flesh no matter the cost. He cast Roots of the Angry Mountain, and then he cast Voice of the Angry Earth as he let his aura loose and roared, "Back off!"

To his glee, both guards—steel seekers!—stopped, and one fell to his knees, his sword clattering on the spell-blasted marble as he slapped his hands to his ears. Meanwhile, Victor *pushed*, and Lifedrinker bit farther through Bayle's magical shield. The king stepped toward Lohanse, perhaps driven by Victor's pressure or the stone-shattering sound of his voice, but the veil walker was there, slapping aside the other guard's attacks and pressing against Bayle's defenses.

The king wielded a huge, thick shield and a one-handed, broad-bladed sword. The shield had to be some sort of artifact because despite Lohanse's mighty attacks—lightning bolts and hammer blows—it kept the king safe. Victor couldn't concentrate on that, though, as his world narrowed to focus on the herculean effort of breaking Bayle's other line of defense: his magical Energy barrier. Lifedrinker screamed her fury and eagerness to break through, and Victor watched as her brilliant edge crackled with Energy—it burst away from her in little explosions and arcs of lightning. He could only imagine the pressure along her magnificent edge.

One of the king's guardians had regained his will and smashed his halberd toward Victor's unarmored neck. Victor dipped his shoulder and tilted his head, letting his Crown of the Dark Colossus take the halberd's edge. The impact rang like a church bell, and the enormous force of the blow might have thrown Victor back, but his Roots of the Angry Earth was in full effect, and he didn't move an inch. Instead, his attacker's weapon rebounded wildly, flying back over the guard's shoulder and carrying him with it for several steps as lava erupted from the stone, bathing the guard in its hot embrace.

"Let's *go!*" Victor roared and drove with everything he had. In the back of his mind, he wondered if he had enough Energy to cast Iron Berserk, but some stubborn part of him wanted to break that damnable barrier without it. Lifedrinker was game, and as his muscles strained like never before, she finally broke free of the resistance. Bayle's Energy barrier came apart like a bomb going off. The waves of force rolled over Victor without moving him, thanks to his roots. Sure, his flesh was burned and torn by the power, but he didn't move.

He squeezed his eyes shut against the blast and held onto Lifedrinker as her sudden explosion of forward momentum threatened to pull her from his grasp. She found her mark, though, biting through Bayle's thick, gem-studded armor and digging her hungry blade into the flesh above his hip. His armor wasn't useless; it slowed her enough to keep her from carving him in twain, but she dug in, and Victor felt her ecstasy as she dragged torrents of Energy out of the king and into herself.

He let go of her and whirled on the two guards, again pressing an attack. With his Gauntlets of the Mountain's Might clenched in enormous metalline fists, he ducked under a great sword cleave and darted forward, inside the halberd's reach. Then he punched upward with everything he had, catching the halberd-wielding guardian under the chin. The man's jawbone and teeth shattered, his eyes instantly rolled back, and he fell—a tree cut free of its roots.

Victor felt the lust of battle and the madness of glory overcoming him. He laughed, darting toward the sword wielder as the steel seeker retreated, his eyes wide, dancing from Victor to his king—now on his knees, coughing blood as Lifedrinker wormed her massive blade deeper and deeper—to his fellow guardians, only two of whom were still standing. Their lives were measured in seconds as Lohanse finished them one by one.

Seeing the end of the battle at hand, Victor burned his Energy again, casting Velocity Mantle to keep his quarry from escaping. He exploded with speed, and then, from the man's flank, he delivered a flurry of terrible blows, crunching armor like aluminum and shattering bones as if they were glass. As Bayle's last guardian fell, coughing blood, Victor delivered a decisive finishing blow to the side of his helmeted head. The gauntlets amplified his already prodigious strength; he might as well have been swinging a wrecking ball, considering how the man's skull came apart.

Victor turned to see Lohanse standing before Bayle, his hands gripping both sides of the king's head. "As decreed by the ancient laws of Ruhnic conquest, you will accept the terms of your champion's challenge. Death." With that, Lohanse's hands exploded with lightning, and Bayle's head smoldered, blackened, and dissolved—ash blowing in the wind whipped up by Lohanse's spell.

Lohanse surveyed the scene, and so did Victor. The crowd had fled the battle, pushing their way up and to the sides of the stadium, piling on top of one another in their haste to escape. Victor looked across the arena to see Queen Kynna and her retinue still there. Arona was standing, her eyes bright with brilliant Energy, and she didn't look happy. Had she wanted to join the fray? Victor could see why the queen would hold her back. The battle would have been catastrophic if everyone piled in—thousands of high-level iron rankers and hundreds of steel seekers. Besides, Victor and Lohanse had made quick work of the rebellion.

"You've done well to exact the justice of the duel, Victor. You may claim your prize." As he spoke, Lohanse none-too-subtly nudged one of King Bayle's hands with his foot, tapping his silver-slippered toe on a thick ring resting on the giant king's thumb.

Victor thought about it briefly, then said, "I want Chenasta's heart, too."

Lohanse shrugged. "Two fights, two rewards. I will allow it."

Victor smiled and ducked his head—the closest he ever intended to come to bowing again—then bent to pull Lifedrinker from the corpse of the fallen king. "Good work, beautiful."

"Mmph, the battle is done, and I will rest. Thank you for the feast, Gore-king."

Victor chuckled, sending her into his new, spacious storage ring. Then he squatted to pull Bayle's ring from his thumb. It was large and heavy, made of something that looked like gold but was even denser. "A storage ring?"

"Aye, explore it later in private." He gestured to the fallen bodies. "Your Energy will be upon you soon. Quite a haul, I'd imagine. You helped to slay four steel seekers, though the king . . ." Lohanse shook his head, clicking his tongue. "The king was close to a veil walker. These others were no champions, but with him to lead the charge—suffice to say, I felt some pressure." He nodded down to the arena sands. "That one was something else. I thought you would die for a moment, but yet again, you surprised me."

Victor reflexively touched his chest, feeling the sting of the tiny void on his middle finger. Lohanse followed the movement, and his eyes narrowed. "Still troubled by Chenasta's attack, I see. Don't let it linger, Victor. That man held a disturbing level of power for a steel seeker. I sensed death and void in him—a deadly combination."

Victor nodded, frowning. Death again—would Death Casters ever cease to trouble him? The air brightened, and he looked down to see glittering silver-hued balls of potent Energy rising from the corpses. A glance to the arena showed him a similar sight near the wreckage of the wall where Chenasta lay buried under the rubble. The crowd had begun to clamor, shouting and screaming, some even cheering, and Lohanse spoke over the noise. "While you're struck dumb by this Energy, I'll calm this rabble and clear the arena. Luck to you, Victor."

He timed his words perfectly, because Victor had barely opened his mouth to reply when a torrent of Energy slammed into him, lifting him high off the cracked, burned arena stands. He spread his arms, soaking it in, luxuriating in the ecstasy of the healing, replenishing influx. His mind wandered of his own volition for a change, and he thought about King Bayle and his attempt to escape. Why hadn't he just run? Why attack Lohanse? Victor had a feeling Lohanse had locked the space down, preventing teleportation.

It made sense, then, why the king and his men would try to kill the veil walker. If they could take him out before others arrived to help, they could try to flee. How confident Bayle must have been in his champion! Victor could only imagine the man's horror when he'd suddenly expanded into the shape of a gigantic, frost-rimed titan. The king's world must have shattered before his eyes when he saw Victor's domain of inspiration and then witnessed Lifedrinker destroying Loss Chenasta.

Even as he hung there, infused with Energy, radiating pleasure at both the physical renewal and the mental savoring of his victory, Victor felt a nagging needle of pain in his chest. It gave everything a bit of a sour taste, like eating an apple, savoring the sweetness as you swallow, only to find a spot of rot in the core—the corpse of a worm or bug. With that unsettling image fresh in his mind, he fell to the ground and blinked, peering at the bright sky and taking in the silent arena.

Lohanse hadn't lied about his intentions; there was no one present. The platform where he'd helped to kill King Bayle was cleared of bodies, though blood and charred marble remained. Victor grunted, climbing to his feet, and then he saw the System messages blinking in the corner of his eye. He focused on them:

*****Congratulations! You have achieved Level 84 Warlord and gained 48 intelligence and 34 vitality.*****

*****Congratulations! You have earned a Class spell: Tactical Reposition, Basic.*****

*****Tactical Reposition, Basic: Casting this spell will allow you to move yourself or a nearby ally to a position within your line of sight. The movement is near-instantaneous and will ignore terrain and enemy interference. This spell cannot be used to move into other objects that occupy the same space. Cooldown: Long. Energy Cost: 10,000.*****

Victor read the announcement that he'd gained two levels several times and then the spell description twice. He wondered how much he could credit to King Bayle. He chuckled, grateful that the ruler had decided to try to fight his way out of the challenge terms. Instead of one steel seeker kill, he'd gotten to help with an additional four others.

"So, what the hell?" he asked the empty air. "I can teleport now?" He focused his gaze down on the sands where the remains of Loss Chenasta awaited and cast his new spell. A torrent of Energy rushed into the spell pattern, and the world *shifted*. Suddenly, he stood on the sand near the wall. "Holy shit!" He laughed, clapping his hands. "Badass!" Almost subconsciously, he reached up to itch his chest and then cussed, pulling his fingers away. "*Pinché*, son of a bitch! This goddamn curse!"

He looked down through his ruined shirt and saw the tiny mote of blackness swirling there. He stared for several seconds, peering closely at how it consumed his flesh, fighting against his regeneration. He wasn't certain, but it seemed as if it might be a tiny bit bigger than when he'd looked earlier—after killing Chenasta. "Speaking of," he grunted, moving over to the rubble. He grabbed two-hundred-pound stones and tossed them like playthings, uncovering the broken, smashed body of his foe.

Lifedrinker had split him right down the middle, and her enormous weight had smashed the guy into the wall so violently that most of his bones and flesh were literally a paste. Frowning in disgust, Victor pulled the fragments of his robes apart, digging through the purple-black flesh and viscous fluids, trying to find the man's heart. "Hell no," he grunted, trying to imagine eating the disgusting slop. Reasoning that the man had been a type of Death Caster, Victor decided to let it go; what if he'd been some undead variant? Hadn't he learned his lesson about eating undead hearts?

Taking a few steps back, he gathered his Energy and cast Honor the Spirits instead. With a satisfied warmth in his heart, he watched his foe's remains flare brightly, consumed by ghostly white flames. As the spirit smoke faded into nothing, Victor grunted his approval. He might not have gotten his heart, but maybe his ancestors could make use of the bastard's foul remains. He hoped Lohanse wouldn't be angry that he took the whole corpse and not just the heart.

Victor turned to the far side of the arena and tried to cast Tactical Reposition again, but the spell wasn't ready. "Damn, that *is* a long cooldown." While he walked, he thought about it and figured the spell's cooldown would shorten as he improved it. If it didn't, he could always try to make an improved variant using elder magic. Ten thousand Energy wasn't a light cost, though; it was nearly a fifth of his total pool, and if he improved the spell with elder magic, he'd probably significantly increase the cost. "I need more Energy," he sighed, trudging down the tunnel to his ready room.

He was almost relieved to find no one waiting for him. Lohanse had been even-tempered and patient with him, even grateful, but he was probably inwardly furious by King Bayle's attempt to kill him. Victor could see him telling everyone to get the hell out. He chuckled, making his way to the teleportation chamber, and with no one to say goodbye to, he stepped through the portal to Iron Mountain.

Almost immediately, he was swarmed with attention. Kynna, Bryn, and Arona, along with the queen's attendants, were all waiting in the portal chamber. They applauded, some cheered, and the queen stepped forward, her face beaming. "You made Gloria proud today, Victor! What an honor to say you bested a great house and then aided the Grand Judicator to mete out justice! Well done, Champion!"

"Hear, hear!" Bryn cheered, and the Queen's Guard took up the cheer.

Victor sighed, waving his hand—half acknowledging the praise and half trying to dismiss it. "Thank you. I appreciate the love—" He absently rubbed his chest through the hole in his shirt, careful to keep from touching the void. It felt good just to massage and scratch the raw, stinging flesh around it. "But I really need to rest after that one. I'll go to my chambers if you all don't need me for anything."

"Of course!" Kynna turned and waved to her retainers and guards. "Give the champion some space. We'll celebrate him soon with a royal feast!"

The crowd cheered again and filed out. Victor reached out to take Kynna's wrist. "Uh, Your Majesty—" He grunted as he accidentally dragged his nail through the void. He pulled his hand away from his chest and continued, "Do you think you could send Florent to my tower? I need to speak to him about void magic." He looked to Arona, who also stood nearby. "I need to consult you, too."

Kynna's dark brows narrowed. "Is something the matter?"

"Nothing too serious, but I think I have some lingering effects from that *pinché* Void Caster's spell." He waved his hand. "Seriously, nothing to worry about."

"Very well. I'll have Florent come to see you immediately." Kynna didn't look happy, but Victor knew what she was thinking: Anything Victor didn't want to tell her would flow like water from a spigot out of Florent's lips. He didn't care; he just wanted to be spared going over the damn curse at that moment.

He nodded his head. "Thank you, Your Majesty. Let's meet soon."

That brought a small smile to her lips, and she inclined her head. "Very well, Champion. Rest well."

Victor waved to Arona and Bryn. "Let's go."

Arona frowned but nodded, and Bryn was all too happy to hurry after him as he stomped out of the portal room and stretched his long legs. He wasn't sure why he was hurrying, but he figured that, on some level, he wanted to get his "Curse of the Void" looked at so he could put it out of his mind, one way or the other. He also had a king's storage ring to examine. Why had Lohanse steered him toward it? He hoped it was more than just riches—maybe it held a natural treasure of some sort. Despite the nagging, itching pain in his chest, a grin spread on his lips, and he slowed to allow Bryn and Arona to catch up. He might be cursed, but at least he had friends.

18

⧉

FIRE TEMPERS STEEL

Florent peered through a square he made with his thumbs and forefingers, staring at the mote of void Energy slowly devouring Victor's flesh. The cursed ball of *nothing* seemed to be almost stable, Victor's regeneration holding it at bay, but he knew that perception was deceiving. It only seemed so because it grew very, very slowly, but in the hour since he'd finished his duel, he could tell it had grown ever so slightly. Would the pace of expansion increase? Why had it grown so rapidly when Loss had first cast it?

Florent frowned and lowered his hands, turning his gaze on Victor's face. "A troubling bit of magic, milord."

"No shit. And?" Victor wasn't in the mood for small talk or beating around the bush.

"And I'll need to study it further. The simple fact of the matter is that void magic, at least to my knowledge, doesn't generally incorporate curses. I know how to destroy matter, teleport, and even sustain myself in the void, but curses—"

Arona interrupted him. "Curses are the province of darkly attuned classes—Witches, Necromancers, Doomspeakers, Occultists, Gravehexers—I could list a hundred more. Most of them have an affinity for death, shadow, entropy, dread, pox—again, I could go on all day."

Victor looked at her as some hope fought to take root amid the dour thoughts dancing through his mind. "You know how to get rid of one?"

"Some, certainly. There are different sorts of curses, though, Victor. There are curses of the flesh, of the mind, and of the spirit. On the surface, this curse seems to be one of the flesh, but if that were the case, I feel like you would have resisted it by now." She frowned, folding her pale arms over the bodice of her dark blue gown. She stared at Victor's chest for a moment, then nodded, and in her raspy voice continued, "We can test the theory, though it will involve some pain on your part."

Victor snorted. "We're past that point. This damn thing hurts!"

Arona nodded, glancing around the room. They were in Victor's parlor, near the balcony doors. He was sitting on the sofa, his legs kicked up on an ottoman. She moved to sit beside him. "If this is a curse of the flesh, if we carve the offending void Energy away from you and Florent destroys it, then you should be well again."

"Okay." Victor nodded, willing to try anything at this point.

"The void Energy would destroy a blade. I can slice it away with this," Florent said, holding out his finger and projecting a beam of void Energy that looked like the absence of a knife blade.

"I'll be precise, and as soon as I've carved it away, I'll simply absorb the void Energy."

"Do it," Victor grunted, gritting his teeth.

Florent nodded and held the slightly crackling dagger of nothingness close to his chest while he splayed the fingers of his other hand. Florent gently, precisely guided his void blade underneath the tiny ball of void Energy in Victor's chest. Victor sucked in a sharp breath as he felt the burning, electric pain of having his flesh dissolve before his eyes, and then it was gone. Florent had absorbed the Energy as soon as he carved it away from him.

Victor stared at the spot on his chest, watching as the bone of his sternum filled in, then the vessels and layers of skin, and then he was whole. He stared at his smooth, pain-free chest for several seconds, then began to smile. "I think it worked—"

"Drat!" Florent sighed, and Arona cursed as the mote of nothingness appeared at the center of Victor's chest and began eating away at his flesh again.

"I was going to say something a lot worse." Victor chuckled, looking at Arona. "Not a curse of the flesh, then?"

She shook her head. "And not of the mind."

"Which leaves spirit, right? I don't get it. How does that work?"

"It simply means that he's bound the curse to your spirit, not your vessel." By way of illustration, Arona tapped one of her polished, perfect nails against the center of her chest. "If I'd had such a curse before I died, it would have followed me to this body."

"I'm a *pinché* Spirit Caster, Arona! How can that *pendejo* put a curse on my spirit?"

She chuckled. "You're a formidable fighter with so many synergies as to make people"—she pointed to herself—"wonder if the gods truly do exist and if they've blessed you. However, something tells me that a steel seeker, one who may have been cultivating his particular brand of power for centuries, might have the upper hand when it comes to a simple battle of wills."

"My will is—"

"Formidable. I know. However, you aren't the only person in the universe who's ever had the bright idea to focus on developing that attribute."

"I . . ." Victor shook his head, frustrated and unable to think of another objection.

"Interesting," Florent said, nodding. "I know that many of my destructive spells, especially those meant to utterly annihilate a foe, can be resisted; it boils down to a battle of wills. So curses operate on much the same principle?"

Arona nodded, still looking at Victor. "Exactly. And now the curse has taken root, and the longer it festers, the deeper those roots will dig and the more difficult it will be for you to carve them out."

Victor groaned. "I have to carve them out? Can't people help? Can't you?"

"Even as a Death Caster, I didn't have a spirit affinity. I wouldn't know how to begin. Perhaps your master?"

Victor frowned, irritated by the term. Hadn't he come to terms with it, though? Hadn't he decided he understood that, for now, Ranish Dar was his master? Things had changed, though, hadn't they? He'd gained significant power since then. He'd had visits from ancestors and spent time with a true primordial titan—a being so powerful as to make Ranish Dar seem a bug. He pushed the thoughts aside and nodded. "I'll message him." He was irritable from the pain and the frustrations he'd experienced as both the people he'd hoped could help him came up short.

"At least it seems to be growing slowly." Arona tilted her head, trying to make eye contact with him, but Victor didn't look at her. He knew she was trying to help him turn his mood around, but he wasn't ready.

"Yeah. It was a lot faster in the arena when he first cast the spell."

"Because he was alive and was feeding it Energy." She held up a finger, and her eyes widened as though she'd just had an idea, but then she shook her head. "I was going to suggest putting yourself somewhere with little or no ambient void Energy, but everything is the opposite of the void. I don't know where you could go."

"I had the same thought," Florent added. "Void Energy is always at a low level unless I go into an actual void or approach an artifact that's rich in it."

"That's why it's growing slowly?" Victor looked at the little mote again. It seemed the same.

"Yes," they both said.

Victor looked at Florent again. "Can't you just siphon it off? Cultivate from it?"

He shook his head. "Have you ever tried to cultivate from another Spirit Caster? This is part of you." He pointed to the spot of void Energy. "Apparently, it's tied all the way through your Core and into your spirit. You would reflexively fight me, and I don't want to battle your will. In the worst case, it would weaken you further and allow this curse to dig deeper."

Victor sighed and ran his fingers through his hair, scratching viciously. "All right. Thanks for the advice. I'm going to write to Ranish Dar now."

Florent nodded and turned toward the door, but he paused. "I'm sorry I wasn't more help, Your Grace, but I will remain near at hand, ready to aid you should you discover a course of action. I will also do what I can to research things on my end."

"I appreciate it." Victor was too preoccupied to say more as he dug through the stack of Far Scribe books in his storage ring, looking for Dar's. He heard Florent leave and was vaguely aware of Arona sitting down beside him, but he'd already found the book and was flipping through the pages. There weren't very many messages; Dar was a "hands-off" kind of master, it seemed. He sneered at himself, mentally labeling Dar that way out of spite.

As he wrote a long, detailed explanation of what he was going through, Arona sat quietly, but when he closed the book, she said, "I should have kept my death affinity."

Victor jerked his gaze her way. "What? *Hell* no."

"I might have been able to research a cure for the curse—a way to lift it. I could have returned to Vesavo and asked for his help. He would have been happy to see I was alive; I could have convinced him I wasn't trying to flee, that—"

"Stop it, Arona. I'd rather deal with this *pinché* thing eating away at me for a hundred years than put you through that. Seriously, though, do you think a Death Caster could help me?"

She sighed and shrugged, her delicate shoulders rising and falling so naturally that Victor really couldn't believe that she was made of metal and crystal. How did it work? Did she only look like flesh and bone, or was she *becoming* flesh and bone? Was that how the spell—

Arona interrupted his thoughts by saying, "It's possible that a veil walker with a class specializing in curses may be able to devise a cure. Spirit curses are notoriously difficult to shake, however. I think your mast—"

"Call him by his name, please."

Victor didn't mean to snap, but his irritation must have been evident, because Arona looked abashed. "I'm sorry! I meant . . ." He must have interrupted her train of thought, because it looked as if she was searching for the words again. Part of Victor wanted to apologize, but another part was tired of apologizing, tired of being nice. He knew he wasn't being cool, but he also knew that he had a curse slowly devouring him and was in constant pain. He decided to cut himself some slack and, rather than apologizing, prompted her.

"You think Dar is my best bet?"

"I do."

Victor nodded and sat up. He was shirtless, but he didn't care. He pulled the thick golden ring off his thumb and tossed it in the air, catching it with a satisfying *thwap* in the center of his palm. "This ring belonged to King Bayle. Lohanse hinted that I should claim it as a prize. What do you think is inside?"

"Hmm . . ." Arona leaned forward, clearly intrigued. "A dimensional ring belonging to the king of a great house?" She held up a finger to indicate she wasn't done. "A king who was prepared to attempt to flee before the terms of a duel could be executed. I think it must be filled with riches. Perhaps his most valued objects!"

Her breathy enthusiasm was a little contagious, and Victor appreciated her efforts to help him forget about his curse. He grinned and nodded. "I was hoping it was something like that, too."

"Well?" she prodded.

"All right, let me see here." Victor sent a trickle of Energy into the ring, claiming it for himself, then expanded his awareness into it. It was an ample space, but nothing so vast as the ring Kynna had given him. At first, he was disappointed when he saw the majority of the contents. He would have been thrilled a year ago, but now, a mountain of sacks containing millions of Energy beads wasn't so exciting to him. Still, he continued to peruse, and then a slow smile spread on his lips.

Nestled among the sacks of beads were six ornate chests. Five were identical—about four feet long by two feet wide and embossed with gold leaf designs. The sixth was smaller by about a third and made entirely of silver. He could feel what was in the five identical chests: Energy Hearts—dozens of them. Each was worth a small mountain of beads; he knew that much, and that was before finding out if any of them had rare Energy affinities.

He couldn't sense what was in the silver chest, so he kicked his ottoman back and summoned it out, placing it on the floor before him. He glanced at Arona and smiled. "So far, I've found maybe fifty million Energy beads and a few dozen Energy hearts."

Her eyes opened wide. "A king's fortune!"

He nodded. "I don't know what's in here, though."

"Open it!" She slid from the couch and knelt beside the chest, watching with wide, bright eyes. Seeing her there on the floor, eagerly awaiting the opening of the chest, reminded him so strongly of a certain Christmas when the cousins had all gathered at his *abuela*'s house to open presents that a powerful wave of melancholy struck him. He closed his eyes and tried to savor the memory. He'd fought with his cousins more often than not, but they'd been happy then.

Everyone had a present to open, and his dear, sweet *abuelita* had made tamales and—

"Victor? Is something amiss? Does the void pain you so?"

Victor realized he had a tear running down his cheek, and he opened his eyes, blinking away more of them. He shook his head and inhaled deeply, shaking his head. "I'm all right. To be honest, it was a happy memory that hit me." He leaned forward and flipped the latch on the chest. "Let's see what's in this sucker." As he lifted the lid and let the hinges hold it open, he stared at the contents and wrinkled his brow in consternation. "The hell is this stuff?"

The chest was lined with black felt, and nestled in cutouts were seven polished, ovoid crystals. Each was about the size of a soda bottle and shone with a faint pink inner light. At the center of the seven crystals, also surrounded by felt, were two other objects: a rune-etched cube of golden metal and a matching sphere about the size of a billiard ball.

"It looks like an array—a, um, formation. You set the crystals up in a pattern, and then those other two objects must be part of it," Arona guessed.

Victor reached into the chest and lifted out the golden cube. Either he was lucky, or some intuition had guided his hand, because beneath it was a rectangle of cardstock imprinted with neat lettering. He set the heavy cube down and picked up the card, reading aloud, "Portable teleportation array instructions for operation." He looked at Arona, who lifted her eyebrows in interest.

"Well? Read the rest!"

Victor grinned. "Step one: Arrange the pattern crystals equidistantly from the control cube. Each crystal will glow with steady, bright light when positioned correctly. Step two: Allow the array to absorb ambient Energy. When the crystals begin to flash with a steady rhythm, the array is ready. Step three: With the destination orb in hand, concentrate on your desired destination. This *must* be a location familiar to you. After completing steps one through three, a portal will appear and remain active until the array pattern is broken."

"Victor! This is . . ." Arona shook her head, apparently lost for words.

"I mean, I've seen portal arrays before . . ." He was thinking of the one Tes used on their quick trip back to Fanwath. He had no idea how rare or valuable such a thing was, but she'd acted as if it was on loan from her order and that it was kind of a big deal.

"Like the portal room in your palace? Or at the arena? Those are very different! They have anchor stones on either end. Someone had to travel to that place to make the link. With this array, you can hold that orb in your hand and go *anywhere* you have ever been. I mean, as long as you remember it."

Victor's stomach dropped as, for the second time that day, he thought of his *abuela*. Could the array make a portal to Earth? He doubted it—there was no

Energy flow on Earth, causing most teleportation means to fail. Still, he could try it. He still hadn't forgotten that Tes said there was a way, but he couldn't remember the details. He just knew he'd have to pack a ton of Energy to keep himself alive, considering his body now sustained itself on it.

"Are you going to try it?"

Victor nodded. "Sure. We could visit my home—Fanwath. We could go to Sojourn. Maybe I'll go there right away if Dar says he can help me." Victor put the card back in the chest and then closed the lid. "I mean, if there's someplace you want to go—"

"No!" She shook her head. "I don't want to see my family, and I certainly don't want to run into Vesavo. I will accompany you where you need to go, though; I'm here to help."

Victor inhaled deeply, nodding as he picked up his Far Scribe book again. "Thank you, Arona, but I honestly don't want you to feel so indebted to—"

She interrupted him for a second time. "It's not just that. I *want* to help you. I want to see you through this problem."

"Well, thanks." Victor flipped the book open, very much doubting Dar would have replied so quickly, but he was surprised to see a lengthy—for Dar—note from the Spirit Master:

Victor,

I'm sorry to hear about your predicament. A curse upon your spirit is no small thing, and this one sounds particularly pernicious. I have some words of encouragement for you and, unfortunately, some words that might bring a bit of gloom to your no doubt already troubled mind. First, the encouragement: You are a Spirit Caster, and a strong one at that. You can beat this curse, but it will take everything in you and some hard work and resources besides.

This is a matter of will. To do battle with the curse, you must enter the spirit plane as pure spirit—set aside your material being and possessions. To carry them over is to mask your spirit, and when masked, you will not see the corruption of the curse. I believe, instinctually, you'll know what to do when you see the aspect of the curse. You will do battle, but, as I said, victory will come with the strength of your will, not muscle. I would not attempt this until you are ready. Retreat is possible, though not guaranteed.

Now for the gloom. I believe I could rid you of this curse, but it would cost you twofold. One, I'd have to cut it away; as I am not you, and I cannot exert my will from within your spirit, I would have to grasp onto the curse and pull—I am certain your spirit would be damaged in the process, which could result in all manner of trauma: lost Energy, a fragmented Core, or even physiological damage such as lost memories or a weakened vessel. As you are undoubtedly aware, your spirit is intimately connected to all aspects of your being. Any damage to it will have repercussions.

I said the cost would be twofold. The other half would be another debt to me. Call me cruel, curse me, do what you will—I have aided you before and will do so again, but this process would not be free. I say this for two reasons. Firstly, you must understand that I have my priorities, and there are many demands on my time. Secondly, I want to encourage you to solve this problem independently. I believe the trials we face push us to our true potential; why do you think you so cleanly thrashed the pampered children of the elite in Sojourn?

I can offer a few bits of wisdom to aid in your success. Most imperatively, do not trust another to solve this problem. Do not seek out a "curse master" or some such thing. I know the spirit well, and I can assure you that any such specialist will harm you at the very least as much as I would. This curse has already taken root, and it will not go quietly.

Once you've come to grips with the situation and found the mental fortitude to commit to solving this problem on your own, you must do all that you can to strengthen yourself. Cultivate your will—if you are near a class change, be sure to choose one that provides a boost to your will and then gain some levels!

If the curse begins to spread too quickly and you aren't able yet to battle it, try consuming a racial or bloodline enhancement treasure! It may slow the progression. The mightier your vessel, the more potent its resistance. And remember, your Spirit Core is linked to your spirit. Cultivate it. Build it. Do what you have been too lazy or too busy to do for so long.

As parting words, Victor, I will remind you that fire tempers steel, young champion. This curse may well be the impetus to significant growth. Good luck. Keep me apprised of your progress. Remember that I can and will aid you, but it should be a last resort.

R.D.

Victor groaned and passed the book to Arona so he didn't have to repeat all of Dar's bullshit. It wasn't that Dar's words had been unhelpful; it was more the tone. It felt almost patronizing, and Victor's constant pain and the vagueness of the advice left him frustrated. He leaned back, pressing his knuckles to his eyes, and tried to distract himself with plans—plans to improve himself and conquer the curse that seemed to be clinging to his very spirit.

19

GETTING ORGANIZED

Victor spent the rest of the afternoon watching Arona experiment with his new teleportation array. He was interested, of course, but he was in a sour mood, uncomfortable, and too mentally distracted to really help. While she moved furniture around to make space and laid the array out on the ornate rug of his sitting room, Victor contemplated his future or the potential lack thereof.

It was hard to forget that he was facing a deadline, what with the painful reminder burning and boring its way into his chest. He wanted to be angry at Ranish Dar but knew he was being unreasonable. Considering the culture the Master Spirit Caster was a part of, he was actually a pretty decent guy. Yes, he put a virtual collar around Victor's neck in exchange for helping his friend, but there were many powerful beings in the Sojourn-controlled part of the universe who would have taken much more.

No, Dar's letter hadn't been overly spiteful or demanding. In fact, he'd been encouraging, and the man had offered to help Victor as a last resort. Sure, he'd said it would cost Victor, but he'd explained those costs, and though Victor thought further debt was a little out of line, he had no real idea; perhaps it would cost Dar, too. Maybe it would take something out of the man to battle the curse in Victor's spirit, or maybe he'd lose significant opportunities by taking the time to do so. The point was, once again, Victor wasn't the person in the position of power, and he couldn't fault Dar for that.

It was that feeling of powerlessness that rankled, multiplied by the pain and—barely suppressed—fear of his current condition. How much stronger had he grown since first being summoned to Fanwath? A hundred times? A thousand? A *million*? Whatever the amount, he was still weak compared to so many. He was weak in the face of his current predicament. Perhaps that was why Dar's words had rubbed him the wrong way—they were true. He had to get stronger. He had to beat this problem on his own.

He'd considered using the dream crystal Tes had given him, reaching out to her for help, but Dar's warning struck true—if someone else solved this for him, he'd lose something. Even if Tes could do it perfectly or knew someone who could, Victor would lose the opportunity to prove himself to . . . *himself.* In the back of his mind, he'd had that option before. Hadn't he gone crawling to Dar? Before reading Dar's reply, he wouldn't have been bothered by that. Now, though, he couldn't stomach the idea—another reason to feel irritated by his mentor.

Dar had made it clear that Victor *ought* to be able to beat this curse, thereby making it impossible for Victor's pride to allow him to beg other, more powerful people for help. No, he had to solve this. He had the means: He was a duke in one of the wealthiest kingdoms on the planet, and aside from that, he'd just gained a king's ransom of treasure. Kynna owed him natural treasures, and he could buy more. He needed to do what must be done to push his advancement.

"I've got it!" Arona said, clapping her hands.

"Yeah?" Victor looked to see she'd arranged the glowing crystal cylinders around the golden, rune-etched control module. Each of the crystals shone brighter than before, and Victor could see them slowly gaining brightness. Presumably, they were charging up. All in all, the array only had about an eight-foot diameter. "I was wondering—how long will the portal last if we pick up everything so we can travel through it? You know, like a one-way trip."

"We'll test that as soon as it's charged up. Here." Arona tossed the destination orb his way, and Victor caught it. It was just as heavy as he'd imagined—a solid ball of gold. He gripped it tightly for a minute, then stood, tossing it back to her. "Don't go anywhere, please. Keep an eye on it while I go and speak to Kynna."

"What about?" Arona made a strange face, and he could tell she felt she'd overstepped, getting into his personal business.

Victor answered quickly so she could relax. "I want to ask her about the fallout from the duel and get an idea of how much time I have before the next. If I'm going to take Dar's advice, I could use a little time."

She nodded, uncomfortable expression melting into a solemn nod. "I'll keep the array safe and wait for you."

"I won't be long." Victor summoned a shirt from one of his rings and shrugged into it. When he buttoned the front, he left the top few buttons open so the spot of void wouldn't destroy it. Thinking about that, he reached for the chain holding his marble-sized vault and key. It hung a few inches above the void, but what if it grew? If he lost the vault to this curse, he'd be furious. He removed it and looped the chain a few times around his wrist, turning it into a bracelet for the time being.

Outside his quarters, Bryn met him, frowning as she laid eyes on the void still swirling, the size of a fingernail, at the center of his chest. She'd seen it when they arrived but had left the room as Arona and Florent tried to help him brainstorm a solution. Victor shrugged. "Still there."

"Hmm." Bryn jerked her chin up and down. "You should cover it. We don't want rumors to spread."

"It'll just destroy my shirt."

She leaned close, peering at the void. "I think not. If your shirt is loose and if you don't press on the spot. It seems to have sunk very slightly below the level of your flesh. Besides, your pectorals are significantly higher than the center of your chest."

Victor frowned, but he supposed she was right. His other shirt had been ruined by his movements and constant reaching up to worry at the itching, burning wound. He buttoned his shirt, and when it didn't immediately dissolve, he nodded and stepped onto the elevator. "Do me a favor and guard that door. Arona's working on something valuable."

Bryn frowned and folded her arms. "I fail to see what sort of threat I could stop that she couldn't."

"Well, maybe not, but you can at least alert her so nothing takes her by surprise." Victor pushed the button to descend and, as the doors closed, added, "Thank you, Bryn."

She continued to scowl but offered no more objection. Once the elevator descended, Victor hurried through the palace to the wing Kynna had commandeered. Her guards led him to her in the same study she seemed to favor, the one bordering the flower garden. When he stepped into the room, she looked up from the divan where she sat, wreathed in the red-orange glow of the sunset. "Victor! Tell me, how bad is it?"

He waved a hand. "It's nothing. I suppose Florent squealed?"

"He was very worried, Victor. Don't hold it against the man."

"Why would I? I counted on him telling you. It saves me the trouble."

"So? Has your other companion found a remedy?" She patted the cushion beside her, but Victor sat down in a wide, comfortable chair with its back to the garden; he enjoyed the feel of the fading sunlight on his neck.

"Not exactly, but your ancestor has given me guidance. This is something I'll need to conquer on my own. However, there are ways that you can help."

She set her wine glass down and leaned forward. "Anything!"

"Well, first, I need you to keep me informed, with as much accuracy as possible, on the dates of my duels. I'll need to accomplish things between them, which will require careful timing."

"I will do my utmost to do so, but you know there are many unpredictable factors—"

Victor waved a hand, interrupting her. "I know. Just do your best."

"What else can I do?" She looked so earnest. Her eyes were so wide and bright, the white flames dancing hypnotically behind their crystalline surface, that Victor struggled not to stare into them. She licked some droplets of wine from her bottom lip and almost seemed embarrassed by the act. It was endearing. "I'm sorry—I was torn between relief and celebration at your victory and then terror and dread when Florent made his report. I turned to the wine to try to ease my mind—"

"Hush, Kynna. I don't begrudge you a bit of comfort. I'd be drinking right now, too, if your ancestor hadn't lit a fire under my ass." He chuckled at her arched eyebrow. "Anyway, the other way you can help me is to do everything you can to gather potent natural treasures or alchemical mixtures meant to advance my bloodline or, more generically, my race. I have to continue to strengthen my vessel if I'm going to beat this thing. Honestly, it's the only reason I'm not dead already. Understand?"

Kynna nodded, and Victor saw moisture gathering in her eyes. "I—" To his horror, a sob choked off her words.

Victor leaned forward and grasped her wrist, pulling her hand to him. He squeezed it. Her skin was soft without the hint of a callus. "I'm not dead, and I won't let this *pinché* curse do me in. All right?"

She sniffed and nodded. "It's worse than you're letting on, though." Victor didn't respond but held his expression steady, staring into her eyes. "I despair because I've been *trying* to find a natural treasure that will aid you. Epic-tier treasures of that nature are exceedingly rare. I will send more envoys further afield. We'll plunder the auction houses of a thousand worlds if we must. I won't spare any expense!"

Victor smiled and nodded. "Thank you. Don't ruin the economy, but yeah, I'd appreciate even one." He inhaled deeply and released her hand, leaning back in his chair. "Now, any idea how long until my next duel?"

Kynna nodded and leaned back on the divan. "I will be extremely pressed with political matters while we work to absorb Alvessia. Moreover, there will no doubt be some repercussions for Bayle's attempt to slay Lohanse. Things have heated up, and when the veil walkers come under fire, their attention on the political goings-on tends to intensify. I believe assassination attempts and other such schemes will be set aside for a while, allowing me more time to negotiate and maneuver. Theoretically, we'll need to work our way from the southern point of the eastern continent to the center where House Khaliday holds sway."

"What's the next logical target?"

"The kingdom that would move us the furthest north would be Voth."

"Yeah? I've heard that name . . ." Victor searched his memory, but Kynna filled in the missing pieces.

"Trinnie Ro's father was once champion there."

"Ah." Victor nodded, his lips curling into a frown as he thought of the champion he'd slain.

"Currently, Voth's champion is a man named Resh A'kel. He's a deadly combatant, Victor—well feared by many other great houses. Bomar Lund, the King of Voth, has used A'kel's reputation to strike many favorable trade bargains in the last few decades; his kingdom's influence has risen quickly among the other houses."

Victor chuckled. "Always trying to caution me. I appreciate your honesty, my Queen. Now, setting aside your concern about Resh A'kel's prowess, if you would work to secure a duel with Voth, can you give me a rough idea of the timeline?"

She sighed and nodded. "Somewhere between six months and ten years. This conquest has been moving far more quickly than usual, Victor, thanks to a series of events that have worked out in our favor, but fights like this—kingdoms vying for everything—don't generally happen overnight."

"Yeah, I'm aware of that. So, let's take advantage of the lull and start pressuring Voth. In the meantime, you can continue to force the other kingdoms on this continent to bend their knees to you. After I beat Loss Chenasta, I don't see any of these lesser houses attempting to resist you. Once we finally take Voth down—hopefully in months rather than years—the other great houses will realize you have more power than they do. You're already, by land mass, a greater force than most of them. I'm sure your economy is growing apace. Yes?"

Kynna nodded. "Yes. However, you underestimate the amount of plundering some of the oldest houses have done over the centuries. Much of the wealth of this continent has already been stripped and taken by them. There's a reason there are no great houses on this continent." Victor opened his mouth to argue further, but she held up her hands. "Nevertheless, your point stands. If I control this continent, they will feel the pinch, especially if I start to deny trade with their nations individually. We can begin to apply true pressure. I'll do my best to accelerate our diplomatic efforts, Victor. In the meantime, you mustn't let people know of your condition."

"Nope. I intend to do some traveling, though I won't broadcast it. Honestly, I'll be in and out of my quarters atop my tower quite often, so don't fear that I'll be disappearing for long periods." Victor stood up. "Stay in touch with me via our Far Scribe book. I'll always have a portal nearby so I can return quickly."

The queen, too, stood, and she stepped toward him, hesitantly stretching her fingers toward his chest. Victor took a step back, and she blushed slightly. "I'm sorry. Please do what you must to recover, Victor. I'll notify you the instant I have an appropriate treasure."

Victor smiled and inclined his head, suddenly feeling much better about things. He felt like he was beginning to build a plan, and having that structure in mind went a long way toward keeping his earlier frustration and the corrupting tendrils of fear at bay. "I'll speak to you soon, my Queen." With that, he turned and marched from her room, barely pausing to acknowledge the folks who called out greetings on his way through the palace.

When he returned to the antechamber to his tower, Bryn was standing watch as he'd requested, and Victor's improved mood must have been evident, because she greeted him with "Something good happened?"

"Some good things are happening, Bryn. Do you suppose I can entrust you with a very important task?"

She straightened up, her golden glaive thumping the polished marble floor. "You know you can, Your Grace!"

Victor chuckled and reached into his storage ring to retrieve the plans he'd drawn up for his cultivation chamber. It was a simple leather-bound notebook with neat scribbles and detailed sketches. His intelligence and dexterity were so far beyond what he'd been born with that his old self, struggling to write neat letters or complete basic geometry problems, would have thought an alien or super genius had written the notes. Victor was no such thing—the super genius part—but he had an uncanny control of his fingers and a mind capable of grasping complicated concepts if he put the effort into it.

"You know I'm having a cultivation chamber constructed in there, right?" He nodded toward his quarters.

"Yes, of course. You've had workers coming and going for weeks."

"Well, I'm still waiting on the amber ore to line it, and the door and artifact chambers, which are being constructed by an Artificer in town, are a ways from delivery." He handed her the book. "Here are my plans. I want you to ride their asses until it's done. Here." He summoned several large sacks of beads from the ring he'd taken from King Bayle and set them on the ground before her. "That's about a million beads. Bribe people if you have to or hire more workers, but get that ore out of the mine and into my cultivation chamber as soon as possible. Tell the artisan to hire more assistants if he needs to. His name's in the book."

Bryn nodded, reaching down to transfer the sacks of beads to her own storage ring. "I can do that. Are you leaving?"

"I'm going to be in and out, which brings me to another point: When I'm not here, there might be an active portal in my quarters. I'll put it in the study, so don't let anyone go in there. Put Feist on the door if you have to, especially when the workers are going in and out."

"Understood. So—" She stopped short, eyeing his chest, and he knew she wanted to ask about his curse.

Victor let her off the hook. "I have a plan to make myself well again, and yes, this is all a part of that. Okay?"

Bryn nodded and saluted again. "You can count on me!"

Victor grinned, reaching out to gently thump his fist on the side of her armored shoulder. "I know I can." He looked into her eyes for several seconds and then entered his quarters. Arona was there, in his sitting area, standing before a magenta rip in the fabric of reality.

"It works," she announced.

Victor saw she held the destination orb in her hand. "Where does it lead?"

"A tranquil deserted little forest on a world I helped Vesavo to conquer a decade ago. I hope you aren't angry. I stepped through to ensure it worked but came right back when I saw the destination was what I intended."

Victor frowned, clicking his tongue as he walked toward her. "I'm not angry, but I wish you would have let me know. What if you got lost or—"

"Someone had to test it. It's the least I can do for you."

"I appreciate your loyalty, Arona, but let's be smart about things, okay?" He bent to pick up one of the crystals. "Help me gather these. Let's see how long it takes the portal to shut down." The two of them walked around, picking up the warm, glowing crystals, and when they had all of them in hand, they watched the portal for nearly five minutes before it crackled and snapped shut with a soft, squelching *pop*.

Victor sent all the portal array pieces into his storage ring and then turned to Arona. "Okay. I've got a plan. I'm going to trust you with another one of my secrets."

"Oh?" She arched one of her perfect, feathery dark eyebrows.

He jerked his head toward his study door. "Let's go in there. We're going to have a chat with a certain dungeon Core named Du."

20

JUST PASSING THROUGH

Wincing a little, resisting the urge to rub the nagging, burning, itching ache in his chest, Victor twisted the key in his miniaturized vault and set it down in the center of his study. As it steamed and jumped, rapidly expanding, he backed up to stand beside Arona. "Just a minute or so," he said, looking past her to ensure the door was closed.

"Is it a travel home?"

"No, more like a vault. At least, that's how I've come to think of it."

"Ah, I understand," she replied, running her eyes over the spherical construct as it surged to its final size, the thousands of bright, flaring runes in the dark metal slowly fading to a dim ochre glow.

Victor stepped forward and turned the key the rest of the way, opening the circular door with a hiss of magical steam. "Just wait here a moment, please." He stared at Arona until she nodded, then stepped inside, peering around the vault in the strange, magenta glow of the silent dungeon Core.

He gathered up the satchel containing his most prized treasure—the ivid royal jelly—and ensured the silk Queen Crystal had given him was still wrapped snugly around the jar. Then he tucked it down into the satchel and set it on the far side of the vault behind some lesser magical treasures and other containers. He trusted Arona, but he remembered how just a whiff of the jelly had affected Tes. Of course, Arona didn't have the senses of a dragon nor the power of a veil walker, so he doubted she would even be able to sense the jelly inside the shroud, but he didn't want to take chances.

Stepping back around Du's floating, spherical, gem-like body, he pushed the door wide. "Come on in." When Arona eagerly stepped past the threshold and peered around the vault's interior, Victor pointed to the floating, softball-sized dungeon Core. "Do you know what that is?"

She shook her head. "Since you brought me here after indicating we'd speak to a dungeon Core, I presume that's what it is; I can't imagine you would have chosen a pink-hued light to illuminate your vault."

Victor chuckled, shaking his head. "Yeah, that's right. This is Du, and he's been pretty damn quiet since I took him out of the dungeon he'd created in the bowels of Iron Mountain." Unconsciously, he began to reach for the sore at his chest, but Arona reached out and snatched his wrist. He looked at her slender, strong fingers and how they failed to close around his thick bones. Still, she'd served to remind him, and he nodded. "Thanks."

She let go, then gestured to the orb. "So how does this being fit into your plans?"

"Well, Du asked me to place him somewhere where he might attract more visitors. I wondered if such a favor would be worth some favors in return—"

"Have I not given you enough?"

Victor grinned and winked at Arona before saying, "Du! I'm so glad you've broken your silence. That's what I wanted to speak to you about. The treasure you gave me was amazing, but so, too, were the challenges I faced in your dungeon. Are you capable of creating as many encounters like that as you want, or does it drain you somehow?"

"These are topics I'm expressly forbidden to speak about."

"By the System?"

"What else?"

Victor grinned at Arona. "So the System grants you certain powers, right? You let that slip when we last spoke. You chose the treasures I earned in your dungeon. Since you've told me that much, you might as well clarify. Can the System even see you in this vault? Will it know you're speaking to me?"

Du pulsed silently for several seconds, and then his voice warbled, *"Oh, woe unto me! Am I held captive in this dimensional space? Thank the fates that my jailor has left the door open, allowing the benevolent System to monitor my plight in this pocket of the universe outside its influence!"*

Victor almost laughed at the Core's antics, but he held his tongue while he turned and pulled the vault door closed. Putting the key into the interior slot, he twisted it until the many locks fell into place with loud *thunks.*

"Oh, wicked jailor! I will answer your questions, but only because you've cut me off from the benevolent System, and I fear for my very existence!"

Victor laughed, looking at Arona to see if she was enjoying Du's theatrics. Her expression was quizzical, though—one narrowed eye, pursed lips, even a finger held up as she contemplated her words. "Is—is this dungeon Core helping you to hide our conversation from the System?"

Victor nodded as he winked exaggeratedly. "No, no. Can't you see he's under duress?"

"Yes! Yes, such wicked duress!"

Victor sighed, his constant pain and irritation resurfacing to supplant his momentary amusement. "So, Du, tell me: Can you repeat what you did for me in the Crucible of Fire?"

"Not exactly, no. I am awarded something called 'influence points' in the System's dungeon management protocols. I earn them passively over time and via certain activities and milestones. In your case, I spent a vast surplus of influence points with abandon to garner your favor, hoping you would return with companions who would then return with their companions, and so on."

"So you're out?"

"Oh, not hardly! I still have many, but more importantly, I'm a high-level dungeon, and even without my influence, the System will continue to allow me to access appropriate treasure; I just won't have a say in what it is."

"So you can make dungeons challenging for me? Like the Crucible?"

"So long as I have a steady flow of ambient Energy, yes. Of course, the type of ambient Energy influences the environments I can create."

Arona stepped closer to Du and asked, "The density of ambient Energy impacts how often or difficult you make your dungeons?"

Du flashed several times, then said, *"Hello, stranger. I am Du."*

Arona let out a raspy chuckle. "Apologies, kind dungeon Core. I am Arona Moonshadow."

"Thank you for the introduction. Were we in an environment of my making, I would know more about you. We dungeon Cores are granted certain insights as we progress through the System's levels. How else would we know what treasures would best suit our visitors?" He pulsed a few times, then continued, *"To answer your question, at my level, I can create low-tier dungeons by the dozens, day after day. If I want to create a high-tier dungeon, I must gather Energy, so yes, thick ambient Energy will speed that process along."*

"If I give you a new home with a ready supply of Energy in the air, will you agree to always offer an appropriate challenge to the people who enter your portal?"

"Victor, there are different types of dungeons: static, meaning they don't change from entry to entry but the monsters and the treasure are always the same; adaptive, meaning they will adjust their level and treasure to match their entrants; and progressive, meaning they keep track of their entrants and can only offer a stronger challenge after each successful completion."

"And you?"

"I am a progressive dungeon. I cannot alter that about myself, though I think it's the best of both worlds. If you fail and must flee the dungeon, I will not increase the difficulty for you, but if you succeed, I cannot open another instance for you until

I've gathered enough Energy to create an even stronger challenge. Like an adaptive dungeon, I can change my layout and encounters, and I can influence the treasures you find. Static dungeons are so dull—I almost pity them."

Arona cleared her throat. "If you meant to have your people use Du to gain levels, it seems like a good fit, Victor. He will challenge them appropriately."

Victor nodded, rubbing his chin. "Well, I'll give you a new home as long as you make a simple agreement with me."

"What are your terms, Sir Victor?"

Remembering some of the more deadly challenges Du had thrown his way, Victor said, "I want to make known to you a few people I care about, and I want you to agree never to give them an encounter from which they cannot flee—no death traps."

"A few, you say?"

Victor nodded. "Yes, no more than ten. If they bring companions, though, don't try to use that as a loophole to entrap them." He looked at Arona to see if she thought he was making a mistake, but she met his eyes and nodded.

"I will abide by your terms so long as you give me a good home and allow access to people other than those on your . . . list."

"I will. I'll post warnings, however. I know how tricky you can be."

"Excellent. An informed entrant is always more fun than a buffoon who stumbles upon me unawares."

"Okay, Du, we'll speak again soon." Victor unlocked the vault and stepped out, holding it open for Arona. When she was out, he locked it and turned the key until it began to shrink again. "I gained several levels when I cleared that dungeon—most of Tier Seven."

"Ah! You hope to use him to gain power and thus be more prepared to battle this curse!"

"Yep." Victor smiled and stooped to pick up his vault, looping the chain around his wrist again. "Can you set up the portal array? I need to send a message." Victor unloaded all the parts to the array, setting them in the center of the room, and then, while Arona got to work laying the crystals out, he summoned the Far Scribe book he shared with Rellia. His message was short and to the point:

Rellia—

I'm coming to visit this evening. I hope you have a page or somebody like that watching this book; otherwise, I guess it'll be a surprise.

—Victor

He closed the book and looked up to see the portal array was already pulsing as it gathered ambient Energy. "You need to get anything together?" he asked Arona. She was perusing one of his bookcases, reading the titles of books his predecessor had put there. "We'll be gone a few days, probably."

"Did you tell the queen? Bryn?"

"Yeah. I mean, I didn't say we were leaving this second, but I've got Far Scribe books with them both. I put Bryn in charge of my little construction project."

"Everything I have is here." Arona held up her left hand, displaying a few gem-studded rings.

"Good." Victor summoned another Far Scribe book—the one he shared with Valla—and looked to see if she'd written anything new. The last message he had from her was a brief note saying she wished she could join him and Tes on Fanwath but was too busy with her obligations to leave on such short notice. He frowned when he saw nothing new written. Had she moved on so completely? Of course, he was aware of the hypocrisy of the thought; she still came to his mind now and then, but he was pretty much over the heartbreak of her decision to put their relationship in limbo.

Arona saved him from further contemplations by saying, "It's ready."

"Cool." Victor stood and walked to the center of the pattern and picked up the destination orb where he'd set it. "I just hold this and think of where I want to go?" Arona nodded, so he clutched the heavy golden ball and pictured the garden behind his home on Fanwath. He focused on the little fountain, the beds of flowering shrubs, the way the peaked, gabled roof of the rear solar reflected the sun's light—

A crackling sizzle sounded as a reddish-pink rip in the fabric of the universe appeared at the center of the array's pattern. "Okay, I'm taking the array with us, so we have to hurry." Victor gathered the crystals, sending them into his storage ring one after the other, then he picked up the control box and did the same. "Ready?"

Suddenly, Arona held a silvery staff, thin and delicate. Its top end, about a foot higher than her head, was adorned with delicate branches of silvery metal that looped and bent into the shape of intricate glyphs. "I am ready."

Victor grinned. "New staff?"

She shook her head. "Not new. It's a more general focus of Energy than my death-attuned treasures. It'll work better with my solar Energy." Without another word or a backward glance, she stepped through the portal.

"She's very direct," Victor said to the empty room, then stepped through the portal after her. To his relief, it deposited them directly where he'd hoped, even though the sunlight was different than in his visualization—it was early morning, and the sky was gray. He gestured to his hermitage. "My house on Fanwath. I need to speak to my governor before our next stop." He unpacked the array and set the parts, aside from the destination orb, on the lip of the fountain. "Can you set it up again? I don't know how long it will take to charge here."

Arona didn't so much as frown. She just nodded and got to work. For a moment, Victor wondered if he was mistreating her in his haste. If he hadn't had a void eating away at his chest, he might have taken some time to show her around and introduce her to people. He wondered if she would have objected to his constant requests if she weren't so convinced that she owed him so much. Things were how they were, though, and he could only resolve to make it up to her later.

He stormed into the house, bellowing, "Gorro! Governor!"

One of the kitchen staff came charging down a dark hallway, eyes wide. "Lord Victor?"

"Yes. Sorry to startle you. I have to speak to the governor."

"He's likely up and about, I'll—"

"I'm here," Gorro said, striding around another corner. He was fastidious as ever despite the early hour. His hair was perfectly combed, and his suit was neat and clean—even his shirt was tucked in. "How may I be of service, milord? Is aught amiss?"

"No. I just have pressing matters and a big job for you. Let's go to the study." Victor led the way, and when he'd closed the door behind Gorro, he began to explain. "I need you to assemble a construction crew. An enormous one with skilled Earth Elementalists. We're going to rebuild the road, the twin citadels, and the bridge leading up to the volcano's caldera."

To his credit, Gorro didn't look stunned or even bothered. He blinked, rubbed his chin, and said, "I suppose Lady Rellia will be funding this endeavor?"

Victor grinned. He knew what the man was thinking; the volcano was north of his borders and fell squarely on Rellia's lands. "Nope. I'm going to buy it from her."

"You're going to buy the mountain?" His eyebrows shot up. "The construction alone will require years to pay for with the income of your province. I'm unsure what we could use as collateral for a purchase of that magnitude."

"No, Gorro." Victor shook his head, chuckling. "I mean me, personally. I'll buy the mountain from her, and here." Victor summoned ten bags of beads from his storage ring, piling them on the rug between them. "Add this to our treasury to pay for the construction. If it's insufficient, let me know. I consider this an investment, and so should you because we're going to be making a lot of income from the project I have planned for the caldera."

"Do you have more detailed instructions? Plans?"

"I will have, but for now, just assemble a crew capable of rebuilding the road and the citadels. I'll have detailed plans in your Far Scribe book before you finish that." He turned to the closed door. "If there's nothing else, I should go and see Rellia."

"Will you visit with Miss Cora? She and Lady Efanie are surely still abed, but I could wake—"

Victor shook his head. "No, Gorro. I'll be back when I have time to relax. Right now, I'm feeling some pressure. Maybe keep my brief visit between—" Victor cut himself off. That was stupid. A servant had already seen him, so everyone in the house knew he was home by now. "Never mind that. Go ahead and tell her I said hello and that I'll be back to visit soon. I'm going to be here a lot more in the near future."

Gorro nodded, clearly relieved by Victor's change of course. "I'll be happy to do so, milord."

Victor shook his governor's hand, then he turned and strode through the house, nodding to the many staff members who happened to have something to do in the hallways between his study and the back doors. He supposed it was both exciting and alarming for him to arrive so suddenly, and he couldn't blame them for trying to get an idea of what was going on.

Outside, he found Arona sitting on the edge of the fountain, watching the crystals pulsing with soft pink light as they charged. They were definitely pulsing more slowly than on Ruhn. "How long, do you think?"

She tapped her fingers on her staff and wrinkled her eyebrows as she contemplated the question. "I think ten more minutes or so. It's about twenty-five percent as fast as back in your palace."

"Perfect." Victor began to summon containers from his storage rings, sorting through a few valuables and preparing for his meeting with Rellia. She'd try to drive a hard bargain; after all, the mountain probably took up a couple of hundred thousand acres—a significant piece of property. More than that, she'd be curious what he wanted with it and likely assume it had some natural value. More than *that*, it was a hell of a landmark. He could imagine it was a bit of a point of pride for her to look at the massive, scoop-topped peak and think of it as hers.

"It's ready," Arona announced again.

"All right." Victor stowed away his treasures and summoned the destination orb. He stood in the pattern and pictured the courtyard outside Rellia's palace as he'd last seen it. A few seconds later, the rip in the universe reappeared. He gathered up the portal array's components and said, "Better let me go through first this time. The portal's probably already surrounded by guards."

Arona gripped her staff and stood ready. "I will be close behind."

Victor held up a hand, grunting in amusement. "But don't attack them!"

She gave him the barest of nods. "As you wish."

Victor narrowed his eyes at her briefly but then nodded and turned, stepping through the portal. Just as he'd presumed, a hundred soldiers surrounded him. Dozens of spear-wielding men and women in Rellia's livery and a hundred or more sharpshooters on the walls. He held up his hands and laughed, "Relax. I come in peace. I'm here to see Lady Rellia."

"Lord Victor?" one of the guards called out.

"Yes! And I have one companion coming through."

"At ease!" the man's voice rang out, and Victor thought he recognized Rellia's guard captain. "Clear a path," the man roared, and the guards began to break ranks. Spears were lifted, and a buzz of conversation filled the air as the soldiers who knew Victor made exclamations and those who didn't asked questions. Arona stepped through the portal, her eyes blazing with brilliant white-yellow light, and Victor stepped in front of her, waiting for the captain, Rellia, or someone of authority to come into view.

"Victor!" Rellia's voice rang out, and he adjusted his gaze upward, where he saw the red-haired noblewoman leaning over a balcony, waving. "Come inside! My chamberlain will meet you at the door." Her voice deepened as she bellowed, "Captain ap'Torrun, clear those soldiers away immediately."

"Yes, milady!" the gruff voice barked. Victor still couldn't see him. The man's face was lost amid the plumed helms of his soldiers.

He turned to Arona and gestured toward the palace steps. "C'mon. Don't worry; we're just passing through here. I need a quick meeting with Rellia, and then we can go and get things started with Du."

The two of them had only taken a few steps, however, when Rellia threw a verbal hand grenade over the railing of her balcony. "I've sent someone to wake Valla! She'll be thrilled you arrived while she's visiting."

21

BARGAINING

When Victor and Arona were shown into an opulent dining room with an amazing fifty-foot polished table crafted from a single slab of wood at its center, he was a little disturbed to see Rellia's servants setting out plates and silverware for four. He could smell the aromas of bacon, fresh bread, and other breakfast foods wafting out of the covered silver trays lining the wall near the place settings, and he was about to object to Rellia's chamberlain, saying he didn't want to stay for breakfast, when the lady in question swept into the room.

"Victor!" She strode toward him, beautiful as ever—no, Victor realized, *more* beautiful; she'd eaten another natural treasure or something. She was taller, her pale blue skin practically glowed, and her hair was like spun red-tinted gold. Before leaving Ruhn, Victor had reduced his size to accommodate the door-frames on Fanwath. So when Rellia enthusiastically embraced him, she could almost look him directly in the eyes. "I've missed you!"

He smiled and squeezed her back. "And I you, Rellia. It's good to see you looking so well."

"Oh my! How cultured you sound! What have they done to my gruff, blunt-speaking Victor?" She grinned as she spoke, her bright crimson eyes narrowed in amusement. Victor was happy to see she was in a good mood, glad to know she wasn't—at least openly—holding some sort of grudge about him and Valla being split. She had to know, right? She knew everything that went on in the Free Marches, and plenty of people were aware of his situation with Valla.

"I'm still in here," he said with a chuckle, thumping his chest as Rellia pulled away, carefully avoiding the aching burn at the center. "I hate to be rude or act like I don't want to spend time catching up, but I'm under some pressure. I have to take care of some urgent matters. I'm not sure breakfast—"

"Oh, hush! You came here for a reason, didn't you? Who's this with you? Shouldn't you make introductions?" Rellia waved away his objection and turned to stare openly at Arona.

Before she could say something too blunt—speculation about his current love life, for instance—he cleared his throat and gestured to Arona. "Rellia ap'Yensha, may I introduce Arona Moonshadow? She's an advisor and close friend."

"Oh! How delightful!" Rellia took Arona's hand and asked, "From whence do you hail? One of the worlds I've heard so much about? Sojourn, perhaps?"

Arona's smile was an easy match for Rellia's as she performed a delicate curtsy, lifting her blue silken robes gracefully. "My Lady Rellia, I'm very pleased to make your acquaintance. Most recently, I've made my home on Ruhn, but yes, I did live in Sojourn for a time. I would hardly call it my origin, though; there were half a dozen before that—worlds that I helped to conquer, many of which I was quite fond of and where I spent years of my life."

"Oh! Then I am honored to host such a world-wise guest for breakfast." Rellia turned to Victor. "Come, Victor, don't be a spoilsport. If you have something to discuss with me, can't we do so over a meal? Valla is—"

"Here," Valla said from an arched opening off to the side of the table. Victor had seen the movement, of course, but he'd assumed it was one of the kitchen staff bringing more food. He looked at her, and his heartbeat slowed to a near stop as something in his gut fluttered uneasily. He felt his mouth go dry and his hands begin to perspire. Some part of his mind laughed, amused that he could be so shaken by her mere presence when a hundred thousand raving enemies only made him eager to fight.

"Valla," he croaked, and she smiled, stepping into the dining room.

"Hello, Victor." She was as beautiful as ever—tall, elegant, dressed in a pale blue silken gown that highlighted the faint tint of her skin and the teal in her eyes, hair, and silvery wings that rose above her shoulders. She looked past him, and her smile broadened as she inclined her head. "Arona. You look different than I remember."

Arona folded her arm over her stomach and bowed slightly. "I've gone through much, but my recovery is nearly complete."

Valla nodded. "So interesting. I wonder how you came to be with Victor. Last I heard, you'd suffered a terrible fate in the Iron Prison." She shrugged, sighing almost wistfully. "Ah, well. No matter." She walked around the table to the chair that would be on the left of Rellia's seat at the head of the table. "Shall we enjoy some breakfast? I'd love to catch up."

"A lovely idea—" Rellia started to say, but Victor brushed past her, moving around the table to stand before Valla.

He held his arms wide, indicating he wanted to hug. "I'm damn glad to see you, Valla. You look amazing."

Some of the stilted frostiness melted on her face, and she smiled more naturally, leaning into him and squeezing him around the ribs. It felt good. It felt like coming home, but Victor knew there was a gulf between them that a simple hug wouldn't banish. Their time apart, their months without communicating, had built that chasm, and though Valla had promised that they'd find each other and their love again, it was clear that it might not be so easy, nor so soon as they might have wanted.

Even knowing all that, Victor savored the familiarity of her embrace—the scent of her, the feel of her arms in the same old spots under his ribs, the way her fingertips lightly caressed the muscles near his spine. "I missed you," he said through a throat thick with emotion.

"And I you," she replied, and he could hear the hitch in her voice. That was when she yelped and pulled her head away from his chest—she had a circular wound above her temple, and as he watched, blood began to stream down the side of her face.

"Damn it!" Victor hissed, reaching up to cup his hand over his chest where his void curse had eaten away his shirt. "I'm sorry, Valla! Do you have—"

She'd already summoned a jar of healing ointment and rubbed it on the spot. "Do you have some sort of armor—a ward? Did it try to defend you?"

"What happened?" Rellia charged around the table, peering at the blood on Valla's face. Her wound was already healed, but the evidence remained.

Victor sighed, shaking his head. "It's nothing—an unintended effect of a small problem I'm dealing with. I'm sorry about that, Valla. I forgot about it for a moment."

Rellia wasn't so easy to deflect. "Why didn't I get hurt when I hugged you?"

Victor chuckled, still holding his hand over his chest. "Because you didn't fold into me the same way. You rested your head here." Victor moved his hand toward his shoulder. "Anyway, I'm sorry, Valla. Excuse me, please, everyone, while I step out to change my shirt." They objected, asked more questions, and even tried to follow him, but he turned and growled, "Really, it's nothing! Give me a moment's peace, please."

As he slipped out the side passage to the kitchens, he heard Arona clear her throat and say, "Lady Valla, I've heard about your adventures among ancient and powerful leviathans. How are your studies progressing?"

Victor stepped around a dim corridor, looked left and right to ensure no servants were approaching, and summoned a new shirt. He sent his damaged one into storage. He'd take it out later to allow the self-repairing magic to work. Frowning, irritated, he shrugged into the clean, undamaged one. Sighing, feeling a little embarrassed, he returned to the dining room, trying to maintain a pleasant expression.

"...have already taught me much, but they insist on me applying their lessons, spending some time *synthesizing* the new knowledge. So I've come home to relax and allow my mind a chance to unpack everything." Valla and the others were already seated, and Victor noted they had left him an open seat to Rellia's right.

He walked around the table, passed behind Valla and Rellia, and sat down. Arona, who was to his right, said, "I'm fascinated by great primordial beings. I wonder if you might pass a message on to your mentor—"

Valla shook her head, lifting a hand to interrupt. "I'm sorry, Arona, but the booraghi are very proud of their isolation; I was warned not to try to use my connection to Oomah, my mentor, to gain favors for any outsiders."

Arona smiled and inclined her head in a stately nod. "No need to apologize; I understand."

"Well," Rellia said, dismissing the topic, "I'm pleased to see you've returned, Victor, and that the unpleasant scowl has faded from those handsome features."

He sighed, shaking his head as he chuckled good-naturedly. "Sorry, Rellia, if I snapped at you." He looked at Valla. "And I'm sorry I hurt you."

She smiled, sipping from a glass of juice. "It was nothing. Is there nothing we can do to help you with your . . . *small problem*?"

"Nah." Victor picked up his own glass of juice and swallowed it down in three large gulps. "It's nothing."

"Thirsty!" Rellia chuckled. She snapped her fingers, and one of her staff scurried over to fill Victor's glass. "So, Victor, while our food is served, tell me what you must speak to me about before running off again?"

Victor shifted in his seat, glancing at Arona, then at Valla. He didn't want to do things this way. Did he want an audience while he tried to bargain with Rellia? Regardless of what he wanted, he had to get it done, so he shrugged and spoke bluntly. "I want to buy the volcano from you. I want to add it to my holdings here in the Free Marches."

"Mount Ember?" Rellia sounded genuinely surprised.

Victor, too, was caught off guard. "Oh, you named it?"

"We named it shortly after you departed for Sojourn. It held the portal to Dark Ember, and we reasoned that the volcano's fires destroyed the portal, so we took ownership of the name. No longer "dark," the mountain and its caldera are now known as Ember."

Victor nodded, tilting his head as he pursed his lips, thinking it over. "Seems fitting."

"So you wish to purchase an entire mountain, hmm? Seems a strange thing to do for a man who's off fighting to conquer other worlds."

Victor shrugged, taking a more measured sip from his glass. "I have my reasons."

"Mother, you should just give it to him if he needs it." As Valla spoke, Victor smiled at her, and Rellia turned to glare.

"Perhaps I was unwise to ask you to bring your business to the breakfast table, Victor."

Valla only ignored her, leaning back to make room for a servant who set a plate of steaming food before her. Everyone was served, and Victor took a bite of some sort of sausage hash, savoring the spicy, fatty mix before he said, "Rellia, name a price you feel is fair. I'm not here to try to coax charity from you."

Rellia chuckled and delicately wiped her mouth with a linen napkin. "I've been making deals for a good long while, Victor. You're the one who wants something. You make an offer."

Victor shrugged. "Fine. A million Energy beads."

"A million Energy beads? For the greatest mountain in the Free Marches and, I'm assuming, its foothills? Why, that must be more than two hundred thousand acres. You think I should sell you my territory for five beads an acre?"

Victor sighed. "Well, how much *are* you selling your territory for these days?" He tapped his fork on his plate while he thought, knowing Rellia wouldn't answer the question. "You gave away homesteads larger than that for favors some of your noble friends owed you back in the Empire. I'm not asking for such generosity, but perhaps a little consideration of our long-standing partnership would be nice." When she only stared at him, he grunted, "Fifty million, then."

"*Fifty* million?" Rellia arched an eyebrow. "Quite a sum to receive all at once. Still, for so many acres . . ."

"It's not like we're talking about prime farmland, Rellia. Those lands are home to rocky crags, boulder-covered hills, and twisted, gnarled thorn woods. The caldera is useless to you; who would build on the site of such a calamitous event? Would you even dare mine those slopes? What if the spirit in that mountain took offense? I'll sweeten the deal by promising to keep the volcano quiet—the Free Marches need never fear another eruption."

"Sounds very fair," Valla said, clearing her throat and wiping her mouth with her napkin.

"Why?" Rellia asked, ignoring her, staring at Victor with her big, bright, crimson eyes. "Can't you tell me?"

Victor smiled. He had her. It was just a matter of making her feel as if she was getting away with something now. "I'll tell you, but then the deal will change—the fifty million will be off the table. This knowledge has value beyond anything I can pay you. Are you sure you want to hear it?" He glanced at Arona, wondering if she wanted to add something—anything—to aid his negotiations, but she held her face passive as she took dainty bites of her breakfast.

"You sneaky barbarian." Rellia chuckled. "You bait me with an exorbitant offer and then tell me the knowledge is worth more?" She cursed, some phrase that the System didn't interpret, clenching her fist momentarily. While Victor stared at her, she relaxed her hand and drummed her manicured, pointed nails on the arm of her chair. "Fine. Tell me what it is!"

Victor grinned, leaning forward. "I intend to rebuild the citadels guarding the road—the bridge, too. I'll rebuild the road and clean out the caldera, constructing a mighty keep there."

"But why? Do you fear another invasion?"

Victor held up a finger, indicating he wasn't finished. "Beneath the keep, I'm going to clear a chamber down in the heart of the mountain, and in that chamber, I'm going to plant the Core of a Tier Nine dungeon."

"Tier *Nine?*" Rellia gasped. "Surely monsters will break free! How can we hope to contain—"

"It's a type of dungeon the System labels 'progressive.' It will create challenges suitable for anyone who enters, and each time they succeed, it will increase the difficulty. The fact that it's Tier Nine only means that it can create challenges suitable for pretty much any iron ranker. Rellia, once the road is rebuilt and the keep is constructed, we can staff it with caretakers who charge entry fees to would-be dungeon challengers. What would you pay to enter a dungeon tailored to you, especially knowing you may gain a handful of levels with each entry?"

Rellia's eyes unfocused as she stared into space. Her mouth opened and closed several times before saying, "A fortune."

"So . . ." Victor reached over and grasped her wrist, so she looked at him. "You give me that mountain, and I'll give you a pair of treasures along with a partnership—fifty-fifty—in the operation of the dungeon."

"Why must you own the mountain?"

"I think it's important for me to own the land where I plant the dungeon. I want to be ultimately responsible for it and what happens with it. More than that, I have a certain kinship with that mountain. I should have argued for it when we first divvied up the Free Marches, but the past is merely a lesson, not something I hope to revisit."

"By the ancestors, Victor! You've *changed.*" Rellia glanced at Valla, perhaps hoping she'd validate her statement, but Valla only smiled softly, staring at her plate as she pushed around some bits of lemon-dressed greens with her fork.

Rellia turned back to Victor. "How often can the dungeon create a pocket realm?"

"Lower-tier ones? Dozens or hundreds a day. As for Tier Nine, I'm not sure. I'll have to test it."

"And something like Tier Six?"

Victor knew what she was thinking—how often could she use it, and how many times could she charge the other powerful people on Fanwath to use it? He smiled and shrugged. "Probably a few a day. I'll have to test it. The dungeon used to be in a more Energy-rich world than this one, but that's another reason I want to put it in the volcano."

"Ah! The Energy! If the dungeon feeds off it, it will keep the mountain calm." She frowned, again staring into space, and Victor could imagine her brain was desperately crunching numbers. Had she made a mistake asking for the knowledge rather than taking his initial offer of fifty million beads? He decided to try to help her understand how much better this new offer was.

"Rellia, when you climb into Tier Six or Seven, you'll learn that access to a dungeon like this is worth every bit of your wealth. There are iron rankers in Sojourn who would give away everything they own to learn from a certain master or gain a few levels in Tier Nine. Trust me, it's better for you to have access to this dungeon than a few million beads. Over time, you'll earn more, anyhow. Besides, I'm going to give you these." Victor reached into his storage container and removed one of the treasures he'd chosen for her.

He set before her a swirling orb of inky black shadows—an Energy heart attuned to shadow, which was Rellia's primary affinity. Next, he piled his old Sojourn armor set at the center of the table: the helm, the gauntlet, the belt, the greaves, and the boots. "I've removed my bond with each of these magical items. It's a powerful armor set that will make you absurdly strong for your level. Moreover, the set will help you resist the primary aspect that the dungeon will use for its environments: fire."

Rellia stared at the shadowy orb for several long moments. Victor looked at Valla, and she met his gaze with a small smile and a surreptitious nod; she thought Rellia would take the deal. Victor loved seeing her face, loved that they were getting along. He wasn't sure she didn't harbor some resentment about his time with Tes. Valla hadn't brought her up, but she'd certainly been a little cold before Victor hugged her. He decided he ought to try to speak to her a bit alone before he and Arona left.

Rellia interrupted his thoughts. "Very well, Victor. I accept—these treasures and an even partnership with you for the mountain. I'll have my people draft up the deed and the business agreement. I assume you'll want me to manage the dungeon access while you're off-world?"

"Oh, I think we can both find managers from our communities. I'm happy to have you oversee them, though." Victor smiled and held out his hand. "A handshake will do for now; I'll let Gorro sign the documents in my stead."

Rellia's eyes widened. "You can't wait?"

Victor shook his head. "I wasn't lying when I said I'm under a lot of pressure." He shrugged. "It's nothing personal—time isn't on my side."

Rellia looked at him searchingly. She licked her lips and darted her eyes toward Valla. "Surely you can spare a moment to speak with Valla alone—"

"Mother, please—" Valla started to object, but Victor spoke over her.

"Yeah, of course I can. Valla? Will you walk with me for a few minutes before I leave?"

She nodded, placing her napkin on the table and pushing her chair back. "I would like that, Victor."

22

MOUNT EMBER

Valla led Victor through her mother's palace to the manicured gardens behind it, and they walked together for several minutes in silence. When Victor felt they were a reasonable distance from the palace and the nosy people within, and when the silence felt just on the verge of being too painfully awkward, he slowed his steps and reached out for Valla's hand. "I'm sorry if it seems like I don't want to spend time with you. I do."

She smiled softly, though her eyes didn't look the least bit happy. "I know, Victor. I can read you better than my own diary. You're holding something back, and there's real worry behind your eyes. Can't you tell me what it is? Is it that . . . *thing* on your chest?"

Victor sighed and gently kneaded Valla's palm with his thumb. "Yeah, it is. There's nothing you can do about it, though. Nothing anyone can—not if I don't want to lose a part of myself. I have to deal with it alone."

"Alone, hmm?" Valla frowned, and her eyes narrowed, but Victor wasn't sure what she was thinking.

"Yeah. Alone. Dar can't help. Tes couldn't help. It's a curse on my spirit, and I have to break free of it."

Valla sniffed and nodded, turning her gaze toward the horizon where, apropos of their earlier discussion, the distant purple slope of Mount Ember lurked. "Will you succeed?"

"Hey, who do you think you're talking to?" Victor tried to put some levity in his voice, but Valla pulled her hand away and turned to glare at him.

"Don't make jokes. Will you?"

"I'm going to do my damnedest. I've got a bunch of ideas, starting with the dungeon I'm putting in that mountain."

Valla nodded, her eyes widening. "I should come and help you."

Victor shook his head. "Valla, I know you're getting stronger, but I've already beaten that thing once. It's going to be brutal the next time I go in."

She folded her arms over her chest. "Arona will join you?"

He gave a half-hearted shrug. "She's Tier Nine."

"Strange that she's here. I could swear you led everyone to believe she'd died in the Iron Prison. How did she come to—" She shook her head, blinking her eyes rapidly. "Don't answer that. I don't want to learn that this is yet another secret you kept—"

Victor clenched his jaw. "Not *my* secret, Valla."

"You do that when you're irritated—say my name like I'm a petulant child."

"Doesn't everyone do that? I'm sorry I'm irritated. I have a lot—"

She shook her head and reached up to cup the back of his neck with her long slender fingers, gently stroking the edge of his hairline. "I know. I'm the one who should be sorry." She smiled, but it was a sad, wistful smile. "We have so much to talk about, and every second I hold you here is a second you could be battling this curse of yours. It's not fair."

"I wish I could spend more time with you. Will you be here long?"

She shrugged. "A month, perhaps? I'll head back once I've passed a test my mentor sent me. However, I'm sure I'll need another break to synthesize his teachings again soon."

"Will you promise to let me know when you come and go? I miss you, Valla."

Her smile brightened a little, and a hint of her old dry humor surfaced as she asked, "You had time to miss me with Tes here?"

Victor clicked his tongue and shook his head. "You're wicked. Anyway, she's gone. I got a speech from her that wasn't too different from the one you gave me."

"Oh? She didn't want to dwell in your shadow?" Her grin tilted higher on one side of her face as she cocked her head at him.

"I think you know it was the opposite."

Her face grew serious again, and she moved her hand to rest her palm on the left side of his chest. "I'm sorry that I tease you. Does your heart ache? I should remember my own pain and multiply it by two—it's not *fair*, Victor." Her hand felt like a balm for his soul as she pressed it over his heart. Her sympathetic tone broke something loose in him, some emotion he'd held buried. He felt it welling from deep within, and he didn't dare speak as tightness gripped his throat and moisture gathered in his eyes.

While Valla looked at him, he stared into her eyes and didn't try to stop the tears that slipped free of his. After several deep breaths, in and out, he said hoarsely, "I can't help it that I love so damn *hard*."

"I know, love," she whispered, gently stroking his chest. "I know. It only makes me love you more. Was I a fool, Victor? Should I have stayed with you? Should I have seen how we might overcome our difficulties? Or should—"

"You're not a fool, Valla. I've changed a lot." He sniffed, squeezing his eyes shut as he let the waves of emotion roll over him. "I have a lot more growing to do. I haven't stopped loving you one little bit, though; I hope you know that. I'm sorry, I love Tes, too, but—"

"Hush." She stretched her other hand up to grasp his neck again, gently stroking. "You've loved her since Coloss. I know you love me, too. It's a big universe, and we've long lives to live. There's room enough, time enough, and you've got love enough. You're not a man who'd stray and bed every pretty face that turned his way." She arched an eyebrow. "*Are* you?"

Victor wasn't exactly sure what she was saying to him, but he understood that question. "No, Valla. If we were together, I wouldn't dream of—"

"I know, sweet man." She tugged on his neck, and that was all the invitation Victor needed. He bent to kiss her, and when they parted, she smiled in a way that reminded him of the happy times before their split. "So, we've both got growing and living to do, but let's remember this love we share and reconnect more often, shall we? I'm counting on you to beat that curse, Victor."

Victor smiled and nodded. "I'm not planning to fail."

"Go on then. Take your secret former Death Caster, and do what you must."

Victor cleared his throat and rubbed his eyes with the back of his sleeve. "All right."

As he turned to retrace his steps through the garden, she called, "And write to me soon!"

"I will!" he called back. As he walked, he tried to make sense of the conversation he'd just had and, as usual, wasn't sure he understood exactly what was happening with him and Valla. He supposed not much had changed other than the fact that they'd both acknowledged their continued love for each other—and Tes. He'd confessed he cared for Tes, and Valla acted as though it was old news. He supposed it was. Hadn't that been her primary objection when they first got together?

He felt stupid and grateful and, as usual, confused. So he resolved to put love out of his mind for the time being and focus on more tangible things—like dealing with the curse eating a hole through him. "And like fighting," he grunted as he strode through the central hall of Rellia's palace. He didn't have to go looking for Arona; he'd asked her to set up the portal array in the courtyard, so he walked directly there.

Of course Rellia was waiting, watching Arona work, and when he strode down the steps into the morning sun, she smiled his way, shielding her eyes in the bright light. "An impressive artifact you have here." She waved a hand at the glowing pink crystals.

"Thank you." He summoned the destination orb from his storage ring. "I'll be heading off, but before we go, can I ask that you add a few stipulations to our deal regarding the dungeon?"

"Oh? After we've sealed the deal, you seek to alter it?"

Victor sighed. "Not exactly alter, but just some fine details. Do you mind?"

"No, Victor. I tease. What is it?"

"I just want it clear that if there's a queue to enter, and I'm sure there will be on some days when powerful parties want to enter, certain people will take precedence. I don't want Deyni or my ward, Cora, ever to have to wait, for instance."

Rellia nodded. "I was already planning something like that. You know I'll want to enter frequently. I'm sure there are others we want on that list. Kethelket? Deyni's stepsisters? Valla? Polo Vosh? I'll make a list, all right?"

Victor nodded, relieved that he had her there to manage things. "Thank you, Rellia. I'd hug you, but let's not risk it this time, yeah? I'll owe you one."

Her eyes squinted in amusement. "Of course, but before you go, may I ask you a question?"

"Sure." Victor squeezed the golden orb and stepped into the array.

"Did you really have fifty million beads to pay me if I'd refused the knowledge about the dungeon?"

He grinned. The answer was yes—he had a good deal more than that, but he wasn't sure exactly how much. Even so, he said, "Come, Rellia, you want me to expose all of my secrets? You taught me better than that."

She laughed, a genuinely joyous sound. "I *did* teach you, didn't I? Ancestors! It feels like a century ago, but it wasn't, was it? Can you recall our battle? It absolutely *ruined* me when you won! I thought I'd never recover."

Victor reached out and grasped her shoulder, giving it a gentle squeeze. "And look at you now."

She inhaled deeply through her nose, nodding. "And look at *us* now. Good luck, Victor."

"Thank you. We'll speak again soon." With that, he focused on his memory of the volcanic caldera atop Mount Ember, and seconds later, the magenta portal crackled into being. He gathered the crystals and the control box, then looked at Arona. "Ready?"

She nodded and, before he could protest, strode through the opening. Rellia laughed again. "She's not one to waste her breath on frivolous things like words, is she?"

Victor chuckled. "Not very often, no." He stepped toward the portal. "Goodbye, Rellia." Before she could respond, he was gone, swallowed by the rip in the fabric of reality. When he emerged, he stood on a blasted plain of dark obsidian and hardened magma. The ash from the eruption was long gone, washed away by the storms that frequently broke on the slopes of the mighty mountain, but the evidence of it was everywhere. Arona stood before him, turning in a slow circle, frowning.

"Can you feel it?" he asked, meaning the heady, magma-attuned Energy that hung in the air.

"Was there a major death magic working here?"

"Ah." Victor chuckled. "Yeah." As he walked around, following the threads of hot, angry Energy, he told Arona about Dark Ember and the invasion he'd helped battle in the Free Marches. He finished the tale just as he stepped into a massive lava tube.

"No wonder the people here hold you in such high regard; you're a war hero to them."

"Ah, don't say that. I made plenty of mistakes." He stooped a little, peering into the dark circular passage. "I think we can follow this down into the mountain. The magma-attuned Energy is practically pouring out of it."

Arona nodded, and before Victor could summon a light of his own, dozens of dancing fireflies that blazed like miniature suns flooded into the shaft, illuminating it for hundreds of feet until it curved too far to see around the bend. He looked at her and smiled. "Flashy."

She smirked and offered a dry, raspy chuckle. "So many of my spells changed or were removed by the System. That's the first time I cast that one!"

Victor nodded, and together they descended. As he'd hoped, the magma Energy in the air grew thicker and thicker, and the dormant lava tube led them downward for hundreds, maybe thousands of feet before it opened into an enormous cavern with still-bubbling pools of lava visible at the center. The air was thick with caustic gasses, but they didn't bother Victor. He looked at Arona and saw she'd wrapped her face in a shimmering blue and gold scarf.

When they locked eyes, she nodded. "I'm fine."

Victor led the way toward a broad stone shelf about a third of the way into the cavern, and once he stood upon it, he unlocked his vault. "I'm going to get Du out," he explained.

"Do you think this is a good place?"

"I do. I'll have Gorro build a passage down here using that lava tube as a guide. We'll build the keep atop it and then close up the other ones."

"Are you going to wait for him to—"

"*Hell* no. It'll take those guys weeks, at *least*. You and I are going into this dungeon now." Victor opened the vault and stepped inside, approaching Du.

Meanwhile, Arona asked from the doorway, "I'm going in with you?"

Victor took hold of Du and prepared for the jolt of lightning that had hit him the first time, but it didn't happen, perhaps because the dungeon Core wasn't currently in a dungeon. He carried the Core out and then locked up his vault, wrapping it around his wrist again. That done, he looked at Arona. "Don't you want to?"

"I—of course! I just thought you would want the maximum benefit possible, and surely you'd reap more reward if you weren't splitting the Energy with me."

Victor shook his head. "Not necessarily. If we can complete it a lot faster, then it balances out. Besides, we don't know exactly how that all works; maybe there's more potential for Energy based on how many people enter. We'll try it, anyway." Victor moved to the center of the stone slab and released the dungeon Core. It hovered in the air as he pulled his hand away. "Du?"

"*Hello, Victor. I'm surveying this environment. The Energy is plentiful, though not as potent as that of Iron Mountain. If the Energy supply remains constant, I will be able to create my Tier Nine dungeon dimensions roughly every fifty hours. Lower-tier instances will be much easier. For instance, I could craft Tier Two dungeons indefinitely. Will you permit me to set my roots in this place? I'd draw much of the ambient Energy, so if you had other uses for it—*"

"That's why I brought you here. Go ahead, Du. Will your portal appear here?"

"*It will. Thank you, Victor.*"

"Hey, Du. Don't forget about my list. Will I be able to give it to you later, or do I have to do that before you, um, set your roots?"

"*Simply speak the names of those you wish me to take extra care with. You may do so now or anytime you enter my dungeon pocket dimension.*"

"Well, off the top of my hand, there's Edeya, Deyni, Cora, Lam—"

"*Wait, Victor!*" Du interrupted, his strange, high-pitched voice warbling. "*It occurs to me that there may be others with the same names as those you care for. I offer you another solution. Do you intend to enter my dungeon immediately?*"

Victor nodded. "Yes, and Arona with me."

"*In that case, should you complete the dungeon again, I will award you twenty tokens of favor. Simply give them to the people you want me to, ahem, favor.*"

Victor chuckled. "All right. Fair enough. Thanks, Du."

Du's pink light blinked rapidly as he replied, "*Thank you, Victor! I'm eager to see what sorts of adventurers will come my way in this new home. Tell me, what is this place called?*"

"This is Mount Ember in the world of Fanwath."

"*Wonderful. Thank you again . . .*" Du's voice faded as he flared brightly and then, with a *pop*, vanished from sight. Victor looked around, squinting into the recesses of the cavern.

"Huh."

"I'm sure it will take a moment," Arona said, though she didn't sound so sure to Victor. He decided to spend the time waiting for the dungeon's portal to appear by getting ready. He summoned Lifedrinker, then, one by one, his pieces of armor. He was happy to see that the aegis was too stiff to press into the cleft between his pectorals where his void curse sat. He was sure his shirt would have a hole in it, but he didn't care.

When he stood before Arona girded for battle, she looked him up and down and asked, "No greaves?"

Victor chuckled. "Not yet. Maybe Du will hook me up."

She nodded. "I meant to tell you before, the crown is impressive. You cut an imposing figure in that armor, and the crown adds a certain quality that a helmet would not."

"I still feel like I'm full of shit when I wear it. I'm not a king anywhere."

Arona tapped a finger to her slightly dimpled chin. "If you styled yourself a king in these lands, who would dispute it? Who *could?*"

"Yeah, but I'm not that kind of *pendejo.* You know?"

"Then perhaps you need to conquer a world of your own."

Victor chuckled. "Now you're talking."

"Or you could marry Queen Kynna. I believe she'd have you."

"*Chingado!*" Victor laughed. "Don't start with that shit. I've got enough trouble with women." As he spoke, something crackled in the air behind him, and when he turned to the noise, he saw Du's fiery portal. "Well? Looks like we're up, Arona. By the way, I think I almost died a couple of times when I did this dungeon alone, and Du didn't promise to pull any punches with us. You sure you're up for this?"

Arona smiled, her eyes bright. "I've levels to regain, and yes, I'd like to be a steel seeker before I meet Vesavo Bonewhisper again. If he holds a grudge, I'll need the weight of that new rank behind my light spells."

Victor nodded. "If he holds a grudge, that piece of shit better be ready to mess with me, too." He held out a fist, and to his delight, Arona bumped it with her dainty knuckles. He locked eyes with her and nodded. "Let's do this."

23

CRUCIBLE REDUX

Victor stood atop a mound of monstrous corpses, watching as Arona fired a beam of sunlight from her outstretched staff, obliterating a great swath of the army that surrounded them. Her eyes blazed with the solar Energy, and a mad smile had affixed itself to her face as she annihilated hundreds of the fire-attuned undead that climbed from the crevasse in a seemingly never-ending onslaught.

Victor chuckled, his Iron Berserk allowing some levity to enter his mind as he took a breather to watch his partner go to work. The encounter was made for her; the destructive power of her solar-attuned Energy seemed to be tailor-made for the destruction of the undead. This was their third gate, and though Victor had done the brunt of the work on the prior two, she was definitely carrying the lion's share of the burden on this one.

It wasn't that Victor couldn't have slain the hordes; she was just faster at it. Watching her, he decided that it was nice to have a partner. He'd been able to experiment with some of his new spells without having to fear burning through his Energy reserves. If he ran low, he just fought with his axe and let Arona do the heavy lifting for a while. He'd created several differently attuned Core Domains, including one fueled by fear, which had been, in his opinion, a literal waking hell. He hoped he wouldn't have to use it in a duel, but if he did, he almost pitied his foe.

Neither he nor Arona had gained a level from clearing the first two gates, but Victor had high hopes for this one. They'd already slain tens of thousands of the undead, and the monsters continued to climb their way out of the massive rift that ran parallel to the road through Du's hellish gauntlet of a dungeon. As Arona finished wiping the field clear of active enemies, her solar beam flickered and winked out, its buzzing hum fading from Victor's ears long enough for him to hear her shout, "Are they endless? Should we seek their source?"

Victor grinned, shaking his head. "I don't think so. Du likes to throw large hordes of enemies at challengers to his dungeon. At least that was my experience."

"Right. You told me about the hundred thousand." Arona's voice was raspy but dry with restrained humor. "I've used nearly half my Core's potential."

"Just take it easy for a while, then. Let me go to work." With that, Victor leaped from the top of his mound of smoldering skeletal corpses and charged a cluster of undead as they clambered out of the fissure. With their numbers thinned for the moment, it was easy to run from group to group, smashing them to bits as they gained their footing. As more and more escaped the chasm, and he began to feel the pressure of their burning, black iron weapons, he'd cast Velocity Mantle for a short burst of speed, slaughtering them en masse, before letting the spell drop to conserve Energy.

He could feel that his Core was getting to the point where it could almost regenerate enough Energy per second to maintain his Iron Berserk indefinitely. Almost, but not quite. As long as he remained berserk, he slowly burned down his reserves, and any additional spell he cast only hastened that process. Despite the ease with which he dispatched the monstrous undead, eventually their numbers began to climb into the hundreds and then thousands again, and he was forced to fight defensively, swinging Lifedrinker in great arcs as he backpedaled toward Arona.

"Ready?" he shouted over his shoulder.

"Yes!"

With her response, Victor sent a stream of Energy into the pathways that ignited his fiery wings, and he launched himself into the air. Immediately, Arona's beam of solar Energy erupted, annihilating the fresh horde of undead. Victor landed beside her, watching as she blasted their enemies into ash. When she was finished wiping the field clear, he charged the chasm again, starting the process over as he pounded the undead clawing their way up onto the stony ground.

They repeated the same strategy a dozen times, and Victor began to think he'd have to cancel Iron Berserk for a while and fight with his natural strength as his Core recovered. As Arona wiped out the horde for the thirteenth or fourteenth time, though, he noted a marked decline in the number of undead climbing forth. He charged among them, slaughtering them with abandon, and in just a few minutes, he found himself with no enemies left to fight.

*****Congratulations! You have cleared the third gate of the Crucible of Fire! Collect your reward inside the gatehouse!*****

Victor couldn't help noticing that he was no longer getting a second message from Du about clearing "group-rated" challenges as a solo adventurer. He'd also noted a marked decrease in the apparent value of the treasures inside the gatehouses. He couldn't blame the dungeon Core for conserving its "influence points," but he hoped he wasn't wasting his time. He hoped he was still making significant progress toward leveling.

It wasn't so easy to tell; he was solidly in Tier Eight now, and according to everyone, Arona included, the difference between Levels Eighty-Five and Seventy-Five was enormous. Even so, as he watched the thick pools of Energy gathering over the slaughtered undead, he felt hopeful that this infusion would push him over. He looked at Arona and arched an eyebrow. "Ready?"

She smiled, clutching her silvery staff. "Always."

He nodded, trying to think of something clever to say, but then the Energy hit him, and he was made senseless, his conscious mind blown free of his body like a feather before a gust of wind. His awareness drifted through what he took to be some sort of cosmic adventure; he saw clusters of stars and icy planetoids, and then, somehow, he swept down through a dense atmosphere, and he saw the toils and battles of great, obscure figures—shadowy giants that carved mountains from the earth and battled serpents whose lengths were measured in miles.

As he slowly came back to himself, Victor wondered if he was seeing the dreams of his primordial ancestors, those great titans that came even before the Quinametzin. His experience with Azforath brought those questions to mind as he recalled the ancient titan's claim to be a "world maker and a world breaker." The disjointed images had a dreamlike quality, but Victor supposed ancient memories buried in his blood—or, more likely, DNA—could be stirring with the massive influx of Energy.

Sitting on the ground, musing over the weird visions, he was vaguely aware of the System message waiting for him to read. He put it off, though, as his mind chased wild theories. He wondered about the sensation of flying through space that he often had during such visions. He wondered if some ancient progenitor had hurtled through the cosmos, comet-like. The image made him smile, picturing a mighty frozen titan smashing into the Earth and spawning a lineage there.

Shaking his head, amused by his fanciful daydream, Victor focused on the System's message:

*****Congratulations! You have achieved Level 85 Warlord and gained 24 intelligence and 17 vitality.*****

*****Congratulations! Your Feat, Warborn Mind, has become Greater Warborn Mind, doubling its effects.*****

Victor stared at the second message for several long seconds. "No wonder people like the Warlord class." Just like that, he'd gained more than twenty extra points for both dexterity and agility. Interested in the actual numbers, he opened his status page and focused on his attributes:

Strength:	680 (780)	Vitality:	870
Dexterity:	280 (338)	Agility:	303 (361)
Intelligence:	292	Will:	673

Thanks to the crown atop his head, his strength had an extra hundred points, and his ever-increasing intelligence was providing fifty-eight extra points to his dexterity and agility. The best part about the feat was that it wasn't conditional on him retaining the Warlord class. He wondered how that would factor into things when he became a steel seeker and had to forge his own archetype.

A burning in his chest brought him out of his daydreams, and Victor touched his aegis, sending it into storage. Peering down at his chest, he frowned, irritated to see the spot of void Energy was slightly larger. He'd hoped gaining a level would set the curse back a bit.

Arona's raspy voice intruded on his dour thoughts. "It's looking worse."

"Nice of you to notice." Victor stood and summoned his armor again, carefully stuffing his arms into it before sealing the seam with a wave of his hand. He looked at Arona, who was staring at the ground, her eyes distant. Had he been too harsh with her? Her social skills were lacking, but he didn't have to take offense just because she was blunt with him. He tried to change the topic. "Did you gain a level?"

Arona shook her head. "No, but I feel I'm close."

"Damn. Four battles and not one level? Tier Nine is no joke, eh?"

"Indeed not." She sighed. "Shall we see if the dungeon will award us anything more interesting?" She gestured toward the distant gatehouse, and Victor nodded, leading the way. So far, Du had awarded them precious metals, sacks of Energy beads, and two Energy hearts—one attuned to fire and the other poison. When they entered the gatehouse, Victor nodded to the chest, giving Arona the opportunity to open it. He'd opened the two before, and they'd had an entertaining discussion speculating on whether it made a difference who opened reward chests.

As the glittering golden steam and motes of Energy faded, Arona peered into the chest and shrugged. "More beads and several diamonds the size of my thumb."

"All right. Take your share."

"I don't need more wealth." She stood and walked toward the gateway to the next section of the crucible.

Victor approached the chest, shaking his head. "I don't either."

"Then give it to your loved ones. Build something in your town. I don't have such things to worry about."

"Not yet. You're not a Death Caster anymore, Arona. You need to consider that you might start building a life you want to cultivate."

She nodded and looked at him, smiling faintly. "Thank you, Victor. I'm not destitute, and I promise I'll speak up if something appears that I would dearly love to have. Until then, I'll save my favors."

Victor nodded and reached down to collect the sack of beads. Considering they were attuned with multiple affinities, he figured the sack's value at around a hundred thousand. The pile of diamonds was beautiful, each cut expertly and, as Arona had said, quite large. He wondered what they could be used for other than jewelry. He would imagine such perfect gemstones could be enchanted with potent magics. With a shrug, he sent them into his storage ring.

When he joined Arona in the gateway, he surveyed the landscape before them. It was another canyon with high walls, but about halfway to the next gate, he saw a squat, dark stone structure. It looked like a keep, though small. "Think we'll need to destroy it?" he asked.

"Perhaps. Or perhaps we're supposed to occupy it and defend it. Will the dungeon tell us?"

"Yeah, it usually does." Victor stepped out of the gateway, and when Arona followed, a message floated before their eyes:

*****Congratulations! You have reached the fourth gate of the Crucible of Fire! Defend the citadel—its destruction will mean defeat.*****

As Victor read the message, dark shadows moved in his peripheral vision, and when he looked up, he saw enormous swarms of black beetles with glowing red eyes pouring out of tunnels near the base of the cliffs. "Were those tunnels there before?"

"No! They make more as we watch!" Arona pointed, and Victor saw she was right; the beetles, each about the size of a small car, were pushing out of the ground, streaming in great numbers toward the stone structure at the canyon's center.

Victor's fiery wings exploded from his back, and he launched into the air. "See you there!"

Arona wasn't going to be outdone. In a blinding flash of white light, she blinked out of existence and reappeared halfway to the "citadel." Victor laughed and focused on the distant rampart, forming the spell pattern for Tactical Reposition. His stomach lurched as he rushed through the gap instantly and found himself hovering over this rampart, his fiery wings dripping magma on the dark stone blocks. He released his wings and hefted Lifedrinker, watching the approaching swarms of beetles.

"I'll take this side!" Arona yelled, and he turned to see her standing on the ramparts, watching the beetles approach from that direction.

"Right!" Victor moved to the other side of the keep, focusing on the wave of dark insects. Looking more closely, he saw smoke drifting from their mouths, and he knew they were going to be spitting or breathing fire. "Shit," he said, a new idea entering his mind. He turned and hollered, "Arona! Don't let them get close! I think they'll explode!"

She nodded, leveling her staff toward the oncoming wave, and as before, a beam of solar energy tore through the air. Victor watched as first one, then ten, then a hundred of the enormous beetles exploded as if they were packed with TNT. "Holy shit!" he laughed, then he stared at the incoming wave on his side. He bunched his legs, leaping at them. Halfway through the air, he cast Volcanic Fury; if he was going to be standing in a horde of exploding beetles, he wanted all the fire resistance he could muster.

As his body surged with power and scorching rage, he roared his lust for battle and killing, and then he smashed onto one of the beetles, crushing it beneath his enormous, powerful form. Fire and heat billowed out of the dead creature, rippling through the teeming horde, knocking them back, toppling them, and generally slowing their advance. Victor laughed and, without thought, stomped his titanic foot, casting Wake the Earth.

Thankfully, he was a hundred yards or more from the little citadel, and when the earth buckled and split, smashing and swallowing hundreds of the giant beetles, only some mortar shook loose from the walls. The resultant wave of explosions filled Victor's rage-fueled heart with joy. He waded among the horde of bugs, ripping his wonderful axe left and right, popping them like ticks under a hammer.

The bugs were single-minded in their desire to get to the keep, but Victor and Arona were thorough—he in his rage and desire to destroy and she in her methodical use of clever, precise spells. Not only did she blast the incoming beetles with rays of solar Energy, she summoned storms of sunlight-filled globes that fell from the sky like brilliant slow-motion raindrops, burning through everything they touched, causing the beetles to explode as their volatile innards were exposed.

If Victor hadn't been so engrossed in his slaughter, enjoying the explosive destruction, he might have been angry or envious or at least frustrated to see Arona slay her horde several minutes before he was done. When the battle was over, and he stood heaving on a blackened, blasted battlefield, she hung back by the keep, staying out of his line of sight; he'd taught her not to tempt the rage in his heart when he took on the mantle of the volcano's fury. For his part, Victor paced the battlefield, desperate for something more to kill until, nearly ten full minutes after the last of the beetles was dead, his anger began to cool.

The surge of Energy from the dead assailants finally sent his fury into complete remission, and Victor found himself standing amid their remains, leaning on Lifedrinker. The only message that awaited him was the one from the dungeon informing him of his victory and encouraging him to find his reward in the gatehouse. He looked at the citadel and saw Arona sitting on the ramparts, staring into space. "Heh." He started toward her, fairly sure she'd finally gained a level.

He focused on the rampart beside her and cast Tactical Reposition. When he stood beside her, he squatted and asked, "Are you still out of it?"

"I've regained Level Ninety-Four."

"Nice one." He held out a hand, and when she took it, he hauled her to her feet. "Do you like your new affinity?"

She smiled at him, genuine amusement in her eyes. "Imagine how you'll feel when that curse is gone."

"That bad, huh?"

"That *good*!" She nodded toward the distant gate. "See you at the reward chest." Then she flashed with brilliant golden light and reappeared halfway between the citadel and the gatehouse. Victor chuckled and launched himself off the rampart, summoning his fiery wings as he began to feel gravity pulling him. He swooped down, black smoke trailing behind him, and skidded to a halt on the stones inside the gatehouse. Arona was there before him, but not by much.

"Go ahead." He nodded at the chest.

"Again?"

"Sure. I opened two. Maybe you'll get lucky."

With a nod and smiling faintly, Arona approached the chest and lifted the lid. When the steam cleared, she exclaimed, "Oh, my!"

"What?" Victor stepped closer, and Arona lifted out a glittering, crystalline scepter. It was about two feet long, and one end was bulbous—a glittering ball of perfectly cut angles that sparkled like a diamond. At its very center, Victor could see a small fiery heart burning like a tiny, miniature sun.

"It's attuned to solar Energy, Victor!"

Victor nodded, rubbing his chin. "Hmm. I think that tricky little guy is still trying to hook us up. I wonder . . . do you think it's solar-attuned because you opened the chest? Would something else have been waiting if I'd opened it?"

Arona shrugged. "I wish I knew how to tell."

"Well, obviously, you should keep that. I'll open the next few to see if something drops that's more suitable for me. That fair?"

"Of course! If you want to sell this at auction, I'm sure it would—"

Victor waved a hand. "Don't be ridiculous. Come on. Let's see what's next." He grinned and hefted Lifedrinker onto his shoulder. "We've got three more gates and then the boss. Hopefully, we'll fight something big."

"Something big?" Arona followed him to the far side of the gatehouse.

Victor nodded. "Yeah. Something like a dragon would be cool."

24

A ROYAL COURT

W ell," Victor said, peering through the gateway into the final chamber of the dungeon, "it's not exactly original, but I'm not going to complain." The cavernous space was much like the one from his previous assault on the dungeon—a vast, high, stalactite-covered stone ceiling stretching over a lake of bubbling lava.

Rocky islands dotted the lake, and on the most distant one, two lava kings frolicked, taking turns diving into the lava and swimming up with some sort of dark-fleshed, dog-sized grub clenched in their jaws. They lay on the stone, lazily eating the things, licking their reptilian fangs as they yawned and stretched, basking in the glow of the fiery lake.

Arona leaned forward, squinting her eyes into the heat wafting out of the chamber. "They're huge!"

"Yeah, and they're savage as hell. When I fought one the last time I was here, the thing bit my foot off."

Arona looked at him sideways, narrowing her eyes. "You can regenerate entire limbs?"

Victor shrugged. "You've seen how my regeneration is staving off this void curse."

Arona sniffed, looking back into the fiery chamber. The two of them had made easy work of the last few gates, and neither of them had gained another level. Victor had opened the chests, hoping for an award tailored for him like Arona's scepter, but all he'd done was add to his wealth—beads, gems, precious metals, and more Energy hearts. Victor felt the rising crescendo of Energy in his body, sure that this next encounter, should they win, would push him to the next level. Arona wasn't so sure.

Aside from levels and treasure, Victor practically salivated at the idea of two more lava king hearts. He'd gained his ability to fly from the last one. What would two more grant him? If nothing else, he was confident they'd help to improve one or both of his Cores. "I'm getting ahead of myself," he muttered.

Arona arched an eyebrow, looking at him again. "Already planning your victory party?"

"Something like that. Can you cope with this heat? The fumes? What's going to happen to you if you fall into the lava?"

"I have an ability that will create a solar shell around me. I can't act from within it, but should I fall, I believe it will protect me from the lava." She pointed to a nearby rocky island. "I can teleport between the islands. If those great beasts cannot similarly teleport, I should be able to keep my distance and use ranged attacks."

"Okay. I'll keep one busy, at least, but if one of them comes for you, I can count on you to keep yourself safe?"

"Yes. My teleport has a relatively quick cooldown."

"And if you run low on Energy?"

She reached into her robe and pulled out a finger-sized vial of blazing sunlight. "I can recharge."

"Holy shit!" Victor laughed. "You know how many times I've thought about how I needed to carry something like that around? It's just that they aren't allowed in the duels, so I've put it off. Sure would be nice to have here, though."

Arona smiled. "I can teach you how to make something similar. Something attuned to you."

"Now?"

She laughed—a raspy sound of genuine amusement. "No! It will take you some practice, and we don't have the proper . . . *setting* for it."

"Right." Victor offered a chagrined smile. "So? You ready for this?"

Arona gripped her scepter and nodded. "I am."

"Okay." Victor hefted Lifedrinker, and she vibrated with excitement. "Let's go, *chica*. You're going to have a feast today." When he stepped through the gateway, Arona was right beside him.

*****You have reached the final conflict in the Crucible of Fire! Defeat the Lords of the Crucible to claim your prize!*****

The two lava kings looked up from their stone island. One spread his wings and launched into the cavern heights, but the other paced, roaring, its voice deep and powerful, echoing over the lava lake. Victor stepped forward and summoned his fiery wings. "I'll hunt the one that flies."

Arona looked at him, stepping away from the heat of his wings. She nodded once, then turned toward the nearby stone island, and in a flash of light that hurt Victor's eyes, she disappeared. As he launched into the air, he saw her striding across the island, scepter outstretched. She was about to volley her first spells at the distant lava king. Victor turned his gaze upward, surging toward the heights, trailing black smoke as his flaming wings snapped and sizzled through the air.

His opponent was up there, clinging to an enormous stalactite. It flicked its black tongue, licking its fangs while one of his bulbous orange eyes watched Victor. In his natural state, Victor was probably a third of the monster's mass, so he cast Iron Berserk as he approached, swelling in size and a furious desire for battle. Of course, his Volcanic Fury would serve him better in that flame-filled chamber, but he had Arona to think of; if he started causing earthquakes and throwing mad temper tantrums, he could potentially harm her.

So, with the heat of his rage tempered by his iron-clad will, Victor surged toward the stalactite, Lifedrinker held ready. The lava king watched him, waiting for him to close the distance, and when he was just seconds away from swinging Lifedrinker at its exposed flank, it shrieked, and the ceiling came apart above him. Stone dust and bits of rock showered down on him, and Victor banked to the left, thinking he'd walked into a trap. In a way, he had, but it was different than he'd first suspected.

The ceiling wasn't collapsing; small tunnels or burrows had opened, and a dozen or more juvenile lava kings—princes?—were pouring out of them, sweeping toward him on fiery wings. Meanwhile, the mature one joined in the assault, screeching again as it belted out a beam of fiery Energy. *"Chingado!"* Victor hissed, diving for the lava lake. "She's a lava *queen*!" The beam of fire narrowly missed him, and Victor arched upward again, hacking Lifedrinker left and right at the swarming, pony-sized lava princes. Despite the rage in his pathways, he almost chuckled at his invented name for the smaller reptiles.

Lifedrinker was not amused; she screamed her fury and hunger, her razor-sharp obsidian blade ripping through the scales and flesh of the juveniles as Victor pushed his wings to their limit, eyes focused on the adult. Fire engulfed him as the smaller creatures poured out their breath; he couldn't evade them all. However, Victor's flesh was sturdy against fire, and his armor protected a large portion of his body.

When he broke through the swarm of smaller reptiles, he was relatively unscathed, and his eyes were mad with battle lust as he slammed into the lava queen. As he hacked Lifedrinker into the tremendous reptile's shoulder, the queen savagely clawed and bit at him. Her hind legs raked his aegis, sliding off harmlessly, but then her great, hooked claws ripped his thighs, shredding his leggings and flesh alike. Victor screamed his fury and pain, but only briefly as the queen's enormous jaws closed on his shoulder, grinding against his armor and shaking him.

Meanwhile, the juveniles piled onto him, clinging to his back, his legs, his arms, and even his head. They tumbled from the heights toward the lake below in a ball of screaming, roaring, fiery flesh. Victor was resistant to fire in his natural state, and he knew his rage would protect him further, but he'd been immersed in lava before. He'd felt the steady agony of the burn and didn't relish the idea. As the scaly monsters clawed, bit, and burned him, he closed his eyes and focused the Energy of his two Cores, summoning the elder magic pattern for Glacial Wrath.

Unlike Volcanic Fury, Victor knew he'd be able to control his impulses with the icy fury of the glacier coursing through his pathways. Moreover, he was immune to ice and fire alike when under the spell's influence. How that worked, he wasn't sure. How the ability would react to his being immersed in lava, he had no idea. He was eager to find out, though.

Even though he'd already been berserk, Victor felt himself swell with the power of the glacier. He expanded in size, gaining another twenty or thirty percent of his former mass. He'd never gone from Iron Berserk into Glacial Wrath before, so it was the first time he realized just how *big* the spell made him. As he fell toward the lava, his skin thickened and grew more dense. His body began to radiate frigid cold, and many of the little lava princes screamed and released their hold on him.

Lifedrinker, still in his grasp, bucked and dug, pulling herself deeper into the lava queen, and Victor allowed it, releasing his grasp on her. Instead, he wrapped his powerful, gauntleted hands around the lava queen's throat, digging his metal-clad fingers into her flesh, crushing her scales so he could grip her thick hide, squeezing his fingers into inexorable fists. She screamed, and Victor glowered into the face of her toothy maw, unimpressed.

Then they hit the lava, and the world exploded. At least, that was Victor's perception as his glacial aspect struck the surface. The collision was cataclysmic; his frigid aura, radiating intense cold, clashed with the molten rock in a violent eruption of steam, shattered stone, and sudden, jagged ice. A thunderous *crack* reverberated through the cavern as the lava instantly flash-cooled, solidifying into fractured basalt around his enormous figure, encasing him and the lava queen in a chaotic shell of half-formed rock and ice-crusted stone.

Plumes of superheated steam burst upward, hissing like tortured dragons, obscuring the air with dense white fog. Shards of volcanic glass, torn from the cooling surface, shot outward in all directions, lethally spearing most of the smaller lava princes and ripping hunks of flesh from the lava queen's enormous, tortured body.

Beneath Victor, the lava's surface continued to harden into a rough, uneven crust that cracked and shifted as his immense weight bore down. The relentless cold of his glacial aura spread outward, forcing the molten lake to retreat in jagged ripples of freezing magma. For a moment, silence hung in the air, broken only by the continual hiss of cooling rock and the labored furious breaths of the lava queen as her pierced, shredded, half-frozen body thrashed in Victor's iron grip.

Then, Victor jerked his arms, ripping great hunks of flesh and half-frozen meat from the lava queen's throat. Hot orange-red blood pumped from the awful wounds, and the light in her eyes faded. His violent movement shattered the frozen stone that clung to his armor and flesh, and it showered to the ground almost musically as it rang against the hollow, bubble-filled stone at his feet.

A tortured roar rang out, and Victor turned his wrathful eyes to the distant edge of the lake where Arona stood, her scepter outstretched, firing a thousand streaming bolts of fiery solar Energy at the lava king. The brilliant little missiles tore through the enormous reptile's flesh; apparently, the sun's heat was enough to burn even the fireproof creatures. Victor turned his icy gaze, scanning the cavern for surviving lava princes. He saw one swimming toward the stone island closest to the entry gate.

He tossed the corpse of the lava queen to the fresh-made basalt at his feet and effortlessly pulled Lifedrinker from the corpse. With the calculated fury of a glacier, he took a step toward the remaining prince. He might have simply walked through the lava, unconcerned about the destruction his frigid aura mixing with the lava would wreak, but his icy rage was too calculating; he knew his time was limited by his supply of Energy, which was dwindling quickly. Instead, he stood near the edge of his titan-made island, watching the prince and timing his next move.

When the smaller reptile was near the island's edge, Victor squatted and then, using Titanic Leap, launched himself toward the poor creature. When he landed, the reptile had just clambered onto the stone, and Victor came down with one foot on either side of it, planting Lifedrinker in its skull, killing it instantly.

He knew no such thing as satisfaction in his Glacial Wrath. He knew only anger, resentment, and the need to visit his dissatisfaction upon the world. When his last enemy was gone, he tilted his head back and roared. His bellow was a vast, mournful sound, the kind of sound a creature might make when it learns it's the last of its kind. He channeled all the fear and rage in his Core, his frustrations and sorrows made incarnate. It was a sound that would break a man's mind with grief and deep, hopeless frustration, wringing tears from even the cold, hateful eyes of a sworn enemy.

To Victor's immense relief, his Breath Core ran dry of Energy, and his transformation faded. He shrank into himself and, still gripping Lifedrinker's haft, he fell to his knees and fought back the urge to weep. He could feel Lifedrinker's despair. He could feel her sadness, her hopelessness, and worst of all, her sense of betrayal. He almost let go of her, afraid their gloomy thoughts would resonate and feed off each other. The idea of leaving her so upset broke his heart, though, and he grasped her more tightly.

"Hush, *chica*. I'm sorry I shared that with you. I'm sorry you felt that."

"Blood-mate, why do you howl with such despair? You aren't alone. We aren't alone. I will never abandon you! Will you leave me to rust at the bottom of an icy lake?"

"What? No! I would never!"

"When you howled, such an image filled my mind! I felt alone and lost and betrayed!"

"It's just my . . . fear and rage, I guess. The Glacial Wrath fills me with those emotions, *chica*. When I howled, you felt it. It's gone now. I'm sorry."

"I rejoiced when you grew so mighty and we annihilated our foes, but if such might comes with such despair, then please, heart-mate, don't use it."

"I'll try not to. I really will. I might need it, though, and if that's the case, you need to remember my love for you. Here." Victor built the pattern for Imbue Spirit in his pathway, weaving courage-attuned Energy to fill it. Then he cast it on Lifedrinker, smiling as warm, red-gold light infused her blade's mirror-smooth, depthless black. "Does that feel better?"

"Yes, love! Yes, battle-mate! I weep with the joy of it! Your spirit entwines with mine, and we dream of blood-soaked battlefields!"

Victor smiled and stood, lifting Lifedrinker to his shoulder, unwilling to send her into a storage container. He looked to the far side of the lake and saw the corpse of the lava king and Arona's hunched figure beside it. She was sitting on a chest, her chin in her hands. Victor couldn't make out the details of her face, even with his titan eyes, but her posture didn't look happy.

He waved away a System message about completing the dungeon and focused on the edge of the island where Arona sat. With a bit of concentration, he cast Tactical Reposition. In an instant, he was standing there, looking at her tear-streaked face. "Shit," he said, realizing his howl had impacted her as severely as Lifedrinker.

"If this is how you always feel, then I thank the ancient dead gods that I'm not a Spirit Caster." She looked up at him with red-rimmed eyes, and he sighed, lowering Lifedrinker so he could lean on her haft.

"It's not always like that. The Glacial Wrath spell takes a toll." He nodded toward the bubbles of misty, ghostlike Energy orbs gathering around the corpse of the lava king. "This Energy will help banish the bad feelings."

Arona sighed shakily and nodded. "That was an interesting strategy you employed—I've never seen a lake of lava explode."

Victor chuckled. "It was only a *part* of the lake."

Before they could banter further, the Energy from Arona's kill and, more distantly, Victor's began to flow into a stream, and he braced himself. Arona's hit her first, and he watched as her eyes rolled back in ecstasy and she was lifted from the chest by the powerful flow. Then Victor's infusion was upon him, and he lost himself to more wild, chaotic visions of things he could barely begin to understand.

For a change, he didn't really try. He just let his mind drift, enjoying the weird trip through space or history or simple fantasy, and when it was over, he found himself sitting on the warm stone with a single System message to read:

*****Congratulations! You have achieved Level 86 Warlord and gained 24 intelligence and 17 vitality.*****

"Well, it isn't much, but it's what I needed. More than halfway through this tier."

He hadn't expected a response, but Arona spoke from off to his left. "I hope I don't spoil your luck, but that's the fastest I've ever heard of someone going through Tier Eight."

Victor looked at her. She was still sitting on the chest, watching him. Her face was relaxed, though, and the evidence of her tears was long gone. "Did you gain a level?"

"I did not. However, I feel I'm very close."

Victor nodded, less than thrilled to see firsthand how slow levels in the ninth tier were. "Well? Should I open it?" He nodded to the chest she was using as a chair.

"Yes!" She leaped up. "Hopefully, Du saved his influence for your final award."

Victor chuckled, stepping close and grasping the lid of the chest, flinging it up with an explosion of golden steam and sparkling Energy. "Let's see." He waved the steam away, impatient, and when it cleared, his smile widened. Du had come through for him. On the bottom of the chest was a stack of golden tokens—the ones Du had promised him that would allow the dungeon to recognize Victor's "favored" guests—and a neatly folded pair of pants crafted from some sort of glittering black scales.

He sent his gauntlets into storage to properly feel the material as he took them out. He looked at Arona, smiling at how supple the leather beneath the fingernail-sized scales was. "Du knew I needed pants."

25

A FORTUITOUS ENCOUNTER

Well? What sort of scales are those?" Arona asked, watching Victor hold the glittering, black-scaled pants out in front of himself.

"Let's see here." Victor sent a tiny current of Energy from his Core into the pants, and a System message appeared before him:

*****Umbral Greaves of the Hollow: Fashioned from the blackened scales of the Ashen Maw, an elder drake that once hunted the souls of fallen demigods, these greaves were first worn by Vrak the Hollow, a warlord who ruled through terror. The Umbral Artificers of Direhold tempered the scales with abyssal ichor and bound them with the sinew of forgotten horrors, ensuring the armor would endure where flesh and steel would fail. These greaves are nearly indestructible, their scales capable of absorbing even the mightiest blows without so much as a crack. Yet their true power lies in the unseen—the dread that seeps from their very essence. The bearer of the Umbral Greaves will find their terror- or fear-attuned spells enhanced, their whispers carrying farther, their shadows stretching deeper. In the presence of these greaves, darkness lingers longer, and the air grows heavy with unseen dread.*****

"Damn, Du! He outdid himself again!" Victor chuckled, turning the supple, scaled greaves in his hands again, looking at them with more appreciation. When he realized Arona was staring at him, waiting for more, he added, "Seems like they're another ancient artifact, and they're a perfect match for me—durable and attuned to fear."

"I'm pleased that he came through for you. I was feeling rather guilty about my scepter, afraid that when I opened the chest, I stole your opportunity for something unique." She wrinkled her nose, watching as Victor continued to examine his new greaves. "They are unsettling, even inert in your hands. I find myself wanting to look away from them."

Victor arched an eyebrow. "Huh. Really?"

She nodded, then gestured to the chest. "You should collect your tokens."

"Right." Victor sent the greaves into storage and then bent to scoop out the stack of little golden tokens. Du hadn't skimped—there were more than twenty of them. As he lifted them from the chest, a crackling, sizzling portal of flames appeared behind him.

Arona asked, "Ready to leave?"

"Not just yet." Victor summoned a large, extremely sharp knife from his storage ring and nodded toward the corpse of the lava king. "I need to collect their hearts." Frowning, he remembered the haunch he still had in storage from the first lava king he'd slain. "I should get some of their meat, too."

"Do you know a recipe?" The way she asked the question—utterly matter-of-fact—made Victor chuckle again as he approached the first of the dead lava kings.

"Yeah, fire-roasted." He wondered if his instinct would tell him that this heart wasn't a fitting prize, considering Arona had slain it. Nothing stirred in his gut, though, and when he carved into its chest and pulled the still-warm organ from the cavity, his mouth salivated hungrily. Perhaps it was because they'd worked as a team that his innate "ritual" still considered the heart "worthy."

Sending the heart into storage, he went to work, carving several hundreds of pounds of flesh from the creature. While he worked, Arona sat on a camp chair she summoned from her storage ring and idly studied her crystalline scepter. When he'd stored away the butchered portions of the lava king's corpse, Victor focused on the island where he'd slain the lava queen and— "No, that's not right."

"What?" Arona looked up.

"The one I killed isn't a *lava* queen; it's an *ash* queen."

"Oh? You've studied these creatures?"

"I had a vision. I, um, experienced life as a lava king for a little while, and I remember being very proud of my 'ash queens.' Heh, it's very strange to hear myself say that." He nodded toward the distant corpse. "Be right back." He teleported to the island he'd created by freezing the lava and got to work, butchering the ash queen as he had the other corpse. Some of the meat was unpalatable—frozen by his glacial touch and then thawed by the scorching environment—and he left it where it lay.

While he worked, Arona surprised him by teleporting to his little island and asking, "Can you tell me about what you do with the hearts? While I watched your duel, the people in Kynna's box were speculating about it; apparently, you've claimed a number of them from your defeated foes."

Victor straightened from his bloody task and regarded her. He could trust her, couldn't he? He wanted to, but he also recognized the need to protect himself; if she were taken and tortured or if, for some reason, she ever turned on him . . . He frowned, remembering that Ranish Dar knew his secret. How many people knew? How many had he revealed his strange ability to? He searched his memories, but as far as he could remember, only Tes, Valla, and Ranish Dar knew the details of what he did with those hearts.

"If it's not something you want me to know—"

Victor shook his head. "It's not that. My mind just wandered off on a tangent. I collect the hearts of my strongest foes because, as a titan, I can gain some shreds of their strength by consuming them. You can imagine how knowledge of that secret could be dangerous, right?"

Arona nodded. "I struggle to see how, but there are old masters who might try to steal this ability from you." She shook her head. "That's not entirely accurate. I've seen Vesavo steal a man's body because he craved his bloodline."

Victor hadn't thought of that. He knew the Warlord had been working on a way to steal bloodlines, but a Death Caster could, theoretically, drive the spirit from a person's "vessel" and inhabit it using their weird phylactery magic. That made two different avenues for someone with power to try to take advantage of his ability. If he'd learned of two, there were probably more, perhaps *many*. "So, never tell anyone about this, all right?"

Arona stood up straight and bowed deeply to him. "I will give my life before I divulge your secret."

Victor studied her as she bowed, and he could feel her sincerity. His instincts weren't warning him about anything, so he grunted his acceptance of her promise and turned back to his work, butchering the ash queen. When he finished, and his storage ring held another few hundred pounds of meat, the two of them exited the dungeon, finding themselves back in the deep, fiery cavern at the heart of Mount Ember.

Du's portal still floated there, but when Victor attempted to enter it again, for no other reason than to see if he could, a System message appeared:

*****The entrance to this dungeon is locked to those of your tier for another 96 hours.*****

"Four days to recharge, I guess."

Arona smiled, tapping her nails on the crystalline ball of her scepter. "A short time to wait if we can gain another level with each run."

Victor rubbed his chin, nodding. She made an excellent point. If they were able to gain even one level per run, he could be Tier Nine in a couple of weeks. He and Arona could be steel seekers in a couple of months. "How long do you think we were in there?"

"With the rests we took between some of the more arduous, lengthy battles, I'd say it was less than two days. Here." She reached into her robes and pulled out a beautifully ornate silver pocket watch. "If I'm right about the days, then we were only in that dungeon for thirty-five hours and seventeen minutes."

Victor sat on a boulder and summoned the Far Scribe book he shared with Kynna. The only update was a short note asking him how he fared. He knew she was afraid his curse was advancing faster than he'd let on, and she probably was wondering if he was dead already. He replied with a quick note, saying he was doing well and asking if she had an update on his next duel.

When he finished, he looked at Arona as he closed the book. "I need to maximize my time between trips through that dungeon. I'm going to find Gorro and drag him out here so he knows exactly where to build the keep to guard this dungeon. I also want to make sure nobody enters it until you and I are done with it. I can't afford swarms of Tier Four and Five adventurers burning up Du's Energy."

Arona nodded, but her face was pensive. After a moment, she asked, "Do you really think gaining levels will help your curse? So far, it hasn't seemed to slow its growth."

"The levels in my current class aren't helping, but that's because I'm not gaining any will. When I hit Tier Nine, I'll hopefully get an option for a class that improves that attribute." Victor sighed and stretched, hating how the burning pain in his chest seemed to expand with the movement. "I also gained two potent hearts in there. I'm hoping they'll help, at least indirectly. Who knows what other treasures Du might send our way?"

"I see. And between dungeon runs? What will you do to enhance your growth?"

"Cultivate, eat natural treasures, and win duels if I have to."

"Then we should keep moving. Shall I assemble the array?" She gestured to the stony cavern floor.

Victor stood and began pulling the teleportation array components out of storage. "Yeah. And, Arona, thank you for going through this with me. It helps to have someone who understands what I'm doing."

"I will be by your side as you battle this curse, Victor. You won't face it alone. I just wish I could help more. Are you certain increasing your will is the path to victory?"

Victor frowned as he set down the crystals for the array. "I'm not certain about anything. All I know is that the reason I have this curse is because that *pendejo*, Chenasta, had a stronger will than mine. The spell took root because I failed to resist it. Ranish Dar says I need to go to the spirit plane to battle against the curse, but he said it would be dangerous and that I'd need to build my strength—basically, the curse will be even harder to get rid of than it was to resist. If I failed the first time . . ." Victor trailed off, shrugging.

Arona picked up the crystals and began placing them in the correct positions. "I understand. You must build your strength before you attempt it. You must build your will."

"Yeah. My will is the big piece, but I think every bit of strength helps. I need to improve my bloodline, gain levels, rank up my Cores—everything."

"Understood." She stepped back, and they watched as the crystals pulsed, gathering Energy. "Will we return to your home in this world? Will Gorro still be there?"

Victor thought about the question. It had been less than two days since he left Gorro. He doubted the governor could have gathered a construction crew suitable for building castles and bridges in such a short amount of time. "Yeah, I think so. We'll go there, then open a new portal to the top of this caldera again and bring him through so we can show him what I want him to build. In fact, we'll bring through a unit of my household guard. They can make sure no one wanders down into the lava tubes before Gorro has time to complete the construction."

"And after that?"

"What time is it?"

"Early morning."

"So, after we get Gorro straightened out, I'll spend a few hours visiting with Cora, my ward, and then you and I can return to Iron Mountain." He grinned, exposing his teeth. "I'll have a feast, and then we can see if Bryn's made any progress with my cultivation chamber." As he finished speaking, the crystals flashed, fully charged, and Victor summoned the destination orb from his storage ring. "Here we go," he said, picturing the garden behind his hermitage again.

When Victor ate the first of his two hearts, he once again glimpsed the fiery domain of the powerful fiery reptile. He had visions of basking with his brood on hot stones, consuming strange subterranean, fire-attuned creatures, and, of course, soaring through the hot gas-filled thermal updrafts of the massive caverns. It seemed a shorter vision than usual, and when he awoke, he was disappointed to find he hadn't gained any new abilities like the flaming wings he'd taken away from the first heart.

Nevertheless, his Breath Core gained a full rank, which would have taken him a month or more of cultivation, at least based on the speed with which he and Lesh were gaining Energy back on Sojourn. When he checked the clock on the wall of his parlor, he saw that he'd only been out for an hour, so, with nothing else to do in the middle of the night, he took the ash queen's heart out of storage.

He might have wondered if he'd be hungry enough to consume another raw heart, but he began to salivate as soon as he laid his eyes on it. Lifedrinker leaned against the couch where he lay, still gleaming with the red-gold light of his Imbue Spirit spell. He'd been reluctant to store her away after their little ordeal in the dungeon, and it gave him comfort to know she'd be there while his visions consumed him. He summoned a bottle of sweet honeyed mead and drank it down, quenching his thirst before lifting the heart to his lips and tearing a third of it off in a massive bite.

The flesh was sweet to him, sweet and tender, and it melted in his mouth as he crunched the juices out of it. He took another bite, and then the third, and his eyes watered with delicious satisfaction. Sweat broke out on his forehead as he swallowed the last bite, and he leaned back, feeling the warm lump in his gut, utterly satisfied. As he closed his eyes, a wave of warmth rolled over him, a sensation of well-being that was far too uncommon in his life as of late.

"What a weary one you are!" a soft voice said in his ear—soft but depthless with profound power that echoed through the hollows of Victor's bones. He snapped his eyes open to see a woman leaning over him. A woman he both knew and didn't know—she was tall and lithe with red-gold skin and raven hair that hung past her shoulders, interwoven with gleaming metallic black feathers. Her eyes shone so brightly they were like little golden suns, and when she smiled, Victor thought his heart would rip to shreds from her beauty.

He didn't have to ask her name. "Chantico."

"It's good that you know me, brave one." She sat beside him, and Victor realized he wasn't in his parlor or lying on a couch, he was on a warm, grassy slope, basking in the warmth of the smoldering yellow sun.

He looked at her again, shielding his eyes from the sun. "I thought you were gone—I mean, from this plane or universe or something."

"Perhaps, but part of me is in here." She tapped his chest, and Victor could feel the potential behind that fingertip, like she could melt him down to his component atoms with a thought. "It creates a bridge. Hmm . . ." She took that same finger and rubbed her chin, grinning with a touch of chagrin. "I wonder if I'll remember this meeting when I wake. My dreams often take me to distant reaches and I don't always recall each step of my journey. Still, I've heard you calling to me more than once. I've felt your threads tugging through the ether. Didn't I send you my fire once?"

"Yes!" Victor leaned forward earnestly. "You saved me!"

Her smile widened, exposing white teeth, and surprisingly large, sharp canines. "You must have deserved it. A one-sided battle perhaps? A repayment for gifts you sent my way? Perhaps both?" She winked, and Victor knew he didn't have to answer. "Why are we meeting in our dreams, though?" She moved her gaze from his face, scanning the length of him. Her smile faded and she sighed heavily. "I cannot save you from the curse that defiles your spirit."

"I . . . I didn't expect you to."

She nodded. "I can see the truth of those words." Suddenly her frown lifted and she smiled again. "You consumed something potent—something to stir your bloodline! My dreams had me close, and so we met! How fortuitous!" She lifted her palm and brought it close to Victor's chest, but he shrank back.

"It'll hurt you."

Her smile only grew broader as she pressed her palm against the painful sore on his chest. "Let's take advantage of this lucky meeting, young warrior. I cannot lift this curse, but I can offer some guidance."

"Thank you," Victor said, looking down his nose at her hand, wondering why she didn't pull her hand back.

"This curse cannot touch me because I make myself into a fortress. My spirit will not allow such corruption. I can see you've begun to understand that concept. You've a touch of the natural resistance of our people. You've learned that the flesh of the Quinametzin is laced with pride—how dare a poison think to corrupt our veins! Yes?"

"Yes," Victor agreed, remembering his vision of the young Quinametzin who'd been poisoned.

"Well, flesh is but a part of your whole, Victor. Your mind and spirit are equally important. As you've embraced the Quinametzin command of the flesh—the insistence that your very blood must drive out corruption—you must learn to do the same with your mind and then your spirit. I can feel your Spirit Core, young warrior. You're closer than you think to solving this riddle. You're right to cultivate your will, but remember, the entity that enslaves you will also limit you. Don't look to it for the answer."

Victor's eyes widened. Was she talking about the System? He opened his mouth to ask, but she held up her hand, interrupting him.

"Gah! I'm not good at this! I'm losing track of the issue at hand." She pressed her palm to his chest again, and Victor could feel the currents of power in her, stirring his blood, speeding the flows of Energy in his pathways, causing his Core to flare. "You'll need a breakthrough. Push your Core, young warrior. The answer to your curse is inward, not outward. What makes you strong? What makes you unbreakable? Answer those questions, and this curse will not be able to touch you."

"What makes—" he began to ask, but then her touch was gone, and so was she. He was alone, staring at the blazing sun. He squinted, looking down the grassy slope toward the thick jungle growth that stretched as far as he could see. Something huge moved through the trees, and he stood, reaching for his axe. When his fingers closed on something soft made of fabric, he blinked and looked down. He was on a couch.

Victor yawned and stretched, realizing he'd awakened. The morning sun was shining through his balcony doors and, for a moment, he thought his strange vision had simply been a dream, but then he saw a System message awaiting him:

*****Congratulations! Your Breath Core has reached Advanced 9.*****

It seemed the ash queen's heart had also ranked up his Breath Core. Two ranks in one evening—no one could complain about that. After he looked at the message, he tried to remember the vision he'd had, but it was foggy and dream-like. A vague impression of a grassy hill and a woman's voice echoed in his mind. He didn't usually struggle to remember visions that had to do with consuming natural treasures. Well, he didn't *think* he did, but he supposed he'd struggle to describe the first few he'd had.

"A woman . . . it wasn't a lava king memory. It was something else . . ." Hadn't she been beautiful? Did he dream of Tes or Valla? No, that didn't feel right. As he struggled to picture the woman's face or hear her words, a faint echo came to him, and he focused on it, clinging to the shred of a memory, until he heard the words again. He repeated them, determined not to forget, "What makes you unbreakable . . ."

26

A LIGHT AT THE END OF THE TUNNEL

Victor spent the next couple of days having meetings with Kynna and her various governors; it seemed running an empire spanning more than a dozen former nations was a tedious and complicated process. She'd asked for Victor's attendance mostly to answer questions and provide assurance that he was ready, willing, and capable of fighting as many duels as necessary to consolidate Kynna's grip on the western continent.

It was mostly for show; once Kynna's representatives saw him with their own eyes and heard his confident words, they would use his past victories to leverage the lesser nations of the western continent to bend to Kynna's rule. Her nation's proximity, at the center of the continent, made her a more immediate threat than the Khaliday Empire and the other great houses. Any of the eastern nations that wanted to curb her influence would have to go through her—something she and Victor invited.

Meanwhile, Bryn continued to pressure the craftsfolk working on Victor's cultivation chamber. He was eager to see it finished because his Breath Core had reached the last rank of the advanced stage, and he hoped that a breakthrough into epic would provide insights and power that he could use to fuel his battle with the void curse. The curse continued to march inexorably toward Victor's destruction—slowly, but very surely growing as it devoured his flesh.

Arona came to his room one morning and announced that it had been ninety-six hours since they'd left Du's dungeon. Victor told Bryn he'd be gone for a couple of days, and then he and Arona returned to Fanwath, teleporting directly into the cavern containing Du's portal. To his surprise, stone walls had been constructed, closing off the lava tubes that gave access to the chamber. One of those walls contained an enormous iron door, and Victor found two of his house guards watching it—one on either side.

It seemed that Gorro ap'Dommic, his governor, had made steady and fast progress with his construction crew. They weren't yet building the keep in the caldera, but according to the guards Victor questioned, the restoration of the citadels guarding the road was well underway. Pleased to see such progress, Victor and Arona entered the Crucible of Fire again, and challenged themselves to complete it more quickly than before.

Du didn't make it easy for them. Victor wasn't sure how the dungeon Core gained levels and power. He berated himself for not getting those details from the Core before setting it free in the mountain, but he had to assume that the Core gained something from having people challenge his creations. Even if Victor and Arona won, completing the dungeon and killing the "boss," it seemed that Du gained power. At least that was Arona's guess when they found themselves facing challenges that were noticeably more difficult than during their previous run.

They faced wave after wave of powerful enemies on the first gate. Like the hordes from Victor's solo run, the numbers mounted into the tens of thousands, but they were stronger creatures with heavier armor and more powerful attacks. It took nearly half a day of constant battle for him and Arona to clear them.

The second, third, and fourth gates went more quickly. He and Arona fought gigantic, powerful creatures, from house-sized beetles to titanic skeletons with blackened bones that smoldered with inner heat. They were more powerful foes, but with only a few to face them, Victor and Arona cleared them in minutes.

The fifth gate was another army of undead, though this time the hordes were sprinkled with elite foes that threw spells or were clad in dense magmatic armor. Victor lost himself in his rage, rampaging madly through the horde, and if it hadn't been for Arona, he would have had no idea how many he destroyed. She estimated that, all told, they vanquished nearly a hundred and fifty thousand undead. And *still* they hadn't gained a single level.

After the sixth gate, they faced a trio of freakish giants. One had two heads, another four arms, and the third moved around like a lumbering, four-legged animal reminiscent of a bear. They were mighty foes, each nearly the size of Victor while under the influence of Glacial Wrath, but they weren't titans. Maybe they were considered behemoths like the gargantuopod Victor had killed in the challenge dungeon in Sojourn, but they died well enough when Lifedrinker did her work and Arona blasted them with fiery solar-attuned Energy. Whatever their nature, Victor claimed their hearts.

For the first time, they didn't face a lava king in the "boss" room of the dungeon. The room was much the same as before—a lake of lava in a vast cavern, but there was only one stone island in the lake, right at its center. When Arona teleported to the platform, and Victor launched himself into the sky, they came face-to-face with a new sort of "Lord of the Crucible."

Tremendous black bones rose from the lava, sizzling and smoking, lifting into the sky as more and more of the monstrous skeletal master of the dungeon came into view. Victor recognized the creature's shape in only a few seconds; it reminded him too much of Hector's skeletal flying mount that had terrorized his army during their assault on Mount Ember. This creature was more enormous, though, and its blackened bones looked like petrified stone, far denser than those of Hector's undead dragon.

The battle with the skeletal dragon was harrowing but not because Victor feared he would lose. The creature was huge and powerful, but so was he, and he could take the punishment it doled out. No, the stress came from Arona. Her magic seemed largely ineffective against the monster's dense, blackened bones, and she had little room to maneuver when it came to avoiding the enormous monster's great claws and snapping jaws. With only one island for her to stand upon, she had to use her teleport and "solar shield" to great effect.

Even with those defensive measures, Victor was forced to save her several times with his Guardian's Rescue spell, shielding her with his Energy and swapping positions with her. It turned out to be a very effective tactic. Twice when he performed the maneuver, he delivered Lifedrinker's deadly edge to the undead dragon's snout when it thought it was about to snap up the much smaller sorceress—Victor had learned that her current class was Solar Sorceress.

In the end, they were victorious, and when the Energy infusion faded and he came back to his senses, he had System messages waiting for him:

*****Congratulations! You have achieved Level 87 Warlord and gained 24 intelligence and 17 vitality.*****

*****Congratulations! You have earned a Class spell: Mental Fortress, Basic.*****

*****Mental Fortress, Basic: Guard your mind from the influence of hostile magics and the pressure of unwanted emotion. This spell will enhance your will attribute with the Energy in your Core. It is costly to maintain, but in times of crisis or when clarity of thought is paramount, there is no greater boon to a general on the battlefield. Energy Cost: Minimum 5000, variable based on duration. Cooldown: Short.*****

*****Congratulations! You have defeated the Unliving Magma Dragon! Search its lair to find your reward!*****

When Victor read the notification, he fell to his back on the hot stone and sighed, a sudden wash of relief leaving his muscles limp. He chuckled softly to himself, closing his eyes as he read the notification again and again. After a while, he heard soft steps beside him and Arona's raspy voice asked, "Did the System tell you a joke?"

"Not exactly, but I think I'm starting to see a light at the end of the tunnel. I mean, where this curse is concerned."

"Oh?"

"Yeah. A new Warlord ability called Mental Fortress. It bolsters my will at the expense of Energy."

"Your will? That's wonderful! How large is the boost?"

Victor sat up and looked at her. She stood before him in ornate, ruby-studded red robes, clutching her crystal scepter. She'd commissioned those robes for Du's Crucible; they granted her a significant resistance to fire. "Good question." He concentrated briefly and cast the new spell. It pulled a thick torrent of Energy from his Core, and he could feel the steady drain as it maintained itself.

Thanks to his ever-increasing intelligence attribute, he had more than sixty thousand Energy. Still, when he looked at his status sheet to monitor the drain, he saw that he was losing several hundred every second. Thanks to his already high natural will attribute, his passive regeneration put up a good fight, but he still didn't think he could keep the spell going for more than an hour or so.

When he shifted his attention to the attribute in question, he laughed, but it wasn't a gleeful sound, more of a chagrined, bitter one. "It's giving me ten will points."

"So few?" Arona folded her arms, idly thumping her scepter against her hip.

"It's only basic. Maybe it gets more efficient with higher ranks."

She nodded. "The System tends to do that, offer a poor version of a spell to encourage the caster to improve it through practice."

"Well, I have other ways to improve it, too. Now that I know it's possible, I can experiment with this pattern as a template."

Arona's eyes widened as she slowly nodded. "Yes, I've dabbled with spell patterns myself, but I've always found it difficult to improve on the System's designs."

Victor wanted to say that he would use elder magic and not the System's standard glyphs and weaves. He wanted to, but he knew better. The System was watching him, and for all he knew Fox and Three were right around the corner, just waiting for him to start teaching elder magic to someone. Maybe someday he could stand up to them and teach who he wanted, *what* he wanted, but for now, he had to use caution; he wasn't as strong as Tes. With that in mind, he nodded and said, "It'll take some work, but I think I can come up with some improvements." He didn't mean to do so, but he changed the topic. "Did you gain a level?"

"I did, though barely! I'm sure you're closer to your next than I am to mine." She nodded to the chest at the center of the stone platform. "Shall we see what treasure awaits?"

Victor nodded, canceling his Mental Fortress spell and climbing to his feet. They'd amassed more wealth and several minor magical items that neither of them would probably use. Victor planned to give them to Bryn, not because she needed them, but to use as incentives for the guards under her command. He nodded to the chest. "You go ahead."

"I will not." Arona proved her intentions by sitting down beside the chest, lithely folding her legs beneath her.

"I opened it the last time—"

"You have more need of the treasures at the moment. If you find something you don't want and think I can use it, we'll talk."

"Heh. Stubborn." Victor smiled at her to let her know he appreciated the sentiment, then he opened the chest. As he waved away the glittering golden steam, he saw immediately that the bottom of the chest was filled with thousands of glittering gemstones. It was enough to make anyone wealthy in most worlds, but to Victor and Arona, it was just the latest installment of their ever-expanding fortune. As he passed his hand through the treasure, sending more than half into his storage container, he looked at her and asked, "How uncommon are Tier Nine dungeons?"

"I know of two on Sojourn and you've been in both."

"The challenge dungeon and the Iron Prison?" When she nodded, he asked, "And the challenge dungeon is only open a few times a year?"

"I see what you're thinking, and you'd be right; the opportunity Du affords us is exceedingly uncommon. On most worlds that could allow a dungeon to grow to this rank, it would be heavily controlled by the powers that be."

Victor nodded as he watched the fiery portal burst into life, expanding from a pinpoint into a large door-sized hole in the universe. "Kind of like Rellia and I intend to do with this one."

Arona nodded. "As is your right."

"Both of those dungeons on Sojourn are static. I wonder how uncommon a progressive dungeon like Du is, especially at this tier."

"Exceedingly, I'd wager." Arona tapped her chin, still sitting cross-legged on the ground. "You know, I begin to understand the ancient King of Iron Mountain—his desire to hide this dungeon. That enormous wall of amber ore makes more and more sense."

"Yeah." Victor held out a hand for her, hoisting her to her feet. "I had the same thought. Anyway, speaking of amber ore, let's get back to Iron Mountain." With that, he stepped through the portal.

The cavern was empty, save for Du's portal and, distantly, the single guard watching the far side of the iron door. When Arona stepped out and began setting up the portal array, Victor walked over to the guard. "Anything happen while we were inside?"

"No, milord, just a couple of shift changes." The guards had a small camp up in the caldera. "Well, actually, something's happening up top. Some engineers and an Earth Elementalist arrived. They're preparing the site for the keep, though they said construction won't begin in earnest for another week or two."

"Good." Victor nodded, turning back to Arona. The crystals were in place and were blinking with Energy as they powered up. "I'll be back soon."

"Yes, milord." The guard saluted, and Victor gave him a good look. He let his vision unfocus and accessed his inner eye the way Tes had been teaching him during her visit, and was surprised to see the guard's Core swirling with green, vibrant Energy. Of course, when Tes showed him the technique, he tried to practice it on her, but never had much luck. With the guard, though, he could see the Core plain as day, swirling in a looping, figure-eight pattern right at the center of his torso.

"Do you have a nature affinity?"

The guard's eyes widened. "I do, milord! I work magic through plant life." Victor stared at the Core for a moment longer, trying to remember its intensity for future comparisons. "Tier Three?" he guessed, having no idea, but figuring one of his household guards would be at least Level Thirty.

"Aye, milord."

Victor nodded. "Good, good. Keep up the good work, soldier."

The man visibly straightened, despite already being at attention. "Yes, sir!"

Victor smiled and turned back to Arona. He tried the trick again as he approached, slightly unfocusing his eyes and reaching out with his inner eye. As with Tes, he couldn't see a trace of Arona's Core. "Ready?" he asked as he approached.

"Nearly so, another minute should do it."

Victor nodded and waited quietly, watching the crystals. Their pulsing was faint, their glow nearly steady, but as he waited it grew even more constant, the tiny waver fading, and then he took out the destination orb and pictured the foyer to his quarters at Iron Mountain. When the portal appeared, smaller, narrower, and decidedly less *fiery* than Du's, he stepped through.

Victor was pleased to find his chambers bereft of the many temporary rugs the workers had put down during the construction of his cultivation chamber. He took it as a good sign that maybe Bryn had managed to see to the completion of the project while he and Arona had been in the dungeon. He walked down the short hallway, into the workshop, and then whooped when he saw the intricate, rune-inscribed amber ore vault door in the far wall.

"It's finished?" Arona asked from behind him.

"I think so!" Victor hurried forward and pulled the door wide. It was unlocked, but he knew, if the artisan had crafted it correctly, that he could lock it simply by pressing his hand to the smooth, slightly raised panel at the center of the door on either side. As soon as he stepped through the aperture, Victor could feel the weird resonance of the spherical amber ore chamber.

He'd used texts given to him by Ranish Dar to plan the chamber. Sixteen areas of the sphere were reinforced by a spider's web of thick amber ore bands that ran around the exterior of the smooth surface. More than that, the interior was worked with System runes to focus and amplify Energy. There was a raised platform at the very center of the sphere, large enough for him to sit on in his natural giant form, which would make him the focal point of any Energy-rich treasures he stowed in the many alcoves built into the chamber's walls.

All in all, it was a lot like the cultivation chamber that he'd used in the Warlord's citadel in Coloss. He hoped it would be better once he placed his treasures and gave the chamber time to gather and focus the Energy. He could feel the thickness in the air, so he was reasonably sure the chamber was already working, capturing ambient Energy and amplifying it. He looked at Arona, grinning. "Can you feel that?"

"I've seen some ornate cultivation chambers in my time—mostly ones built by Vesavo—but this is the first one I've seen crafted completely of amber ore." She looked small standing in the doorway in her human-sized body. He imagined that was what he and Valla had looked like when they used the Warlord's chamber. Victor's chamber had a radius of twenty feet, but there were only a few steps leading up to the central platform—plenty for his giant-sized strides.

He summoned the two Energy hearts that were attuned to his Breath Core Energies, holding them in the palms of his hands. "I'm going to work on my Breath Core first; it's at the peak of the advanced tier. Theoretically, I could cultivate Energy for all of my affinities at once, but the chamber will gather and focus more of the blue ice and magma if these are the only treasures inside."

"Logical." Arona nodded, clasping her hands as she watched him place one Energy heart on the left in the centermost alcove and the other on the right.

"I can feel it gathering the Energy already. I'll let it build up overnight, and in the morning, I'll do some cultivating." With that, he returned to the door and followed Arona out. He pushed the vault door shut with a resounding *thunk*, and then pressed his hand on the central plate until he heard the locks engage.

He and Arona were walking back through his parlor when he heard knocking on his door. He briefly closed his eyes and let his inner eye peer out into the world. To his pleasure, he recognized two Energy signatures outside his door. Smiling, he said, "It's Bryn and the queen."

Arona nodded, gesturing toward the sitting area near the balcony. "Shall I give you some space?"

"What? Why?" Victor waved a hand, negating the idea. Raising his voice, he called, "Come in."

Bryn stepped through, wearing her ornate dress uniform and wielding the golden glaive he'd given her. "May I present Her Majesty, Queen Kynna Dar, ruler of—"

"That's quite enough," Kynna said, breezing into the foyer. She wore a glittering, deep blue gown, and her crown sat proudly on her head. Despite her gruff interruption of Bryn, she was smiling, and when her eyes found Victor, the smile deepened. "Victor! We've managed to acquire an epic-tier natural treasure. With luck, it will have a profound effect on your bloodline!"

27

A SOLITARY MEAL

At Kynna's words, Victor felt his heart rate quicken. "Really?"

She nodded, her smile broadening further. "Yes! One of the envoys I sent to Sojourn has returned bearing an item won at auction. Of course, I wanted to present it publicly, along with more commendations for your valor, but I know time is of the essence. You'd more likely be more annoyed by the ceremony than grateful, in any case, so . . ." She shrugged, allowing her sentence to go unfinished, and then she held out her hand, and a polished black wooden box appeared in her palm.

Victor stepped closer, first looking at the box, then shifting his gaze to Kynna's face and the white flames flickering inside her crystalline eyes. "I appreciate the lengths you've been going to. I know epic bloodline treasures are uncommon. What is it?"

"Take it and see." Again, Kynna proffered the box, and Victor nodded, taking it from her hand. It was square—about the size of a Rubik's Cube he'd gotten from one of his aunties that he'd never had the patience to solve.

"Should I open it?" He asked the question because he knew some natural treasures lost their potency rapidly when exposed to the air. Kynna nodded, her eyebrows tilting up in the center with eager anticipation. Victor lifted the lid off the box. It was delicately crafted and lined with black velour padding. Inside sat a walnut about the size of a tennis ball. Clearly, it wasn't exactly a walnut. For one thing, the shell was dark brown—almost black. And while the nut had the wrinkles in its shell similar to a walnut, it was too round.

Victor's nose instantly picked up the woodsy, coffee-ground scent of the nut, and underneath that strong odor, a hint of sweet vanilla that made his mouth water. He lifted it to his nose and sniffed, his eyes going wide with the wonderful aroma. "It makes me want to try to crunch that shell with my teeth!"

Kynna laughed. "The authentication documents say that anyone who catches a whiff of the meat inside that shell will be powerless in the face of the temptation."

Victor smiled and held the open box out toward Bryn. "Smell that."

She leaned close and sniffed. Her mouth dropped open, her eyes bulged, and Victor saw a trickle of drool begin to slide out of the corner of her lips. He laughed, and pulled it back, holding it out to Arona. She took a step back, shaking her head. "You think it's funny to torture people. Look at poor Bryn!"

Victor clicked his tongue, continuing to chuckle as he put the lid back on the box. "I dunno, I'd want to know what it smelled like if I was standing in Bryn's shoes."

Bryn laughed, nodding good-naturedly, even as she blushed. "I did! I was desperate to know!"

Victor looked at Kynna. "Thank you, my Queen. What's it called?"

She produced a small black card with gilded silver letters on one side. She squinted at them and, haltingly, pronounced, "A Yan'grovashee World Tree seed." She shrugged and handed Victor the card. "I hope it helps you, Victor. I hope it provides some insight into your curse, or perhaps greater resistance."

"I do, too." Victor sighed and, with a shrug, sent the magical seed into his best storage ring.

Kynna looked from Bryn to Arona, perhaps judging whether she should ask for some privacy. Apparently, she decided not to; she looked at Victor and asked, "Any progress?"

"Um, a bit, yeah." He shrugged. "I'm doing what I can to gain strength and, if things go well, I'll try to battle the curse on the spirit plane soon. I imagine I'll be out of it for a while when I consume your gift. Do you have any news regarding my next duel?"

Kynna shook her head. "I continue to pressure House Voth, but Bomar Lund has stockpiled enormous resource caches, and the other great houses support him. I believe he can resist my efforts to force a duel for a very long time. As I consolidate power on this continent, however, I know it rankles House Khaliday; every week their empire diminishes. They won't stand for it, not for long. Soon they'll pressure one of the other houses to come forward with a champion they hope can slay you."

"Your Majesty," Arona said, stepping a little closer to the two of them, "don't you fear assassination?"

"The veil walkers are still on war footing after the attempt on Lohanse's life. They limit movement between continents to the established teleportation networks, making sneaking a kill squad into Victor's duchy much more difficult. Moreover, even if such an attempt were made, we've spent the last half year reinforcing the defenses of this keep." She smiled and looked around, her eyes lingering on the stone walls of the tower. "The bones of this place are ancient, and they run deep. It's well situated atop this hill, and having the city five miles away is a tactical advantage my palace in Gloria lacks."

Arona looked at Victor, pressing her palms together as she performed a strange half-bow, something he'd never seen her do before. In her raspy voice, she very solemnly said, "I will stand guard over this place while you undergo whatever that potent seed does to you."

Kynna cocked her head to the side, making it clear that her tall crystalline crown magically held its position. "That's very noble of you, Arona Moonshadow."

Arona turned to the queen, her palms still pressed together, her head still bowed. "I owe Victor much, and I intend to do my part to see his mission on this world completed."

"Then, if Victor is willing, I will name you a Champion of the Realm. It's only fitting that you have the respect your actions demand." She looked at Victor, an eyebrow arched questioningly.

Victor shook his head. "No, my Queen. Make her a captain of the Queen's Guard if you want, but not a champion. If this nut knocks me out for a month and you need someone to fight one of the champions of the great houses, I won't have Arona step into that role."

Kynna's mouth partially opened, and Victor wasn't sure if she was going to deny that intention or if she was going to argue that he should allow it, but she must have thought better of her words in either case. She closed her mouth, nodding. "I understand."

"Thanks." Victor turned to Arona. "Thank you for watching things around here while I'm out of it, though."

"Um, Your Grace," Bryn said, shifting so her golden glaive sizzled and flickered with Energy, "let's not forget that quite a few capable folks are already guarding this palace!"

Arona turned to Bryn, looking up from her solemn bow. "Of course, Baroness. I meant no offense."

Bryn nodded, cheeks flushing, clearly uncomfortable speaking up in front of the queen. "None taken."

Victor felt he needed to put an end to the impromptu little meeting before someone *did* take offense, so he cleared his throat and motioned vaguely toward the door. "I suppose I should consume this thing right away. The sooner I do, the sooner I'll be done with whatever ordeal it puts me through, right?"

Kynna nodded. "I wouldn't have immediately brought it to you if I disagreed. Will you do it here?"

Victor nodded and absently rubbed his chest near the constant, roiling fire at the center of it. He honestly didn't know how he was able to chat and laugh;

it felt as if he was being branded with a hot iron on a constant basis. Someone, maybe a coach, once told him that a person can get used to any level of misery over time. Victor wasn't sure that was true, but he was definitely less grouchy than when the curse had first afflicted him. "Yeah," he said after a few seconds of thought. "In my cultivation chamber. It's secure, and the thick Energies should help stave off the void."

Kynna watched his hand where it pressed against the edge of his pectoral, carefully avoiding the center of his breastbone. "Is it terribly uncomfortable?"

Victor cocked a lopsided grin and lowered his hand. "Nah, it's not bad."

"Liar," Bryn muttered.

Kynna looked at her sharply, then at Victor with more concern. "Hiding the truth from us will not make anything easier." She stepped closer and reached out to grasp his shoulder, her fingers surprisingly strong as she gripped his muscles. "Let us in, Victor."

Victor took a long deep breath through his nose, then shrugged. "It's awful. I'm worried something is wrong with me. How can I periodically forget about something this fucking painful? Am I losing my mind? I was laughing earlier. I was excited about my completed cultivation chamber! My stomach was rumbling and I was thinking about barbecuing some lava king flesh to eat—long story. Still, how can I do all that when this is going on?" He reached up to his collar and ripped his shirt open, revealing the marble-sized sphere of nothingness that was eating his flesh, just a tiny bit faster than it could regenerate.

Bryn hissed through her teeth and blurted, "It's so much bigger!"

Kynna looked at Bryn and then Arona. "Is it?"

Victor answered before his friend had to. "Yeah, it is. It's nothing like when Loss cast the spell, though. It's only growing a tiny bit every day, but I guess if it's a percentage, the pace will become unmanageable." Victor summoned the treasure Kynna had given him and held the polished box up. "Hopefully, this will help. Maybe it will improve my regeneration. Maybe I'll have some other kind of breakthrough."

"Hopefully," Kynna agreed. "Even if it does, or if it doesn't, you need to rely on us more. I am a queen, yes, but I'm also your friend. You wouldn't have that curse if not for me—my kingdom."

Victor shook his head. "Nah, Kynna. This is on me, and maybe a little on Ranish Dar." He chuckled ruefully. "You've tried to stop me half a dozen times."

"She's right, though," Arona rasped, her dry voice cutting through any nonsense. "I owe you everything. Let me help you more. If nothing else, you should feel comfortable enough to vent to me. Your mind isn't broken, though; I can tell you that right now. Your subconscious knows you can't do anything about the pain. When you don't think about it, part of you is tuning it out so that you can continue living and hopefully find a solution to the problem."

"She's right," Bryn added. "My father tamed a fellhawk when I was a girl. We watched it hunting the slopes near our home for months before he finally coaxed it close enough to get a good look at it. He had a broken-off arrow in his wing—the barbed arrowhead had scar tissue grown around it, but even so, every time he flapped his wings, the blades would cut his flesh. I remember thinking how difficult it must be to hunt with that constant pain. My father told me that the mind and body can adapt to much when it comes to survival."

Kynna looked at Bryn with an appraising expression. "I've never heard you speak so much at once, Bryn. I'm impressed—and heartened—by your story. Do you hear that, Victor? It's natural for you to learn to function through your pain."

Victor forced a smile, though he wasn't feeling very jovial at the moment. Even so, he appreciated what the three of them were trying to do, so he said what they wanted to hear, "I know you're right. I should confide in you more."

"Go then!" Kynna said with a firm nod. "Go." She turned to Bryn. "You'll keep me posted on his status?"

"Of course, Your Majesty." Bryn straightened into attention and saluted for good measure.

Kynna turned to the door. "Come see me when you're done, Victor, and don't worry about us. Everything will be fine while you're busy."

"I will." Victor watched her leave, then turned to Arona. "I guess I'll be in my cultivation chamber."

"No one can open that if you lock it, Victor," Bryn said as though he'd forgotten.

"Exactly." He deftly tossed the box with the priceless treasure inside it from one hand to the other, then turned and walked back to his workshop. Naturally, both women followed him.

"What if we need to help you? How will we look in on you?" Arona asked.

"Here." Victor held his hand to the smooth section of amber ore on the door. After the locks disengaged, he kept his hand there until a circle of faintly glowing silvery runes appeared. He removed his hand and said, "Put your hand there now, Arona." Arona quickly stepped forward and held her palm on the metal. A moment later, the silvery runes flashed and faded. "Now you can lock and unlock the door."

Arona lowered her arm and leaned her shoulder against the door. "Bryn should have permission, too."

Victor shook his head, looking directly into Bryn's eyes. "I trust Bryn, but she's not as strong as you—yet. Someone could force her to open this door against her will. You understand, Bryn?"

The former guardswoman nodded, smiling reassuringly. "I do, Victor. It's enough that one of us can reach you."

Arona still stood between Victor and the door, and when she didn't move, he said, "Well?"

"Are you sure you want to do this now? An epic bloodline treasure could take weeks for your body to process."

"Yeah, I think the last one I ate was about a week." Victor shrugged. "I mean, I'm hungry. I was going to go and cook something; that much was true. I have snacks in my ring." He didn't mention that the "snacks" were behemoth hearts. "I'll probably sit in there and meditate for a while. I'll have a solitary meal, and then I'm going to eat this magical nut for dessert." He held up the box. "There's no point waiting." He gestured to his chest where his ripped shirt hung open. "Every day this thing gets bigger."

"We'll be here, Victor," Bryn said, thumping the butt of her glaive's haft on the hardwood flooring.

"Thank you." Victor reached past Arona and pulled the door open, forcing the much smaller woman to step away hurriedly. "See you two soon." He could tell Arona wanted to say something more, but she didn't, and he didn't want to drag the moment out any longer. He stepped into the vault, looked into each of their eyes one more time, then pulled it closed with a resounding *clang*. He touched his hand to the smooth surface at the center and held it there until the locks *thunked* into place.

Already, the air in his cultivation chamber was thick with the elemental Energies of blue ice and magma. He could feel them as he inhaled, seeping into the wide pathway leading from his lungs and into his Breath Core. It was very satisfying, and he thought he could feel a slight relief in his chest where the void busily worked to eradicate his flesh. Was its influence lessened there in his cultivation chamber? Did the thick currents of Energy make it harder for the absence of *anything* to assert itself? He hoped so.

He climbed the steps to the platform at the sphere's center and sat down. The platform was large enough for him to sit comfortably, and he thought there was even enough room left over to lie down. Sitting there, he decided to make good on his promise to eat something. He summoned one of the behemoth hearts from his last dungeon run. The thing was enormous, though not as large as the gargantuopod's. Even so, Victor didn't think he'd be able to eat more than one at a time.

Without any ceremony or hesitation, he began to bite hunks out of the hot, tough flesh. He chewed absently, enjoying the flavor as always, but his mind wandered. He thought about Kynna and her words, about how concerned everyone seemed. He thought about Valla and Rellia and felt a little guilty for not seeing them again while he and Arona were on Fanwath to run the dungeon. In the back of his mind, he knew why he was having those thoughts: Some part of him wondered if he might die in that chamber.

If the treasure knocked him out for weeks and did nothing to slow the curse's progress, it could grow large enough to consume part of his heart. Could his regeneration keep him alive as his heart was constantly eroded? He swallowed the last hunk of the behemoth's heart and summoned a flask of wine to rinse his mouth.

The meat in his gut was hot and full of Energy, but no vision overcame him. He didn't lose consciousness, and he didn't get any System messages. Nevertheless, he felt those deep wells of Energy flow into his Core and flood it with power. It swelled and strained, fighting against the pressure that kept it from advancing.

His Spirit Core was on the third rank of the epic tier, and Victor had a feeling another heart like the one he just ate would push it into the fourth. Considering some of the people he'd met on Sojourn spent years trying to cultivate enough Energy to advance through an epic rank, Victor wouldn't complain about that.

As the heat in his gut dissipated, and he finished the flask of wine, he picked up the box containing the natural treasure. "Time for dessert, I guess."

28

THREADS OF FATE

Victor took the seed from its case and again held it close to his nose, gently inhaling the intoxicating aroma. Shivers ran down his spine, and little lights exploded behind his closed eyes as the potent scents filled his mouth with saliva. His body *wanted* him to eat the thing as much or more so than any other natural treasure he'd been exposed to. Wondering if he'd be able to control himself long enough to get the meat away from the shell, he contemplated the best way to open it.

Not being a nut connoisseur, nor having any of the tools such a person might employ, he simply shrugged and crunched it with his powerful fingers. Desire instantly clouded his judgment as the true nature of the seed's potent flesh made itself apparent. The heady scent made him swoon as the world tilted sideways and began to dip. He felt as if he were hanging upside down from a strangely undulating amber ore platform. With a concerted effort of will, Victor ignored the weird sensations and nearly overwhelming hunger that had seized his guts.

Focusing on the feel of the broken shell in his fist, he carefully opened his hand, almost surprised when the fragments of shell and meat didn't fly off into the spinning, warped, psychedelic landscape that had overtaken his senses. He felt nausea and hunger simultaneously. He was dizzy and euphoric at once. Still, he narrowed his eyes and stared at his hand, forcing himself to focus on the strange white meat surrounded by crunched, broken, near-black shell.

Delicately, with forefinger and thumb, Victor painstakingly pulled the shell fragments away from the meat and then, before he lost himself in the hallucinatory haze the aroma had struck him with, he plopped it into his mouth. He experienced a fraction of a second of euphoria as he bit into it and swallowed. Then his consciousness was thrown from his body, whirling away into the universe on waves of chromatic light that buoyed him, cradling his psychic projection as it hurtled into another reality.

Xolotlkan stood atop the verdant hill, the sun's heat soaking into the flesh of his broad, scarred back. He watched as, a hundred thousand strides distant, Tlalquemeh sank to his mighty knees, flattening the jungle beneath his enormous girth.

"He will sleep," Tzitzimani said, her voice hushed as she came to stand beside him.

Xolotlkan looked at her, his heart filling with pride at her beauty. Her hair was like the feathers of ravens, and her eyes were brighter and more lustrous than the purest gold. She was marked by the battle, her flesh slowly pulling itself together to leave fine scars from her many wounds. Beneath the black warpaint that covered her eyes, her chin and lips were dark with drying blood, evidence of the heart she'd already feasted upon. "Will he sleep or will he die?"

She looked at him with narrowed eyes, her lips twisting in a way that was almost derisive. "He cannot die!"

"Just because he has always been does not mean he will always be." Visions of Tlalquemeh's battle flashed through Xolotlkan's mind's eye. He saw the dragons as they landed on the primordial titan's back, digging their claws into his flesh, emptying their lungs of acid and fire. He saw the great being's blood and heard his roars of fury and pain. Then he saw him hurl the dragons to the horizon or into the earth, carving canyons through mountains and displacing entire lakes with the impacts.

Tzitzimani sighed, her voice quiet and a little morose as she replied, "His life is sad. He misses his love, and the only time he wakes is to fight those who challenge him. Perhaps he wants to die."

Xolotlkan looked past Tlalquemeh to the purple slopes of the great mountain, Ocelhuatzin—the burial site of the primordial titan's love. "Is she dead?"

"My mother tells me she sleeps. When her heartache grows too heavy to bear, that is when her tears flow like fire."

"She weeps for her children," Xolotlkan agreed. "Are we Quinametzin not enough for her? My father says his grandmother could trace her lineage to Ocelhuatzin."

Tzitzimani took his hand in hers and leaned her soft cheek into his sun-hot shoulder. "Love is a strange thing."

"And us? If I ever feel sorrow like Tlalquemeh"—he nodded toward the slumped, kneeling figure on the horizon—"then I would rather die."

"You're too small to have feelings that big!" she teased, tilting her chin so her lips were there, waiting for his kiss. Of course, he obliged, leaning slightly to press his lips to hers. Savoring the sweet scents of blood and rose oil.

"I feel much," he grunted, reaching a hand around to her back, groping downward for the soft flesh beneath her supple leather leggings. She pushed him, pulling away from his eager grasp.

"Always so hungry for my flesh after a battle! You must feast on other flesh, though! You have hearts to claim. If you ever hope to be half as great as that one"—it was her

turn to nod toward Tlalquemeh—"then you must seize every opportunity to nourish your body and spirit."

Xolotlkan folded his arms over his chest and peered toward the ancient titan. "Is it possible? My father, my grandfather, even my grandfather's grandfather—none of them have approached such might. Are we too far diluted from his ancient blood?"

Tzitzimani stepped close again, resting her fingers lightly at the nape of his neck, gently scratching the short hairs there with her sharp nails. "His blood is in us—his blood and many other great ones, besides. We must cultivate and awaken it. We must grow strong from the hearts of our foes. We must gather the Tonalolia in our heart-suns, and we must find and claim the treasures of the world. Our parents and grand-parents are great, but we will be greater. Let their wisdom be our stepping stones to move beyond them."

Xolotlkan turned away from the sorrowful titan and looked down at his wife. "I am too lucky, Tzitzi. I am too lucky to have you. Why would you spend your time with this worthless one?" He smiled as he spoke, knowing she'd protest.

"Hush, Xolo!" Her use of his pet name made his heart thump, skipping a beat. "You're the greatest of our generation. I'm the lucky one."

"We're both lucky." He put his arm over her shoulder and pulled her into him, squeezing her tightly. "Tlalquemeh claimed most of the kills, but you're right. I have three dragon hearts to feast upon. Will you join me as I claim them?"

Victor floated in darkness, but he wasn't cognizant of himself. For a long time he struggled to separate himself from Xolotlkan. For what seemed an eternity, he yearned for Tzitzi's gentle touch. If he'd had eyes to see with, they would have been blinded by endless tears. If he'd had a heart to ache, it would have torn asunder as he experienced hopeless loneliness and loss. Gradually, though, pieces of the puzzle that was *Victor* began to fall into place, supplanting the memories and essence of Xolotlkan.

He began to recall his own life—his mother and the crushing loss of her; his *abuela* and the love and support she gave him; his struggles to fit in and, just as he was finding his place, his rude, unexpected departure from Earth. He recalled the battles he fought, the friends he made and lost, and more than any-thing, he felt the rich, surging love that boiled in his heart, eager to be shared. He saw Thayla, Chandri, and Teil; his thoughts even lingered on Kynna for a while.

Then his mind came round to an image that had been on the periphery, slowly working its way toward the focal point. He saw Valla, and his nonexistent heart swelled as if it would burst. As he remembered their time together, color entered his void in streaks and bursts, only to be washed away by more grim darkness as he recalled her decision to separate. Then, on a wisp of a breeze that swirled out of nowhere, came the flickering, hope-filled image of a blonde-haired woman. She ran ahead of him, looking over her shoulder, laughing as the wind tossed her ribbon-strewn hair and colorful skirts.

"Tes," he grunted, though with what mouth and what vocal cords, he had no idea. The hope she gave his poor, battered heart was palpable, but he wondered—was it real? Hadn't she left him, too? Wasn't his love unrequited? He had so much to give, so much to *share*. Why couldn't it ever work out? Despondency reasserted itself, and he pushed thoughts of women and love away, dwelling in the empty void and content not to think.

He drifted for another eternity, no longer Xolotlkan, but not exactly Victor, either. He'd pushed them both away, and he was content with nothing. Why shouldn't he be? The void didn't hurt or ache. It was nothing.

After a minute or a million years, a voice drifted to him, familiar and foreign, *"What a strange place to find you again. I thought I was alone with my thoughts, but here you are. What strange threads of fate have tied us together through eons and galaxies? Are you, too, seeking solitude?"*

Victor racked his fractured, neglected memories for the voice; finally it clicked, and he thought, *"Chantico?"*

"Oh, are you so far gone? Your thoughts are sluggish."

"I'm . . . not sure what I am."

"Do you seek this void, or are you lost?"

"I had a vision. I saw my ancestors, I think. No, I was my ancestor."

"Oh? Something interesting at last! Tell me of your vision, little brother."

"I . . . I was Xolotlkan, and I knew happiness and love . . ." Victor let himself relive his brief time as the ancient Quinametzin. As he described his feelings and the loss, he began to understand why it had affected him so profoundly. He hadn't only stood in Xolotlkan's shoes for a few minutes, he'd *been* Xolotlkan. He'd felt everything in his life, including his love for Tzitzimani.

"How cruel!" Chantico cooed. *"To feel such love and then have it ripped away? But why not embrace your true self?"*

"I started to, but then I remembered my own failed loves." The words came easily. Victor hadn't consciously realized how stubborn he'd been, how he'd pushed himself away and embraced the nothingness.

"Ah, the heart. When spears, blades, and clubs fail to break us, sometimes we do the work for them, hmm?"

"Yeah, I guess . . ."

"You guess? What a strange young titan you are! Perhaps it's your big heart and desire to love that binds us. I, too, suffered many terrible heartaches over the years. Yes, perhaps that is the thread that ties me to you. I sense a kindred spirit in you, more than our blood ties. What else ails you? Why do you hide away in this void?"

"Why do you?" Victor fired back.

"Oho! Fair enough. Let the elder share first, hmm? I seek solitude to contemplate my existence. Long have I toiled for more and more power. Long have I loved and lost. I've ascended through more than one veil, little brother. Now I wonder if it's time to forget some of this. Perhaps it's time to start anew. Such weighty decisions require peace and clarity of thought. Your intrusion was unexpected, but I can't blame you for fate and karmic ties. I wonder, was I simply meant to advise you on matters of the heart?"

"I don't think so. I, um, didn't find this void purposefully. I have a curse . . ." Victor haltingly called up and recited the memories necessary to share his problem with Chantico. Though she didn't speak, he could feel her presence. A *thing* in the nothingness. A weight and warmth where nothing should exist.

When he finished, he heard her click her tongue. *"I remember now. I spoke to you about this centuries ago, did I not?"*

If Victor had a mouth, he would have smiled. *"To me it was just a few days."*

"Time moves strangely for me as I drift. My mind is free, unfettered by physical laws, much as yours is now. Let me think. What did I tell you before? You asked me why the void would not harm me, and I said I made a fortress of myself. Was that not helpful?"

"It feels like a dream, big sister." Victor wasn't sure why he called her that, other than she was calling him little brother, and he liked it. *"It's not clear to me. I had trouble remembering your words."*

"Well, you'll remember this time, provided I can help you to get home. I said to make yourself strong—unbreakable. I told you to seek out that which does so. I don't mean to speak in riddles, but I don't know you enough to tell you the answer. I begin to think I have a clue, however. Victor, when you set yourself adrift in this void, was it your curse that sent you here?"

"No . . ."

"Was it fear of responsibility or, worse, fear of a foe?"

"No . . ."

"Was it fear of death?"

"No!"

"No, little brother, it was your poor, wounded heart. When you awaken, ruminate on that for a while."

"How will I—"

"Hush. Let your big sister do something for you. Follow my voice." With that, Chantico began to sing. It was a beautiful melody, otherworldly and devoid of language, but full of meaning. The sound drifted away, and he strained to listen, following it without thought. The song evoked images of grassy meadows dappled with wildflowers of every shape and color. He felt the sun's heat, good and right, and he heard the laughter of children as they played.

Drifting through nothingness, pulled along by Chantico's hauntingly beautiful voice, Victor's self-imposed isolation faded as his spirit, his *self*, found his body and slipped back home. Instantly, he was wracked with horrific pain, and his eyes snapped open.

He was lying on his back, the smooth dome of his cultivation chamber high above him. His chest burned with near-blinding, scalding pain as his nerves were endlessly devoured, regrown, and devoured again. With a grunt, Victor lifted his head and peered past the System message in his eyes, trying to get a look at the void. His eyes widened with horror when he saw it. No longer the size of a marble, the black ball of nothingness sat in a baseball-sized hole in his sternum. "*Pinché* son of a bitch," he hissed, lying back down.

Trying to tune out the pain, to find the place where he could ignore it in his mind, he focused on the System messages:

*****Congratulations! Your Quinametzin Bloodline has advanced to Epic 6.*****

Victor laughed bitterly, shaking his head. "All that for one *fucking* rank." With a grunt and an inadvertent gasp of pain, he struggled to a sitting position. His shirt was open, unbuttoned, which reminded him that he'd been wearing a shirt *without* buttons that he'd ripped open before eating the magical seed. Someone had changed his shirt. He looked to his cultivation chamber's vault-like door and saw it was closed tight.

Taking a deep breath, bracing himself for more pain, Victor prepared to stand, but stopped. The air in the chamber was absolutely *thick* with Energy attuned to magma and blue ice. He could feel it almost like when Mount Ember had erupted and the magma had hung heavy in the air. How long had the Energy been gathering? How long had he been lying there?

His pain forgotten, Victor surged to his feet and walked to the vault door, slapping his hand on the lock. It clicked open, and he pushed the door wide. His workshop had changed. A bed had been moved into it and someone had installed a sink and toilet, along with wood-framed silk screens to wall off the little bedroom from the far door.

He didn't have to wonder who had done it for long. A muffled yawn sounded from the piles of bedding, and a moment later, a bleary-eyed Bryn sat up. When she saw him standing in the doorway of the cultivation chamber, she leaped to her feet. She was clad in her uniform pants and an undershirt, and Victor wondered if she always slept in her clothes. "Victor! Your Grace!"

He nodded, grimacing as the pain in his chest surged. "Bryn. What the hell is going on?" He gestured to her bed.

"I found it easier to keep an eye on your chamber from here. After the first month—"

"*Month?* How long have I been out?"

She didn't look him in the eyes, fidgeting a little as she stepped closer to her boots. "Nearly six months, Your Grace."

"*Six months?*" Victor hissed, stepping out of the cultivation chamber's doorway and slamming the massive door shut with a thunderous clang. "Six fucking months?" he asked, with a little less vehemence.

Bryn nodded, slipping her feet into her boots. "We feared it would be longer—nothing changed for so long, Your Grace."

"Will you cut that shit? Why are you being so formal?"

"I—" Bryn shook her head, sighing. "I don't know. I suppose with the passage of time, I've built you up in my mind. I'm just so happy that you've risen. Kynna has been measuring your curse, and as it grew, she became . . ." She trailed off, shaking her head. "She despaired." Suddenly her eyes flew wide and she hissed, "Victor! You have to hurry! She and Arona are meeting with the Queen of Kuria. They're negotiating terms for the duel!"

Victor glowered. "Lead the way, Bryn, but start talking. What the *hell* do you mean she and Arona are negotiating terms?"

Bryn grabbed her glaive and ran for the door. Victor hurried after her, his pain, his vision of Xolotlkan, even his conversation with Chantico forgotten. All he knew was that there was no damn way he was going to let Arona fight a duel for him, especially if it was Queen Livessa—House Kuria was one of the true "great" houses. Something had to have happened to bring her to the table.

He didn't have to speculate. As they ran to his elevator, Bryn said, "Somehow word got out that you were incapacitated. Rumors at first, but Queen Kynna thinks the veil walkers let the truth out. An assassination attempt was made." She paused to open the elevator. "But Arona was there and foiled it. When word spread that the queen was attacked and you were nowhere to be found, Livessa issued a challenge."

"Why didn't the queen refuse?" Victor slammed his fist onto the button to lower his elevator.

"She played coy, agreeing to the duel, but scheduling it for nearly four months into the future. She thought you'd surely be awake by then."

Victor growled, his pathways filling with rage as he waited for the elevator to descend. "What time is the meeting?"

"Noon. I think we have time. We can teleport directly to the arena complex; they're meeting on neutral ground."

As the doors opened and Victor took the lead, jogging through the palace to the portal room, he could hear Bryn sprinting behind him. He wanted more information, but he needed to hurry. He was furious at Arona for sticking her neck out, but he was also worried and guilty. It was *his* fault he'd taken so long.

He'd lingered in his void of nothingness for a long time. If Chantico hadn't found him . . . He didn't want to dwell on it. He was *lucky*. He was lucky that something was tying his fate to hers or vice versa.

"We'll see how lucky," he growled, sprinting down the long subterranean corridor to the portal room. He blew past several guard posts, but their stammered challenges and halting greetings fell on deaf ears. Victor was lost in his urgency. When the door to the portal room was in sight, he cast Tactical Reposition, snapping into existence among six startled guards.

He threw the door aside, strode into the chamber, and, seeing the heavily guarded crackling portal already open, strode toward it, brushing aside the guards who didn't move out of his way quickly enough. "Sorry, soldiers. I'm in a hurry," he grunted as he practically dove into the portal.

29

⚜

CONFRONTATION

Arona shifted in her seat, trying to remain impassive but wholly unnerved by the presence of the Death Caster standing behind Queen Livessa. When Queen Kynna told her about the meeting to discuss terms, Arona hadn't been sure what to expect. She'd come in and sat beside the queen, and Kynna hadn't mentioned that, apparently, champions often stood behind the head of state. Drok the *Skull* certainly did, and it was readily apparent where he got his name. His head bore no flesh.

Sitting there, under the gaze of the baleful red orbs that served as his eyes, Arona cursed herself for insisting Kynna ignore Victor's admonition, adamant that she take Arona on as a champion in his stead. As the deadline for the duel drew closer, first months away, then weeks, and Victor still lay unconscious, Arona had contemplated a hundred ways to extricate him from this situation. She'd planned routes by which she might abscond with him—servants she could bribe to help her carry and hide him from view.

She thought perhaps she could get him to the System Stone in Gloria. She had plenty of funds with which to pay the System's exorbitant teleportation fees. Of course, it would have been simple if Victor had left her in charge of the portal array. Unfortunately, like all of his treasures, it was locked away in his dimensional containers, accessible only to him. It didn't matter, though; she'd failed to act, too worried that he'd wake in a fury, stung by her betrayal in allowing his efforts on Ruhn to fall to ruin.

Of course, it hadn't helped that she'd been hopeful, up until the very last day, that he'd awaken. She'd dreamed that he'd come out of his deep hibernation with some miraculous answer to his curse, stronger than ever, ready for the duel. What a fool she'd been! Was it the solar Energy at her Core? If she'd had her death-attuned Energy influencing her, she would have been far more pragmatic!

It also hadn't helped that she'd developed quite a friendship with Kynna. The months she'd spent with her, getting to know the ins and outs of her court, had opened Arona's eyes to Kynna's truly *good* nature. She was kind to her people and hopelessly naive to the schemes of the nobility, including her own relatives. Seeing the makings of more than one assassination plot, Arona felt the need to step in and help Kynna see what her heart hid from her. More than one of Kynna's cousins and an uncle had been banished as a result.

It was natural, then, as the day approached and Victor still slumbered, for Arona to step up and offer to stand in his place. Of course, Kynna had other champions, but Arona had taken their measure, and she knew she was stronger. Victor and Trobban had seen to it that her Core was powerful—easily a match for her old one. More than that, Arona had been driven by a cruel but talented master for nearly a century. She knew how to battle, and some of her new solar spells, converted from her epic-tier Death Caster spells, were rare and unnaturally effective.

She was not yet a steel seeker, but Arona had nearly been the match of Ronkerz's Big One. She was stronger now, wasn't she? She should be able to stand against a Death Caster. Wasn't solar-attuned Energy particularly effective against the undead? That was what she'd *thought*. Back when she'd learned that Livessa's champion was a Death Caster, she'd been quite confident and had conveyed that confidence to Kynna. Now, though, in the presence of Drok the Skull, she didn't feel much death-attuned Energy. What she felt was pure, abject terror.

Drok was, indeed, undead, and he definitely had the grave-like aura of death about him, but it was *clearly* a secondary affinity. He absolutely *oozed* terror. Poor Kynna had been beset by trembling fits as she reviewed the terms of the duel, struggling to complete sentences, her eyes wide and fearful. Livessa was perfectly at ease, of course. She sat, beautiful and regal, in her chair, calmly clarifying the terms she offered for the duel.

"As you know, Kynna"—they had agreed to forego titles early on—"I'm offering you banishment. We of the great houses are impressed by you. We don't want to snuff out your potential. What a show you've put on! That being said, you've already agreed to this duel. We've set the date; this meeting is a mere formality. Your reluctance to sign this final agreement will not protect you from the wrath of the veil walkers. If your champion isn't in that arena tomorrow morning, the terms will be upheld regardless. The veil walkers are on my side in this matter."

"Yes, I understand, Livessa. We agreed to a duel, and all I'm asking for is another few months to put my house in order." Kynna had gone over her strategy with Arona. She'd stall for time, using her very real fear and doubt to convey a grudging acceptance of her fate. The more time she could buy, the greater the chance Victor would recover. Livessa wasn't giving an inch, however.

"A few months? What do you hope to accomplish in that time? Judicator Wesper is here, Kynna. She knows the strife the people of our empire are enduring because of your succession war. She knows that every day people go hungry. Every day trade suffers and wealth is lost. Bandits feed on our contested borders, our usual peacekeeping forces unable to respond. This cannot continue. Wesper will see this document signed, or you will face worse than banishment."

Kynna licked her lips, a trembling hand turning the pages of the terms. Arona could sympathize; Drok the Skull's presence was overwhelming, even for her. The waves of terror hit on a visceral level, making the flesh of her new hands clammy, her mouth dry. Dead Gods! Why did Trobban make such a perfectly vital vessel? Could he not have given her more control over the emotions of her new mind? She knew he couldn't have. She wouldn't have been *her*. Even her spiritual projection had carried with it her emotions and quirks. Without allowing their transference into a new vessel, she would have struggled with the shock of the duality—a separation of her old self and the new. Death Casters often went mad from such incomplete transfers.

"If you could just see your way to understanding—"

Kynna's latest objection was cut short as the door behind them flew open. As Arona shifted her gaze to look toward the disturbance, the veil walker Livessa had mentioned, Judicator Wesper, appeared at the head of the table and held up her right, gauntleted hand. "Everyone, remain still. I will not have violence at this meeting."

At her words, Arona found her body locked, held tightly by the force of the veil walker's will. She could still see the door, though, and, despite Wesper's command, an enormous figure stooped low to duck under the lintel, stepping into the room. It was Victor.

The people of Ruhn were large folk, nearly all of them between ten and eleven feet in height. Therefore, the doors were usually around thirteen feet high to accommodate them with plenty of space to spare. Victor, even standing with a forward-leaning stoop and doing a poor job of hiding his pain, had to be close to fifteen feet tall. It had been a while since Arona had seen him on his feet, especially at his true size, so the sight of him like that—gaunt, eyes sunken and shadowed, straining against the veil walker's aura—was a little shocking.

"How dare you defy my will?" Wesper asked, stepping closer to Victor. She was an imposing woman, clad in gleaming silver plate studded with diamond-like gems that seemed to find every stray particle of light and reflect it a thousand times over. Her helm had great azure wings that swooped back and undulated as if they were alive. They echoed the blazing blue of her eyes, which at the moment were narrowed in anger.

"You asked for no violence," Victor said, grinding the words out through clenched teeth. "I intend none."

"I asked for people to be *still*. Why do you intrude on this meeting?"

"I am Queen Kynna's champion. I'm here to relieve that petite woman beside her."

Suddenly, a dark wave of terror emanated from the other side of the room. It was like a curtain of nightmares, sounds, and *things* that Arona couldn't and wouldn't name. She found her heart racing as her poor body tried to both obey Wesper and flee from Drok the Skull. The undead champion had pushed closer to the table, straining against Wesper's command. His eyes blazed with brimstone fires as a deep snarl emanated from his skeletal mouth, echoing and reinforcing the nightmares brought about in his aura.

Kynna swooned, falling forward onto the table, her mind unable to cope. Livessa, too, was affected, her mad dog of a champion apparently failing to keep her out of the waves of dark terror rolling out of him. She began to whimper, unable to speak or flee, thanks to Wesper's powerful will, but so blasted by Drok's nightmarish Energy that tears rolled like rivulets down her cheeks.

Victor seemed unbothered. He leaned forward, towering over the veil walker, but rather than a threat or a promise to behave, he said, "You should control that guy. I'm just here to watch Kynna sign her contract. He seems to want a fight."

Wesper whirled on Drok, and when her gaze was squarely directed toward his fiery-eyed skull, the flames dimmed, and he stumbled back. "*Be still!*" she hissed, and the waves of terror immediately faded. Arona let out a long, shaky sigh. When Wesper swung her gaze back to Victor, the fury on her beautiful face was palpable. It rolled off her in the waves of her aura and either it was enough to cow Victor, or he thought he ought to show some respect, because he bowed his head and didn't move.

Wesper glared around the table, and when her eyes rested on Arona, she jerked her head to the door. "Wait without." Suddenly, the bonds of the veil walker's iron will fell away, and Arona was free to move. She pushed her chair back and hurried out, hardly sparing a glance for Victor. He didn't look at her, but she could see his breaths were ragged, his eyes squeezed shut. It had cost him to fight the veil walker's will—that or his curse was paining him terribly.

She stood in the hallway, pressing her back to the wall beside the door. She breathed heavily, glad to be away from Drok and out of the veil walker's focus. She was hopeful the door would be left open, but it slammed, and she was left in the dark.

As the door slammed, Victor felt the veil walker's aura retract and the terrible weight on his own will fell away, allowing him to properly resist the curse again.

The knot of void Energy destroying his chest shrank back enough for him to breathe without agony, enough for his heart to beat without shredding with each outward expansion. He'd wondered if he could live with the void touching his heart, and he'd just learned that he could, though every second was torture.

He could feel his flesh knitting, gaining ground on the curse, at least for now. How much had it cost him, though? How much bigger was the void than when he'd walked into this room? It didn't feel much worse than when he'd awakened in his cultivation chamber, but he supposed he'd have to look at it to be sure—after all, pain was relative. He opened his eyes and looked up, only to see the veil walker glaring at him. Her expression was as much puzzled as angry.

"You're not well," she said, clicking her tongue.

"I'm fine."

She didn't respond to him, but her eyes said she knew he was full of shit. She turned back to the table, and Victor did as well. Kynna was sitting up, rubbing her forehead, clearly disoriented. Victor was pretty sure she'd fainted under the onslaught of the Death Caster's aura. He looked at the other champion, unable to keep the amusement from glinting in his eyes. What a *creepy* son of a bitch! The other queen, Livessa, was also out of sorts, hastily working to hide the tears that smeared the makeup around her eyes.

"This disturbance is unacceptable," the veil walker said. "I'm of a good mind to bar both of these champions from battle tomorrow. It would be within my rights to put off this duel and force both of your houses to find new champions." Livessa started to speak, but the veil walker held up a finger. "However, the council of which I am a member, those of us who watch over this beautiful world, grow weary of this conflict, and we are eager to see it progress toward its inevitable end. That said, I will allow you to make good on your promise, Queen Kynna, and sign this agreement so these two champions can settle things in the arena at dawn."

Kynna looked up at Victor, her crystalline eyes moist with unshed tears, clearly still bothered by what she'd felt from Drok. She looked confused to see him and was clearly unsure how to proceed. Despite his pain and exhaustion, Victor smiled and nodded. Trying to portray confidence. With a shaky hand, Kynna picked up the pen and scrawled her signature on the document before her.

"*Ha!*" Drok laughed, his voice unnatural and hollow as it emerged from his fleshless mouth. "*Ha!*" he repeated, turning to open the door and glide out, his black, feather-covered robes obscuring the movements of his limbs. Livessa stood and frowned at Victor, but then she turned to Kynna. "Make peace with your people, Kynna. Tomorrow, they'll be my subjects." She turned and swept from the room, trailing a dozen feet of silken material behind her gown. Victor saw servants outside the door stoop to pick it up and hurry after her.

"Champion?" the veil walker said, staring intently at Victor until he brought his gaze around to her.

"Yes?"

"You would be wise not to challenge a judicator's will again. Such defiance after the events that occurred at your last duel cannot be tolerated."

"You mean when I saved Lohanse?"

"You *aided* Grand Judicator Lohanse, yes. This is precisely why I have allowed you to go unpunished for your actions today." She glared at him for a long few seconds, then let her gaze fall to his chest, where his shirt hung loosely over the ball of void Energy. "Make your peace, Victor. I believe your time on this world is near an end." The air shimmered around her, and then she was gone.

"Victor!" Kynna said, pushing her chair back and shakily standing.

"My Queen," he said, wincing as he straightened up. When she walked toward him, Victor was suddenly aware that he was his full natural size. He wasn't used to looking so far down to meet her gaze, so he concentrated momentarily and cast Alter Self, reducing himself to twelve and a half feet or so—just short enough to clear the doorways without ducking.

"Elder gods! We feared you'd never awaken. How fortunate you did so just as we prepared for the duel!"

"Hmm. Fortune? Fate? Some divine intervention? I don't know what to call it, but yeah, I guess it's a good thing." Victor could *feel* Arona's presence on the other side of the door, so he stepped over and pulled it wide. She stood close, clearly trying to hear what was happening. When she saw Victor, she peered past him.

"They're gone?"

"Yes," Kynna replied. "I signed the paper, Arona. How can . . ." She shook her head, unable to voice what she was thinking. "If you flee, they may still allow my family to escape with banishment."

"Oh, stop it." Victor chuckled. "You think I can't kill that *pinché* Death Caster?"

"Victor," Arona hissed. "Did you not feel? He's more than a Death Caster! He has a powerful spirit affinity. The terror—"

She broke off her words as Victor chuckled. He would have laughed more robustly if not for the pain in his chest. "I forget; you weren't there when I beat your team, were you?"

"My team?" Arona looked at him, puzzled, for several seconds, and then her eyes widened. "In the challenge dungeon! Before you broke the place, you turned into a dark, winged creature! I saw it in the recording Vesavo took!"

"Heh. Yeah, something like that." Victor put one broad hand behind Kynna's shoulders and ushered her toward the door. "Anyway, don't worry about me with that guy. He's strong, and I'm very glad he won't be fighting you, Arona, but don't worry about me."

As they walked away from the meeting room toward the portal chamber, Victor teased Arona, "I can't believe you're not a steel seeker yet. I gave you *six months* to get ahead. Did you make any levels?"

"Victor!" Kynna whirled on him, her eyebrows drawing down angrily. "Do *not* tease her. She saved my life from assassins, and before that, she helped me to root out corruption in my court."

"Oh?" Victor turned to Arona. "You were advising the queen? Maybe Dar doesn't need to send anyone to fill that role—" He cut himself off as he remembered six months had passed since he'd looked in any of his Far Scribe books. "Shit! *Did* Dar send anyone?"

Kynna shook her head. "Not yet. He's slow about anything. He moves in years, not weeks or months."

Victor nodded, rubbing his chin. "I need to read my Far Scribe books. Arona, I guess you're off the hook for your slow advancement."

She smiled half-heartedly, but Kynna wasn't having any of it. "Your levity is out of place! Arona and I—everyone!—were worried to the point of madness. I was sitting in that room ten minutes ago, suffering under the weight of that foul, skull-faced demon's evil aura, preparing to sign away everything and everyone I care about. Arona was bracing herself for the possibility of a duel to the death with him. Now you're here, suddenly, and things are naught but a jest!" She stepped to the side, grabbed his shirt, and forced him to stop walking and look at her. "Do you understand?"

Victor liked to think he was an understanding guy. He could put himself in others' shoes pretty easily. Nevertheless, he was in pain, and he wasn't exactly happy with things, either. When she scolded him like that, his tongue got away from him, and he said exactly what he was thinking. "I get it, Kynna. I get it more than you think. I ate a damn *nut* that you gave me, and then I went through a fucking mental trip that took six months. I woke up with *one* more rank in my bloodline and found out everything I'd worked for on this world was about to be lost. I *ran* here, by the way, with a void curse eating my goddamn heart out, so, yeah, give me a little while to come to grips, all right?"

He pulled his shirt free from her hand and stalked down the hallway. He could see Bryn ahead, standing by the door to the portal room. He heard Arona, clear as day, say, "He suffers, Kynna. Don't blame him."

Kynna was just as easy to hear as they followed him. "That's the thing: I blame myself. I should put a stop to this whole war."

Sighing heavily, Victor stopped again and turned to face the two women. "This might be a blessing in disguise."

"How could it be?" Kynna asked, her eyes moist again.

"If we were the ones pushing the duels, how many would I have had to fight to get to Kuria?"

Kynna sniffed, looking to the side, avoiding his eyes. She'd clearly had this thought before—likely back when the duel was offered and she had been confident Victor would awaken. "This has saved us seven duels against the great houses," she said. "If we beat Livessa, we'll be on the doorstep of House Khaliday."

Victor smiled. "I'm feeling better about those lost six months already. Think about that! Two fights, and I'm done."

"Victor, you big, bombastic fool." She sighed, clicking her tongue. "Drok the Skull stood against that veil walker just as you did. He's a thousand-year-old monster who's purposefully steel bound. Khaliday wouldn't have allowed Kuria to come to me with a duel if there was a chance he could lose."

Victor stared at her, ready to cuss and fume. How many times was she going to doubt him? Drok the Skull might be a monster, he might have come from off-world, but they'd known about him the last time they'd had this discussion, hadn't they? Even Tes had warned him about the "monstrous Death Caster" she'd seen. Still, everyone had been on board with him pushing ahead with the duels then, right? Were they losing faith because of the curse? Looking at her, he had to ask himself why he cared. Why was he pushing this stupid conquest?

What was driving him? Was it a desire to see Dar's request that his descendant rule this world fulfilled? No, he didn't give a shit about that. Was it some misguided loyalty to Kynna? A desire to put her on a throne she didn't really want all that much? No, that wasn't it either. He wasn't entirely sure about the conquest, but he knew about this duel. "Listen, Kynna," he growled. "That piece of shit challenged me in there. He fucking *laughed*. If I have to fly my ass to Kuria, I'm going to kill him, so you might as well let me fight him in the arena. As for House Khaliday, we can talk about that when I'm done."

Kynna stared at him, her eyes wide at his vehemence. After a few seconds, she nodded and pressed her lips together firmly. "I, too, would like to see that demon brought low."

Arona stepped beside her, resting her delicate little fingers on Kynna's forearm. "I'll add my support for that, too."

"Then," Victor said with a fresh grin, "I will gladly present his skull to you both."

30

TERROR

Grand Prince Troyssas sat in his box, high on the northern wall of the arena, his throne-like seat overlooking the spectacle with a vantage no other could boast. To his left, halfway down to the sands, was the box where his distant cousin, Queen Livessa, sat with her retinue. On the other side was the upstart, Queen Kynna. The two women were impressive, but Troyssas didn't have eyes for them. He watched the strange champion, Victor, as he swayed on the sands, seemingly unsteady on his feet.

He stood hunched, his tall, muscular frame encased in powerful artifacts. His brow hid his eyes as he leaned forward, but the dark circles surrounding them were apparent. His bronze flesh glimmered with a sheen of sweat, and his mouth hung partially open as he took short, pain-filled breaths. Even his mighty axe resembled a crutch more than a weapon as he leaned heavily on the haft.

"What ails him?" Troyssas rumbled, his voice like falling boulders as it emerged from his chest.

Savinicus, his Master of Revels, was quick to respond, "None know, Highness. He was missing for months. Some speculate that he suffered some mortal malady in his battle with Loss Chenasta."

"How can we not know?" Troyssas pouted. "Do we not employ the best spy masters in the world?"

"Naturally, Highness; however, if none know, then even the best spies cannot suss out the truth of the matter."

"Well, it's good that he will die, but I had hoped to be entertained." Troyssas hadn't wanted Livessa to issue the challenge. He hadn't believed the champion had died or been replaced like so many had insisted. Even if he *had* been, why should they rush things? Plenty of champions in the great houses might have killed Kynna's champion, whoever he or she may be. Why put Drok on the sands? If the unthinkable happened and he lost, Khaliday would be exposed.

Troyssas swung his enormous arm to his left, jostling Carpecus's seat. "Well? You're my chief advisor—advise!"

"Grand Highness, Queen Livessa is as astute as she is striking, and her unwavering faith in Drok the Skull remains unshaken. I am confident that today's duel will decisively quell this regrettable insurrection. With the downfall of Kynna Dar's house, we may commence the arduous yet necessary task of reaffirming the allegiance of the lesser nations to House Khaliday."

"You'll stake your life on it?"

"I, um, well, no, Highness, such bravery is beyond a simple administrator like myself. Why, I would—"

"Be still." Troyssas waved his arm, sending the man cowering into silence. He leaned forward, pressing his chin into one thick fist, shifting his vision to the undead fiend who had come from off-world to serve Livessa. He was an imposing figure, certainly. "*Steel bound*," he muttered, remembering what Savinicus had told him about the fellow—a creature of conquest, a monstrously evil spirit that had subjugated a hundred worlds. He claimed to be steel bound by design and wanted to remain at that tier for various reasons. "Why?"

Savinicus was astute enough to know he was being spoken to but didn't understand the question. "P-pardon me, Highness?"

"Such tedium. Why? Why is the fool avoiding the veil?"

"Ah! Drok? He claims there are challenges, dungeons, worlds—like our own—where he'd be barred should he advance. He claims that he seeks to experience all he can before pushing himself beyond the reach of such places."

Troyssas gathered a wad of phlegm and spat to the side, unmindful of the servant who scurried forward to collect the precious bit of *him*, storing it away in a shielded dimensional container. "He sounds like a coward to me. He works himself to a pinnacle of power and then goes about smashing those still climbing the ladder. Of course he's accumulated an impressive tally of victories with such methods."

"That's certainly a valid viewpoint, Highn—"

"Do you patronize?"

"N-never, Highness!"

Troyssas waved a hand dismissing him, still observing the Death Caster as Grand Judicator Lohanse began his usual spiel. Drok was clad in dark robes adorned with glistening feathers. He looked more like a shaman than a proper champion for one of Ruhn's oldest, most powerful houses. Still, that skull was impressive, and he had a certain darkness about him, a strength of aura, that Troyssas could feel even from his seat, a thousand strides away. He tapped the control rune on his armrest, and the air wavered before his eyes, bringing his view closer.

Drok turned his skull-faced gaze directly toward him, the orbs in his eye sockets roiling with flames that promised pain and despair. To his shame, though he'd never admit it, Troyssas looked away, widening his perspective so he could see both champions at once. Again, he turned to his chief advisor. "My sister is prepared for every eventuality?"

"Naturally, Highness. Empress Matessa has plans within plans, and she was in close counsel with Queen Livessa prior to her issuing this challenge."

"Good." Troyssas couldn't imagine the sickly giant would win, but something about the man put him off—a discomfort of the mind that he wasn't accustomed to—and he didn't like it.

Victor stood on the sands, his mind wandering. The sounds of the crowd and Lohanse's long-winded speech were lost to him. He was fixated on the puzzle of his curse, and as he thought about it, he let his thoughts drift down mental roads toward his strange meeting with Chantico and her message to him. She'd said they'd met before and discussed his curse, but Victor only had vague dreamlike memories of that encounter. This more recent one, though, was vivid and clear.

He could hear their conversation as plain as day, even now, while the crowd roared, the wind howled with the horns, and the sands shook with the thuds of the great drums announcing the imminent commencement of the duel:

"Victor, when you set yourself adrift in this void, was it your curse that sent you here?"

"No . . ."

"Was it fear of responsibility or, worse, fear of a foe?"

"No . . ."

"Was it fear of death?"

"No!"

"No, little brother, it was your poor, wounded heart. When you awaken, ruminate on that for a while."

Ruminate. He'd sat up all night doing so. After all, why would he sleep? He'd just done so for six months. No, it would be a while before he once again allowed himself sleep. What was she talking about? His wounded heart? Love? Was he hiding from love? Is that why he'd failed to awaken? His heart? But . . . despite his struggles with love, he *still* loved. He still loved Valla. He still loved Tes. He still loved all the people he'd grown close to. He wouldn't hide from *that*, would he?

Cold shadows swirled around him, accompanied by the vague cackling of the Death Caster he'd met the day before. Had the fight begun? "That's right," Victor sighed, remembering the horns and drums. Waves of horrific Energy rolled over him—terror. He saw things that should have stopped his heart:

monstrous incarnations of his *abuela*—flesh sallow, eyes oozing maggots. His mother rushed at him, her face a skull-like mask of death, her limbs too long, tipped with razor claws.

Victor swatted them aside, smashing them with Lifedrinker. They were horrible, but he was all too familiar with the threads of fear that twisted his reality. He could feel and taste the Energy in the air. It was thick and rich; had Drok created some sort of terror domain? Shadows clutched at his ankles, roped around his neck, pulling him like a torture rack. Victor's thoughts were elsewhere, though, as he contemplated the fear.

Drok couldn't have known his mother and *abuela*. No, the spell he'd cast must have been designed to bring his own fears to life. "My fears . . ."

More monstrosities came at him out of the darkness—twisted versions of Valla and Tes, Edeya, Lam, and Deyni. They were corpses, broken and rotting, with jagged claws and teeth filed to points. They leaped at him, climbing his legs and torso, clawing at his flesh as the shadows pulled him taut. His armor was gone, somehow stripped from him by the same shadows that bound him. The corpses of his loved ones tore his flesh, scooping bits of him into their mouths.

The pain was immense, but Victor had felt pain. He'd felt constant agony for, apparently, more than half a year. He wondered if this torture and the sight of his loved ones in such a state was meant to break him. Was this a spell that Drok the Skull had used to conquer armies? Could he create a domain like this and allow his victims' fears to break their minds? Victor was more interested than horrified. Was this what he feared most?

Kynna clenched her fists, looking into the arena, horrified by the spectacle. Victor had hardly tried to fight! He'd smashed the first couple of horrors Drok summoned, but now he stood, stretched like a sacrifice, while more and more horrors crawled over his body, clawing at and feasting on his flesh. "What happened to his armor?" she whispered, looking at Arona, who sat close beside her.

"I . . ." Arona shook her head. "It can't be real. These must be phantasms, projections of Victor's subconscious. I say Victor's and not Drok's because I recognize some of those poor, broken creatures. What we see are manifestations from Victor's mind, twisted by Drok's terror-attuned magic."

"Is he helpless?" Bryn asked, far more comfortable addressing Arona than she ever had been Kynna herself.

Arona shook her head. "I don't know. Victor keeps many secrets, even from me. Look at his face, though. He doesn't look like a man being eaten alive by the corpses of his loved ones."

"Loved ones . . ." Kynna whispered, looking more closely at the undead creatures crawling over him—naked, rotting, ghoulish. "How awful!"

Meanwhile, the Death Caster stood exactly where he'd been when the duel began. His arms were uplifted, and dark shadows poured forth from them, filling the arena with the cloying reek of terror. If not for the veil walkers'—Lohanse had companions in attendance after the last duel's disastrous ending—magic, the power of their auras, shielding the spectators, Kynna was sure everyone would have fled by now. Even through their power, she could feel the stomach-turning twinge of fear. "And Victor is in the thick of it."

"Does he punish himself?" Bryn asked.

Kynna looked at her sharply. "What?"

"He lets those shadows pull him taut. His axe lies in the sand. His eyes are distant. Does he invite this torture?"

Kynna looked at Arona, wondering if the woman had some insight. She frowned, her pale eyebrows narrowing over her sparkling blue eyes. "I wish I knew."

Victor felt as though he was onto something. Why had Chantico been so insistent that fear drove his self-isolation in the void? Had she felt it? A piercing coldness entered his stomach, distracting him, and he looked down to see one of the terror manifestations—poor, sweet Deyni—pulling the flesh of his stomach aside with her clawed hands, stretching a bloody hole into which she could crawl. Something woke in Victor's chest at the sight. Hot anger began to flow into his pathways.

How did this bastard dare to mock and defile his mental image of Deyni like this? Was this supposed to break him? Was he supposed to be terrified? Should he fall to his knees and weep for the mercy of death? If that was the man's goal, he'd picked the wrong man to try it on. Victor was intimately familiar with fear. It was his strongest affinity, after all. The falseness of the horrors was plain to him. The idea that they would break him suddenly sparked something in his chest that began to cook with his indignation, boiling out of his mouth in a mirthless laugh.

"You think you know fear, *Death Caster*?" For even though Drok used terror, a spirit affinity, Victor could feel the cold touch of death laced in every one of the nightmare creatures and shadows that clung to him. He could taste the corruption of the grave in the thick, terror-attuned Energy in the air. "I can show you what pure fear is like."

Victor washed the rage from his pathways and opened himself to the broad band of fear-attuned Energy encompassing his Spirit Core. He let it flow like a river into his pathways, and then he shaped the pattern for Aspect of Terror. To someone observing, they might think Drok had finally broken through, that Victor was succumbing to his dark magic, for, indeed, shadows enveloped him.

They sprouted from the ground, his flesh, and the very air around him, swathing him in a ball of roiling darkness that spread into the arena.

Victor's fear-attuned shadows compounded the darkness of Drok's death-tinted terror, and the sun, barely peeking over the eastern edge of the enormous arena wall, seemed to dim as an unnatural chill fell on the arena, quieting the crowd as people hugged their arms close and murmured their unease.

As Victor's nightmarish alter ego manifested, trying to push his conscious mind into submission, he fought hard to keep some semblance of himself in control. The Aspect of Terror fought, but, in the end, it acquiesced. They were one—a duality—that would feast and slaughter together. So, as his body broke and twisted, reforming into something horrifying, Victor was aware of the process as he'd never been before. He knew that his understanding of the spell in the past had been wrong.

He wasn't becoming something that reflected the fears of his foes. No, he was creating a manifestation of eldritch terror, something that existed in the primal minds of most sapient creatures. Worse, the shadows that flowed from and with him would amplify the horror, bringing forth visions tailored to the minds of any being unfortunate enough to witness his presence.

As his bones snapped and twisted, reforming into wings, feathers, and scales, he sent out probing shadows to clutch Lifedrinker, drawing her into himself to form a beak and talons that would ruin his foes. He slipped free of the bonds Drok had worked so hard to weave; they were to him like water to a fish.

The nightmare creatures, the beings representing those he loved, were simply twisted bits of terror. He drew them in, pouring their Energy into his Core, strengthening himself. As his transformation completed, and the world became a gray plane inhabited by the brilliant spirits meant for his feasting, he lifted his great beak and shrieked, a sound amplified rather than muffled by the dense shadowy Energy that hung heavy in the arena air.

"Dead Gods!" Troyssas hissed, feeling something strange happening in his guts. What was that twisting, bubbling sensation?

"Highness, we should depart! That sound!" Savinicus was on his ass and he turned, scrabbling on all fours up the stairs toward the exit.

Troyssas scowled at him, then looked at his personal guards. They were on their feet, weapons ready, but they weren't as affected as his master of revels. It dawned on him then that Savinicus was a mere iron ranker. "Get him out of here," he said to Brinnit, the captain of his guard.

"Yes, Highness." She moved from the door to grab Savinicus by the collar, hauling him up and out of his private seating area.

Troyssas turned back to the arena, scowling. It had gotten so *dark*. "Was that screech something from Drok? Another of his terror creatures?"

"I've no idea, Highness," Carpecus replied.

Troyssas frowned, watching the roiling shadows. Another shriek split the air, twisting his guts further. Was that . . . Was that fear? "Impossible," he muttered. When Brinnit reappeared, he pointed toward the arena floor. "What makes that sound?"

"I believe it's Gloria's champion, Highness." She stepped toward the ledge of his boxed-in seating area, peering with her sharp, silver-lit eyes. "He's transformed into something terrible. A creature of shadow and scale. He—" She stepped back, gasping. "He's in the air! Look!"

Troyssas followed her pointing finger and saw a ball of shadows hurtling into the air, swooping in a slow, lazy arc. As he watched, the shadows began to stream behind it, filling the air with deep darkness that blotted out the sunlight entirely. For a moment, Troyssas caught a glimpse of a glowering, angular red eye, and the knot in his guts wound tighter. "Dead Gods," he hissed again, repeating a curse he seldom used—why should he remind himself that there are or were beings beyond his ken?

Victor reveled in the terror-thick air. He took it in, bolstering his Core, feasting on it. The brilliant spirit on the sands below was kind enough to continue making it, feeding him as he gathered his strength. As he swept through the air, amplifying and spreading the fear, blotting out the unpleasant light of the sun with his shadows, his eyes fell on the countless brilliant spirits surrounding him. They were ripe for harvesting.

He would reap their fear, and with it powering him, he'd rip a hole in the veil bridging the plane of nightmare with this world, creating a realm meant for—

A ball of icy death smashed into his wing, and he banked, shrieking again, turning his baleful gaze on the spirit below, the one who had been feeding him. It wielded death as readily as terror, it seemed. *"You first,"* he hissed, pumping his terrible wings and falling like a hawk on a mouse. More terror manifestations emerged from the brilliant, icy-blue spirit, but Victor only drew them in, shrieking his laughter as his prey fed him.

Then he was on the spirit, clutching limbs with talons, snapping his beak through metal and cloth, peeling away roiling, shadow-filled feathery robes. He pinned his prey to the sands and stared into its orange, hate-filled eyes, savoring the sensation as the hate and anger gave way to more fear. *"Yes!"* he hissed, drawing out the "s," as he pulled the fear and terror into his Core, discarding the death to fall like frost on the sand, inert and useless.

The Energy was so *rich*. His prey fed him directly from its Core; the spirit was made of terror already, and so, so much of it! It was filled with more terror, by far, than Victor's own Core held fear! He couldn't help the ecstatic joy as he screamed, howling in ecstasy as his fear-attuned Energy swelled and pulsed, pushing his Core up a steep cliff, climbing toward a breakthrough he was sure to reach—his prey wasn't even half-drained!

Even better, the waves of fear-laced shadows flowing out of him as he feasted and the echoes of his shrieks were having an effect on the tens of thousands of bright spirits around him. They bled their own fear and, like a vortex, that Energy began to spiral downward into him. He swelled, his nightmare form stretching, growing, looming over his victim. He pulled and pulled, greedy for the deep well of terror that lurked within it.

Victor knew he was slipping. He could feel the Aspect of Terror trying to assert itself. Part of him wanted to let it. He felt *good* for the first time in months. His pain was a tiny thing, a minor annoyance easily ignored, next to the euphoria of accumulating his prey's rich, delicious Energy. The air was filled with fear-attuned Energy; he was *swimming* in it. He knew his Core was close to a breakthrough. He knew his prey was helpless underneath him. Why not let go? Why not run with it? Wasn't this one way he might beat his curse? If he feasted on an entire *world*—

He broke the thought off, unfinished. He knew he couldn't. He had to remember who he was. Growling, shrieking involuntarily, he refocused on his prey—Drok—and drew his Energy into himself. *"No!"* he shrieked. *"I'll finish with just you."* His words—more shrieks laced with intent—had the effect of further wilting the Death Caster. He shrank under Victor's talons, his Energy flowing as if someone had opened a floodgate. Victor soaked it up and felt his Core breakthrough, but he didn't pause. He wouldn't stop until Drok was utterly annihilated.

31

NO DOUBT

Grand Prince Troyssas watched as the ruination of House Kuria played out before his eyes. The judicators were evacuating the arena, ushering the nobility to the portal rooms in the building, or, in the case of the tens of thousands of low-born iron rankers, out to the streets where they could make their own way home. It hadn't taken long for Troyssas to realize it was fear that was stirring his guts. His very *heart* had begun to thud with an unseemly urgency at the creature's shrieks, so he and his guardians had asserted their will, pressing their auras against the terror-filled Energy. Things were stable—for now.

Another shriek split the unnaturally dark air, and Troyssas gritted his teeth, more angered by the sound than fearful now. "He makes a mockery of us," he growled.

"Us, Highness?" Brinnit asked, her gleaming great sword shining brightly against the unnatural dark.

"The great houses. Kuria is cousin to Khaliday! This should not be happening!" Troyssas dismissed her attention with a flick of his wrist and said, "*Wesper*, I know you listen. Come. *Speak* with me."

The air shimmered beside him, and the veil walker appeared, frowning down her elegant nose, her arms folded over her silken gown, hiding the smooth curves of her cleavage from his probing eyes. Troyssas had always been enamored with her, and the fact that she'd shunned his touch for more than a century only made him more intrigued. While she scowled, he smiled, resolving to have several of his courtesans play-act as her when he returned to the palace. "You should not summon me so, Grand Prince. I'm not the only veil walker listening for your voice in the arena today."

"Well? Are you going to do something?" Troyssas nodded his enormous head toward the railing that overlooked the arena and the battle being waged.

"What would you have me do?" The genuine puzzlement in her eyes only infuriated Troyssas further.

"You'll allow Kuria to end like this?"

"Queen Livessa entered this arrangement of her own free will. She *asked* for it."

"And yet you made certain guarant—" Troyssas continued to speak, but no words emerged from his lips. Fury brought the blood to his clean-shaven head, darkening the flesh like a deep red wine. Despite his fury, despite the deep wells of power in his Core, Wesper's aura held him like a vise. She gripped everyone in the box that way—frozen, deaf, and dumb. Then her words came to him, slinking into his ears without the hint of a sound, but rather the intent of her will to make them known to him.

Shut your fat, stupid mouth, fool. I made no guarantees, only suggestions. I only shared what I knew. I made no promises. Even that would have me banished from this world if Lohanse caught wind, so be silent, or you and your sister will lose what aid I can give.

As the last of her words slithered into his ear, echoing strangely before sinking into his mind, the oppression of her aura disappeared like a bubble popping, and she was gone. The people in Troyssas's box shifted uncomfortably, likely unaware of what had happened to make them suddenly nauseous. Brinnit confirmed as much when she muttered, "That damn fear—it wears on me."

Troyssas cleared his throat, embarrassed and angry in equal measure, but impotent to act on his feelings—at least with Wesper. "Can you see them? The combatants? Does Drok have a hope of recovery?" As he asked the question, he scanned the arena seating, amazed at how quickly the veil walkers had cleared the audience. Only the two queens remained with their retinues, undoubtedly shielded by a veil walker's aura.

Brinnit leaned over the rampart, her eyes blazing with Energy. "The nightmare yet squats atop him, talons piercing his flesh. Drok's Core grows dim, and he is listless. Barring some sort of intervention, he will be drained and dead shortly."

"Then let us depart. The empress will need to prepare her strategies. Let us hope the champion she bought is worth his fee." With that, Troyssas hoisted his great bulk from his throne-like chair and turned his back on the arena. He couldn't help feeling he was turning his back on Livessa, too, and despite the hardness in his heart, he felt a twinge of something he hadn't felt in a very long time—melancholy, perhaps. How long had it been since they were raised together in the capital? A thousand years? They'd grown apart, but she was still one of the few people left on Ruhn who could remember Grand Prince Troyssas, he of the Iron Yoke, as a child who begged fruit pies from the kitchen staff.

* * *

When the vast well of his prey's Energy ran dry, Victor, terror incarnate, released his grip on Drok's brittle body, spread his great, shadow-drenched wings, and tilted his razored beak to the sky, screeching his triumph. Scanning his surroundings, he was disappointed to see the throngs of bright spirits were gone. Only a few lingered and they were dim, shrouded by some sort of veil.

He cracked his wings, launching himself into the air, swooping left and right, but as he dove toward a grouping of spirits—only a dozen or so—the air grew thick, and his passage slowed. He furiously beat his wings, but the more he approached his new prey, the slower he moved and the denser the air became. The spirits grew ever dimmer in his monochrome vision, and, frustrated, he banked left, pumping his wings to send him higher. If these spirits would elude him, he'd find other prey farther afield.

To his great agitation, the air above him was similarly dense. No matter how he pumped his wings and screamed his fury and bottomless *hunger*, he made little progress. Eventually, he began to tire. The duality of his nature became lopsided, and Victor began to assert himself more and more. Eventually, his human feelings returned, and he pushed his hunger aside. He was victorious, yet weary, and he could feel the pain in his chest once more as he glided to the sands and sent the Aspect of Terror away, back to the corners of his mind where it dwelled, unquiet and ill-tempered.

As he came back to himself, cloaked in shadows, screaming his agony as his bones snapped and his limbs rearranged themselves, Victor thought about his battle. He thought about how he'd feasted on Drok and how he'd yearned to feast on *everyone*. Despite those urges, he'd been in control for the most part. Only after gorging on Drok's rich supply of terror-attuned Energy had the Aspect pushed him into the passenger seat. Even then, its control had been tenuous; it hadn't taken much of an effort of will to get back in control.

When he was fully *Victor* again, he found Lifedrinker lying at his feet, massive, powerful, and quiet; she'd taken her share of Drok's Energy during the battle. They'd been merged, with her impossibly dense metal forming his natural weapons, his talons and beak, perhaps more—hadn't there been a scythe-like blade on his tail? "*Tail!*" Victor chuckled, his voice raw as he stooped to send his slumbering axe to her storage container.

Would he have been able to stop from feasting further, though, if the veil walkers hadn't walled him in? He was assuming that was what had stopped him. What else could it be? He sighed, noting System messages waiting for him, though he knew he might have more after the System awarded him for slaying the steel seeker. With that thought, he ignored them, looking toward the stands, unsurprised to find them barren.

He looked to Kynna's viewing box and saw her and Arona staring at him, wide-eyed, silent, and unmoving. The others were gone—Kynna's courtesans and guards, even Bryn. Arona's face was washed of color. Had his feasting been so disturbing? Was she not a century-old former Death Caster? Had she not seen worse? Shifting, ignoring the raw, burning pain in his chest, he turned to look up at Livessa's box. A dozen veil walkers stood there, enforcing the terms of the duel; Lohanse wasn't taking any chances.

He moved toward Drok's skeletal corpse. The Death Caster's feathered robes lay in tatters, ripped apart by Victor in his feeding frenzy. His pale flesh was like paper over his bones, and it smelled more like a graveyard than a corpse. Nevertheless, the System was ready to honor Victor's triumph; bubbles of rich, shimmering, silvery Energy were gathering over the corpse. Victor sat down, folding his legs under him as he waited.

He wasn't sure how to feel. Shouldn't he feel triumphant? Shouldn't he want to lift Lifedrinker overhead and rail at the sky, announcing his might, reminding his ancestors that he was victorious once again? He could feel the swelling of his Core, but again, he resisted the urge to look at it. He'd wait until after the System fed him his due. That was his last thought before the Energy hit him.

After his six-month slumber, he was leery about losing himself, so he fought to remain present and cognizant. The struggle was monumental against the tide of Energy, though. Drok may have been a steel seeker, but he'd had a well of Energy unlike anything Victor had yet encountered. How long had that man lived? How much terror had he spread on how many worlds? How many millions had he slain?

At last, with those thoughts, Victor felt a touch of pride. He'd done something good. He'd removed a stain on the universe when he'd vanquished Drok. As he fell back, his eyes closing at last, Victor had the disquieting thought that he had to be careful not to fill Drok's void with his own darkness.

His visions were strange and muted, unlike any he'd had before. He saw figures that might be his ancestors or might be anyone—blurry, colorful people seen through a haze that made them as watercolors. They laughed and ate, they slept and toiled, but always together, always with the heat of life and love at their cores. As the visions faded, Victor awakened to the familiar, constant, howling pain in his chest.

He grunted, sitting up from the hot sands, peering at the blazing sun in the pale blue sky. He'd been lying there for hours, at least. No one was nearby, not even Drok's corpse. He touched his armor and sent it into storage, then peered at the void in his chest. If it was larger than before his fight, it wasn't enough for him to measure with a glance. His vision was blurry, in any case, thanks to the System messages waiting for him to focus on them. At last, he acquiesced, reading through the bothersome words:

*****Congratulations! Your Spirit Core has advanced: Epic 8.*****

Victor stopped reading, blinking at the message. He remembered feeling a breakthrough as he drained Drok, but he'd thought he'd gained a single level for his Core. He'd gained *five*. No amount of cultivation could come close to such a gain. It was unheard of. Even Dar had cautioned him that ranks in the epic tier would come slowly and painfully. How could draining one man increase his Core's power so much? He continued reading:

*****Congratulations! You have achieved Level 89 Warlord and gained 48 intelligence and 34 vitality.*****

Victor stopped again, his mouth opening in disbelief. A single opponent, a man he'd rather easily thrashed, had just given him two levels—in *Tier Eight*! Yet another message awaited him:

*****Congratulations! Your spell, Aspect of Terror, Advanced, has evolved: Abyssal Tyrant, Epic.*****

*****Abyssal Tyrant, Epic. Prerequisite: Fear or related affinity. You no longer wear the illusion of terror—you become it. Your form twists into a manifestation of primal fear, shifting between flesh and shadow, embodying nightmare itself. Those who gaze upon you tremble beneath the weight of true horror, their will eroded, their bodies failing under the presence of dread made real. Fear-attuned Energy no longer simply feeds you—it obeys you, flowing to your call, shaping itself into force, binding your enemies, or fueling your power. Your strikes carry the weight of fear realized, rending flesh and soul alike. Energy Cost: Minimum 5000, scalable. Cooldown: Long.*****

"*Chingado!*" Victor hissed. When he'd taken on the form of the Aspect of Terror, when he'd realized it wasn't an illusion meant to evoke his enemy's personal fears, had he made a discovery? Had he unwittingly evolved his spell? His eyes focused on a particular line of the description: **Fear-attuned Energy no longer simply feeds you—it obeys you, flowing to your call, shaping itself into force, binding your enemies, or fueling your power.**

Did that mean he'd have more control—that he had finally mastered the spell he had feared to cast almost as much as his enemies feared to behold it? He hoped so, because, after all, fear was his most potent affinity, even if he hated to acknowledge the fact. As he waved away the last message from the System, he realized Lohanse was standing on the sands before him, watching with arms folded.

As Victor grunted, pushing himself to his feet, Lohanse rumbled, "I see you yet live."

"I do." Victor pulled the hem of his undershirt, tugging it away from the hole in his chest so its self-repairing magic would begin to work.

"That doesn't look pleasant."

"It's not."

"Not feeling talkative, hmm? Even after that enormous Energy infusion? I'd think it would make you positively gregarious."

"Well, I'm sure you saw the nature of my victory." Victor sighed and shrugged. In his mind, Lohanse was smart enough to understand that channeling all that fear and terror took a toll on a man.

The veil walker didn't disappoint. "I've seen many fights, Victor, and participated in even more. I've known my share of Spirit Casters, but I've never seen something like that *manifestation* of terror. Ancient Gods, but those poor fools chose the wrong champion to stake everything on, didn't they?"

"Well, Drok was impressive in his way." Victor shrugged again. "But yeah, he picked the wrong *pendejo* to try to terrorize." Victor wasn't sure why he spoke so openly with Lohanse. Perhaps it was the way the Grand Judicator had taken him aside in the past and given him words of advice. Whatever it was, Victor wasn't in the mood to play coy, especially with the constant agony in his chest. He'd been hopeful that his victory and subsequent gains would have given him some relief, but the curse was there, persistent as ever.

"Victor, Drok was a *monster*!" Lohanse chuckled. "That demon had a well of Energy as deep as many veil walkers. The *work* he must have done to cultivate his Core!" His chuckle became a laugh as he clapped Victor on the shoulder. "You're the talk of the aerie. I hope you'll survive to finish this drama; I'd love to see Kynna Dar raised up over House Khaliday. Already, she's within rights to label House Dar as great."

Victor smiled, surprised by the man's candor. He said as much. "You're being awfully open about your support."

"Ha! My fellow veil walkers have departed. You're the last one in the arena, and I've taken the time to mask our conversation—something I didn't do before."

"Well," Victor said, looking around the sands, "I'm assuming he didn't have anything worth claiming?"

"I'm afraid he was unadorned by artifacts—not a single ring or jewel. As for his organs, the devil's heart was a pile of dust, so I didn't think you'd mind me removing his corpse."

Victor waved a hand dismissively. "I don't care. Listen, Lohanse, I'm sure Queen Kynna is curious about my state of being, and I wouldn't mind a bit of rest. Thank you for staying with me while the Energy ran its course."

"Of course. I have a small word of caution for you regarding your queen." Victor had begun to walk toward the tunnel leading down to the ready room, but he stopped in his tracks, turning to hear the veil walker's words. "Several of my fellow guardians escorted her to the portal room. There were words spoken about the dangers of a Fear Caster. Of course I scolded them, and voiced my dissenting opinion, but I fear they may have undermined the queen's confidence in you. Perhaps not; I believe she's quite fond of you, but the display you put on—the need for an evacuation—can't be dismissed easily."

"So, the veil walkers aren't as neutral as they claim?" Victor arched an eyebrow, clicking his tongue as he turned to continue walking.

"We have favorites, but we mustn't act on them!" Lohanse called after him, and Victor smiled at the implication; Lohanse had already said he hoped Victor won. He went down the tunnel, into the corridor beyond, and then to the portal room. Lohanse hadn't been kidding when he said they'd cleared the arena out; not a soul crossed his path. When he came through the portal, though, it was a different story: Kynna, Bryn, Arona, and all of the Queen's Guard were in the chamber, awaiting his arrival.

"Victor!" the queen exclaimed, forcing everyone else to hold their greetings out of decorum. She stepped forward, reaching for Victor's hand, and he gave it to her, trying to smile as she took it between hers. "We feared something nefarious; it's been nearly two hours!"

"And yet you waited?" Victor looked around the room. "You all let the queen stand here? For hours?"

Bryn straightened, bristling. "Her Majesty stands where she wills, Your Grace."

"Go easy, Victor." Kynna squeezed his hand, staring into his eyes. "Are you well?"

Despite the pain in his chest, he tried to smile again and nodded. "I'm no worse, if that's what you're asking. I made some significant gains, thanks to Drok." He shrugged, looking around the room again. "Would you mind sending your guards out, my Queen?"

Kynna didn't look away from his face as she said, "Out."

As soon as the armored figures filed out and the door closed, Kynna tapped her crown, summoning her dome of secrecy with a crystalline *ping*. "What is it, Victor?"

"Well, I need to catch up on my correspondence and make plans for my first attempt at conquering this curse. I'm very close to a new tier, though, so I might work with Arona to attain it. Will you be all right for a week or so?"

"Of course! The Veil Walker Council will enforce peace while I take control of Kuria; it's a massive undertaking—the first great house to fall in centuries. Meanwhile, now that Gloria will share a border with Khaliday, the empress will be forced to come to the table. This will be a lengthy process." She paused, breathless, as she leaned closer. "Victor! Already, another of the great houses has sent me overtures. Khaliday's support is fracturing."

Victor squeezed her hand before letting go. "That's good news, my Queen." He looked at Arona. "Shall we?"

"Of course," she rasped.

As he moved toward the door with Bryn and Arona in tow, he paused and looked back at Kynna. "Don't worry about my fear affinity. I have others to balance it out."

She nodded, her crystalline, fire-filled eyes gleaming with sudden, surprising moisture. "I have no room in my heart for doubt where you are concerned, Victor. I trust you."

32

PLEASANTRIES

When they were in Victor's elevator, Bryn cleared her throat and asked, "Your Grace—" She glanced at Arona. "Victor, that didn't sound like you."

Victor looked at her, puzzled. "What?"

"When you said you would *attempt* to battle your curse."

Arona lifted her hand to her mouth, masking a nearly inaudible snicker. Victor arched an eyebrow at Bryn. "What do you mean?"

Bryn cleared her throat again, looking to the side, and then, in a faux deep voice, growled, "I will *crush* this curse! How *dare* it soil the spirit of one such as I?" When she turned back to him, her smile was huge, her cheeks red. "That's what I *thought* you'd say."

Victor didn't feel much like laughing. In fact, a petty part of himself reared its head and demanded he be insulted, that he remind them he didn't think his very possibly fatal curse was much of a laughing matter. He fought it down, though, and managed to force a weak chuckle. "All right, Bryn. You got me. Maybe it's the duel, or maybe it's this constant fucking agony in my chest. Maybe this curse is breaking me down, bit by bit. I'm not *trying* to sound pathetic. You make a good point; some confidence wouldn't hurt."

While he spoke, Bryn's face fell, and Victor realized his attempt at *not* sounding pathetic had been pretty pathetic. "I'm sorry, Victor, I—"

"You're fine. Come on." Victor gave her shoulder a nudge just as the elevator stopped and the doors opened. "Forget it." He exited first, walking with a perpetual slouch that he'd developed to keep his clothing from touching the cursed void in his chest. He went into his chambers and immediately felt the urge to go and sit in his cultivation chamber. He knew why: The Energy in there was rich, leaving little room for ambient void-attuned Energy. He wondered how much worse the curse would have been if his six-month-long vision trip had occurred outside the chamber.

Arona closed the door behind them, and he turned to see that Bryn had followed them in. He'd said, "Come on," hadn't he? He nodded to the sitting area. "Get comfortable if you want. I have some Far Scribe books to look through." He was relieved when both women took their seats, leaving him alone. Before tackling his correspondence as promised, he called up his status sheet, curious to see the totality of his Energy levels since expanding his Core and gaining nearly fifty intelligence:

Energy:	73105/73105

He chuckled when he realized he couldn't remember exactly what it had been before. Somewhere around fifty thousand, he thought. It was undoubtedly an improvement. He figured he ought to be able to maintain his epic elder magic spells significantly longer. More than that, with his intelligence now at 388, his Greater Warborn Mind feat was giving him 77 points in both dexterity and agility. As far as he was concerned, taking the Warlord class had been worthwhile, if only for that feat.

"Something's funny?" Arona called from the sitting area.

Victor waved a hand, dismissing the question as he walked over to join them, sitting in an armchair adjacent to their couch. He dug out his Far Scribe books, setting them on the table, and while Arona and Bryn had a glass of wine, he read through them, one by one.

His six-month absence hadn't gone unnoticed by any of the many people he corresponded with, though only a handful seemed concerned. Of course, Valla and Rellia had sent him several messages asking for an update as to his well-being. Valla's most recent message, sent nearly a week prior, was particularly desperate-sounding:

Victor—I swear, if you don't respond soon, I will lose myself in despair. Please! Don't make me come looking for you!

Of course, the short note had been preceded by several longer, far more detailed letters about her studies and how much she'd enjoyed seeing him again, among other topics. Victor figured he ought to reply immediately:

Valla,

I didn't mean to leave you in the dark. I ate a natural treasure that kept me unconscious for six months. I know that sounds like madness, but it's true. As for my health, it's not changed much since I last spoke to you. Don't worry about me.

Love,

Victor

It was a short, almost lazy reply, but at least it would keep her from panicking and doing something stupid. He wrote something similar to Rellia. Then he took a while to read through notes from Edeya, Lam, Thayla, Efanie, and Gorro ap'Dommic, his governor. Everyone was well. Everyone was missing him. The keep guarding Du's dungeon entrance had been completed nearly a month ago, and Deyni, Cora, and Chala were getting along well. Everything was . . . *good*. It brought some peace to Victor's mind as he sat there reading through those missives.

When he set the books aside and looked up, he realized Bryn and Arona had been watching him. Far more relaxed than earlier, he offered a genuine smile. "How long was I reading those things?"

"More than an hour, but it's fine. We've been drinking some of your good wine." Arona held her glass up to illustrate the point. Bryn giggled, and Victor had a feeling the wine was hitting her pretty hard. He chuckled, and, realizing they'd set a glass on the table before him, he picked it up. He held it high, leaning toward the two women.

When they hurriedly clinked their glasses against his, he said, "Here's to you two. Thank you for putting up with me. I only woke up yesterday, and then I jumped into a duel. I haven't heard about the toll my absence took on you."

"I'll drink to us!" Bryn laughed and tilted her glass back.

Arona was slightly more reserved, simply raising her glass in salute before sipping. Victor took a gulp of the impossibly smooth alcohol, then leaned back in his chair, trying to pretend his chest didn't surge with fiery pain at the movement. "Go on then," he said. "Tell me about what you did while I was slumbering away."

They drank away the afternoon and the evening, and by the time midnight came around, even Victor was ready for some sleep, having consumed several bottles of potent wine. He'd told himself he wouldn't sleep for a while, not after having wasted six months doing so, but after he'd said goodnight to Bryn and Arona, he felt the weight of his eyelids and was struck by powerful, wracking yawns as he shuffled into his bedroom.

As he lay down, an urge possessed him, and he summoned the special ring Tes had crafted for him before leaving. It was made of simple silver, but the band was thick and wide, meant for his thumb. She'd intricately carved hundreds of tiny runes into the metal and shaped it to hold a beautiful ruby-red crystal. The stone was cut perfectly to capture light and disperse it in a weird, beautiful, misty glow that covered most of his hand when he wore it. It was a dream crystal, and if he wore it when he slept, so long as Tes also wore hers and slept, they'd meet on the plane of dreams.

They hadn't made any sort of schedule, and Victor had slept with the ring on his thumb several times with no result, but he didn't mind. He didn't like the idea of a schedule, and Tes agreed—she was, at heart, a romantic like him. She'd said that if they were meant to meet, fate would arrange things. He'd loved the *idea* of those words, but, in practice, it wasn't so satisfying when fate had, thus far, not seen fit to bring them together. Would that night be different? Drunk Victor was hopeful.

He put the ring on his thumb and flopped onto his pillow. He had to lie on his back; his curse was too painful in other positions. Usually, that restriction made it hard for him to fall asleep, but that night, he was soundly slumbering almost as soon as his eyes closed. Unfortunately, rather than a meeting with Tes on the plane of dreams, he had fitful, disquieting dreams about things he only remembered in fleeting glimpses and feelings—someone was missing or lost, he was stuck trying to complete something futile, and strangest of all, he was trying to prepare dinner, and the food was badly overcooked.

When he dressed and emerged from his room, he found Bryn and Arona sitting at his dining table, eating a breakfast served by two of his household staff. "Thought you'd be sleeping in late, Bryn," he said by way of greeting.

"I feel fantastic, Your Grace."

Victor sat down, and one of the servants placed a platter before him. It was stacked high with scrambled eggs, bacon, sausage, and three different types of tart. The kitchen staff had grown accustomed to him having a near-bottomless appetite. Sadly, despite his long slumber with nothing to sustain him other than Energy, he just didn't feel all that hungry. While Bryn and Arona chatted, he listened and picked at his food.

After a while, Arona set her steaming tea down and asked, "Are you not hungry, Victor?"

He shook his head. "No. When you're finished, let's set up the portal array."

She took her napkin from her lap and primly dabbed at the corners of her mouth. "I'm ready now."

"Are you leaving, Victor?" Bryn asked, willing to be informal now that the staff had left.

"Yeah, but just for a few days. I'm close to a level, and I want to go and earn it before I . . ." He looked up from his plate and locked eyes with her, grinning. "Before I kick this curse's ass."

She smiled, pushing her chair away from the table. "I'll be sure to let the queen know. Is there anything you want me to work on while you're away?"

Victor shook his head. "No thanks, Bryn. Just keep things running smoothly as you have been. I appreciate your hard work."

With that, Bryn departed, and Victor and Arona went to his study, where they set up his portal array. Just a few minutes later, they emerged into the deep cavern at the heart of Mount Ember near the crackling, fiery portal to Du's dungeon. However, things had changed: Du was no longer in a vast cavern but in a small, stone-lined room. The walls and ceiling had clearly been built around the portal, locking it behind a massive, rune-inscribed door constructed of a dense, dark gray steel alloy.

Victor approached the door and rested a hand on it, assessing the depths of Energy in the metal. It was certainly impressive, but nothing like amber ore. He was confident he could rip it from the hinges if he wanted to. Even so, it must have cost Rellia—and him—a pretty penny to install such a barrier on Fanwath. "I guess Rellia's taking security seriously."

"Should we visit the keep and the custodians?"

Victor nodded. "I suppose that would be the right thing to do." He looked at the door again. "One problem."

Arona laughed. "You don't have a key."

Victor laughed along with her as he set up the array again, and they waited a few minutes for the crystals to charge. Not long after that, they stepped through the weird magenta hole in the universe into the caldera proper. Things had changed a great deal atop Mount Ember. Victor had used the destination orb to choose a spot he remembered well—the slope overlooking the caldera from the old roadway before it had been ruined. Now, however, a new road had appeared, paved with meticulously fitted cobbles, featuring raised berms and proper masonry culverts.

Behind them, a guard station had been built at the top of the rise—a small keep in itself. When Victor turned to regard the construction, horns blared, the door at the base of the little keep flew open, and several soldiers in Rellia's livery charged out with polearms ready. Victor waved dismissively, content to let them approach at their pace, and turned to regard the caldera.

The road ran at a gentle grade down toward the center, where a large, gray stone keep squatted. It was a square building with a central tower and a wide parapet, from which Victor could see soldiers patrolling. The portcullis and gates were open invitingly, though, and Victor saw a dozen or so outbuildings, including more than one inn and a separate tavern. It seemed Rellia was intent on making prospective dungeon-goers comfortable.

More than the road and the buildings, it looked like she had Earth Casters hard at work revitalizing the grounds within the high cliffs that encircled the caldera. He could see dark, rich soil sprouting with green shoots everywhere. They weren't crops but tiny trees. Nodding, smiling at the changes, Victor inhaled deeply, sampling the air. Magma Energy was still prevalent, but it was far more subdued than before. That was to be expected, however; Victor knew that Du would siphon off most of the volcano's rage-filled fire. It made the place more pleasant—more . . . *stable.*

"Sir!" a gruff voice challenged from behind him. Victor didn't have to turn; Arona was there to help.

"Calm yourself, fool. Lower your weapons. Do you not recognize the lord of these lands?"

Victor started forward, walking toward the keep, only partially listening as Arona answered a few questions from the soldiers. A moment later, she caught up to him, and he glanced at her, smiling. "Thanks for that. My patience has seen better days, and I didn't want to chat with those men."

"It's nothing."

When they reached the keep, only about a five-minute walk, a retinue had already formed in the gatehouse, and at its head was Rellia herself. When Victor was only twenty yards distant, she abandoned decorum and ran forward, her long crimson hair streaming behind her, her shapely, blue-tinted leg slipping through the sizeable slit in her gown. She was a striking woman, Victor mused, his mind going to stranger and stranger places thanks to the dreamlike disconnect he was forced to affect to ignore the pain in his chest.

He remembered how Rellia had flirted with him after his victory over her in the arena back in Gelica. He wondered how his life might have changed had he stayed in the city and pursued her rather than wandering off to help Thayla and Deyni reach the Shadeni clan. The thought was strange, considering his relationship with Valla and Rellia's subsequent motherly role with him, but his life was strange, so why not entertain a strange thought now and then?

He brushed the random tangent of meandering thought aside nonetheless, and gave Rellia an appropriately chaste hug, turning his side to her slightly to avoid her pressing against his curse. "Victor!" she exclaimed, her eyes narrowed and scolding. "You should have communicated more frequently. I was worried! Oh, dear, I can tell from the dark hollows of your eyes that you're not well."

"I'm just the same, Rellia. Don't worry." Victor waved her off and gestured to the keep. "You're doing a nice job here. It must have been costly to construct things so quickly."

"Nonsense. We've plenty of resources in the Free Marches now, and your governor has been rather loose with the sizeable purse you left with him."

"Oh yeah?" Victor chuckled. "Well, that's good, I suppose." He realized he'd been ignoring Arona and stepped to the side so he could look at Rellia and her together. "You remember Arona?"

"Of course. It's lovely to see you, milady." Rellia took Arona's hand.

"Likewise, Lady ap'Yensha."

"Just Rellia, dear. Well?" She turned to Victor. "Will you join me for a meal?"

Victor grinned, clicking his tongue and peering up at the keep. "Is Valla waiting inside to ambush me?"

"You only *wish* she were, brute!" Rellia slapped his shoulder. "No, she's busy with her strange studies under the oceans of a distant world." She sounded a little bitter, and Victor, for the first time, wondered what she *really* thought about Valla's current circumstances.

"I *do* wish it, if I'm honest. Oh well, I'll settle for lunch with you." He winked, finally finding some real humor, and Rellia laughed musically, tickled by the playful jab.

She took Victor's hand, tugging him forward. "Very well. Please follow me, and we'll have a rustic meal in this most rustic of keeps."

Victor allowed himself to be led into the bulky edifice, and there, he and Arona spent a lovely morning visiting with Rellia, touring the keep, and talking about all she'd accomplished with regard to the volcano and the dungeon. After a couple of hours, they sat down to a "rustic" meal consisting of grilled steaks—Victor wasn't sure what kind of animal—stewed vegetables, and fresh bread and butter. It was good, and something about the company or the setting helped Victor's appetite, and he cleaned his plate.

Afterward, Rellia guided them downstairs, where she'd set up offices for the managers of the dungeon. She'd hired people to create a calendar and manage the various tiers of dungeon applicants. After letting the clerk on duty know that Victor and Arona would be using the dungeon, she guided them down a long, black-marble-lined corridor that wound its way into the mountain, descending several flights of stairs along the way. "We closed up the lava tubes entirely. This is the only access to the chamber now."

When they reached the underground cavern, Victor was impressed to see dozens of enormous stone columns lining the perimeter and, from their tops, grand stone arches that spanned the entire ceiling. "That looks like it was hard work."

"You would think so, but a few Tier Four Earth Casters make short work of such tasks." Rellia nodded to the squat stone building at the center of the cavern. "We built that around the dungeon portal. There are only three keys to that door." She nodded to the metal door Victor had already discovered from the inside. "One that the custodians hold, one that I hold, and this one"—she held out her hand, summoning a heavy, dark gray key with a dozen intricate tines—"which you will hold."

Victor took the key and pocketed it. "Thanks, Rellia. I think you've done an outstanding job here. Tell me, though, have you tried the dungeon?"

She looked up at him with narrowed eyes. "You wrote to me in the Far Scribe book, but now I see you didn't read my letters to you!"

"I did, but when I awoke, I had so many—"

"That you skimmed a little?" She laughed, letting him off the hook. "To answer your question, no, I've been waiting to speak to you because I didn't know if there was some hidden danger or if you'd be angry that we used the dungeon's Energy."

Victor nodded. "Well, I appreciate that. You can use the dungeon. Just don't let anyone above Tier Six go in. I don't think you'll need to worry about that, as we haven't told anyone about the dungeon here, and—"

"No one in the Free marches is beyond that tier," she finished for him.

"Right." Victor gestured to the door. "Well, speaking of going in."

"Very well, Victor. Thank you for spending some time with me. I hope you'll see me again soon, and please, will you encourage my daughter to visit more often?"

Victor laughed. "I'll try, Rellia; I really will. Don't count on my skills of persuasion, however."

Rellia smiled; her crimson eyes were dark in the dimly lit cavern, but she looked genuinely happy. He was almost envious. Wouldn't it be nice to settle in one place for a while and watch it grow and improve? "Until we meet again, then, Victor." She turned to Arona. "Keep him out of trouble."

Arona's raspy voice was light with amusement as she replied, "I can only try. Thank you for the lovely meal."

With that, Victor hugged Rellia again, and then, using his new key, he and Arona stepped into the portal chamber and re-entered the Crucible of Fire.

33

ALMOST TOO SCARY

Victor wasn't sure what to expect in the dungeon this time around, as far as gaining levels went. Advancement had felt increasingly slow since he'd crossed into the upper half of Tier Eight, aside from his incredible gains after killing Drok the Skull. Nevertheless, if he'd been concerned that he wouldn't claim that final level, his worries were for naught. It was after the third gate, as he and Arona finished slaying nearly a hundred waves of magma sprites that poured endlessly from a chasm of bubbling lava, that the System announced his triumph:

Congratulations! You have achieved Level 90 Warlord and gained 24 intelligence and 17 vitality.

Congratulations! Your Feat, Greater Warborn Mind, has become Peerless Warborn Mind, doubling its previous effect.

Level 90 Class refinement is available. Class refinement is permanent. Quinametzin Energy cultivators will next be offered a Class development opportunity at Level 100. To view your options and make your selection, access the menu through your status page.

Victor would have fallen over with excitement if he hadn't already been knocked off his feet by the infusion of Energy he'd just received. He stared at the messages, focusing on the one about Warborn Mind, reading and rereading it to ensure he hadn't made some sort of mistake. There it was, though, as plain as could be: He was now getting nearly half of his intelligence attribute applied to his dexterity and agility. Just to confirm, he pulled up his attributes:

Strength:	680 (780)	Vitality:	957
Dexterity:	280 (445)	Agility:	303 (468)
Intelligence:	412	Will:	673

Much had changed since he'd gained Level Eighty. Most notably, his intelligence had more than doubled, and thanks to his Warborn Mind feat, his speed attributes had staggeringly improved. Meanwhile, his vitality had pulled further ahead of his will, which used to be his greatest attribute. The numbers were worth celebrating, but a voice in the back of Victor's mind kept wondering if he'd be suffering from his current *cursed* predicament if he'd chosen a class at Level Eighty that focused on will.

"Spilt milk," he said with a sigh.

"Did you gain your level?" Arona asked, reminding him that he wasn't alone.

Victor nodded, shifting uncomfortably as his armor pressed against the curse. In frustration, he touched the aegis and sent it into storage. "Yeah—Tier Nine."

Arona shook her head, summoning a plain wooden chair to sit on. "So quickly! I still can't believe you weren't yet Tier Eight when you came to Ruhn. I know you have unorthodox means for cultivating Energy and gaining levels, but still, your Energy affinity must be high."

Victor shrugged, nodding. He couldn't deny that it was "high," but that didn't mean he'd tell her what it was; he'd been conditioned to keep those numbers to himself. "It's true; I've been lucky in many ways."

Arona cleared her throat and shifted, and Victor wondered if he'd made her uncomfortable with his blunt interpretation of her words. After a moment, while he sat quietly, trying to decide if he'd look at his class refinements right there in the middle of the dungeon, she said, "I don't mean to take away from your accomplishments. I hope you realize that."

"Thanks, Arona. It's true I've accomplished a lot, but let's be honest. I was born with a potent bloodline, and some combination of my parentage and upbringing developed this Core that rages inside me. That part was good luck, or maybe bad luck, but it was luck. As for what I've done with what I have . . ." He shrugged, smiling. "I guess I can take some credit."

"You've made hard choices, and no matter the gifts you were given, your decisions were good. Think of the many powerful people on Ruhn and the thousands of other worlds connected to Sojourn. So many are born with everything given to them, yet most will never earn a name worth remembering. You, Victor, have made an impression on everyone you've met."

"All right!" Victor grabbed one of her chair legs and shook it, rattling her. "You're making me uncomfortable with all those sappy words."

She laughed, gripping the seat until he stopped. "Fair enough. I shall stop." She cleared her throat again, crossing one of her legs over the other. "Well? Are you going to tell me about your refinement options?"

"You think I should look now?"

Arona's eyes bulged out as she stared at him, agape. "You haven't *looked* yet?"

"Well, we're in a dungeon, and—"

"When I reached Tier Nine, even if I'd been beset by a horde of unquiet undead, I would have found a way to peek!"

Victor laughed and nodded. "Okay, I take your point. Just a minute . . ." He summoned his status page and selected the Class refinement tab, scanning through the options:

*****Class refinement option 1: Doomforged Tyrant, Mythic. Prerequisites: 1. Prior Class levels in Warlord. 2. At least two of terror, rage, despair, or related affinities. 3. A history of reshaping the fate of battles through your presence. 4. Sufficiently advanced will and strength attributes. 5. A Core tempered by conflict, bloodshed, and the cultivation of your foes. 6. Widespread recognition as a conqueror.**

You are not merely a warrior or a leader—you are a force that cannot be denied. Rage fuels your strikes, and fear walks in your shadow. You do not need the favor of fate; you crush it beneath your heel and carve your own path. Every battlefield is your domain, every war another monument to your legend. Those who stand against you do so only until their spirits break, their courage drains, and their bodies crumble beneath your wrath.

Class attributes: Will, Strength.***

*****Class refinement option 2: Cursed Dreadnought, Mythic. Prerequisites: 1. Prior Class levels in Warlord. 2. Terror and Rage or their related affinities. 3. Lived and conquered while suffering under the malady of a curse—a strength of will proven by your refusal to succumb. 4. Sufficiently advanced vitality and will attributes.**

Your body fails, but your will refuses to break. The curse gnaws at your flesh and wears at your mind, but it cannot stop you. You are the unyielding force, the battle-scarred warlord who marches through ruin, crushing all in your wake. What should have killed you long ago has only made you an immovable, unstoppable presence on the battlefield. Even when your body falters, your rage will carry you forward, refusing to let you fail. You are the cursed warrior who will not die, no matter the cost.

Class attributes: Vitality, Will.***

*****Class refinement option 3: Warborn Titan, Mythic. Prerequisites: 1. Prior Class levels in Warlord. 2. Titanic, behemoth, or other related, primordial bloodline. 3. A history of engaging in and triumphing against overwhelming odds. 4. A sufficiently high affinity for rage or a related attunement. 5. Sufficiently advanced strength and vitality attributes. 6. Widely recognized as a conqueror on the battlefield.**

You are no mere general—you are war itself, given flesh and power. Titans, behemoths, and ancients whisper your name, recognizing you as one of their own. Your sheer physicality dominates battlefields, and your presence alone shatters morale, reshapes tactics, and turns armies to dust. You no longer lead warriors—you stand as the vanguard of war itself, a juggernaut who strides through destruction unfazed. Where others command armies, you are the army.

Class attributes: Strength, Vitality.***

*****Class refinement option 4: No Refinement. You are pleased with the path on which you find yourself and choose to continue until your next refinement option.*****

When Victor failed to speak or move, not even blinking for perhaps an hour, Arona finally seemed to lose her patience and cleared her throat. "Are you unwell, Victor?"

"Um, no, not unwell." Victor blinked, realizing his eyes were dry from staring at the System's text. "I think I understand why the Warlord class is so sought after."

Arona smiled, nodding. "Ah! Did it open up some interesting refinements? Any legendary ones?"

"Not exactly . . ." He trailed off, unsure if he should even mention that he'd been given three "mythic" options. He could only assume mythic was better than legendary—

"Victor! Don't be coy! I want to help you, and I promise I won't share your secrets." Victor looked at her, interested in her sudden insistence. She was usually quite deferential when he wanted to be secretive. His face must have conveyed his thinking because she sighed, shaking her head. "I'm sorry. I worry about you and am very interested in how this class change might affect your . . . *situation*. I'm also something of a scholar and won't deny my rabid interest in class choices and descriptions."

He smiled, waving a hand. "Don't worry about it. The thing is, I didn't get any legendary options, but I got three *mythic* ones."

Arona snorted, clicking her tongue. "Fine, if you want to keep it to yourself, then go ahe—" She stopped speaking when she noticed his expression. "You don't jest?"

He shook his head. "No, I'm not kidding."

"Mythic," she whispered. "Vesavo taunted us—his apprentices—with promises of a mythic spell. He claimed to know several. I haven't heard of a mythic class, though, Victor. There must be more to these offerings than your Warlord class, no? Are there other prerequisites?"

"Yeah," he grunted, "many." Rather than make her drag the information out of him, he began reading his options aloud. When he finished, she stared at him for several long minutes, and he was content to stare back, his mind busy with the implications of his offerings.

Finally, she said, "I've never seen such lengthy class descriptions. Usually, it's a sentence or two—maybe only a pair of phrases." She inhaled deeply and slowly let it out as she leaned back. "How *strange* that you've been given an option that requires you to be *cursed!*"

"Heh, yeah."

"Are you leaning toward any of them?"

"I like the sound of the last one, Warborn Titan, the most, but I don't really have a choice." Victor shrugged as though his decision were obvious.

Arona narrowed her eyes at him. "What do you mean?"

"I have to deal with this curse, which means cultivating my *will,* and the only class that puts will as the primary, number one attribute is the Doomforged Tyrant." He laughed, shaking his head. "As disturbing as that sounds."

"But aren't you going to battle your curse now? Your class won't matter until you make some levels to earn those improvements to your will. The second class is *based* on you being cursed; perhaps it will come with skills or feats to help you cope."

"Arona, that's a thought I had as well, but I'm not looking to *cope.* I'm not looking to spend ten levels—which may drag on for years and years based on what everyone tells me—being cursed. I'm fucking sick of this thing." Victor made the mistake of thumping his chest where the void curse lay under his shirt, and he hissed, pulling his fist away. He held it up, watching the skin regenerate over his thumb and forefinger.

She nodded, wincing in sympathy. "I can understand that. The third option also doesn't offer any will. I can see your logic now—if you should fail in your first attempt to break the curse, you won't have an easy path for building your will if you take that option. We shouldn't contemplate failure, though."

"Yeah, I know. But, as nuts as it sounds, Doomforged Tyrant is the *safe* bet."

Arona smiled, chuckling softly. "*Nuts.*"

"You know what I mean, though? The System didn't translate that to 'crazy' for you?"

Her eyes widened. "Ah! *Crazy!* I thought it was more of a curse."

Victor shrugged. "Maybe the System did, too." He wasn't unhappy with the options—obviously, considering the "mythic" ranking and Arona's excitement, he'd been given great choices. It was just that Victor was annoyed that he felt steered toward one option, and he knew it was the *right* choice; his gut wasn't arguing with the logic he'd expressed to Arona. On top of that, his curse was bothering him, and he was just *weary* on a level that didn't make much sense, considering his extended downtime before his duel and the enormous Energy infusions he'd received since.

"Are you certain, then?"

He nodded. "Afraid so." Without waiting for his resolve to falter, Victor selected the first option: Doomforged Tyrant.

*****Congratulations! You have refined your class: Doomforged Tyrant.*****

*****Congratulations! You have earned a Class Feat: Presence of the Tyrant.*****

*****Presence of the Tyrant: Your aura is heavy, laced with the weight of your fear-attuned Energy. Moreover, those who consider you an ally will feel the weight of your rage in battle and be moved by it, sharing a small part of its benefits.*****

Victor didn't realize it initially, but a change had come over him. He'd swollen with the power of his new class—not physically, but somehow, his power was magnified and seemed to make him more formidable. To him, it felt as though he was flooding his pathways with Energy, gearing up for a battle, but when he turned his eye inward, his Core was at rest, and his Energy was safely wound tightly in its usual formation.

Then he realized what it was; his aura had expanded, but rather than stretching out, slamming into Arona and anyone else who might be near, it had filled *him* with its extra density. Moreover, he felt a renewed control over it. He could expand and contract it with just a flick of his will, and, as he'd learned to do by accident back on Sojourn, he could wrap it around his Core space, shielding it from prying eyes far more effectively than before. As he did so, the System confirmed what he knew:

*****Congratulations! Your Aura Veil skill has improved: Epic.*****

"Huh," he grunted. "So easy." He looked at Arona to see that she'd shrunk back, looking at him wide-eyed. "Does my aura cause you discomfort?"

"It's not that. You—you're different." When he continued to stare at her, she added, "It reminds me of a veil walker, Victor. Should an iron ranker have such . . . *gravity?*"

"I'm holding my aura in . . ."

"It's not that. It's not pressing on me. It's . . . like you're pulling me! Haven't you ever stood next to a great master and felt this way? I find myself feeling I should bow and back away, apologizing for troubling you!"

"Ah, what the *hell?* That's not what I want. Relax, Arona. And yeah, to answer your question, I've been in the presence of people like that. Dar used to make me feel that way when we first met. Then there are *others* . . ." Victor's mind turned toward Crystal, the ivid queen, and Azforath, the primordial titan. "Anyway, sorry if it's uncomfortable."

She rallied, leaning forward and smiling, her blue, gem-bright eyes glinting in the orange-red glow of the dungeon's ambient light. "I just need to get used to it. Are you eager to try out your new abilities?"

Victor stood and stretched, realizing that his curse didn't seem so bothersome. He lifted his shirt and looked at his chest, grinning at what he saw: The ball of void Energy was about half the size it had been, back down to something between a golf and tennis ball. "Ha!"

"That's wonderful!" Arona leaned close. "Perhaps the weight of your aura provides some extra resistance!"

"Yeah, I think you're right." Victor summoned his armor and shrugged into it. Then he summoned Lifedrinker. As soon as his hands wrapped around her haft, she spoke, "*Heart-carver! Champion of the blood typhoon! I feel your power has increased again! Your strength flows into me! Let us dance our bloody dance, heart-mate!*"

Victor laughed, his mood buoyed as usual by his wonderful axe—his wonderful companion. "We will, *chica*, we will. It's good to hold you and hear your voice." He lifted her to his shoulder, resting her there as she continued to exude feelings of excitement, adoration, and pride. She didn't need words to convey how much she loved being with him, and it brought moisture to Victor's eyes to feel those raw emotions.

"Your axe is pleased with you?" Arona asked, looking at him sideways.

Victor blinked, clearing his throat and looking away. "Uh, yeah." He nodded toward the gatehouse. "Shall we?"

Arona nodded, and they advanced. The rest of the dungeon went much the same as the last time they cleared it. It might have been a little more difficult, but with Victor's renewed strength and the enthusiasm with which he waded into battle, the hordes of enemies fell to their combined might, and the final boss—another skeletal dragon—was no match for them.

Arona reported that his aura pushed her toward violence in the battles, and she had to fight to restrain herself lest she run out of Energy. When he asked if it was too much, though, she shook her head and grinned, claiming she quite enjoyed the vitality it bestowed upon her. Victor wondered if, when he was berserk, his aura would help her heal quickly, but she never received a single injury. Anytime she was in trouble, she'd create her solar shell, and Victor would cast Guardian's Rescue, taking her place in the path of danger.

In the end, Victor learned what people meant by the steep curve of leveling requirements. Despite completing more than half the dungeon after he'd gained Level Ninety, as they finished, he was still Level Ninety. Worse, Du failed to provide any unique or seemingly potent artifacts. Their wealth increased, nonetheless, and Victor was still intent on challenging the curse when they left. He wanted a good night's sleep, and then he planned to lock himself in his cultivation chamber and perform the Spirit Walk, which would hopefully mean the end to that irritating phase of his life.

"And if I fail," he said, explaining his plans to Arona as they built the teleportation array, "at least I know how to build up my will some more—gain levels."

She *tsk*ed. "You shouldn't put the idea in your head that you can fail. You know that."

He frowned. He *did* know that. Hadn't he learned that since he'd been a wrestler? Always visualize the win! What had gotten into him with that damn curse? It wasn't the first time he'd thought of battling it as an "attempt." He looked at Arona and nodded, trying not to glower. "Thank you for that reminder. This curse wears on me in secretive ways."

She placed the last crystal and then stood back, watching them charge. "I will always be truthful with you and say what I believe needs saying." She looked at him and grinned, an unusual look of mischief in her eyes. "Even if you are almost too scary to look at directly."

34

A GIFT OF TIME

When Victor and Arona stepped out of the portal into his study, his impulse was to seek solitude in his cultivation chamber. He wanted to do some thinking, and he often did his best thinking when he was cultivating. Arona wasn't ready to be so quickly dismissed, however. "Victor, if you're set on doing battle with that curse on the morrow, then perhaps some preparation is in order."

He narrowed his eyes. "Yeah, that's what I've been doing."

"Well, I had some thoughts for more explicit preparations—as I understand it, the strength of your will is paramount in this battle, yes?"

He didn't bother responding; she knew the answer. "Go on."

"When did you last drink a tincture brewed to enhance your will?"

Victor chuckled, thinking back to the last time he'd sought out tinctures meant to improve an attribute. When had that been? Coloss? "Never, I guess. My will has always been far stronger than I needed it to be." He shrugged. "What's the most I can hope for? Ten or twenty points?"

"With a will as strong as yours, it may be less than that, but wouldn't every point be worthwhile? Moreover, we could acquire a short-term enhancement potion that you should consume prior to your Spirit Walk. Some of them are quite effective, if short-lived."

Victor nodded, unfolding arms he hadn't realized he'd folded. "Yeah, that's smart, Arona."

"Perfect. Then, may I use this portal array? I shall visit the auction on Sojourn."

Victor narrowed his eyes. "Sojourn? Are you sure that's wise? What if Vesavo—"

"My Core is brightness and light; trust me, if he sensed my presence in the city, he would think it a mistake, a coincidence that a being such as I felt similar to his long-dead apprentice."

"You're certain? I don't want to have to come and rescue you—"

She laughed, shaking her head. "That won't be necessary. I'll create the portal in a grove outside the city, a place I know well—secluded and quiet. From there, I shall make hasty flight to the auction hall, where I'll easily hide my presence. As for the return portal, I'll simply rent a room in one of the inns that provides safe haven to all guests."

"You've thought this through, huh?" Victor nodded. "All right. Let me get you some beads—"

She waved a hand. "Nonsense! We've made millions in that dungeon, and I had a stash *before* that. These items won't be overly expensive, in any case."

Victor shrugged. "All right. Thank you, Arona. Here." He summoned the various parts of the portal array, handing them to her, one by one. He knew he was putting a valuable treasure in her hands, and so did she. She took each piece reverently, especially the control orb, as he gently placed it into her open palm. He didn't say it, but he knew she understood that he was trusting her with a great deal. Why wouldn't he, though? Hadn't she looked over his slumbering form for six months? Hadn't she risked her life standing by Kynna's side when he couldn't?

"I'll be back before morning. May I create the portal here?"

"Yeah, of course." Victor stepped toward the door to his workshop. "I'm going into my cultivation chamber."

She watched him go through the door, and before it closed behind him, she said, "I'll see you soon, then."

Victor sighed, stretching his neck and back as he walked across the workshop to the cultivation chamber door. He pressed his hand to the lock and pulled the door wide, smiling as the rich, magma- and blue-ice-attuned Energy washed over him. Inside, he closed the door and sat on his pedestal, taking a few minutes to let his mind settle.

He had much to think about, and the curse was only the most pressing of his many concerns. He wondered how Kynna was doing. It had been four days since he'd spoken to her. How were things going with the veil walkers and the transition of power for House Kuria? Had there been any talks about the next duel? He wondered about that. His *next* duel might be his last. Could they really get House Khaliday to commit? How confident could they be in their champion after what Victor had done to Drok the Skull?

He only knew that their champion was from off-world, and according to Tes, he was a dragon. He couldn't be as strong as she was, though, could he? Wasn't she basically a veil walker? If this champion, dragon blood or not, was still working inside the System, that meant he was no more than a steel seeker. Victor frowned. Shouldn't he have more information by now? Shouldn't Kynna have delivered a dossier on the champion?

He supposed it was very possible that she had. It could be sitting on a stack of missives in his study, for all he knew; he hadn't exactly looked around to see what he'd missed while he'd been insensate for six entire months. It didn't matter anyway; regardless of what he learned, Victor wouldn't back away from the fight. Hadn't his ancestors feasted on the hearts of dragons? Was he any less of a Quinametzin? "Ha," he chuckled, pleased to feel the familiar old pride surging in his chest. His class change had been good in that regard. The strength of his aura was pushing the despair of the void curse down to manageable levels.

Of course, that thought made him contemplate his new class. "*Doomforged Tyrant!*" He clicked his tongue, shaking his head. He'd never have predicted he'd embrace a class so dour-sounding. He wondered if the "Doomforged" part had to do with his curse. *Was* he doomed? He knew the "Tyrant" part wasn't literal. He didn't feel tyrannical anywhere but the battlefield, and he was sure that was what it referenced. He was meant to dominate in war and combat, and that was fine—it was welcomed.

Sighing, Victor realized his meditations were going nowhere. His mind was too busy, so he summoned his Far Scribe books and looked through them, wondering if any of his loved ones had something interesting to share. He smiled when the first one he opened, Edeya's, had a lengthy new entry. He summoned a big bottle of honeyed mead and took a long drink before nestling the book in his lap and reading through the letter:

Dear Victor,

I was pleased to get an update from you, finally! I'm sure you could tell by the tone of my earlier messages that I was worried. You said you'd be gone months and maybe years, but the reality of it hadn't sunk in until you'd been silent for months and months, and then the one-year mark slipped by. Anyway, it was wonderful to hear from you, and I'm glad things are still progressing for you there regarding the succession war. I'm amazed that you were unconscious for six entire months! I've read stories about great heroes eating treasures and sleeping away the years, but I'd always thought they were fanciful tales to impress children.

Things are going very well here, in case you were worried. Lam and I are getting along—better than before. Of course, you know about my reservations, as I spilled my silly heart out to you in letter after letter, but I finally took some of your advice and was honest with her about them. Wonder of wonders, she understood! I wish you could see my smile as I write this. Anyway, Lam agreed that, despite her deep love for me, it wasn't healthy for me to be everything to her.

We're still together, and we still adventure together, but we've both taken up hobbies apart from each other. We've developed friendships that give us a little space to grow the other aspects of our personalities. You won't believe this, but I've become very close with your cousin, Olivia. She's a fascinating woman! She's very passionate about everything, and I often wonder if that stems from her incredible affinity for the elements. As great as her passion is, she's also very analytical, and, with her help, I've begun to develop new spells—she's been sharing her texts from Fainhallow with me.

Victor! She wants to talk to you about creating a school in the Free Marches to rival the other great academies on Fanwath. She speaks in strange terms—colleges and universities, even schools for children to prepare them for "higher learning." I think it's all fascinating, of course, and I'm sure you could convince Rellia to help fund the endeavor. Wouldn't it be wonderful to have academies to compete with those in the Empire?

As for Lam, she and Lesh are like two peas in a pod these days. They've expanded on the sparring schedule Lesh maintained with other iron rankers in Sojourn. Now, they treat it almost like a martial sect, and Dar's lake home has become known as the premier place to practice one's weapon skills in Sojourn.

I'm sure you're wondering about Darren. I'll tell you a secret, but only if you promise to repeat it to no one! Usually, I'd assume you wouldn't have anyone to whisper to, being on another world far away, but I know you keep Far Scribe books with many folks other than myself. Anyway, I trust you, so don't let me down! The secret is that Darren has confided to me that he intends to marry an avian woman native to Sojourn. Her name is Bree Lansa, and she's sweet and pretty—as far as avians go.

I don't mean to sound prejudiced, but you know how they are with their beaks and big eyes, their clicking sounds, and . . . oh, listen to me! I am being prejudiced! I don't mean it that way. Let's see—the positives: Her feathers are sky blue and glisten wonderfully in the sun. She has a pale yellow beak, much smaller than Darren's, and her voice will move you to tears when she sings. Anyway, Darren is lovestruck, and though he's still intent on gaining levels, he's slowed his adventuring to spend more and more time with her.

What else can I tell you? I haven't seen hide nor hair of your master. The servants say he's at some place called the "Arcanum." I guess I've been there before, but it was when my spirit was fractured and again when it was newly made whole, and I don't remember it at all. It's wonderful that we can still live here at the house, so if you correspond with him, please convey our gratitude.

Please let me know if you have anything else you'd like me to write about. Of course, that would require you to write more than a cursory note letting me know you're alive. Did you take note of the biting wit in that last sentence? Next time we're together, you can expect more of that in person, but with a bit more venom followed by a big hug and even a slobbery kiss on your gigantic, stupid, handsome cheek.

I miss you, Victor!

Love,

Edeya

Victor sighed happily, closing the book. He sat that way, visualizing Edeya and the others in Sojourn, living their lives. The idea that Darren Whitehorse, the asshole politician from First Landing, was now a *Thunderbird* and planning to marry an avian woman on Sojourn was so bizarre to him that he couldn't help but chuckle as he contemplated it. He was glad that Lam was finding some balance for her passionate infatuation with Edeya, too. Edeya was young—so was he, but who was counting?—and she deserved a little space to explore other aspects of herself.

He sent the book into storage, but when he looked around his cultivation chamber, the thought of actually cultivating no longer appealed to him. His mind was relaxed, and he felt the weariness of his ordeals in the dungeon. He felt the weight of his new Class, and to his delight, a deep, heavy yawn gripped him. "Good," he grunted, content to lie back right there in the dim, ambient light of the heavily enchanted amber ore.

Always hopeful, though not expecting anything to come of it, he summoned the ring Tes had made him and slipped it onto his thumb as he lay there on the hard surface of his cultivation platform. His body didn't mind the unyielding surface; his flesh was resilient, his bones like titanium. The curse burned in his chest, but it was a minor thing—an annoyance he'd grown used to, especially when he was flat on his back. He closed his eyes and let his mind drift through the fanciful ideas of children from the Free Marches going to schoolhouses in the villages and towns dotted around the countryside.

He slept heavily, but after a while, his consciousness became aware, and he found himself walking on a cobbled path in a moonlit garden. Everything had a strange, otherworldly luster, an underglow of silvery light that reminded him a little bit of the spirit plane. The colors were vivid, though, and the songs of nightbirds and the aromas of cherry-scented blossoms told him he wasn't on that twilit plane.

Victor paused while walking and took a minute to look around. The path meandered through tall shrubs with long dark leaves and aromatic white and orange blossoms. In the distance, he heard the tinkling music of a fountain, and when he turned to look behind him, he saw a slender figure approaching. She wore soft lavender skirts, and her pale yellow hair was tied back with matching ribbons.

Tes smiled when she saw him looking and skipped forward, arms wide, reaching for an embrace. "At last!" she said breathlessly, hugging him tightly. In that strange place, they were a good match, size-wise. Her cheek rested on his shoulder as he pressed her close, savoring the softness of her and the gentle floral scent of her perfume. "Fate has finally seen fit to bring us together," she murmured as he squeezed her gently.

"I have to admit, I was starting to think this crystal you made didn't work," he said with a chuckle.

"Such little faith!" she teased, grasping his shoulders and pushing herself back to look him in the eyes. Suddenly, her face grew grave, and her brows narrowed with concern. "You've changed."

"Yeah." He shrugged. "I guess I have."

"Your aura is heavier. You've gained much strength, but you're hurting. What ails you, Victor?"

Victor smiled, reaching up to take her hand, lifting it off his shoulder. Holding it gently, he said, "Let's walk through this pretty garden and not waste our time discussing things we can't do anything about." He turned to start walking, but Tes tugged her hand, stopping him.

"If there's a problem, then let me be the judge about what can be done."

He looked back at her, at the hardness in her eyes, the firm set of her jaw. Of course, she wouldn't let him blow past the issue, so he tried to minimize things. "It's nothing, Tes. I'm dealing with it. Isn't that what you wanted me to do—build my strength, my independence? This is one of those things I need to handle on my own."

"You'd use my words against me so? Victor, please, at least tell me what ails you."

Her fingers were warm in his hand, and her eyes were plaintive. She was so beautiful and obviously cared a great deal about him, but Victor found that some stubborn streak in his heart didn't *want* to tell her about the curse. He knew a big part of it was his pride; she'd left him to grow in power so they could stand together, unashamed in the society she called home. Well, that meant he needed to deal with his problems on his own. Another part of his reluctance was worry—worry that she'd insist on trying to help even though Dar had cautioned him that such help would, ultimately, do him harm.

He let go of her hand and folded his arms over his chest, frowning. "No, Tes. I won't have us waste this time together going round and round about something I'm going to handle on my own."

"But, Victor, if you're handling it, why would we go 'round and round'? Just tell me and trust that I'll respect your wishes. You trust me, don't you?" She stepped forward, resting her delicate fingers with lavender-painted nails on his crossed arms.

Victor's conviction crumbled, and he decided she had a good point. If nothing else, this would be a good test of her respect for him. If she insisted on trying to help, he supposed that would tell him much about how she viewed him. So, with a single nod of his chin, he said, "All right, Tes. I'll tell you, but then let's drop this subject and enjoy this gift of fate, agreed?"

She stared at him for a long, quiet moment and then mimicked his single nod. "Agreed."

"A Void Caster has put a curse on my spirit, and it's slowly devouring me. I've spent the last half of a year building my strength, preparing to battle the curse on the spirit plane, and I will do so when I wake up from this dream." While he spoke, she maintained eye contact with him, and though she didn't react with any change of expression, he saw moisture gathering in her eyes. More plaintively than he liked, he said, "I need to do this on my own, Tes. Do you understand?"

Her fingers tightened on his arm, and for the briefest of moments, he felt her control slip. He felt the depth of her power and the weight of her draconic aura. He'd felt it before when she'd teased him back on Coloss. Back then, it had been awe-inspiring and a little terrifying. Now, he could acknowledge that it was impressive, but it paled next to Azforath or the ivid queen. It wasn't much worse than standing before the full weight of Lohanse's aura. He smiled as she regained control, and it faded.

"I understand, sweet Victor. I understand." She slid her hand down his wrist to entwine her fingers with his. "Let's walk and talk and make the most of this wonderful gift of time together."

35

TIDINGS OF WAR

When Victor awoke the next day, it was midmorning, and he felt very rested. More importantly, though it still felt rather dreamlike, he remembered his time with Tes. Of course, if he were a cynic, he might wonder if his mind had invented the encounter—if he'd truly been dreaming and not "dream walking." Victor was a romantic, though, and if ever there was a bane for a cynic's take on the world, it was the romantic's. In his heart, he was certain he'd been with Tes, certain she'd chosen to respect him *almost* as an equal, and certain they'd spent hours walking, chatting, and simply *being* together.

When he emerged from his cultivation chamber, he found Arona and Bryn waiting, sitting together at one of the workbenches, perched on tall stools. Bryn jumped up when he stepped into the room, and Arona chuckled and said, "I told you he was only sleeping."

Bryn blushed a little, looking down. "I thought perhaps you'd already begun your battle with the curse."

"No," he said with a yawn, gently probing the tender flesh around the ball of void Energy. "I've yet to face this thing."

Arona nodded, pointing to a polished wooden box on the workbench. "Well, it's good you waited."

Victor stretched his neck until it popped and walked over to stand beside her. "You found what you were looking for?"

Arona smiled, drumming her fingers on the box. "Yes! Two tinctures to improve will and a potent potion for a temporary boost."

"I can't believe you haven't hit the ceiling on tinctures," Bryn said, moving to stand on the other side of him. "I think I was still a teenager before they stopped affecting me enough to make them worthwhile."

Arona clicked her tongue, chuckling. "Oh, I think if you searched wide enough and spent enough money, you'd find a tincture that still had a significant effect."

Bryn narrowed her eyes, glaring at the former Death Caster. "I did say *worthwhile*, yes? I don't intend to spend my family's fortune trying to eke out a few more points here and there."

"Fair enough." Arona nudged Victor. "Well? Open it!"

"Right." He yawned again. "Take it easy, ladies! I just woke up!"

"You *do* seem particularly groggy this morning. I don't think I've ever seen you in a state like this. Was it a good sleep, or were you tormented by . . ." Bryn trailed off, frowning awkwardly, as if she felt she'd put her foot in her mouth.

"Relax." Victor patted her shoulder. "I slept really well. Good dreams." Smiling to himself, he opened the box, revealing two silver vials stoppered with black wax, and a larger glass bottle containing lustrous golden liquid that sparkled and gleamed with an inner light.

"The two vials are the most potent will tinctures I could find," Arona said. "I'm sure the second one will have a much reduced effect, but that's all right. The potion is supposed to grant a tremendous boost that will last for up to an hour. I couldn't get any more specifics."

Victor picked up one of the small silver vials. "Should I drink these now?"

Arona's blue, almost crystalline-looking eyes sparkled with enthusiasm. "I don't see a reason not to."

"I'm curious," Bryn added.

"All right." Victor cracked the wax seal with his thumbnail and then pried the stopper out. A waft of vanilla with an acrid after-scent assaulted his nostrils. He tossed the contents into his mouth, swishing the liquid once before swallowing. It had the texture and vapors of an alcohol, and when it went down, it was sweet at first but fiery as he breathed. He coughed, chuckling as his eyes watered. "Potent."

"Do you feel it?" Bryn asked.

"My stomach is hot and—" Victor closed his mouth as tendrils of fiery heat spread upward along his spine and then encased his skull. It was like getting a scalp massage from a fire elemental. Not truly—it wasn't *quite* painful, but it was almost unpleasant as the spiderwebs of heat sank into his brain. He groaned, clenching his fists as mild convulsions racked him.

Arona looked at Bryn. "I'd say he's feeling it."

Bryn didn't laugh or take the chance to tease Victor. She grasped his shoulder and steadied him. "You'll be fine, Victor. We're here."

Perhaps shamed by Bryn's compassion, Arona nodded, grasping one of his clenched fists in her much smaller hands. "The reaction is lessening already."

She was right. The heat was fading, and his tremors were nearly gone. Victor opened watery eyes and coughed again. "Shit," he said with a chuckle. "Honestly, now that the fire is fading, I've got a nice buzz. Probably pretty expensive to use these to get drunk, though."

"And the effect?" Arona asked, her gaze intense.

"Right." Victor called up his attributes on his status page:

Strength:	680 (780)	Vitality:	957
Dexterity:	280 (445)	Agility:	303 (468)
Intelligence:	412	Will:	694

"Hey!" he laughed, clapping Arona on the shoulder, sending her stumbling off her stool. "Oof, sorry about that. Anyway, I gained twenty-one points!"

"That's impressive," Bryn opined. "These must have cost you dearly."

Victor shook his head. "Didn't cost me a thing." He hastily grabbed Arona's elbow, steadying her as she regained her stool. "Arona bought these for me."

Bryn's eyes widened further. "Oh? A good friend, indeed!"

Arona waved a hand, dismissing the comment. "It's nothing. I earned the beads fighting beside Victor, and you've no idea the debts I owe him." She pointed to the box. "There's no sense putting off the second tincture. If you waited for another racial advancement, it would be more potent, but you don't have time for that."

Victor burped, still feeling the inebriation brought on by the first vial, and shrugged. He picked up the second tincture, broke the seal, and tossed it back, coughing and thumping his fist on the workbench as the fire spread through him again. Either he was getting used to the effect, or it was, indeed, less potent because he hardly shook at all, and the heat seemed to fade far more quickly. When it was over, he pulled up his attributes again:

Strength:	680 (780)	Vitality:	957
Dexterity:	280 (445)	Agility:	303 (468)
Intelligence:	412	Will:	699

"Oof," he wheezed, his throat still raw from the drink. He swallowed, giving his regeneration a chance to address the issue.

Meanwhile, Bryn grew impatient, nudging his shoulder. "Well?"

"Only five points that time."

Arona smiled smugly, seemingly pleased by the less-than-ideal result. When she spoke, though, it became clear why. "I nearly bought a third. I'm glad I didn't—it likely would have garnered a single point."

"Well, I'm damn glad you suggested this, Arona. Twenty-six points is a significant gain." He made sure she was looking into his eyes and then added, "Thank you."

"You're welcome." She inclined her head slightly, and Victor could see she was pleased.

"Well, now I feel like a heel." Bryn sighed, folding her arms over her chest. "I should have thought of some way to help you with your—"

"Oh, stop it." Victor laughed, turning away from the workbench and walking to the door. "You help me every day. Just knowing you're here to cover for me with Kynna or to manage the palace staff—it means a lot. "Now, I'm going to take a shower, get some clean clothes on, and eat a hearty meal. Then I'm going back into that cultivation chamber, and I'm going to kick this curse's ass."

"Wait," Arona called. He turned, and she held up the potion. "Take this with you. Remember to drink it before your Spirit Walk." She tossed it to him, and he snatched it out of the air. Some might think that would be a risky thing to do with a glass bottle filled with an extremely expensive potion. Considering his superhuman adroitness, however, the risk was next to nonexistent.

Victor sent it into his storage ring, then performed a silly half-bow with a flourish of his arm. "Thank you!"

Bryn giggled. "He *is* in a good mood. Victor, do you want me to have the kitchen prepare anything special?"

He shook his head. "No, I'm going to barbecue some meat." He paused by the door and chuckled. "I'd invite you two, but it's lava king meat, and I'm cooking it with magma." He laughed at their expressions, shaking his head as he left. He *was* in a good mood. He supposed it had much to do with his dreamwalk with Tes, but he was also feeling some tension release—tension he'd been building steadily over the weeks and months he'd suffered under the curse. He was finally going to face it, and one way or another, he would be done with the damn thing.

He made good on his promise to shower and change, and then he left his chambers. After thumping Feist's shoulder and congratulating him on being awake for a change, he took the elevator up to the roof. The top of his tower was landscaped like a garden with paved pathways meandering between cedar planters that grew high with all manner of interesting plants. The groundskeeper could access the roof via the elevator, and Victor had run into her a couple of times as she trimmed and repotted various plants.

On that day, however, he was all alone on the rooftop, and when he walked to a large iron fire pit surrounded by comfortable cedar chairs, he savored the quiet and the warmth of the morning sun. After a while of basking, he summoned a large hunk of meat he'd cut from a lava king's thigh. He still had hundreds of pounds of the meat in his storage ring, and, thanks to the magic of the dimensional container, it wouldn't spoil.

He'd cooked his meat with his fiery breath more than once, and a few times, he'd tried seasoning it, but the magmatic fire of his breath wasn't kind to herbs. He supposed, if he took enough interest, he might try marinating the meat beforehand, but the truth was that some primal part of him loved it just as it was, blackened and charred by his breath on the outside and red and bloody at the center.

He put the roast-sized hunk in the firepit, gathered his breath, and blew a stream of magma into the basin, utterly scorching the meat. He wondered if there might come a day when he'd have more control over his Breath Core. Maybe he'd learn to control the temperature or thin out the spray of super-heated molten rock and gas. As it was, just a short burst was enough to sear the flesh, and if he kept it going any longer, he'd ruin it.

On an academic level, Victor knew that his fiery breath weapon existed as magma in his Breath Core, but that, as soon as it emerged from him and sprayed out onto the world, it was lava. He wasn't sure when that understanding had clicked for him. He supposed it was something he'd learned in a science class or seen mentioned in a movie or on TV, and as his intelligence increased, he simply accessed that distant bit of trivia: Magma is molten rock under the earth, and lava is molten rock after an eruption.

He chuckled at the idea that he was considering his Breath Core as "beneath the earth." There was more to it, of course; as he breathed the Energy out, it was laced with far more volatile gas than afterward. The lava cooling in the fire pit was far less explosive than the stuff in his Core. These were the sorts of thoughts that ran through his mind as he chewed his meat, sitting on a lounge chair and enjoying the morning sun.

As he finished, he stood and faced the iron fire pit. He inhaled and exhaled a stream of blue ice onto the cooling lava. It froze and shattered, allowing him to scoop it out of the fire pit and saving the groundskeeper from having to replace it. He was just finishing piling the thin shards of basalt on the side of the pit, easy to collect and dispose of, when a familiar voice startled him.

"An interesting trick, that."

Victor whirled, scowling, suddenly made furious by the intrusion on his peaceful brunch interlude. "Lohanse." He didn't mean to make the word sound like a curse, but it did.

The veil walker held his hands up, palms out. "I come in peace, Victor. In fact, I put myself at great risk to come here like this."

Victor frowned, trying to gather his temper. His aura was surging inside him, begging to be let loose. He flexed his will, though, and settled it. After a moment's pause, he cleared his throat and said, "You startled me."

"I see that. In any case, my time is short, and I have troubling news. Will you hear me?" Lohanse wore a matching tunic and loose, flowing pants crafted from silvery thread that shimmered in the sunlight. It was too flashy for Victor's tastes, but it looked like something a master tailor had sized and crafted. He had to admire how the fabric hung, without a single wrinkle, on the veil walker's frame.

"I'd be a fool to say no, wouldn't I?" Victor folded his arms over his very fine yet very mundane shirt.

"You seem changed. You've overcome a difficult milestone, perhaps. Hmm." Lohanse folded his arms but lifted one hand to scratch his chin. "No matter. Listen, Victor, things aren't well in the aerie." Victor knew the "aerie" was what the veil walkers of Ruhn called their domain—a floating island where none but they were authorized to venture.

"Yeah?" He almost added, "Why would I care?" but knew better.

"Yes. There are seventeen veil walkers—seventeen seats—on the guiding council of Ruhn. Over the last few centuries, through laziness, hubris, or sheer stupidity, we have allowed relatives of House Khaliday to occupy eight of those seats."

"Does that matter? I thought you all swore neutrality."

"Sadly, while bound by an Energy contract, that oath can be overruled by a two-thirds vote, and it's disturbingly specific in its limitations; there are ways to undermine it."

"So they only need three more votes?"

"Indeed. Three more votes, or a few dead or missing veil walkers."

Victor looked up to the blue sky, then around his garden. Was it quieter than it should be? "I take it you're masking our conversation."

"Of course. I'm as much a target as any."

"So the veil walkers are fighting?"

"Not openly, but Brishae Ri is missing. As you might guess, she was—is, I hope—aligned with me, proud of our neutral service to Ruhn. I fear things will become more and more . . . *muddled*. If the Khaliday faction takes control, then it's very likely they'll find a way to help Empress Matessa. They may refuse your right to a duel. They may simply look away while the Khalidaysian champions, warlords, and assassins assault Kynna en masse."

Victor growled, grinding his teeth. Had he really expected an empire that had held power for thousands of years to follow the rules? "What am I supposed to do, Lohanse? If the veil walkers are killing each other off, maybe you ought to bring help in from outside Ruhn. I could message Ranish Dar. I could—"

"Victor, just hours ago, my supporters and I locked Ruhn behind a dimensional barrier, a barrier meant to keep our citizens safe from incursions from hostile worlds. As Grand Judicator, I had that power, requiring only two others to engage the seal. The artifact structure that creates the barrier uses and amplifies my Energy, but it takes me out of the fight. I have very little left in reserve, and should the Khalidaysians come for me, I will have to flee, effectively giving up my seat."

"So unlock it and get some help," Victor pressed.

"Do you think we would be the only ones to bring in reinforcements? It would be the ruination of our world, Victor. Millions would die."

"Okay," Victor sighed, lowering his arms. "I'll ask again: What am I supposed to do?"

"You cannot flee. Not with the barrier in place. I suppose I came here to warn you. To give you a chance to prepare. The Dead Gods know that House Khaliday is preparing; if anyone is privy to the intentions of the Khalidaysian faction of the veil walkers, it would be the empress. With luck, my actions are driven by simple paranoia, and Brishae Ri will be found, restoring the balance of power. If, however, the Khalidaysians manage to eliminate or, through intimidation, turn more members, the fate of House Dar may soon be out of my hands. It will be all I can do to keep the veil walkers from openly participating in a conflict."

"Do you *think* you're being paranoid?" Victor asked, stepping closer to the other man.

"As evidenced by my engagement of the barrier, I do not. I have a feeling—a deep, sinking feeling—that things are changing, that the world I know is being pulled out from under me."

Victor's mind returned to the man's worst-case scenario. "Did you say champions? Plural?"

"As you've heard, House Khaliday has a new champion, but the empress's stable runs deep. She can call on half a dozen or more powerful steel seekers. Then there are the other warmongers that feast at her table—fiends like her brother Troyssas—and her assassins." Lohanse shook his head. "That's to say nothing of the allies to House Khaliday. While some great houses are eager to see them brought low, others will stand by their side. I wish I had better tidings, but I truly fear the best I can hope for is a stalemate in the aerie, and that would mean we'd have to let things play out down here."

Victor nodded, his scowl deepening. "You keep the veil walkers out of it, and I'll deal with the rest. Kynna might not have the kinds of monsters that the empress does in her stable, but she's conquered many nations. We can pull together an army to defend her."

Lohanse smiled, but it was a pitying smile, as if he was humoring Victor. "Of course. I'm sure you'll put up a magnificent resistance. I must leave now before my absence is noticed. Good luck, Victor. I will do everything in my power to forestall or turn aside the scenario we've discussed." He held out a hand, and Victor took it instinctively, without hesitation. It felt good to have Lohanse look him in the eye and shake his hand. He was a powerful man with an admirable code of honor. Victor hoped that wasn't the last time he would look him in the eyes.

36

INTO THE FRAY

Victor strode purposefully down the corridors of his palace with Bryn and Arona hurrying to keep pace. He hadn't explained anything yet. He knew better than to speak openly about Lohanse's warning—not before he was under the protection of Kynna's crown. There were plenty of devices to shield a person from scrying, but Kynna's crown was special, crafted by her husband as he ascended to the status of veil walker. It had enchantments that Victor hoped even other veil walkers would struggle to pierce.

When he reached the wing where the queen had set up offices, the guards pounded their spears and halberds on the marble floors in salute, and one of Kynna's aides hurried forward from his station. "Your Grace, how may I—"

"Where's the queen?"

"In the garden study, milord, but—"

Victor strode past him, the rest of his words lost, dismissed by his subconscious as Victor's mind raced through the implications of Lohanse's visit. He was at war with himself with regard to his curse. Should he still try to resolve it? Should he wait and prepare as best he could for the—in his opinion—inevitable attack? The problem was that he had no idea of the timeframe. Lohanse was good to warn them, but how *much* warning did they have? Was the empress sending her killers even now, or did she wait, hoping her partisan veil walkers would take control?

His long legs and hurried strides didn't allow for much contemplation time before he came to the study, and the guards outside snapped to attention. "I need to see her."

"Of course, Your Grace. One moment," one of the guards said, turning to open the door. "Your Majesty? The duke—"

Kynna's voice rang out, silencing the guard, "Come in, Victor." Victor walked into the room, scanning to see if the queen was alone; she was. He held the door for Arona and Bryn, then pushed it closed. "What is it, Victor? Are you unwell?"

He knew the queen asked that question because of his curse, but it still rankled. He hated having people doubt his health or readiness or . . . He shook the thoughts away. This wasn't the time for self-pitying irritation. He approached the queen's desk and beckoned for Arona and Bryn to come close. "My Queen, I'm well, thank you. Please activate your crown's ability to protect our privacy."

Kynna reached up and tapped the central spire of her tall crystalline crown, and a chime rang out as the shimmering shell of the crown's protection surrounded them. "What is it, Victor?" She looked from him to Arona and Bryn, who seemed as confused and concerned as she was.

"I was visited by Lohanse."

"What?" Kynna's eyes flew wide, and she leaned forward in her plush chair, uncrossing her legs as though she might leap up.

"He came with a warning . . ." Victor looked at Bryn and Arona. "This is not something you can repeat outside of Kynna's protection." He tapped his ear in illustration, and they both nodded. While they hung on his words, breathless, Victor recounted Lohanse's warning about what was happening with the veil walkers of Ruhn.

As he finished, Kynna slumped into her seat, defeated. "So this is how it will end, then? Will they not at least give us the option to flee Ruhn? If Lohanse will lift his barrier—"

"We aren't defeated yet," Victor growled.

"How can we win, Victor? You are mighty, but the great houses have champions that can, at least, challenge you. How can you face ten or twenty? If Matessa rallies her allies, it will be more like fifty or a hundred. Can you face so many steel seekers?"

"I will stand with you, Victor," Arona said, her raspy voice firm.

"As will I, of course!" Bryn sounded fierce, and Victor smiled, touched by her bravery. She wouldn't last long in such a battle.

"I didn't bring you here because I doubted your bravery, Bryn. Nor yours, Arona. I know you'll do what you can to help." He turned to Kynna. "You must rally the other champions you've gathered from our victories. You have to bring every person who might be able to fight for you to this palace. I don't mean soldiers, I mean powerful Energy wielders like that cowardly asshole, Thorn, who betrayed you. More importantly, you have to bring everyone who means *anything* to you here. We must keep them close and protected; otherwise, Matessa will use them against you."

Kynna's pale, slightly gray flesh paled further. "She'd force me to surrender by threatening their lives."

"Or she'd try to break you by impaling them outside your gates," Arona said flatly. Victor wondered what horrors she'd seen in the wars Vesavo made her wage.

"How much time do we have?" Kynna asked. Before Victor could answer, she added, "Truly, though, if they'd let us surrender, many lives could be spared—"

"Kynna," Victor said with a heavy sigh, "they'll want to make an example of you. Do you think they'd let you live? Do you think they could break every law of this world and let those they betrayed live to spread the tale? How could they pretend to have an egalitarian system when those meant to protect you orchestrated your downfall?"

"You're speaking of the veil walkers." Kynna's eyes unfocused as she made the connections. "If they allow Matessa to do this, they won't let me or mine live to tell the tale."

Victor folded his arms, nodding, swallowing a wince of pain as he pressed his arms against the curse. "It's a matter of survival now, Kynna. There isn't an option where we can walk away without a fight. Lohanse believes he can hold the Khalidaysian veil walkers to a stalemate, keeping them out of the fight. If we win—if we destroy the empress and her champions, they'll have nothing to fight for. With luck, they'll flee, and Lohanse can rebuild the Veil Walker Council." Victor was making things up, but he didn't care; as far as he could reason, that was what Lohanse hoped for.

"How long?" Arona asked.

"No idea. We have to hurry. Kynna, you must order everyone you care about, everyone who can fight, to come here. Arona and Bryn will help you prepare."

"And you, Victor?" Kynna stood, moving around her enormous desk to stand closer to him.

"I'm going to have a Spirit Walk. I have to be at my strongest, and that means removing this curse."

"I agree. You must rid yourself of it," Arona said, some metal entering her raspy voice. "Go, Victor. Let Bryn and me advise the queen. They will not find this palace an easy stone to crack."

Victor looked at Arona, saw the determined set of her brows, then turned to Bryn. She was trying to look brave, but he could see in her eyes that she was spooked. She was crumbling inside. She was being asked to stand against the most dangerous fighters on the planet, people she'd celebrated and revered as a child—great champions and families whose names echoed with gravity in the history books of her world. She must be thinking her end was at hand.

"I'm not going to let them destroy what we've built," he said, trying to sound confident. To help, he cast Imbue Spirit on Bryn, sending her a shard of his spirit laced with courage-attuned Energy. Her eyes lit up with golden Energy, and her back straightened as her fear fell away, replaced by determination. "Do you feel that?"

She clenched her fists and nodded.

"That's how I feel. That's how certain I am that we can win. *Remember* that feeling when you have doubt. Remember it when the men and women you command begin to falter in their resolve. I'm going to be here, and you can believe me when I say those motherfuckers haven't yet had a taste of what I can bring to a fight."

"I will be ready!" she said through her clenched, determined jaw.

Victor nodded, turning back to Kynna. "Listen to Arona, Kynna. She's fought wars."

"I was trained by one of the most devious and vile military minds ever to exist," Arona added. "I'm not proud of what he made me do, but we'll use that experience." She turned to glare at Victor. "Go! Let us prepare. The sooner you face your curse, the sooner you'll be ready to fight."

Victor nodded, inwardly quite pleased that she was taking charge. Without another word, and despite Kynna's intake of breath as though she might want to say something more, he strode out of the study. He figured he'd leave his Imbue Spirit active on Bryn until the last minute, but he'd need to cancel it before he spirit walked. He'd need every ounce of his strength.

When he returned to his chambers, he paused before entering his cultivation chamber. He'd caught a glimpse of Iron Mountain through his balcony windows and stepped outside to view the enormous peak more clearly. The sun was bright and the sky clear; it was easy to forget the executioner's axe hanging over Gloria. He pondered the great mountain, its shoulders high among the clouds, its peak scraping the firmament of Ruhn. It was a sight to behold, even for someone who'd traveled to several fantastical worlds.

It was easy to believe a primordial titan had settled down to rest there under that mountain. He wondered if he should have gone to Azforath for advice. Dar had cautioned him not to seek help, but he didn't know that Victor was, literally, on the doorstep of a being like Azforath, nor that the ancient titan was at least *inclined* to be friendly. Even so, Dar's advice about conquering this problem for himself held true. This was something Victor ought to face and defeat on his own.

As he turned, closed the door, and walked to his cultivation chamber, a voice in the corner of Victor's mind told him that line of thinking was bullshit. What if he'd been Level Twenty or even Fifty when Loss Chenasta cursed him? He'd be dead. What if he'd been a steel seeker? The curse probably wouldn't have taken hold. So, why was it so crucial that Victor face it alone now? Was it simply because he'd been cursed at the right time—a challenge he *could* face? "Bah!" He shook his head, throwing the philosophizing to the side. He had enough to worry about.

Inside his cultivation chamber, Victor summoned his Terror-Scale Boots. The supple black leather and glistening scales gleamed in the faint glow of the amber ore as he pulled them on. He wasn't sure they'd help him with this particular voyage onto the spirit plane, but he figured any little advantage was worth exploring.

Then, he summoned Lifedrinker and the potion Arona had purchased for him. He set the axe before him on the platform as he sat cross-legged on the unyielding surface. "Sorry, Bryn," he muttered, severing the connections to Imbue Spirit and Alter Self. His Energy came back to him in a rush as he surged in size, and the bits of himself he'd sent into Lifedrinker and Bryn returned. He stretched out a hand, lightly stroking the axe. "I'm sorry to call my spirit home. I need it to fight this curse."

"War-heart, I yearn for your touch, but I know you must conquer a most vicious foe. Bring me! Together, we cannot fail!"

Victor smiled and lifted the axe, something he would have struggled with a year prior, and laid her gently across his knees. "Of course you're coming." She radiated excitement and pleasure. "You're never afraid, are you, *chica?*"

"Never when I'm in your hands, blood-mate!"

Victor smiled, then ripped the cork out of Arona's potion. He tilted it to his lips and drained the bottle in two gulps. Warm tingles infused his spine and skull, and when nothing else happened, he looked at his attributes:

Strength:	680 (780)	Vitality:	957
Dexterity:	280 (445)	Agility:	303 (468)
Intelligence:	412	Will:	699 (769)

It seemed the potion was boosting his will by about ten percent. "Not bad," he grunted. Then, clutching Lifedrinker, he built the pattern for Spirit Walk and, bracing himself for anything, filled it with Energy. As always, the world shifted to shades of twilight, and the material forms of his cultivation chamber and even his palace fell away, replaced by grassy plains and, in the distance, an enormous, gloomy forest that stretched up the sides of a mountain that reached into the stars.

Victor was dumbstruck by the sight of Iron Mountain on the spirit plane, amazed by its majesty and the clarity of the twilight sky that revealed the firmament more clearly and, much closer to hand, moons and *other* structures that floated above the world, narrowly missing the tremendous peak. His fascination was cut short, though, when something cold and biting snaked around his neck and began dragging him backward over the grass.

Victor gasped and tightened his grip on Lifedrinker's spirit form. She was glossy black but filled with light like that you'd see shining down from a moon.

When he rolled onto a shoulder, swinging her around in an arc at whatever gripped his throat, she whistled through the air like the wind itself and bit into the thick rope of inky blackness. Victor gasped, and though his body was a construct of his spirit and mind, he felt the need to heave his chest for air as the constriction faded.

As his head cleared and he gained his feet, he saw what had come for him, and horror filled his mind. A swirling *blob* of nothingness as big as a house squatted on the grassy plain, half embedded in the earth and half exposed. The exposed half writhed in the air, waving hundreds or thousands of tentacles like the one that had seized his neck. They wriggled out and down, snatching up bits of twilit grass and soil, pulling them into the blob where they were destroyed or absorbed—Victor couldn't tell.

"*Chingado,*" he hissed, stepping back. He held Lifedrinker ready as more of the tentacles snaked through the air toward him. Was this the representation of the curse on the spirit plane? He wondered why it wasn't attached to him, but he found his answer as he tried to dodge back and felt everything get . . . *thicker.* He was bound to the monstrosity. His image, his projection of himself, looked like his physical form on the material plane, but he was *more* than that. He'd entered this part of the spirit plane from his body, and that was where the curse and *he* were anchored.

As he tried to move away, the air felt like water, then it felt solid, and he simply couldn't move more than a hundred yards from the blob. Even the ground sucked at his feet. "Okay, then. Let's fuck this thing up, *chica.*"

"I yearn to taste it again!"

Grinning, Victor stepped forward. He summoned his Banner of the Champion, blasting the landscape with brilliant golden light, and then he cast Iron Berserk, expanding in size and flooding his pathways with the blazing heat of his rage. Stomping forward, he unleashed his aura, letting it flow outward as he approached the blackness of the void that was feasting on his spirit, among other things.

Tendrils of blackness snaked out as he approached, eager despite his heavy, rage-filled aura. He swatted them with Lifedrinker, and she sheared them to bits with every swipe. In his full, titanic glory, Victor stood even with the top of the blob, but it was vast, its mass enormous. He wasn't sure cutting pieces off was the strategy to employ, but it was what he did best, what his instinct demanded when he began a fight, so he leaped into the work with a vengeance.

Tentacles snaked out and tried to ensnare him, but he ripped them apart with his movements; his titanic figure was unstoppable. Lifedrinker cut and cleaved, ripping great hunks of the blob apart. Victor was surprised; he'd expected the blackness to be void-attuned Energy. He'd expected that it might hurt Lifedrinker to cut into it, but she didn't recoil or seem harmed.

He hacked her in great, sweeping arcs, biting deep into the gelatinous meat of the blob, but even as he did so, the cuts filled in, and the bits he shaved off rolled and slithered over the grass to join with their mother. "Fucking *hell*," he roared. "How do I hurt this *pinché* son of a bitch?"

The harder he fought, the more futile the effort seemed. And Victor backed off, hoping to conserve some strength. Several long tentacles of ropy blackness followed after him, but he slashed them, and they retreated. Growling, his rage magnified by his frustration, Victor concentrated and, with an effort of will, canceled his Iron Berserk.

Lifedrinker's blade wasn't enough to kill the blob, and he wasn't willing to risk her by leaving her embedded in the mass of . . . *stuff* to attempt to drain it. That meant he needed a new tactic. As soon as he felt his Core regenerating, and after cleaving another seven or eight probing tentacles, Victor built the pattern for Volcanic Fury. The magma- and rage-attuned Energies flooded his pathways, and he surged in size, roaring his awful madness into the air.

Peering with sepia-toned vision toward the mound of quivering hateful sludge, Victor felt his fury multiply. He screamed his passion, stalking toward it, and as soon as he was within a dozen strides, he gathered his breath, filling his lungs and opening the pathways to his Breath Core. Hot magma licked his lips as he exhaled, sending a gout of the fiery, steaming Energy to splash against the quivering mass of tentacles.

The sound of the lava impacting the curse was like an egg hitting an over-heated frying pan. It sizzled and popped, and hot gasses burst from the impact. As the matter that made up the blob absorbed the heat, it bubbled and quivered, solidifying under the lava as it, too, cooled to basalt. Victor roared out that breath as long as he could, the longest blast he'd ever given without the aid of his ancestor's fire.

When he stopped, his vision clouded by steam and smoke, gasping for air, he was thrilled to see a great section of the blob had fallen still, its tentacles all burned to stubs. "Ha!" Victor howled in victory. He lifted Life-drinker and stalked toward the hardened, dead section of the blob, intent on smashing it apart, exposing more fresh innards for him to burn with his next blast.

He was one step away, axe held high, when the solidified part of the blob shivered and sank, wholly absorbed by the thing. Fresh, glistening black jelly appeared, and new tentacles grew out. Worst of all, the blob seemed larger. Victor, maddened by his Volcanic Fury, *knew* something was wrong, but he only felt rage and a renewed determination to slaughter the thing before him. So, he went at it, screaming and spitting his madness as he hacked Lifedrinker into the blob again.

He focused on a single thought like a terrier outside a rat hole: Maybe something was hiding from him in there. Maybe he could carve his way to the center and kill whatever it was. Roaring, cursing, spitting fire, he hacked, kicked, and burned his way into the blob. Despite the fury that had overridden much of his logic, a small part of himself managed to wonder if he was being foolish, but he wasn't ready to listen to that tiny voice. He was a titan, and this damn thing needed to feel his *wrath*!

37

ON HANDS AND KNEES

As Victor waged his war of madness, hacking Lifedrinker left and right, encouraging her to drink and feast on his shapeless, gigantic foe, he slowly came to grips with the realization that he was making no progress. Worse, it seemed he'd ensconced himself in the thick, clinging, burning, freezing *stuff*. As he swung and railed, jerking his arms, kicking his legs, breathing his magma and blue ice, he made a pocket for himself, but the black gelatinous stuff *kept coming*.

It was only when he found himself fully immersed, hundreds of tentacles clinging to his arms and legs, his torso, and his neck, that they began to show their true nature. The gelatinous surface seemed to sublimate into a hissing, burning black steam that *wasn't* steam. It wasn't *anything*. It dissolved his spirit flesh with a touch in a fiery, torturous cascade a million times worse than the single point of void he'd suffered with on the material plane. However, his own suffering was nothing compared to the tortured scream Lifedrinker wailed out as the void began to dissolve her spirit form.

The sound brought a shock of panic to Victor's heart, and his pain was forgotten. His rage faded as fear surged into his pathways. How could he be so foolish as to risk Lifedrinker? What would he do without her? If she died there, if her spirit was consumed by his curse, he'd never forgive himself. As his panic mounted and Lifedrinker's screams echoed through his mind, Victor summoned every ounce of control he could, trying to silence his racing thoughts, trying to tune out the horrific pain of his flesh being dissolved, regrown, and dissolved over and over.

He focused on his Core space, dragging the fear out of his pathways and commanding his inspiration to flood them. As his grip on that positive, white-gold Energy intensified, he shaped it into his Core Domain spell and unleashed it in the heart of the cursed miasma. Inspiration-attuned Energy exploded around him, reshaping the very soil and air of the spirit plane, and Victor was granted a reprieve as the void Energy struggled to gain purchase.

Lifedrinker's wails subsided, but the agony that still racked her came through her haft into Victor's hands, and he screamed his horror and guilt for having done that to her. His cries raged into the glittering, brilliant domain he'd created, and he spun, desperate to find an egress, a way to get Lifedrinker to safety. His Core was much more potent than when he'd learned to create his domain, but it still bled Energy at a frightening rate.

How long could he hold the void at bay? How long could he . . . *feed* it? Suddenly, it clicked, and Victor realized his folly. He'd bought himself and Lifedrinker a moment of respite, but at what cost? His Core was gushing Energy into the void, and the damn curse was eating it up! Growling with frustration, mostly at himself, Victor pulled magma-attuned Energy from his half-depleted Breath Core and sent it into the pathways for his fiery wings. As they burst, crackling with glorious power, from his shoulders, he launched himself up, hoping to escape the curse before his Spirit Core was drained.

When he reached the edge of his inspiration-attuned domain, he smashed into the gelatinous substance of the curse's solid form and blasted a tunnel with his magmatic breath. At the same time, he cracked his blazing wings and surged upward, streaking out of the curse, trailing black smoke that faded into glittering mist on the spirit plane. The curse reached for him, sending giant, ropy tentacles after him, grabbing his legs and feet. He ignored them, flying with every ounce of Energy he had, pulling them with him, stretching the *stuff* of the curse like great rubber bands behind him.

He was clear of the body of the curse and knew he was close to the limits of his movement, thanks to how the curse bound him to this part of the spirit plane. Lifedrinker was part of his heart—a partner through everything. He'd die before he let her be consumed by the void. If he held on, if he failed with her in his hands, she'd die.

Fighting back tears of frustration and guilt, he screamed, "I'm sorry, Lifedrinker!" and hurled her past the boundary. Without him, she was free to burst free of the curse's domain, and she flipped through the air, sailing a hundred yards before smashing into the grassy, twilit plain. There she rested, her blade in the ground, her haft standing high, waiting for his grasp, close but impossibly distant.

As he'd fled his Core Domain, the spell had shattered, so Victor's Core was no longer draining at a precipitous rate. Still, looking inward as he fought against the pull of the curse's tentacles, he saw his Core was dim, and he knew if he looked at his status sheet, he'd be down to something like twenty percent of his maximum. As he stared, his mind numb at the utter failure of his assault, Victor's Breath Core ran dry, and his wings sputtered and faded.

He fell to the grass with a ground-shaking thud. With his feet firmly planted, he could more easily resist the pull of the tentacles still gripping his legs. He stared down their ropy lengths to the bulk of the curse, and despair gripped him; it was twice the size as when he'd arrived on the spirit plane. He had no weapon to cut the tendrils around his legs. He had no breath, and worse, it wasn't regenerating.

Frowning, he checked his Spirit Core again—still dim. Why couldn't he regain his Energy? That had never been the case on the Spirit Plane before. He had to assume it was the way he was bound to that spot, in close proximity to the enormous, surging void. It drank the spirit plane's ambient Energy like a sponge in blood—quiet but insatiable. Frustrated, furious, and worried about Lifedrinker, Victor tried to end his Spirit Walk.

He felt it start to happen; he felt his spirit bleeding through the veil, back to the material plane, but the cursed tendrils gripping his legs pulled him back. Victor reached down to grasp one of the tentacles. He grabbed it with both hands, crushing the squishy substance in his fists as he pulled, ripping it away from his leg. It stretched rather than broke, though. No matter how he pulled, more of the substance pumped through the tentacle to fill in the narrowed section. Soon, he had a knee-high coil near his feet, and then *that* began to erupt with smaller, grasping tendrils.

"*Chingado!*" Victor hissed, stumbling away from the nest of writhing, grasping, miniature tentacles. Once again, his fear began to escape the confines of his Core, seeping into his pathways. This time, Victor embraced it. If he couldn't rip the tentacles off, perhaps he could rend them. He built the pattern for Abyssal Tyrant and let the fear-attuned Energy flow through him.

As Victor's body surged with the power, convulsing—*changing*—he screamed, first in agony, then in frenzied hunger—a screech that echoed through the spirit plane, sending any spirits lingering near scurrying. His joints twisted, and his limbs expanded. Great talons exploded from his shadow-wreathed hands, and enormous black-feathered wings burst from his back, trailing smoky shadows in their wake. Sharp spines burst from his flesh, even as that very flesh turned dark, obscured by oily shadows and scales that clung to him like tattered robes.

He arched his back, lifting his black, depthless eyes to the twilight sky, screaming such a sound that the very grass quailed away from its echoing horror. Victor's face, cloaked in those same inky shadows, elongated into a black hooked beak, though his teeth remained in the back, sharpening to needles as they multiplied.

There he stood, a nightmare incarnate. He was a creature of night and shadow, terror and despair—fifteen feet tall, with a wingspan to match. His arms were too long, though hard to see in the shadows that obscured him. Though his talons lacked Lifedrinker's enhancement, they were ten inches long, razor sharp, and curved. The spines that dotted his scaly, smoky flesh dripped inky shadows that sizzled as they fell to the grassy plain.

Again, he screeched, casually swiping his talons through the tentacles that bound his legs. They fell apart in tatters. Victor, a tyrant of fear, cracked his wings, exploding into the air. Deep in his mind, some part of him rebelled at what he'd become, but the tyrant didn't care. The hunger drowned everything. He scanned the gray landscape, searching for color, but seeing only darkness. There was nothing close by to feast upon. He shrieked again, confident his cry would bring some fear to the surface or flush some bright spirit out to flee.

His survey was cut short as he hit *something*—a thickness of the air that refused to let him pass. Frustration mounted as he shrieked again, fighting against the barrier. Failing to make any progress, he turned back toward the ground, scanning the grayscale landscape. Of course, he saw the heaving mountain of blackness, and part of his mind knew it was his enemy, that it wanted to destroy him.

He vaguely recalled his earlier fight with it. He remembered how it had hurt his most loyal companion. It made him furious, but he was an Abyssal Tyrant, and hunger was paramount. That blackness, that *emptiness* held no sustenance for him. Every second he existed cost him something; every movement of his terrible form drained his stores of Energy, and he saw *nothing* to feast upon. Swooping left and right over the mountainous void, he tested the limits of his boundaries and found he was running out of space.

As his Core spent itself to maintain his existence and his lack of sustenance weakened the tyrant in his mind, Victor began to come more and more back to himself, and he knew what he had to do. As much as it rankled, as much as it was antithesis to his very nature, as much as it would shame him, he had to flee. It was a conclusion he'd already made once, but for some reason, wearing the primal skin of the Abyssal Tyrant made the torment to his pride all the more visceral.

With a frustrated, infuriated screech, Victor, still soaring on wings of shadow and midnight black feathers, ended his spirit walk, the taste of failure thick in his throat. That bitter taste was soon forgotten, replaced by the coppery suffocation of blood and the horrific pain of a body being consumed. "*Gack!*" he gasped, blinking his eyes, trying to make sense of what he saw. His vision was tinted crimson, and it pulsed, black tunnel walls threatening to encase him with each agonizing thud of a heart that was constantly being destroyed and regrown.

He turned to his side and coughed out a gout of blood, only to have it come up again, choking him. He peered down and saw, through the ruins of his shirt, that the void was enormous—large enough to consume his lungs and heart and eat into his spine. His titanic body and behemoth regeneration fought against it valiantly, but it was a losing battle. The fact that he lived at all was a testament to the durability of his bloodline.

His cultivation chamber was dim, the pedestal on which he lay smeared with blood, but he was alone. He tried to stand, but his legs only worked intermittently. He reached for Lifedrinker's haft, hoping—praying—but she felt cold. Inert. Her spirit was trapped on the other side. Despair and defeat overwhelmed him then, and Victor's mind found the darkest corner possible and crawled into it.

He lay there for a while, trying to make himself numb to the pain of the constant destruction of his body. The void was directly responsible for the worst of it, but his body was failing in other ways. His blood flow was intermittent, his breathing, too. His body was largely dependent on Energy, but it still needed oxygen. It still needed his organs to *function*. A constant stream of blood dribbled from his mouth, the result of repeatedly ruptured vessels and arteries.

While his body suffered, Victor's mind drifted away from it. He thought about all the mistakes he'd made. He thought about the foolishness of going onto the spirit plane ready to do battle as though a dragon awaited, and not a curse. It was clear that the thing wouldn't be killed by conventional means. *Could* it be killed? He'd taken the idea of "battling" with it far too literally. There must be another solution. Even with his gains, though, his will was clearly not up to the task.

The thought that followed that line of thinking was nothing short of pitiful; he was helpless to improve now. The fight was done. Why not succumb to the damn curse and put an end to the suffering? The thought wasn't serious. Not at first. It wasn't in Victor's nature to give up. Perhaps he asked the question so that he could review *why* he fought. Down that road lay *people*—always people. He never fought *just* for glory, did he? Wasn't he always trying to accomplish something for . . . *someone?* Sure, he stood to gain, but did anything matter if he was alone?

If he didn't have people around him, people to share in his victories, what was the point? If he gave up now, those people would be gone. Would they be all right? Some of them would, but would *he?* His mind drifted into a fantasy, imagining another life, another existence, and running into Tes or Valla again. They'd be different, and so would he, but . . . on some level, wouldn't they *know?* Wouldn't they know he'd given up? If they wouldn't, he damn well would. It would be a mark on his spirit.

"*Fuck* that," he grunted, spitting out another gout of blood as he pushed himself to his hands and knees. His palms were numb. His legs, too. It felt as if he was gliding on waxy air as he crawl-fell down the steps to the cultivation chamber door. As he crunched his face against the unyielding metal, he reached up to slap his hand on the control panel. A moment later, the door bolts thunked open, and he pushed it wide with his shoulder.

Sunlight came through the high windows of his workshop, blasting into his bloodshot eyes. He felt relieved when he saw the workshop was empty. Bryn's little makeshift bedroom was vacant. He could see her bed was made behind the screens—had she stopped sleeping there? He honestly didn't know. He'd assumed it was temporary while he'd been unconscious, but then why was her bed still there? Why was there a dress uniform neatly folded atop the chest beside it?

Victor coughed up another gout of blood and shook his head. Why was he focusing on things that didn't matter? Grimacing, he crawled out of the chamber and then, leaving a streak of blood in his wake, toward the center of the workshop. He unwound the chain for his vault from around his wrist, then, trembling with the effort, he turned the key and set the vault down. As it hissed and steamed, he crawled back, collapsing twice before he was far enough away to be clear of the vault's rapid growth.

Gasping for breath, he lay there for a few minutes, waiting for the vault and then gathering his strength for the next push, for his next effort. As he lay there, panting, he heard boot heels on the floor and opened his eyes to see Bryn come around the side of the vault, peering at it, clearly puzzled. "Bryn," he choked, spitting more blood.

"Your Gr—*Victor!*" She sprinted the last few steps toward him, falling to her knees at his side.

"Careful," he grunted. "Don't touch the void."

"It's, oh, *ancient gods*, Victor!" Tears sprang into her eyes as she gingerly put her hand on his shoulder, gently squeezing.

"Looks worse than—" He broke off, coughing out another gout of blood. He tried not to get any on Bryn, but it was a losing fight; he could barely control his body's movements. "Sorry," he croaked.

She was openly sobbing by then. "What should I do? Should I get help?"

"Nah, nothing anyone can do. Listen, I'm not done yet." He paused to cough up some more blood. "See my vault there? Open the door for me."

Blinking back tears, Bryn looked at the vault, then, sniffing, stood up to approach the door. "Just turn the key?"

"Yeah. When it's open, take the key out and give it to me." He watched as she opened the door and then pulled the key out. She peered at it with interest as she handed it back to him. "Thanks, Bryn." Victor began the arduous process of crawling into the vault. There wasn't a huge space inside, but he could fit with room to spare even at his normal, giant size. It didn't really matter as he was crawling, anyway.

"Sh-should I come in with you?" Bryn asked from the doorway. Victor hated that she was watching him crawl. He wished he'd managed this part alone.

"No, Bryn. Listen, I—" He paused as an intense wave of pain washed over him, and the black tunnels encroaching on his vision nearly closed in.

"*Victor?*" Bryn started forward, but he held up a hand.

"No. Listen. I'm going to do something crazy, but it's my last option. I think. Shit, Bryn, I don't know. T-tell Kynna I'll do my best. If—if I don't come out of here, I'm sorry. I promise I won't give up. I'll try to the end. Tell Arona that."

"Victor . . ." Bryn stood by the door, clearly vacillating between coming into the vault or running for help.

"Thanks, Bryn. I'm damn glad you were assigned to me when I got here. Go on, now. Push that *pinché* door shut for me." Victor was on his hands and knees, blood drooling from his mouth, and he knew she probably thought he'd lost his mind. Gathering his strength, he looked up, locked eyes with her, and roared, "*Do it!*"

She jumped, eyes flying wide, then grabbed the heavy door and swung it shut with a clang that echoed with a note of finality. Victor used the vault wall to steady himself as he lifted his torso high enough to reach the lock. He stuck the key in the hole and twisted it until the locks engaged. "There," he gasped, falling back onto his butt. He turned and, unsure whether he was about to save himself or seal his fate, crawled toward the satchel containing the ivid royal jelly.

38

A GUIDING HAND

Arona looked from the sealed vault door to Kynna. She stood with arms folded, one hand under her chin, lips pressed into a thin line. Her eyes were narrowed, and the white flames that burned in their crystal orbs were dim. Arona turned to Bryn, whose expression was anything but guarded. She, too, had crossed her arms, but in her case, it was more like she was hugging herself. Her lips trembled, and her eyes were red from the tears she'd cried.

Arona stepped closer and gently grasped Bryn's wrist. "His words, Bryn—tell them to me again."

She sniffed and, with a quavering voice, replied, "He said to tell the queen he'd do his best. He said he wouldn't give up. He told me to tell you that he'd try to the end."

Kynna stepped forward, resting her palm on the cold, glyph-inscribed metal of Victor's vault. "Can we open this, Arona?"

"You could ask Trobban his opinion, but I think not. It's Fae-craft—true elder magic. I don't know where Victor found it, but it's far beyond my ability to breach. I think the Energy required would destroy this palace and anything inside."

"*Trobban?*"

"The Artificer Victor employed. I'm sorry; I thought you knew him." Arona could see the queen was struggling to maintain her even demeanor. She could see the cracks along the edges of her veneer—a hastily made fist to quiet trembling fingers, eyes blinking just a touch too rapidly, an inability to maintain eye contact, and, most of all, a refusal to look at or question Bryn further about Victor's condition.

"Ah, yes. I remember now." The queen didn't say more but leaned her forehead against the vault and closed her eyes. "Why did he *lock* himself in?"

"My Queen," Bryn blurted, "you should have *seen* him. He was barely alive, he—"

"Hush," Arona said, tightening her grasp on the woman's wrist. "Victor might have looked terrible, but he's a very hard man to kill." She looked toward Kynna. "I can think of a few reasons he might have sealed the vault." When the monarch didn't respond, she continued. "He may believe that what he's doing will take a while. He knows we might come under attack and wouldn't want us to expend resources protecting him. There's also the possibility that whatever he's doing in there is dangerous. Perhaps he doesn't want to expose us to it."

"What *could* he be doing?"

"He had treasures in there—things I only glimpsed in their containers. Perhaps there was something he was saving as a last resort. Something he thought would be better *not* to use."

Again, the queen didn't respond, but Arona could see her lips moving as she continued to press her forehead against the cold vault door. Was she praying? Did the people here pray to gods? Arona scraped her memory but couldn't recall any worship—just the old curses, the muttered names of dead powers. She cleared her throat. "Queen Kynna, we must continue as planned. There's naught else for us to do. We cannot flee this world. If Victor said he would fight to the end, then we must do so as well."

She turned to Bryn, pulling her wrist to unfold her arms. "You must be strong for Victor now. You're a warrior, Bryn, and we'll need you to inspire the troops. Do you remember Victor's words to you when we met in the queen's study?"

Bryn blinked her eyes and looked down at Arona. In her current state of distress, the fighter looked softer than usual, more delicate. Arona knew better, though; Bryn was a strong woman. Perhaps Victor had made a mistake granting her so many titles and lands—so many privileges. She had much to lose now, and she could feel everything slipping through her fingers. It was a weighty thing, responsibility. She smiled and said as much. "Things were easier when you were a simple member of the Queen's Guard, weren't they?"

Bryn sniffed, set her lips into a firm line, and shook her head. "I'm up to this, if that's what you're asking." She cleared her throat and spoke more forcefully. "My Queen, I've drafted the missives, and the messengers are set. Shall I put things in motion?"

The queen was silent for a while, still pressing her forehead to the vault. Arona began to wonder if she should prod her to action again, but then Kynna stirred and stood up straight. She turned, reaching up to adjust her crown. Her face was set in a stern glower as she nodded to Bryn. "Go. Gather our heroes. Gather our loved ones. We'll make our stand here, and, with luck and the love of the fates, Victor will emerge to join us against our foes." With that, she walked around the vault and toward the exit. She paused and said, "Arona, please find me in my study this afternoon. We've many plans to discuss."

"I will, Your Majesty." Arona listened as her steps receded, then turned to Bryn. "You can do this. We must."

"You could hide. You could go to another city. The—" She stopped speaking, knowing she couldn't name their foes without Kynna's crown to shield their conversation. "*People* don't even know you exist."

Arona smiled and shook her head. "I'd never do that to Victor. I promised I would help, and so I shall. My life has been long and dark, Bryn. These last months on Ruhn have been bright enough to outshine a hundred years of darkness. I owe that to Victor, and I won't deny that I've grown fond of some of the folk here." She held out a hand, and Bryn took it. Her palms were warm and a little clammy—stress would do that to a person. "Come. I'll keep you company while you speak to your envoys. My preparations will take some planning, and you can help me with that when you're done."

Bryn nodded, forcing a smile as she gripped Arona's hand. Together, they departed the workshop, leaving Victor's vault to brood there in silence. It was like an egg—full of potential, but also bearing a distinct possibility of failure. Would it open, or would it fade into myth, buried in the ruins of a once mighty kingdom?

Victor sat in his vault, his back to the wall. A streak of blood ran from the door to where his feet twitched, his muscles spasming regularly thanks to the sorry state of his body. In his lap was a silk-wrapped package, impossibly small considering the power that dwelt within it. He remembered it being bigger— *heavier*—but then, he'd been smaller the last time he held it. He closed his eyes and tried to remember the moment Crystal, the queen of the ivid, gave it to him.

He remembered her eyes—iridescent like pools of rainbow—and how her voice, like crystalline chimes, had sounded in his mind. What had she said? He racked his memory, and her voice came back to him, clear as the day he'd first heard it:

"My gift is potent and, outside our hive, something that would be nigh impossible to acquire. I'm giving you a sample of the royal jelly my attendants fed to me in order to make me a queen. It's the same substance they will feed to my replacement. I do not feel it will threaten our hive at all to give you this small sample. You will take it away to your world, and soon, we will be separated from your universe. For this reason, I'm willing to risk the unknown effects it will have upon you. It will be up to you to decide if you are willing to take that same risk."

The idea of "unknown effects" and "risk" had once been enough to make Victor wonder if he'd *ever* eat the jelly. Now, though, as a roiling void sought to consume him, they seemed like trivial concerns. Of course, he'd hoped to save the jelly for a greater need. Hadn't Tes impressed upon him how valuable and potent it was? Would it have made the jump to steel seeker, or perhaps to veil walker, trivial? He had no idea. Maybe it wouldn't help him much at all. Maybe it would destroy him.

Carefully, he unfolded the silk that encased the crystalline globe. He'd struggled to look at the stuff back when he'd first found it, but now, despite his pain and weakness, he found he could stare at the strange, golden, gelatinous substance inside the crystal. It was heavy for its size, but he wasn't sure if that was the magical container or the jelly. It looked tiny in his massive palm—only about the size of a baseball. He could see a nearly invisible seam near the top of the globe, and he figured he was meant to unscrew it.

He didn't do so, though; despite his mental assertion that he could withstand the jelly's pull, he found himself staring, unable to move. His mind was caught up in the weird, reflective swirls of the substance. It wasn't all a consistent golden color. Parts of it were amber, tinting toward red. If his throat hadn't been constantly filling with blood, he would have realized he was salivating madly. It was that blood that broke him from his trance; he began to choke, and he jerked his head to the side, coughing out a gout of foamy red liquid.

He put his hand over the globe to save his mind from slipping away again, and then he had a disturbing thought: What if, when he swallowed the jelly, the void consumed it? The damn curse was right at the center of his chest and was clearly devouring at least part of his esophagus on a continual basis. He resolved that he'd have to simply hold the jelly in his mouth, hoping it could find its way into his blood if he held it under his tongue. Would it make it less potent? He'd have to hope not.

Squeezing his eyes shut, lest he lose himself to the jelly's pull again, he took a deep breath and held it—he didn't want to be sent into a coma or something when he smelled it. Then he gripped the top of the crystal sphere and twisted. The ivid were clearly more clever craftsfolk than he'd anticipated. The top came away instantly, without any effort, as though it knew he wanted to open it. Victor didn't hesitate; the time for that was past. He lifted the little orb to his lips and turned it, pouring the stuff into his mouth.

It didn't *pour*, exactly. It kind of flopped out like a hunk of semisolid jelly. When it touched his tongue, Victor could no longer hide from its potency. His eyes sprang open, every vein in his body dilated, and stars exploded in his vision. A sound like a tornado rushed through his ears, deafening him. Then, as the ivid royal jelly dissolved in his saliva and sank through the pores of his flesh and into the tiny vessels of his mouth, Victor felt a rapid expansion of tingling, fiery euphoria spread through his body. Before he could savor the feeling, his mind was ripped free of its physical bonds.

If Victor had been conscious to watch what happened to his body, he would have seen golden steam erupt from every pore in his body. He would have watched as it gathered in a cloud around him, obscuring his figure. Then, he would have seen that steam solidify, encasing him in a golden, crystalline cocoon. He wasn't cognizant, though, and even if he had been, his eyes were obscured. He couldn't see or taste or breathe; he couldn't hear or even wonder how the cocoon wasn't affected by the void that it had encased.

Victor drifted on a cloud of Energy. Unlike other times when he'd been swept away for a vision of this ancestor or that, or sent hurtling into the void, bodiless and unaware, he felt very much like he knew who and what he was. He knew he was Victor, and he knew he'd just consumed something incredibly potent. What he wasn't sure of was whether or not he was alive. He felt a lot like he did when he performed a Spirit Walk.

He could see his body, somewhat ethereal and luminescent, and he could see that he stood on . . . *something*. He wasn't sure what, however. All around him was a dense fog of Energy so rich that when he tried to quantify or categorize it by shape or color, he couldn't. It escaped his attempts, slipping from conscious thought just when he thought he had a grasp on it.

He tried walking, and that worked, but it took him nowhere. He tried sitting on that strange surface, and his body complied, though, again, it accomplished nothing. Was he meant to do something? Was he just meant to wait? Was he transitioning through the veil? "Ha," he muttered, surprised to find that his voice worked though it traveled nowhere. Wouldn't it be ironic if his attempt to continue fighting had been an elaborate way to kill himself?

As that bitterly humorous thought passed through his mind, Victor was sent down a spiraling mental trip of regrets. Valla and Tes featured prominently. Deyni and Cora, Chala and Chandri. Of course, his other friends paraded by: Thayla, Tellen, Kethelket, Olivia, Edeya, Lam, Lesh, and even Darren. He thought of Kynna and Bryn and the thousands of people depending on him to defend them. He thought of Arona and hoped she'd win free. If anyone could escape to tell his loved ones what became of him, she would be the one.

Eventually, he stood up and continued walking . . . nowhere. He had no other plans and nothing else to do, so he figured it was better than sitting around sulking. Maybe he was worried about nothing. Maybe the royal jelly was just doing its thing, and he'd wake up healed and powerful. He shook his head. Why, then, would he be conscious? Why wasn't he dreaming? He wished he had someone to guide him, some person he could seek counsel from—Dar or Khul Bach, or even Azforath. No, he decided, if he could have anyone to help him in that moment, it would be Chantico. He *liked* her and the way she called him "little brother."

He sat down again, bored with his endless trip to nowhere. He thought again about Chantico and the advice she'd given him regarding his curse. Hadn't she said to make himself like a fortress? She'd said he should contemplate what he feared, what had kept him floating for six months in the void. He'd vastly improved his control over his fear, hadn't he? He'd built up his Core by draining enough terror-attuned Energy to grant him two levels. He'd reached Level Ninety and gained a far more powerful aura.

Was his aura not an extension of *him* and everything that made him up—his Core, his affinities, his accomplishments, his spirit, and his *will*? That had been his understanding—so many of his feats affected his aura, and apparently, so did his class. Were those just parts of his history? Was his aura like the rings on a tree? Again, he found himself wishing he had someone to ask.

Dar had spoken to him about those topics over the months Victor had prepared for his trip to Ruhn, but the man was cagey and often spoke in riddles. Didn't they all, though? Khul Bach, Azforath—even Old Mother. Victor smiled, remembering her and the love she'd shared with him. She really *had* been a wonderful person, and he'd found her at just the right time in his life. Naturally, that thought made him think of his *abuela,* and he *longed* for her voice and her gentle pats on his cheek when she'd say something like, "*Qué bueno eres, mijito.*"

Victor's eyes were suddenly moist, and his chest heaved for breath. Was she really *gone?* The idea was so gut-wrenching that he realized he'd been avoiding *really* thinking about it for ages. He'd kept his mind busy with just about any other kind of worry or thought. Sitting there, in a cloud of potent Energy, he closed his eyes and *remembered* his grandma. He remembered her voice, her eyes, and how she'd been his rock when everything in his life turned upside down.

Hours or days could have passed; he didn't know. He was lost in his contemplations, savoring the rich fragrance of his *abuela's* cooking, the songs she would sing to wake him up for school, and the way she would scold him and tell him to be proud of himself when he felt like giving up. When his melancholy ran its course and he found himself smiling at the memories, he opened his eyes to find he wasn't alone.

Chantico sat cross-legged in front of him, her golden-brown skin glistening in the strange shimmer of the Energy around them. Her eyes were like polished amber gems, but their depths were wells that could absorb a person's soul. To his utter disbelief, Victor realized that Chantico's cheeks were moist with tears. Her dark brows, sharply angled and severe, tilted upward as she said, "What a strange place you've summoned me to, little brother. It was wonderful to relive some of your memories with you. That kindly woman reminded me of my own great-grandmother."

"Chantico?"

"Has whatever ails you stolen your wits?" She smiled to soften the words.

"I didn't mean to—"

"Pull me from my reveries? Disturb a hundred years of meditation? Worry not, little brother; I'm interested in this affair." She looked around, narrowing her eyes. "You've done something foolish, haven't you?"

"Um—" Victor shrugged. "I don't think I had a choice."

She smiled, pulling her lips back to reveal perfect, white teeth with canines too sharp to be human. Was that what a pure Quinametzin's teeth were like? "I will give you some guidance, Victor, but I can feel something building between us—what once was a simple karmic tie is becoming a karmic burden. It will weigh on your spirit if I continue to aid you without some reciprocity. Will you promise to do me a favor in exchange for my aid?"

Victor didn't hesitate, and if she knew him well, she would have known the question was redundant to his nature. "Of course."

Her brilliant eyes twinkled as she nodded, continuing to smile at him. "Okay, little brother, let's see what's going on in here." As she spoke, she stretched out her long, sharp-nailed fingers to rest her fingertips on his forehead. Her touch was gentle, but it felt as if someone had connected a high-voltage line to his skull. Victor stared into her eyes as the electric waves continued to pulse through his head.

Perhaps because of the connection she'd made, Victor thought he saw glimpses of her thoughts and memories in those eyes. He saw her standing over a battlefield that spanned a continent. He saw her charging into the arms of not one but a dozen lovers over the span of an eon. He saw her transform into a tremendous golden-feathered eagle and soar into space. More memories were there, waiting for his gaze, but then Chantico took her fingers away from his head and folded her hands in her lap.

"I see what's happening. I can guide you through this process, little brother, and protect you from much of the worst of it, but I have to warn you: This will not solve the riddle of your curse. It remains and will eventually destroy you, even with the reprieve this treasure has granted you. Perhaps, if we talk further, we can discover the weakness that allows it to gain such a foothold on your spirit."

"I—"

She smiled and reached out to take his hand. "Don't worry about the advice you were given. I won't fight this fight for you, but I might help you understand how *you* should fight it."

"Thank you." Victor smiled as he grasped her hand with his "big sister."

39

INTROSPECTION

Arona paced the walls of Victor's palace at Iron Mountain, scanning the countryside. The structure was atop a high hill, with steep grades leading down grassy plains into dense forest. To the east, some five miles distant, lay the city of Iron Mountain. Southward, the entire horizon and most of the sky were dominated by the mountain itself. Being near that peak made it easy to forget that the palace was on elevated ground.

The mountain's great shoulders rose toward the firmament, fading into obscurity in the atmosphere. That peak, that *place,* had meant something special to Victor . . . The thought interrupted her contemplations of the countryside, reminding her of *him,* and she turned, looking over the courtyard toward the tall spires of the palace. Her gaze drifted upward to the top of the tallest, broadest tower. His vault was up there, and he was either lying within, undergoing some sort of personal battle, or he was dead. She wished she had a way of knowing which.

Of course, Kynna had employed her most talented scryer to attempt to see within the Fae-crafted vault—tomb?—but she'd been unable to pierce the dense magics that protected the contents. Arona hadn't been surprised. The Fae employed elder magic, and such artifacts were beyond most modern practitioners.

She turned her attention back to the lands outside the palace walls. Kynna's engineers were hard at work, fortifying the magical wards. Their enormous excavations dotted the landscape in a mile-wide radius. They were burying warding monoliths designed by Arona's old master, Vesavo.

Arona knew the designs well, but she'd had to employ Death Casters from the various kingdoms under Kynna's rule to create them. They made a barrier pattern that would sap the Energy of enemies passing near them, draining it away. Because of the size and density of the stones being used, Arona had been able to create sinks for hundreds of Energy types. Of course, they could be destroyed, but burying them would make that a painful process. Any sappers Kynna's foes sent forward to deal with them would be easy targets.

It wasn't that the palace's warding wasn't already robust. For instance, Arona had found that the footings for the walls went as deep into the earth as they soared into the sky. They'd been married to the bedrock by powerful Earth Elementalists long before anyone currently living in the palace had been born. The enormous stones used to build it were enchanted in such a way as to be nigh indestructible, and the anti-flight patterns and spatial shielding made it unlikely that anyone short of a veil walker would be able to enter the keep by other means.

No, the empire's killers and champions would have to come through the gates or spend tremendous amounts of Energy and time trying to breach the walls. Meanwhile, they'd be giving Kynna's people a chance to make the assault as costly as possible.

Arona sensed her contemplations were about to be interrupted again; she felt Bryn's approach before she heard her boots. "How do things look?" the one-time Queen's Guard asked.

Arona turned to regard her. Bryn wore a gleaming silvery breastplate and a matching helm adorned with golden wings, complementing the golden glaive Victor had given her quite nicely. She looked strong, which was exactly what they needed; it was important for the leaders to project confidence. The palace grew more and more crowded every day, and the civilians and fighters alike knew something dire was coming, despite Kynna's refusal to breach Lohanse's trust by telling them what exactly it was.

"Arona?" Bryn prodded.

Arona blinked, chuckling softly. "Sorry, Bryn, my mind runs in many directions these days. Things look good. The monoliths are all in the ground, but the Earth Elementalists still work to cover them. It takes time to draw the massive boulders through the earth, but we want the monoliths buried in stone, not soft soil. They've assured me they'll finish by week's end."

"Will the, um, *malaise* be active immediately?"

Arona shook her head. "The monoliths are tied to a control stone here in the palace. If we were all Death Casters, we'd let it run unchecked, but we don't want to turn Iron Mountain into a death-attuned horrorscape, do we?"

Bryn pressed her lips together, the corners turning down in distaste. "Definitely not."

"And the queen? How was your meeting?"

"She's as well as can be—more determined than last week when I met with her. She had some good news; one of the other great houses, Voth, requested teleportation access. Kynna refused, of course, but King Bomar wasn't put off;

he's sending his champion here to parlay, and Kynna wants you and me to determine his intentions."

"He's coming overland?"

"Flying, I assume."

Arona nodded, her dark brows turning down. Could it be an assassination attempt? "What's his name?"

"Resh A'kel. Bomar used him in several duels *against* the other great houses in the past. They were only trade wars, and no one lost their lands, but his aggression wasn't well-received by House Khaliday. Kynna's hopeful that Bomar might want to aid us."

Arona turned to regard the excavations on the plains again. "If this Resh A'kel wants to join our fight, he's welcome, but we must be careful. I won't allow him in Kynna's presence."

"No." Bryn moved to stand beside her. "I agree with that sentiment. I'm already nervous about some of the champions Kynna brought in from the kingdoms she conquered. I feel their loyalty is less than absolute."

"Their oaths are quite binding, but I agree we shouldn't bet on them giving their all."

Almost whispering, Bryn leaned closer to say, "I wish he'd emerge."

"We all do, Bryn. I pray every day that he will, that he's not dead in there." Arona meant it. She prayed to any great powers that might be listening—she prayed to fates and to Victor's ancestors. She didn't think anyone would listen; she'd long lost any belief that true gods existed. Vesavo had broken her of such notions, but being with Victor had sparked something in her that didn't used to exist—hope.

"You do?" Was all Bryn said, likely wondering about her use of the word.

Arona didn't want to expound on her strange, nebulous faith. Instead, she just turned to her and nodded. "We must remain hopeful, Bryn. I can feel it coming, though, can't you? It's like a storm I can't see, though the pressure of the atmosphere bears down on me."

"Yes," Bryn said softly, lifting her eyes toward the overbearing presence of the mighty peak, "I can feel it."

Chantico, still sitting before Victor, lifted her arms and let the weird, nebulous Energy play along her fingertips. "Tell me, little brother, what natural treasure did you find?"

"Is that what this stuff is from?"

"Yes, this *stuff* is Energy attuned to the aspect of *potential*—incredibly difficult to cultivate. It's meant to be directed by a mind far different from yours or mine. I've seen similar, though never so much at once or quite so . . .

alien." She stared at him, her eyes boring into his, and Victor shrugged almost sheepishly.

"An insect queen gave it to me. Her species was on the verge of creating its own universe where they intend to *ascend* to another plane of existence or something along those lines."

Chantico clicked her tongue, a wry smile turning up one corner of her lips. "It's no wonder you make waves through the universe. The threads of fate that weave your road are thick and multilayered, stretching to strange and consequential places and beings. Every step you take vibrates through the ether. I wonder how so many knots were woven under and around you. Was it a chance encounter? Many? One choice leading to another and another, accumulating through momentum and luck? I'm glad my blood runs in your veins, Victor. It pleases me that I had this chance to meet you before I finished my contemplations and left this plane."

"Are you so sure you must go?"

"I've lived well and long, Victor. I've tasted all that this existence has to offer, and I grow increasingly intrigued by what lies *beyond.* However, I'll admit to some pleasure at the none-too-gentle tugs on the threads that connect us." She smiled and reached out to grasp his hand again. "Let's speak about what's happening to you."

"You mean with the curse?"

"No, not that yet. Let's talk about this." Again, she lifted her hands to run her fingers through the dense, nebulous Energy surrounding them. "This Energy needs directing. I can help it on its way, and so could you if you took a hundred years or so to study how traits are tied into a person's blood—the impossibly small, impossibly dense instructions written on the tiny structures that make up our skin and bones and hair." She smiled. "Something tells me you don't want to sit here and contemplate such matters for so long. You have things to do back in your life, yes?"

Victor nodded. "Yes, if I stay in this vault for a hundred years, many of my loved ones will suffer."

She thumped a fist on his knee. "Just so. I will help this Energy on its way, at least much of it, but you ate something very, very potent, Victor, and there will be more than your body can absorb. We'll have to talk about your Core, too, and that will take effort on your behalf."

"I'll do anything needed."

"I know you will. So—" She reached out and brushed her fingers across his forehead, sending lightning tingles arcing through his skull. "I've already taken a long look in there, little brother, and I've seen that you've made good use of our bloodline's ability to absorb the strengths of our enemies. You've unlocked some potent bloodline traits—regeneration, fiery wings, even a Breath Core! That's nothing to say of the many lesser ones."

When she paused, Victor thought she wanted him to say something, so he said, "I've done my best. I always wanted to please my ancestors."

Chantico's smile broadened. "Such an *earnest* young titan. I like you more and more, Victor. I'm also pleased to see you've advanced your bloodline itself; it's nearly pure in you! I believe that's why this treasure you consumed hasn't killed you outright. A lesser vessel would come apart under the strain of all this potential."

She waved her hand around, and this time, some of the Energy gathered around her fist, balling up around it into a globe so bright that Victor couldn't look directly at it. "So, we'll take some of this Energy and send it into your cells—the tiny building blocks of your body—with the mission of awakening the deeper parts of your ancestry. Do you know what I mean by that?"

"You don't mean the Quinametzin?"

"Ah, we Quinametzin are titans, to be sure, but we descended from other, even more potent beings—primordial titans born of fire and chaos, beings that built and destroyed entire worlds." She grinned and winked at him. "You've met one—well, two, if you count me."

"You're a primordial—"

"I was born Quinametzin, but like you, I sought to enhance my bloodline. Over centuries, I did so, awakening the deeper parts of my ancestry." She gestured to herself, indicating her figure and appearance. "I wear this form most of the time because that was how I looked during my formative years. As you'll soon learn, however, a primordial titan's blood and bones are bursting with the vast weight of incalculable potential. If I wish it, I can stand a thousand feet tall, wearing the scales of my conquered foes and breathing fire that would make a volcano shudder with shame."

"*I'll soon learn . . .*" Victor trailed off, trying to comprehend exactly what she was saying.

"Perhaps not to such a degree immediately, but this will awaken much." She gestured with her hand, still clouded in brilliant Energy. "I wish you'd gained more traits from slain foes, but you've gained many. You'll benefit greatly. You will have to learn to *will* yourself to be a certain way. Natural laws must be browbeaten into submission."

Victor narrowed one eye, confused. "What do you mean?"

"Your bones and flesh are going to be very dense. If you try to stand on the structures of lesser beings, you'll destroy them, even if you maintain your usual size. You have to *will* yourself to be lighter. When I looked through your mind, I saw that you've learned some control of your aura, yes? It's much the same.

Simply take command of your body and assert your desires. It will listen. You'll find this easier on worlds with less ambient Energy. It takes power for a primordial titan to expand to her—or his—full potential."

She waved her hand, gathering a bit more Energy, then pressed it to his chest, closing her eyes briefly. Victor felt a tingle through his entire body, but it faded rapidly. When he looked down, the Energy was gone. "That was it?"

She laughed, a musical, lilting sound, and shook her head. "I sent that Energy into your cells to do their work, but it will be a process. Luckily, your mind is free, here with me." She waved her hand. "Look around! Do you see? More than half of the potential is gone, sent into you to work its magic, digging for the hidden lines of instruction that will unfold the secrets of your ancestors."

Victor felt some relief, as though he'd been rescued from a math exam he hadn't studied for. "Thank you, Chantico."

"We aren't finished. We must address the rest of this potential; you'll have to absorb it, and to do that, you'll need a much stronger Core." She smiled slyly. "I have a hunch we're going to accomplish two goals with this work."

"Two goals?"

"Patience. Let me lead you there." She put her hands on her knees, palms up. "Put your hands in mine." Victor did so, once again feeling electric tingles permeating his flesh at her touch. Was it power? Was it her Energy merging with his? Was it psychosomatic? Before he could ask, she said, "Now, close your eyes and take me into your Core space."

Victor had no reason to argue or delay; he was eager to see what she would show him, so he did as she asked. When he opened his inner eye and turned his gaze inward, he was acutely aware that he wasn't alone, though he saw neither himself nor Chantico. All he saw was the beautiful, pulsing heart of his power, the Spirit Core he'd so painstakingly built with Ranish Dar's guidance back on Sojourn.

At the center of his Core space sat the blazing, throbbing, white-gold sun of his inspiration-attuned Energy. Around it, arrayed in concentric rings, were his other affinities—first, a golden, sparkling band of glory-attuned Energy; then, around that, the thick, glowering crimson ring of rage. Finally, surrounding them all, was a ring of darkness, shadow, and dread—his fear-attuned Energy.

"You've done good work here, little brother," Chantico said, her voice echoing in the space, under the constant hum and buzz of his Energies. "I was very pleased to learn you had a Spirit Core."

"You were?"

"Yes! I have one, too! I believe emotions and feelings are what make people special. If two people see a woman's death, they both may objectively experience the same event. It's how they *feel* about it that makes them special or unique.

You have big feelings; I know this about you from my glimpse into your memories. It's no surprise that you have such potent affinities. I think you're missing something, however."

"I am?" Victor frowned, his mind racing through the many conversations he'd had with different beings about his affinities. Most prominent among them was the bear spirit, Thunderbite. It seemed a lifetime ago when the long-dead bear had helped him to form his fear affinity. Hadn't he sort of indicated that Victor didn't have any more strong affinities? Or maybe just one other? Wasn't it glory? Even Dar hadn't thought Victor's Core was lacking. But then, Dar had been trying to help him perfect what was there. Had he really *looked* for something else?

"Yes," came Chantico's answer. "Something vast. Something underlying all of this." He thought she was waiting for a response, but before he could say anything, she asked, "Tell me about your inspiration, Victor. When did you find that?"

"When my Core was broken. I was in a dark place—a slave, weak and alone. I thought of Lam, who at that time was more of a slave master than a friend, but she'd done something that, in my mind, was incredible. I saw her in battle, and I remembered how it made me feel, and that emotion and that *inspiration* resonated with me. Of course, that was just the first of many images that I used. When I recognized it, I thought of others who'd inspired me, and that helped me to form my affinity."

"So, would you agree that your inspiration affinity helped to pull you out of despair—out of a dark, fearful place?"

"Yes, of course."

"Excellent. Tell me about your affinity for glory, Victor. Why do you crave the recognition of others so?"

Victor's eyes were on his Core, but his mouth—or the representation of it in that strange place—turned down at the corners. Was that what his glory was? Was he just trying to be recognized? It felt deeper than that—more meaningful, more . . . glorious. Still, she had a point: at its core, glory couldn't exist without others to witness his actions. If he were the last person, alone in an empty world, nothing he did would be "glorious." It required the recognition of others. "I . . . don't know, I guess."

"Oh come, you're more clever than that. Think it through."

Victor wanted to argue, wanted to say it didn't matter. He had to consider why he felt that way, though. What was so difficult to face? Mentally buckling down, he forced himself to confront the question: Why did he seek the recognition of others? What did he love about the crowd's cheers? Why did he crave hearing his name in other people's mouths? "I guess . . ." He struggled to finish, hesitating with the hard truth that was on the tip of his tongue.

"I'm here, Victor." Chantico's hands clenched his more tightly, and that electric surge intensified.

With an effort of will, Victor bulldozed through, admitting the answer that felt somehow shameful. "It makes me feel safe. It makes me feel like I'm not alone and that people want to be around me."

"A wonderful insight, little brother, and nothing shameful at all! No one wants to be alone—not all the time." She squeezed his hands again. "One more. This one will be easier for you because you've admitted it before. Tell me where your rage comes from."

Victor sighed, feeling some stress bleed out of him. She was right; he'd made this admission more than once. "My rage comes from fear. Thunderbite helped me to see that."

"A clever spirit!" Chantico's thumbs caressed his palms, a comforting touch that did much to keep Victor relaxed as she said, "So, you can see, I'm sure, what this means: your three *lesser* affinities are rooted in fear, your *strongest* affinity. Inspiration to pull you *out* of fear and despair, glory to help you *fend off* your fear, and rage to react to the *things* you fear, smashing them to bits."

Victor couldn't argue, though it felt reductive; his use of rage wasn't really about fear anymore, was it? He supposed that wasn't the point—that was where his *affinity* was rooted, and he knew that was true. His early fights, his early troubles with family and school, were all rooted in fear. "That's right."

Chantico's voice echoed around his Core space, radiating approval and confidence. "Excellent. Now, little brother, we need to talk about what your *fear* is rooted in."

40

DARKNESS AND LIGHT

Victor stared into Chantico's eyes, waiting, but she didn't speak again. She wanted him to draw a conclusion or ask a question, no doubt. It wasn't as if he hadn't contemplated his fear affinity before. When he'd first unlocked it, building that dark, malignant ball of Energy in his Core, he'd hated the idea that he was so attuned to it. Thunderbite had chastised him, reminding him that without fear, he couldn't be brave. What had his words been? Something about those without fear being "bold," but that only those who conquered fear could be brave.

That idea had mollified Victor, helping him come to grips with the idea that, despite his great inner well of fear, he persevered. He took action and did the right thing more often than not, and it seemed to him those actions were more meaningful in the face of his fear affinity. None of that answered the question, though. What was the root of his fear? Where did it come from? If his other affinities were byproducts of his fear, could his fear, then, be a byproduct? Is *that* what Chantico meant?

He supposed she could mean something else. His fear affinity could be the base of his other affinities, but perhaps she simply wanted him to explore where his fear came from. Was this a supernatural, otherworldly, out-of-body counseling session? Was he supposed to confront his demons and find out—

Perhaps she sensed he was drifting, because Chantico spoke then—her voice calm, soothing. "Victor, when do you first remember being truly afraid?"

The answer came immediately—memories of bright lights, hushed voices, adults talking over his head as if he weren't even there. He'd known something was wrong. He *knew* what *pobrecito* meant, and he'd seen the sorrowful eyes of his *abuela* and his aunties. He'd recognized the hard looks his *tíos* kept giving each other. Yes, he decided, when his parents died, he'd known his first, true taste of fear. Any arguments or scolding or trouble up to that point became meaningless. Nothing was like the cold finality of his parents—his *mother*—being gone from the world.

"Did you find it?" Chantico prodded.

"Yes."

"Good. Victor, you're an intelligent man. I think you would have come to this process on your own eventually, but I believe you've been avoiding it. I don't mean recently, either; I believe you've been avoiding these thoughts your entire life." She chuckled, her voice rich in a way that made Victor think of his *tío's* expensive guitar. "I speak as though you've been hiding for centuries, but you're a young man. I'm sorry to push you so before you've had a chance to truly live and come to grips with these thoughts in your own time."

"It's not your fault, big sister."

"So. Use that brain of yours, think about your fear and the times you've had it. What was it rooted in? What did you lose? What were you afraid of losing? What about your rage? What made you the most furious? When did that start?"

Again, Victor let his mind drift back to his childhood, and just as Chantico said he would, he began to make connections. His first fear was rooted in the idea that he wouldn't see his parents again. He'd never feel his mother's hand on his forehead, hear her gentle voice, or see the smiling approval on her face. After that, he felt fear constantly. In those first, early years, Victor feared disappointing his *abuelo*, but then the grizzled old man had died, and Victor found himself fearing he'd lose his *abuela*, who'd stepped into the void his mother had left behind.

After that, he'd feared being ostracized by his cousins and the scolding, disappointed looks on his aunties' faces—the way they talked about his mother's family, rightfully disgusted by the fact that they wanted nothing to do with Victor. Those were the first memories that helped him see the connection between his rage and fear. He fought when he felt unwanted—when fear whispered that no one liked him, no one cared. He'd taken on cousins years older and earned himself quite a few good beatings. Still, the pain of kicks and punches was easier than that of rejection.

That line of thinking—the thought of *rejection*—helped Victor to see more clearly how his glory affinity was tied to his fear. What was the rejection related to, though? What was he afraid he wouldn't have? Acceptance? Friendship? Family? Love? He supposed it was all of those things and more.

Putting aside his youth, Victor tried to focus on more recent feelings. What did he fear now? Most people might, very reasonably, say they feared death. Victor couldn't say the same—not since he'd learned about the spirit plane and his ancestors. He knew this life wasn't the end of everything, and that made it impossible to truly fear death. At least not death *itself*. He'd be a liar if he said he didn't fear missing out on things in this life if he died. Wouldn't he like to see what became of Deyni? Wouldn't he like a chance to make sure Cora had a good life? What about love? If he died, he'd lose any opportunity to—

Something gripped Victor's heart then, and he knew he was onto something. Why did he *love* so hard? Why did he so desperately want things to work with Valla? Why had it crushed him so when she'd left? What about Tes? Why were his feelings, so profound and visceral, *real*? Was he just trying to fill that void that had begun to grow in his spirit when his parents had died?

He thought about that word, *void*. Was it a coincidence that he'd used that term when that was the type of Energy he'd been cursed with? Was the figurative void in his heart somehow related to his weakness to the curse? He frowned, concentrating, trying to make the wispy, fragmented thoughts more solid, more concrete. It became clear how fear and rage fed the emptiness—the *void* in his heart.

Glory, too, he supposed, was the same. When he experienced those "glorious" moments in his life, he felt whole. He felt the rush of adoration, of belonging. What about inspiration? He felt it had a lot to do with hope—when he was inspired, he felt as though the hole wasn't bottomless.

Was that it? Was everything related to the *void* that had begun to grow when his mother died? A hole stretched wider by his inability to fit in with those he loved? An emptiness that deepened with each failed love, each fleeting victory on the mat—short-lived glory that vanished the moment the crowd stopped cheering?

Short-lived. The word resonated with Victor, and he contemplated his earlier notion of how inspiration was like that, too. When he was inspired, he forgot about the void, but it didn't last. How often did he turn to rage or fear when the inspiration he'd gotten from an exemplar—Lam—or a wise word—his *abuelita*—failed to keep him going through his troubles? For a long time, Victor thought about that. He ran through the memories of his life, remembering his fights, his triumphs, and his constant efforts to fill the missing parts of his heart—his spirit.

After a while—he couldn't have guessed how long—he turned his gaze inward to his Core, and it seemed to him that it didn't look right. Why was glory, a presumably positive influence on his spirit, encircled by rage and fear? Had Dar set him on a faulty path? Why was inspiration, the most positive of his affinities, so much weaker than the others? It seemed to him that—

Victor's eyes flew open, and he looked at Chantico again, locking his eyes with her. "I don't think glory and inspiration are right."

She smiled, revealing those sharp canines as she slowly nodded. "Go on."

"My inspiration Energy is wonderful; it's easy and helpful. It helps me when I'm stuck, but it's fleeting. It doesn't fill that emptiness—the hunger that fuels my rage and fear."

She raised an eyebrow but didn't speak.

"Glory, too, is fleeting. Worse, I think I'm getting the wrong thing out of it. When I feel people see my accomplishments—spectators, fellow soldiers, even my ancestors—it fills that void, but only briefly. It's not a lasting connection."

"You've done well to see so much, Victor." Chantico squeezed his hands, and Victor realized he'd forgotten she was holding them. "Everyone has darkness and light in their spirits. Yours is very bright, indeed, but you've let the things feeding on the emptiness in you grow too strong. You've broken up your light. Think about it: inspiration and glory . . . they're echoes. Incomplete. Inspiration is a spark—steel on flint. It burns fast, and then it's gone. And glory? That's a reflection of light—borrowed, bounced from others. It's not real unless it's shared."

"A reflection of what?" Victor frowned as he contemplated her words. "I feel like everything is sort of related to love—the love of my mother, my grand-mother, my love of so many others, and that *desire* to be loved. It doesn't feel right, though."

"That's because we're talking about something *missing*, Victor—an empti-ness in you, a hollow spot, a *void*. Yes, that void was first brought to life early on when you lost something or someone dear, but it's been growing. Your other affinities are a reflection of it. You fight to regain what you lost and what you *fear* you'll lose. It's not just love; it's friendship, camaraderie, a sense of belong-ing, a place in this world or the next.

Victor sighed. "So, yeah, love is another incomplete answer. Like inspiration or glory."

"That's right. Think about it: Can you fill a void with love? Perhaps, but not your own. Your need for love is immense, but it's fed from the outside. You give love, but when it isn't returned—when it's lopsided—the emptiness grows instead of healing. No, the light in you must be self-generated and lasting, something that can stand against any darkness. Don't you see it?"

Chantico's implied insistence that the answer was right in front of him frus-trated Victor, and it must have shown on his face, because when he grunted and shook his head, she smiled and squeezed his hands again.

"I wish I could make you see what is so plain to me without my guidance, but I fear you're too close to the subject. Maybe with time and more life experi-ence, you'd find it, but I think you've done enough. You're right on the precipice. Let me, then, nudge you over. What you're truly attuned to—what's always been there—is *hope*.

"Think about the times you refused to give in. When you stood alone on a corpse-strewn battlefield, bloodied and unbowed. When you wrestled with an ancient being of fire in his own lava-filled home. When you stood, defiant, against not one, but many, who have pierced the veil of power. Again and again, you refused to surrender.

"Beyond the battles, beyond the defiance, you *believe* in love. You believe you'll find it. You want to *share* it. You want to lift others. None of that says inspiration or glory to me. It says *hope*. The kind that burns bright enough to light a world."

When she stopped speaking, her voice echoing like music through his mind, Victor stared into the strange, shifting currents of Energy for a long time, trying to see if there was a flaw in her logic. Was it true? Was he so hopeful? Were his love and courage rooted in hope? Was that how he defied his fear? Was that why he felt inspired? "If I really have an affinity for hope," he said, frowning, "and it's strong enough to fill the void in my heart—or my spirit, or whatever—then why hasn't it?"

"Victor, how do you think you have such a wonderful life? Why do you think people love and follow you? Your hope is there! It works in the background, helping you to survive and thrive. You just need to fix your Core to properly reflect reality."

"Fix it?"

Chantico nodded. "As I said, everyone has darkness and light in them. I think it's fortuitous that your rage and fear are splitting your darkness. Your light, however, should stand unified before them. You should combine your glory and inspiration and properly build your true affinity, a light that will outshine the darkness in your heart."

Of course, Victor liked the sound of that. He liked the idea that he had a more potent, positive affinity that could properly balance his rage and fear. He didn't like the idea of giving up inspiration, though, and, despite what Chantico said, he *liked* his glory-attuned Energy and spells. She must have seen his thoughts written on his face because she chuckled, shaking her head.

"Change is difficult and *frightening*, Victor. Will you give in to your fear now?"

"*Chingado!*" Victor chuckled. "You know the right buttons to push." He shrugged and then nodded. "All right, big sister, how am I supposed to do this?"

Arona stood beside Bryn inside the gatehouse, the closed amber ore portcullis behind them. A man approached—a man who'd leaped from a hovering airship and fallen like a feather to the road. He wore a platinum-colored fighting gi that made her squint as it reflected the noontime sun, and she could see a long black-handled sword jutting up behind his left shoulder. She knew who it was: Resh A'kel, the champion of Voth, sent by King Bomar Lund to parlay with Kynna. Arona had no intention of letting him anywhere near the queen.

She could feel Bryn's nervous energy and didn't blame the woman. Even from some hundred yards distant, Arona could feel the man's aura—he had a certain vitality and grace, a deadliness that went unspoken, like a predator cat among grass-eating lesser creatures. She had the pattern for Solar Shell prepared, ready to instantly deflect an attack, and she knew Bryn would be quick to strike with that deadly glaive Victor had given her.

Between the two of them, she had confidence they could hold him at bay long enough for some of Kynna's other champions—waiting atop the wall—to join the fray. She dared to hope that her fears would prove unfounded. She wanted to believe that he'd come to offer aid, though her experiences in her past life told her that it was doubtful. Bomar Lund was power hungry, and even if this man were here to help, there'd be a catch.

The man, Resh, stopped twenty strides from the gate and surprised Arona with a respectful bow. He was tall, though not a giant, and his platinum garb extended to a band of matching cloth he'd used to cover his left eye. Was it missing? When he bowed, she caught a glimpse of his blade—a longsword that flowed and reflected the sun like liquid silver. After his bow, he stood straight, waiting.

"Speak," Bryn called. "We'll hear your intentions."

He cleared his throat, and in a smooth voice, devoid of malice, he called back, "May I approach?"

Bryn looked down at Arona, and she nodded. Bryn called out, "Come closer, then."

The man glided forward; it seemed he took two steps, but then he was there, just an arm's length from the two of them. Arona fought to control her reaction, not wanting to look surprised, but poor Bryn inhaled sharply, and her glaive tilted forward before she caught her reflex and steadied herself.

"I am Resh A'kel," the man announced, nodding in a much more reserved bow.

"I am Arona Moonshadow, and this is Baroness Bryn of House Dar. What is your business here?"

Resh nodded, narrowing his one eye. He was a handsome man with a strong jaw, though his grooming left something to be desired; it looked as though he'd missed shaving for a day or two. Still, his smile was pleasant as he said, "I had hoped to parlay directly with Queen Kynna."

Arona inclined her head. "I'm sure, things being as they are, you can understand why that won't be possible. Her Majesty has given us permission to speak on her behalf regarding your visit."

Resh pointed to a tiny silver bell hanging from the sash around his waist. "If we're to parlay here, in the open, may I employ this device? It will make our words difficult for prying eyes and ears to discern."

Arona arched an eyebrow. "Do you mean to imply that the queen would—"

"No, no!" Resh held up a hand, shaking his head. "The reason for my caution will become plain if you'll allow me to proceed."

Arona nodded. "You may."

Resh unfastened the bell, then held it high over his head, flicking his wrist. Tiny tinkling sounds poured out of the device, echoing, rebounding, and resonating. Soon, the tinkling rose to a crescendo, then a muted heaviness filled the air. When Resh spoke again, his voice was clear, but it sounded somehow smaller. "We should be safe to speak freely now."

"Speak *plainly* then," Bryn growled. Arona couldn't help but half smile; the warrior was covering her nerves with bravado.

"Very well. King Bomar Lund would like Queen Kynna Dar to know that the empire moves against her. Even now, a host of champions and assassins gathers, preparing to move against this palace. The veil walkers will not intervene, as they, too, are at war. King Lund knows this because Empress Matessa Khaliday invited him to have me join in the slaughter. He reserves the right to do so but makes an offer to your queen, hoping for another outcome."

Arona wasn't surprised by any of that news, though she was surprised by the frankness of his speech—he must place a great deal of trust in that little bell's magic. "Go on," she said.

Resh smiled, summoning a small rolled parchment sealed in gold-flecked purple wax. Again, he bowed as he held it out to her. "King Lund asks for your queen's hand in marriage. If she agrees, I will join the fight on your side, and King Lund will rally some allies to strike your foes from the flanks while they assault your palace."

41

THE OTHER SIDE

Gathering his will, Victor meticulously pulled his fear-attuned Energy away from his singular Core construct, once again forming it into its own globe. He remembered the herculean effort it had been to force the fear to bend to his will back on Sojourn when he'd rebuilt his Core, and, in comparison, this seemed almost effortless. Had he grown so much? It didn't seem to him that his will was *that* much greater than when he'd left Sojourn; however, he *had* gained many levels and undergone many trials and tribulations.

"That's good, Victor," Chantico said, her voice reverberating through his Core space. "Your fear-attuned Energy responds well to you. I can see you've done much to master it." Her words drove home the point that his control over his Energy was impacted by more than just his will attribute. His domination of Drok the Skull and subsequent feasting upon his terror-attuned Energy had led to more than one breakthrough.

As he pulled the last of his fear away from his central Core and compressed it into the dense, glowering, purple-black globe, he turned his attention to his rage. Once again, he went through the process of separating the looping, swirling ribbon of crimson Energy from his central Core, and, once again, he found it easier than before. He focused his will and, over the course of what felt like minutes to him, drew the Energy away, building another dense orb near the fear-attuned one.

When he finished, he opened his eyes and looked at Chantico, who sat patiently, holding his hands in hers. He knew she was being supportive, but he also knew the contact allowed her to see what he was doing in his Core space. "Is this taking longer than it seems? I spent days working to pull that energy into those bands."

"Likely, yes. Time is strange here; we're in a world of your making. Just as memories of whole days or years can pass by in a blink of the eye, your time at work on your Core may be compressed by your mental perception."

"Wouldn't you notice?"

"Not while my spirit wanders here." She shrugged. "In a way, I'm in your nascent spirit world, Victor. This is a place that you control, though you haven't learned how to do so consciously. It matters little to me, however. I could leave if I so desired, but I find you and this process fascinating. Honestly, I've come to more personal revelations in my time with you than I managed over decades of contemplation."

"Will that balance the karmic debt between us?"

Chantico grinned crookedly at him, narrowing her beautiful amber eyes. "You're clever, but not *that* clever. Don't worry, dear little brother; the task I will ask of you will align with your goals—another thick thread of fate that drew my curiosity."

Her smile fell away, and she squeezed his hands. "Now, the hard part will begin. You must abolish your affinities for glory and inspiration; this will be an arduous process that will prove more and more difficult as you proceed. Much of your determination is rooted in those two affinities, and you'll be forced to rely on other aspects of your character to power through. It's imperative that you don't stop until the work is complete."

Victor narrowed his eyes in determination. "I did plenty of difficult shit before I had inspiration or glory."

"I know. If you must rely on your rage, then do so."

"So what do I do?"

"When you created your fear affinity, did you not learn to strip a portion of your Energy of its affinity?"

"Ah, yeah." Victor nodded. "So I do the same thing with my inspiration and glory?"

"Yes. Glory first, I'd say. Then, your inspiration in stages. Do you understand my meaning?"

Victor nodded. He understood, and he wasn't as worried as she was. He'd built his inspiration out of nothing, hadn't he? He'd lived most of his life relying on rage—he could do so again for a short time. He knew, without her telling him, that fear was not the Energy he should feed to his spirit when it came to a difficult task. Rage, though? Rage could do the job. He closed his eyes, focused on his Core space, and pulled the glory-attuned Energy away from his brilliant orb of inspiration.

It flowed easily, far more malleable than fear or rage. When he had it built into a glittering, spectacular orb of Energy, Victor focused his will and bore down on it, pressing with all of his figurative might. As he destroyed this source of positive, wonderful Energy, Victor made war with himself, wondering if he was making a terrible mistake. He trusted Chantico; she'd come through for him more than once. Still, he'd worked hard for this glory. It had worked hard for *him*.

How many times had he waged war under the banner of his glory? How many times had his enemies felt the burning glare of his glorious, bloody sun? How many times had the crowd's cheers regenerated his exhausted, weary body? How many times had those cheers filled the emptiness that gnawed at the core of his being? Growling, Victor fueled his determination with rage, letting it simmer with depthless heat at the base of his will construct. He encircled his glory-attuned Energy with that relentless force and snuffed it out, crushing it into gray, lusterless Energy, eradicating every trace of the Glory that once had been.

"Good, Victor!" Chantico's encouragement bolstered Victor, and despite the increased sensation of emptiness making him feel somewhat listless, he channeled more rage into his pathways, strengthening his resolve as he siphoned half of his inspiration-attuned Energy out of his core, squeezing it into a separate orb. As he bore down on it, compressing and annihilating that wonderful white-gold glow, he wept. Tears that glittered with the strange light of that spirit world poured down his cheeks, and Chantico gripped his hands tighter.

Victor thought of all the times his inspiration-attuned Energy had served him so well, and he nearly faltered. He nearly stopped. Somehow, some fear leaked into his mind, and he began to wonder if this was some sort of trick or trap. Was this being, this woman guiding him, truly Chantico, his ancestor? What if she were some manifestation of his curse, deceiving him into destroying the best parts of himself? What would he be without his inspiration? As the thought crossed his mind, he relaxed in his efforts, and the orb of inspiration-attuned Energy flared more brightly.

"Little brother," Chantico whispered, "look into yourself. Know the truth of things—that Energy isn't what makes you who you are; it's a reflection of one aspect of your being. When you build up your new affinity, it will encapsulate that part of you and much more!"

Victor nodded, gritting his teeth, then he opened the floodgates on his rage, using that furious Energy to bolster his will. He focused past that pain-filled tunnel, past the blurry confusion, to where he knew he would stand whole again. Yes, he was destroying a vital part of himself, but it was like breaking a crooked bone in order to set it straight and give it a chance to grow stronger than before. He could visualize it—a Core more powerful, with a positive Energy that outshone his fear and rage, one that wasn't overshadowed by them.

With a pulse of despair and self-loathing, he used his prodigious will to crush the white-gold brilliance from the globe, leaving him with another pool of listless gray, unattuned Energy. Groaning, struggling to maintain his hopeful spirit, Victor focused his attention on the other half of his inspiration-attuned Energy. Once more, he brought his will to bear, surrounding the much-reduced orb and pressing down, squeezing the attunement out of it.

His mind had become numb by then, and he no longer wept. He felt robotic, but he knew that wouldn't do; he couldn't crush the attunement out of so much Energy without a little passion. Once again, he called on his rage, as he always used to do when things were dire. He thought of the people who'd wronged him. He thought of those he cared about on Ruhn and how the corruption of the veil walkers was threatening their very existence.

Despite the unreal nature of his body in that place, just as he'd shed tears, he began to simmer with rage. His flesh grew hot, his breathing grew ragged, and a low, deep growl formed in the pit of his stomach. He visualized breaking free of his self-entombment and slaughtering his foes. He knew that, to make that vision a reality, he had to crush this ball of Energy. He had to break his affinity. Just like that, with the force of his will, bolstered by the fury in his heart, Victor snuffed out his inspiration, and a fresh, raw wave of hopelessness overcame him, washing the rage from his pathways.

He might have wallowed for years or centuries, but Chantico's soothing voice came to him, "You did it, Victor. The hard part is over." She released his hands and leaned forward to grasp his shoulders, shaking him. "There's no time to wallow, Victor. Push through this brief despair. Just because your Energy is gone doesn't mean your inspiration is. Tell me, does losing your glory-attuned Energy erase all of your glorious deeds?"

Victor realized he was staring into the space between them, focusing on the weird shifting Energy in the air. He blinked and lifted his gaze, peering into her eyes. He took a minute to remember what she'd asked him, but when he reviewed her words, he found himself shaking his head. "No. I still beat those *pinché* sons of bitches."

"That's right! Do you need love-attuned Energy in order to love?"

Victor inhaled deeply, expanding his chest and pushing away the ennui that had begun to cloud his mind. He nodded, forcing a smile. "I get it. I didn't give up my inspiration; I just broke my affinity for it."

Chantico nodded. "But remember, Victor: your inspiration and glory were echoes of something greater. Let's build your new affinity, shall we? Gather up that unattuned Energy and push it into your pathways; circulate it through your body. While you're at it, cultivate this Energy around you; this *potential* will make the process much easier. That treasure you consumed was the perfect thing for such a momentous task. We'll build your Core stronger than ever before."

Victor closed his eyes and did as she asked. He took the sluggish, uninspired gray Energy in his Core space and pulled it into a long thread, dragging it out into his pathways. Then he reached out with his will, drawing in the Energy around him through the pathway openings in his palms. He'd never tried to cultivate Energy that didn't match or at least wasn't closely related to his attunements, but this Energy wasn't exactly *not* attuned to him.

The Energy both was and wasn't attuned to everything. It was potent, too, and as Victor wound it around the unattuned Energy already in his pathways, drawing it deep into himself, he began to vibrate with its power. He knew this wasn't his physical body; it was a representation of it, but he wondered if the real thing was going through those reactions, too. Wasn't his body already being affected by the potential-attuned Energy? Wasn't it waking up his deepest ancestral traits? Could he survive that *and* his Core alteration at once?

"Victor! Be careful of your stray thoughts! The goal of this is to imprint your desired affinity on the Energy in your pathways. Now is the time to remember your life. Remember the times you fell into despair and fought your way out. Think about the things you believe in and the goals you have for yourself. What do you hope for, Victor? What hopes keep you going when all else is darkness?

Chantico's words had the desired effect, and Victor's mind turned toward more positive things. He thought about how, when he was a child, desperate for the love of his mother, his *abuela* had stepped into that void, and he began to *believe* that things would get better. He remembered longing to fit in with his cousins and the desperate, misguided attempts to make that hope a reality. He never gave up, though, did he? In the end, he'd earned his cousins' respect and even their love. Hadn't they been there to cheer him on at his matches?

He remembered how he'd trained—how he'd run to school instead of taking the bus. He was the first to set out the mats and the last to get off them. He was the one who'd insisted his older cousins wrestle with him on the dried grass in the back of his *abuela*'s house. How they'd *punished* him for it! Even so, he'd loved every minute of it. Why? Because he'd set his mind on winning state before he graduated. He was *driven*, but what was behind that drive? It had to be hope, right? He'd hoped that he could win; he'd hoped that people would be impressed—he'd hoped that the recognition would fill the void he hadn't really known was there.

Maybe it hadn't been the healthiest way out—but it had worked. It could've been worse. If he hadn't found that hope and hadn't latched onto it, what kinds of trouble might he have gotten into? He turned his mind to his life since leaving Earth. He thought about the time he had spent fighting at the Wagon Wheel. What had kept him going then? He'd fallen into despair more than once, but he always found a glimmer of hope, didn't he? He never truly believed he was stuck.

When he'd been sold to the mines, his Core broken, he'd kept fighting, right? Was it just determination? Resolve? But those things had to have something behind them, didn't they? He had to have something to look forward to, and it had always been freedom. He'd never lost hope that he'd get out. When he saw Lam and felt that inspiration, what he'd really seen was a physical representation of the hope he'd been holding onto. She'd been a living, breathing example of what was possible.

His mind drifted that way for a long time, remembering the many brushes with death that he'd endured. Then, he thought about how, when he unlocked his Quinametzin heritage and learned of his ancestors, he'd been driven by the hope that he could impress them enough to earn a place among them. That thought brought him around to the idea that he'd always been looking, *hoping*, for a place to belong and for people who loved him.

He thought of Thayla and Chandri, he thought of Valla, and, of course, he thought of Tes. Didn't he, even now, hope that he could become the kind of man that could stand proudly by her side? It was just one example of the kinds of hope that kept the despair in his heart at bay. It was what balanced his spirit and pushed against the fear and rage, keeping them from overtaking his personality. Despite every hardship he'd ever had, he'd bounced back, hadn't he?

Victor could see the Energy in his pathways was moving more quickly, taking on a faint luster, though it still seemed colorless and primarily gray, even with the potential-attuned Energy intermixed with it. He needed to find that feeling, that construct of his hope, and focus on it to give this unattuned Energy its shape. He didn't have to look far. Chantico's fingers twitched in his hands, and he remembered her sitting there. He remembered the time she'd first come to him.

He'd been fighting the reaver army from Dark Ember. He'd faced them alone, desperate to stop them from annihilating the reinforcements that had been coming to aid the Ninth. Glorious, brutal, unforgettable—he'd fought to his last ragged breath, and when he'd been sure it was over, when there were still hundreds of reavers around him, he'd still been proud. Even when he thought he was about to die, he'd held onto hope. What had he yelled? Something like, *"Come on! You pinché rat fuckers!"* He'd wept tears of blood as he screamed, *"Abuela! Ancestors! I'm coming to you!"*

He might not have held out hope for winning that fight, but he'd certainly hoped he'd earned his place among his ancestors, hadn't he? That wasn't the key, though; that wasn't when he'd felt true hope bloom in his chest. No, that had come when he'd been answered: *"Is your bloody work over? I don't think so, child of the Quinametzin. I am Chantico, brave son, and I lend you my strength and my fire. Stand tall among these undead fiends. Teach them what it means to corner a titan!"*

As he remembered those words and the hope that had blossomed to life in him, Victor felt an answering surge of life in his pathways as the thick ropes of Energy flowing through him took on a shimmering, silver-blue hue and radiated warmth and positivity. Relief washed over him as he gasped, fresh tears springing into his eyes. He'd done it. He opened his eyes, smiling as he saw Chantico's answering smile.

"Nicely done, little brother. Now you must reform your Core with this new Energy at the center. Your old tutor had the right idea. Put this positive Energy closest to your spirit and put the others outside; make your fear and rage orbit your hope."

Victor nodded and refocused on his Core space. He pulled the dense river of silver-blue Energy out of his pathways and slowly coiled it around itself, forming a loose ball at the center of his Core, then he compressed it with his will. It wasn't the same as squeezing the attunement out of it. He just had to break down the individual strands and form them into a proper sphere. When it was done, he could feel the resistance fall away, and the orb of brilliant, silver-blue Energy snapped into place with a gravity of its own.

Pulling back, Victor looked at the three spheres in his Core space and smiled. The hope-attuned Energy was larger and denser-seeming than even the dark, glowering orb of fear. He hoped that was a good sign that his affinity would be even higher. It was certainly easier to manipulate the hope-attuned Energy than his other ones.

With renewed optimism, Victor got to work, dragging his rage- and fear-attuned Energies back into position, stretching them into bands that encircled his pulsating Core of hope. Rage was first, and when it was done, Victor stared for a long while, fascinated by how tendrils of the crimson, angry Energy stretched down like lightning strikes on the smooth, silvery-blue orb of his hope. Those red tendrils never penetrated far.

Then he pulled his fear into a more expansive, thicker band that encircled his Core perpendicular to his rage. It cast a dark shadow on the soft, smooth surface of his hope-attuned Energy, but it was just a shadow; it was clear that the calm, silvery blue Energy was unaffected. When it was done, he *felt* different. He could feel the vast potential in his Core, and though it was hard to quantify, he felt as if he had more control over his fear and rage.

"You've done beautiful work, Victor. That's a Core to be proud of, but we're not done."

Victor opened his eyes and looked at Chantico. "We're not?"

She gestured around them, at the remaining potential-attuned Energy. "You must make use of this. It's time to cultivate—you must expand your Core and your pathways in order to sustain the changes that your body is undergoing."

Victor nodded, feeling much relieved now that he had his new affinity in place. "I think I'm beginning to see the light at the end of the tunnel."

Chantico's eyes narrowed as her smile broadened, and she nodded. "An apt analogy, Victor. Let's get you to the other side."

42

XELHUAN

Arona, Kynna, Bryn, and ten members of the Queen's Guard stood atop the second tallest tower in Victor's palace, the "Mountwatch Spire," named for its unobstructed view of Iron Mountain. They weren't observing the mountain, however; they were watching the Khalidaysian forces struggling to deal with the perimeter stones that Arona had devised.

There wasn't a great army arrayed before them. Instead, there appeared to be no more than fifty individuals who'd come to fight. They were fifty monsters, though, each of whom, individually, was probably a match for the entire Queen's Guard.

At the moment, they were delayed, the sickly malaise of Arona's death-attuned perimeter wards holding them at bay. Even the handful of Death Casters out there knew better than to push through the field—the stones under the earth would drain them just as readily as those with other affinities. Meanwhile, the cold, lifeless Energy permeating the air made it difficult for the Earth Elementalists to work. They were trying, though; ten high-tier individuals brought to support the Khalidaysian champions were channeling from a safe distance, working to pull the perimeter obelisks out of place.

"It won't be easy for them," Arona said, turning to look into Kynna's smoldering eyes. "We anchored them deeply with amber ore chains fastened to the bedrock. Even so, if they are relentless, eventually, they'll pull enough stones out of the pattern to disrupt the field."

"You did well, Arona," the queen replied. "You've bought us precious time. I yet hold out hope that the veil walkers will settle their feud and put an end to this unlawful attack."

Arona nodded, turning to scan the ramparts, ensuring that none of the queen's staff had joined them unannounced. When she saw they were still alone, save for the queen's most loyal guardians, she asked, "And have you considered King Lund's offer?"

"Of course I have! I consider it every minute." Kynna leaned forward, peering past the crenellations to the right so she could see the solitary blue tent set up in the field outside the gates. Resh A'kel had made camp there, refusing Bryn's offer of accommodations inside the palace. "That champion would be most welcome in the coming fight, let alone the others Bomar has promised. Still, it rankles to be held hostage in such a way. I've never liked Bomar Lund, and I like him less for taking advantage like this. No, I'll hold out a bit longer. Have you any idea how much time we have before they can directly assault us?"

Arona shrugged. "Days? Perhaps a week or, at most, two. Unless the empress sends more Earth Elementalists—perhaps one with a proper metal affinity to deal with the chains. If that were the case, I'd say two days."

"Even with an airship, they'll need at least four days to travel here. So let's assume we have six days before those killers can assault the palace." The queen looked past Arona to Bryn. "Have you received the report? How do our defenders match up?"

Bryn turned to face the queen as she spoke, her words clipped and formal. "Our champions outnumber theirs nearly ten to one, but they have several individuals whom we cannot match. Most prominent among them is the Imperial Champion, Dro Vah."

Kynna nodded, muttering, "Dro Vah'lash'rokeen'anam. My spymaster tells me he's an actual dragon."

Bryn frowned, perhaps irritated that the queen was asking her for information she already had. She'd never say so, though. Instead, she cleared her throat, nodded, and replied, "None have seen him take on a dragon's form, my Queen; however, it is rumored that he breathed acid upon two lesser champions from the imperial stable, killing them outright. It's said that he was offended by their lack of respect."

The queen shook her head, sighing. "I understand you two intend to fight with our champions, but I must insist you stay by my side. If our superior numbers fail against the might of their most potent fighters, then you may be my last line of defense." She gestured toward the field. "Besides, if they breach that formation of yours and begin an assault on our walls, I'll likely accept Bomar's offer, and then we can count on Resh A'kel to stand against Dro Vah. Hopefully, my husband-to-be will bring enough other champions into the fray to offset the other elites Khaliday has sent against us."

"Do you believe Resh can defeat Dro Vah?" Arona asked. She herself was doubtful. The truth of the matter was that there were fifty steel seekers out there. Fifty champions, each of whom could likely defeat her in a one-on-one battle. Meanwhile, the queen had some five hundred Tier Eight and Nine iron rankers and only a handful of steel seekers to defend her. If the iron rankers were like Victor, they might have a chance. The odds of that, though, were slim. Arona felt confident she could defend against any of those steel seekers for quite some time, enough to escape or get help, but defeat? No, things weren't looking good for the queen's forces.

"I've no idea," the queen replied. "He is respected and feared, but no one knows exactly what Dro Vah can do."

When they'd begun preparing to resist the Khalidaysian onslaught, everyone had estimated that the empress had seven or so steel seekers she would send against them. They'd assumed that a few of the great houses would send one or two more to assist them. They might have had a chance if they'd been correct, if only fifteen steel-seeker champions were out there. Fifty, though? Arona knew very well that the queen would have to accept Bomar's offer if they were to stand any chance at all.

Nevertheless, she understood Kynna's reluctance. Things weren't over yet. The queen's hope that the veil walkers might end their conflict and come to her aid wasn't so far-fetched. They'd maintained order for thousands of years, hadn't they?

Her review of their impossible situation was cut off as Bryn, ever hopeful, pointed to the tall tower standing to their right. "Do you think he's gone?"

Kynna sighed. "Bryn, must you put salt into the wound? It's been nearly three months. You said he was on death's door when he crawled into that vault. Even his gigantic axe is inert, lying dead in that cultivation chamber he built. We must find a way through this without him, and the time draws nigh when we'll have to see if King Lund will be our path forward. It's not so much to ask, really. I've married a man I didn't love before. My first husband. Do you remember?"

Bryn shook her head. "It was before I was born, my Queen. I know my history. His name was King Yvan, right?"

"That's right. They won't teach you in the history books that my father desperately tried to stop that marriage. He didn't believe any individual should be sacrificed for the good of the many, even a royal princess. He thought it morally abhorrent. I swore to him, though, that I loved Yvan. I did it to forestall a war with Frostmarch, and it worked, for a time. Unfortunately, Yvan was a coward and a lecherous dog, and he was killed in a duel when I was still very young."

"Wasn't it King Vennar of Frostmarch who killed him?" Bryn asked, her voice tentative.

"Indeed." Kynna clenched her jaw, and Arona felt she was done with the subject. The queen made that clear when she said, "I'll go and write some missives and spend some time with my journal. You two should do the same. Even if I take Bomar Lund's offer, I fear it's likely our days are numbered."

Arona opened her mouth to try to argue or at least offer some encouraging words, but the queen turned on her heel and strode toward the stairwell without pause or another glance.

When she and her Queen's Guard had all filed out, Bryn cleared her throat, shifting uncomfortably. "Something I said?"

Arona snorted, smiling wryly. "Gallows humor, Bryn? I'm impressed."

The onetime Queen's Guard smiled and put one of her arms over Arona's shoulders, jostling her gently. "Come now; how many times have you had to bolster my spirits over the last few months? We've time yet. If the queen accepts King Lund's offer, the threat of his champions might force the empress to negotiate; perhaps she'll be willing to settle for banishment."

Arona nodded. "I had the same thought. I've enjoyed my time in this world, but if we can all leave with our lives, that might not be so bad. It would be different if . . ." She trailed off, once again glancing at Victor's tower. Bryn only nodded, squeezing her more tightly as she followed her gaze.

For the thousandth time, Victor painstakingly dragged a great swath of potential-attuned Energy into his pathways, straining and stretching them to near bursting, then cycling it through, into his unified Core construct. He pressed with his will, watching as the Energy compounded, slowly expanding the limits of his Core, each of his affinities pulsing rapidly, building to a crescendo until it broke through another barrier, becoming denser and slightly larger.

It was the sixth time he'd broken through to find a new plateau, and though the Energy in his "spirit space" was growing thin, he knew he'd already pushed his Core to heights he hadn't imagined. He could feel the heaviness of it, the throbbing power. The first breakthrough had been trivial, but the second had taken him hundreds of cultivation cycles. He knew why: his Core had been at the eighth epic tier when he'd consumed the royal jelly, so the second breakthrough had pushed him beyond epic.

He'd asked Chantico if his Core would be "legendary" now, but she feigned ignorance, saying she didn't exist within the confines of the System, nor would she ever bow to its categorizations. Her attitude reminded him of Azforath's, and Victor knew it was useless to press the issue with her.

"Very good, little brother. I believe you've taken all you can. This remaining potential is slowly sinking into your being, drawn by the process I started when I first arrived. Your Core is much more potent than when we first began, largely because of how we balanced it, but also because of this unseemly gift those insects gave you. Ivid, you say?"

"That's right. They use this jelly to make their queens."

"And their queen is much, much stronger than the rest of the hive, yes?"

Victor nodded. "Yes. When I gazed at her with my inner eye, it was like looking at the sun."

"Ha! Amazing. Your path is truly blessed, which is something we should discuss before this Energy is fully absorbed by your body and you awaken."

"My path?"

"Yes. Recall the favor you promised me, little brother. If you follow through, that favor will dictate your path in the near future."

Victor nodded. He felt so much better than when he'd arrived in that place—not physically; he couldn't feel his body yet—but mentally. Chantico's time with him had been invaluable. The help she'd given him to see that he had another affinity, one that could encompass all of the best facets of inspiration and glory while providing a stronger balance against his fear and rage, couldn't be overstated. If he'd been alone, struggling to figure out what to do with all of the potential-attuned Energy in his spirit space, he might have lingered for centuries before he came to grips with it. He might never have found a solution so elegant as Chantico's.

He was grateful to her, and a favor to her felt like a gift to himself— something he'd take pleasure in doing. "I won't back out of my promise."

She smiled, tilting her forehead forward, acknowledging his words. "I knew you wouldn't. It's something I should do myself, but my heart will not allow it. It's a great shame of mine, something that binds me to this universe. It's the primary obstacle to my ascension."

Victor stared into her eyes, giving her his full attention, but he didn't speak. When she saw that he was waiting for her to continue, she nodded again and said, "I've had many children in my long life, Victor—many and many. My first lover and I had five sons and four daughters. This was back when I was a young Quinametzin. I was the pride of my people—a great fighter and hunter, and a leader, too. Over the centuries, those children grew and had their own children. I took other lovers and had more children, too. Still, those first nine sons and daughters of mine hold a special place in my heart.

"One of my first sons, Xelhuan, had an affinity for death magic. He grew very powerful and built a kingdom of darkness in the deep, primal forests of the great continent where we Quinametzin first thrived. I won't bore you with a thousand-year tale, but suffice it to say that his people and his magic clashed with most of the Quinametzin people. He even made war against me and mine, slaying his own father." Chantico's voice grew tremulous as she spoke, and thick, glistening tears ran from her eyes. Victor reached out to grasp her hands, holding them as she'd held his during his struggles with his Core.

"When the Energy grew thin on the world of our origin—the world you call Earth—most of the Quinametzin left. Xelhuan remained, ruling over his kingdom of death. He made many followers and gained many allies—other death worshippers who'd stayed to rule over the dark, fear-filled world. When the Energy faded further, nearly entirely gone, they built a great portal and traveled to another, bigger, richer world—one with a docile population which they soon enslaved, adding to the hordes of thralls they brought with them."

Chantico had said he was connected by fate to the favor she needed, and, with that clue, it was easy to guess where this was going. Frowning, he said, "Dark Ember."

"Yes, Victor! The *Great Masters,* as they call themselves, are the death worshippers from my—and your—world. Chief among them is my own son, Xelhuan."

"You want me to stop him?"

Chantico nodded. "I ask much, I know. He's stronger than the one you call a mentor—the one who helped you to build your previous Core construct. Still, you're stronger now, too. Soon, you'll reach the point where you must hone your spirit and build an archetype for yourself. Perhaps you're there already after consuming this mighty treasure. I know you'll do well, Victor. Moreover, I know your new affinity is exactly what Dark Ember needs. Millions wallow there, hopeless. Bring them the light that shines in here!" She pulled her hand from his and pressed it to his chest.

Victor enjoyed her praise but was doubtful he was up to the task. "He's ancient, though. You're saying he's stronger than a powerful veil walker?"

"*Veil walker.* I've heard this term before. That would be an appropriate title for his rank." She nodded, contemplating. "He'd be a powerful veil walker." She kept her hand pressed to his chest as she continued. "The Great Masters each hold sway over vast swathes of land. Kill some lesser masters and build your strength as you free the thralls who live in despair. Like most of his ilk, Xelhuan wallows in his vile experiments, hiding away in his dark lair. He and the other masters have no love for one another. Conquer one, and the others will eventually try to claim those lands, but they won't come to another's aid."

"They don't have alliances?"

"No. They have peace agreements that are fragile, at best. They'd just as soon kill each other as help one another against a threat. They're a loveless, horrible lot, and the sooner they're brought low and the suffering of their enslaved peoples ends, the better." She moved her hand back to his, squeezing. "You've already sworn to help the people of Dark Ember, Victor. I can see it plainly on your spirit, wrapped deeply with resounding karmic bonds. I offer you another reason to do what you already want."

"Can I really do it, though? Even if I'm a steel seeker, can I face a veil walker?"

Chantico's eyes narrowed as he spoke. "*Steel seeker, veil walker!* You are a titan! You are a Spirit Caster with a powerful hope affinity! If anyone can free that world, it will be you. The fates pulled us together for a reason! Xelhuan is a Quinametzin, true, but he's forsaken his heritage. He hasn't tried to find the deeper roots of his bloodline. No, he, instead, performs dark rituals, ever distancing himself from our kind. Stay true to yourself, Victor, and you will prevail against him."

For the first time, Victor had an inkling of doubt about Chantico's motivations. It almost felt as if she'd guided him toward a hope affinity so that he could better face the challenge of defeating the undead masters on Dark Ember. Was that the case, or was it just as she'd said—fate? Was he destined to go there and face the evil wrought by one of his own ancestors? He decided it didn't matter. He'd made a promise, and she was right; he had always intended to go there anyway. "I'll do it."

"I knew you would, little brother." Again, tears welled in her eyes, and she looked down, then up again, blinking rapidly. "I feel ashamed."

"Why?"

"Because I ask so much of you. Because I am to blame for Xelhuan's existence. Seven times, I stopped others from slaying him—seven times, before he grew powerful enough to dissuade assassins. Those are long tales, though, and our time grows short. Look!" She gestured to the air around them, and Victor saw she was right; the potential was almost gone. Just a few stray wisps remained. "I will await you on the spirit plane. I know you yet have to battle your curse. When that is done and when you've finished your business on Ruhn, will you come to me? I can show you the way to Dark Ember."

Victor could feel something changing in the air. He could feel something changing in *himself*. Something was pulling, tugging at his consciousness. She was right—he was about to wake up. Hastily, he nodded, leaping to his feet and pulling on her hands. "Let me hug you, big sister! Thank you for your guidance."

She embraced him, pulling him tight with powerful arms. When they separated, she locked eyes with him again. "It was my pleasure. I know I call you *little brother*, but somewhere along the line, I am your ancestor, Victor, and I am very, very proud of you. I'm sorry to lay my burden upon you. I hope you know how grateful I am."

Victor didn't reply, but he smiled, staring into her depthless amber eyes as the world grew dim, then black, then bright again as he took his first deep breath in months and opened his eyes.

43

AWAKE

Grand Prince Troyssas sat in his high pavilion, watching the distant spectacle playing out beneath the towering walls of Iron Mountain's seat of power. He'd nearly left, bored to tears by the painstakingly slow progress of the Elementalists as they worked to remove the boundary stones Queen Kynna had put up. When he'd volunteered to lead the assault force, eager to see the slaughter of the House of Dar, he'd expected it to be a quick thing—a jaunt in the countryside punctuated with a few choice moments of violence.

He wondered how Kynna had known to prepare for them. Not only had she enhanced the palace's already formidable defenses, but she'd also gathered up every member of her extended family—anyone who might have been used against her. In the end, it wouldn't matter. At least they were all gathered here; it would make the executions convenient. They'd have to watch for blood poppies growing in these fields in the years to come.

Things were finally moving along, in any case. The boundary stones had been dragged free, opening a wide passage for assault, straight at the walls and gate. This was the kind of thing Troyssas lived for! If left in peace, his champions could hammer down those gates with their might. Therefore, Kynna's defenders were forced to do battle. What entertainment! The landscape was a blasted ruin, but the walls and mighty amber ore gates held firm. Still, what fun to watch the pitiful defenders throw away ten lives only to wound or kill one of Matessa's champions!

"You summoned me, Highness?" A deep, gravelly voice asked, and Troyssas looked down from his raised platform to see his sister's new pet, the champion she'd brought in from off-world.

Dro Vah was shirtless. In fact, he wore nothing but black, silken pantaloons, and when he folded his well-muscled arms over his chest, the pose emphasized his stunning physique. A lesser man might have been impressed, perhaps even intimidated. Troyssas, however, was a giant among giants, and he thought the display pathetic. He was tired of the showboating stranger. What had the self-proclaimed dragon done to earn any of the vast wealth his sister had showered upon him?

Troyssas gestured toward the keep, waving one massive arm so his heavy, gem-encrusted bracelets jangled. "Why aren't you participating?"

The man shrugged, tilting his chin up and to the right so the wind caught his shoulder-length sable hair and blew it out of his face. He turned his emerald eyes toward the wild showcase of magical abilities and martial prowess taking place near the palace gates, and in a lazy drawl, replied, "It's a bit beneath me, don't you think? Let the pups sharpen their fangs on those foxes and wildcats. I'll wait for a lion."

"Ah, I see." Troyssas nodded, feigning conviviality. "You're content to wait for something more challenging?"

"Of course, Highness."

The man's lazy use of the honorific made Troyssas bristle, but once again, he contained his irritation, pouring honey into his voice. "I'm so pleased to know you don't grow bored. I couldn't help but note that several of my courtesans have come and gone from your luxurious camp house. I trust your needs have been met?"

"Well, a dragon's needs are great, Highness. I make do, however."

Troyssas nodded, choking back an angry retort. He was ready to explode, but the moment wasn't perfect yet. "And, dear dragon, should a champion worthy of your attention fail to appear, you're content to rest here? Is the pay sufficient? Will my personal attendants and lovers be enough?" Some of his ire leaked into his voice with that last question, and Dro Vah turned his sharp gaze upward, narrowing his brows, perhaps recognizing the game Troyssas played.

"Do you think your sister's wealth and faith are misplaced?"

"Let me consider." Troyssas brought one of his enormous hands up to his chin, rubbing a thumb through his soft, feathery red beard, feigning deep introspection. After a long moment, he stood and leaped down from his platform with an earth-shaking rumble. He stepped close to the shirtless champion and leaned forward, putting his enormous head mere inches from the smaller man's as he growled, "Why, yes, Dro Vah. I *do*. I think you're a colossal waste of time and a fraud to boot! If my sister hadn't explicitly forbidden it, I'd kill you myself. Know this, dragon boy—if you don't make yourself useful during this assault, I'll see her mind changed on the matter."

Dro Vah didn't flinch. He didn't seem angry, either. "Troyssas, I was hired to fight a man your other champions feared. I came to this assault hoping to face a titan. If he appears, I will kill him. Regardless of that, however, your sister has a gift for Queen Kynna, and I believe, when it's delivered, I will have another man to slay. When that fight is done, if you still have the stomach for it, I'll be happy to entertain your challenge."

Oddly, by the time Dro Vah finished speaking, Troyssas found himself looking up at *him*. Had the man grown? Had he been concealing his actual size? The prince took a step back, glowering, but the supposed dragon's confidence had cooled his lust for violence. Rather than bluster or threaten further, he asked, "A gift?"

The champion nodded, his perfect lips stretching into a wide smile that exposed oversized, silver-capped canines. "That's right. A little something for the queen that, if delivered with proper timing, should drive home the hopelessness of her situation." He turned to glance at the battle again. "Let her valiant, overmatched defenders kill a few more of your champions, and then I'll deliver it. You'll enjoy the reaction."

A moment of disorientation overcame Victor as he peered around the dim interior of his vault. The color of the ambient lighting seemed off, more tinted toward orange than red, but when he blinked, he realized it might be an effect of his eyes. Everything seemed sharper and brighter. When he focused on the key in the lock, he could see the tiniest details as though he held it under a magnifying glass. He shifted his gaze downward, toward the smear of dried dark blood he'd left as he'd crawled into the vault. He could see the tiny flecks peeling away from the inviolable surface of the floor.

Blinking, he focused on the enormous string of System messages blinking at the corner of his vision, demanding his attention.

*****Congratulations! You have refined your race, evolving your Quinametzin Bloodline into that of a Nascent Primordial Titan, Legendary 5.*****

*****Your feat, Epic Quinametzin, has evolved to Legendary Titan.*****

*****Legendary Titan: As a result of breaking through to the legendary levels of your titanic bloodline, all of your attributes have permanently increased by a further 100 points.*****

As Victor read the description for "legendary titan," he blinked, pausing his perusal of the messages, as the words sank in. Improving his bloodline to legendary had just given him six hundred attribute points! It was an absurd amount—nearly twenty levels' worth of points in a legendary class. More than that, it didn't seem he'd lost the points the "epic" version of the feat had given him. "And I've got a shitload more messages to read," he muttered, pushing aside his urge to check his status sheet.

*****Your feat, Behemoth's Regeneration, has evolved to Primordial Behemoth's Regeneration.*****

Primordial Behemoth's Regeneration: You have inherited the ancient, undying vitality of a primordial behemoth. Your flesh no longer merely heals—it reknits with relentless, elemental force. You will now rapidly recover from wounds that would be fatal to others, including severed limbs and organ damage. This regeneration adapts to repeated injury, accelerating over time and resisting attempts to suppress it. It continues to complement and magnify similar benefits gained from other sources.

Your feat, Wyrm's Fervor, has evolved to Primordial Wyrm's Fervor.

Primordial Wyrm's Fervor: Consuming flesh seared by the fires of your Breath Core awakens the dormant potential within your primordial flesh and bones. This practice offers a steady—if gradual—path to strengthening your primordial bloodline.

Your affinity for glory-attuned Energy has been lost!

Your affinity for inspiration-attuned Energy has been lost!

Congratulations! You have gained an affinity for hope-attuned Energy!

Your spells, Inspiration of the Quinametzin and Banner of the Champion, have been merged into: Standard of the Last Light.

Standard of the Last Light, Epic: You manifest a glowing standard—the final light against the dark—that floats behind you. Allies who see it will be filled with hope, gaining endurance, resistance to fear, and a bonus to their will attribute that increases the longer they stand their ground. The more desperate the situation, the stronger the banner's effect. Enemies who attempt to extinguish that hope suffer mounting penalties the longer they remain in sight of the standard. Energy Cost: Minimum 1000, scalable. Cooldown: Long.

Your previous methods for manifesting certain types of Energy are no longer available to you. Removing all spells dependent on such Energy.

You have lost your ability to cast: Heroic Heart. Removing.

You have lost your ability to cast: The Inevitable Huntsman. Removing.

Congratulations! You have advanced your Spirit Core: Legendary 5.

Despite more messages waiting, Victor paused, taking a minute to absorb everything he'd read. The improvement to his bloodline was incredible but not unexpected. He'd known that Chantico had guided a considerable portion of the potential Energy into him with the purpose of unlocking his primordial titanic traits. Still, he hadn't expected to gain *ten* ranks of his bloodline, something that would have required a hundred fortunes' worth of lesser natural treasures.

In all honesty, that was an understatement; Victor had no idea how difficult it would be to acquire legendary-tier natural treasures. The value of that royal jelly had truly been incalculable. Then there were the changes to his feats—not all, but some. His regeneration was much improved, which made him wonder . . .

Victor looked down at his chest, and sure enough, the curse was still there, but it was smaller, driven back by his will, his aura, or just the nature of the royal jelly in his system, perhaps. Whatever the case, it was back to the size of a baseball, and it *struggled* to consume his flesh. What was more, his flesh regenerated so quickly as to look almost whole as the little void flailed against it.

"Ha." Victor pressed a finger against the void, and though it stung and began to eat away at his skin, it was nothing like when he'd last touched it. Victor pulled his hand away, clenching it into a fist before him. He could *feel* the density of it. He could feel the . . . *potential*. If he weren't already cramped in the vault, he might have tried to release some of it to see if Chantico was right—could he control his body with the force of his will? Looking at the door, realizing he was already too large to go through it easily, he tried the opposite.

Victor could feel his aura tightly wrapped around his Core space, an integral part of him now that he'd gained his epic-tier Aura Veil. With a flex of his will, he moved it outward, around him, wrapping it around his body and then compressing it. To his amazement, he shrank. He *folded* more of his simmering potential onto itself, increasing his density and reducing his size. Still, he knew he'd be enormously heavy when he stepped outside the vault, so just as Chantico had suggested, he *willed* himself to be lighter.

He could feel it working. He didn't have a means to measure it, but the ponderous weight of his limbs faded, and he moved more like his old self. The best thing about his new nature was that he didn't have to maintain the pressure of his aura and will. The change persisted, though he could feel the potential in him, ready to be unleashed.

Smiling, Victor resumed his evaluation of the changes that had been wrought over him. His loss of Heroic Heart and The Inevitable Huntsman irritated him, but he knew he could get them back. There had to be a way to weave courage and justice with hope; he just had to discover the pattern. He was pleased with his new Standard of the Last Light but wondered how much he'd miss inspiration. Was there a way to cast inspiration-type spells with hope-attuned Energy? Hadn't Chantico said they were related?

He pushed the questions aside; they could wait for a time when he wasn't so pressed. He was nearing the end of the System's messages, so he carried on reading:

*****Congratulations! You have achieved Level 91 Doomforged Tyrant and gained 24 will, 24 strength, and 5 vitality.*****

Victor stared at the message for a moment, slowly nodding. The class was "mythic," which made it better than legendary—forty-eight attribute points per level rather than thirty-six, not counting the five vitality from his Titanic Constitution feat. He was a little surprised that strength and will were boosted equally, but he wasn't going to complain. He read on:

*****Congratulations! You have achieved Level 92 Doomforged Tyrant and gained 24 will, 24 strength, and 5 vitality.*****

*****Congratulations! You have earned a new Class spell: Dread Imperative, Epic.*****

*****Dread Imperative, Epic: With a burst of fear- or rage-attuned Energy, you project your will in an area attack. Enemies in range of the spell will be forced to confront the inevitability of defeat. Foes who fail to resist will suffer crippling morale loss. They will find attacking you a daunting proposition, and depending on the strength of their will, they may flee or freeze up entirely. Energy Cost: 15,000. Cooldown: Medium.*****

*****Congratulations! You have achieved Level 93 Doomforged Tyrant and gained 24 will, 24 strength, and 5 vitality.*****

*****Congratulations! You have achieved Level 94 Doomforged Tyrant and gained 24 will, 24 strength, and 5 vitality.*****

*****Congratulations! You have achieved Level 95 Doomforged Tyrant and gained 24 will, 24 strength, and 5 vitality.*****

*****Congratulations! You have earned a new Class spell: Maw of the Broken Will, Legendary.*****

*****Maw of the Broken Will, Legendary: With a surge of focused will and fury, you tear open a rift in the ground, forming a jagged chasm that howls with the screams of the conquered. This pocket dimension, born of fear and rage, lashes out at all nearby enemies.**

Weakened or demoralized foes will be pulled into the maw by unseen hands, trapped in a pocket realm of torment where they experience the twisted echoes of their worst defeats, fears, and failures, losing health and Energy and suffering permanent damage to their will attribute. Once ejected, your foes will be stunned and broken.

Your allies will be immune to the spell's effects, though the battlefield will change while the maw is open. Energy Cost: 55,000. Cooldown: Very Long.***

As Victor finished reading the last System notification, he realized he'd stopped breathing. *"Chingado!"* he hissed. The spell sounded horrifying, but . . . *awesome. Both* of the spells he'd gained from his new class seemed great. It was almost enough to make him lose sight of the fact that he'd gained *five* levels in the ninth tier! Chuckling, giddy with the heady rush of achievement, he pulled up his status sheet to review all the numbers:

Status				
Name:	Victor Sandoval			
Race:	Nascent Primordial Titan: Legendary 5			
Class:	Doomforged Tyrant - Mythic			
Level:	95			
Breath Core:	Elder Class: Advanced 9			
Core:	Spirit Class: Legendary 5			
Breath Core Affinity:	Magma: 9; Blue Ice: 9		Breath Core Energy:	6300/6300
Energy Affinity:	Hope 9.4, Fear 9.4, Rage 9.1, Unattuned 3.1		Energy:	208226/208226
Strength:	1000 (1100)	Vitality:	1057	
Dexterity:	380 (585)	Agility:	403 (608)	
Intelligence:	512	Will:	919	
Points Available:	0			
Titles & Feats:	Titanic Rage, Ancestral Bond, Flame-Touched, Greater Titanic Constitution, Titanic Presence, Desperate Grace, Unyielding Challenger, Elder Magic, Born of Terror, Battlefield Awareness, Battlefield Presence, Aura of Command, Legendary Titan, Mountain's Resilience, Primordial Behemoth's Regeneration, Blood Supremacy, Primordial Wyrm's Fervor, Peerless Warborn Mind, Flight of the Lava King, Presence of the Tyrant			

Skills:	
System Language Integration	Not Upgradeable
Spirit Core Cultivation Drill	Epic
Breath Core Cultivation Drill	Advanced
Cooking	Basic
Animal Taming	Basic

Unarmed Combat	Basic
Knife Mastery	Basic
Spear Mastery	Advanced
Bludgeon Mastery	Improved
Axe Mastery	Epic
Breath Weapon Mastery	Improved
Tactical Mastery	Basic
Grappling	Advanced
Sovereign Will	Epic
Titanic Leap	Improved
Aura Veil	Epic
Spells:	
Iron Berserk	Epic
Channel Spirit	Improved
Prismatic Illumination	Epic
Project Spirit	Improved
Spirit Walk	Advanced
Tether Spirit	Basic
Abyssal Tyrant	Epic
Imbue Spirit	Improved
Honor the Spirits	Improved
Alter Self	Improved
Velocity Mantle	Epic
Wild Totem	Advanced
Impart Nightmare	Improved
Guardian's Rescue	Epic
Volcanic Fury	Improved
Wake the Earth	Basic
Roots of the Angry Mountain	Advanced
Greater Spirit Binding	Advanced
Voice of the Angry Earth	Basic

Locate Ally	Basic
Core Domain	Epic
Glacial Wrath	Epic
Tactical Reposition	Basic
Standard of the Last Light	Epic
Dread Imperative	Epic
Maw of the Broken Will	Legendary

When he saw his Energy level, his eyes bulged out. When he'd consumed the royal jelly, his maximum Energy had been around seventy-six thousand. Now, he had more than *two hundred* thousand. Had cultivating his Core into the legendary ranks really boosted it that much? There wasn't any denying the report.

He was also surprised to see that his hope affinity wasn't any higher than his fear. He'd thought it would be stronger, based on how it was represented in his Core space. It certainly *looked* stronger. Then he recalled that he'd split his negative affinities into rage and fear, and he remembered how Chantico said it would be a good idea to keep them that way. Seeing his affinities represented as raw numbers drove the point home—if he hadn't done so, his fear would be a match for his hope.

He wondered about his "race." What did it mean that he was a "nascent" primordial titan? He was just emerging? What would it be like if he ever became a true primordial titan? Would he be like Azforath? Was that what would happen when he advanced to the "mythic" tier, assuming there was such a thing?

Victor took one more look at his much-inflated attribute values, and then, shaking his head in disbelief, he closed the status sheet. He knew things were urgent, that Kynna and the others were no doubt worried about him, eager to see him emerge from the vault, but he wasn't done yet.

He could put off dealing with the curse, but that would mean leaving Lifedrinker on the spirit plane, possibly wounded and definitely alone and worried. Even if he put his feelings aside, he knew it would be foolish to go into battle without her—not when he was likely outnumbered and facing enemies with all manner of unknown capabilities. So, that decided, he shifted into a lotus position and closed his eyes, clearing his mind. Then, as he'd done so many times in the past, he formed the pattern for Spirit Walk and once more went to battle his curse.

44

WHAT HONOR DEMANDS

Arona and Kynna stood atop the Mountwatch Spire, watching the wild battle taking place on the plain before the palace's gates. Of course, Arona hated that she wasn't helping—so did Bryn and all of the Queen's Guard. She knew they'd be able to help, but how much? Five of the thirteen Queen's Guard were nearly steel seekers, and, together, they could surely slay a few of the Khalidaysian champions, but then they'd be lost. It was the same story for Arona and Bryn. They served the queen better by staying alive—for now.

"It's fortunate the wards make flight impossible above the palace," Kynna observed, watching the champions flit about down below—many were winged or had other means of flight. However, if the enemy tried to fly over the walls, the powerful wards would rebuff them, likely causing them to crash. That hadn't stopped them from trying—what was a fall from great heights to a steel seeker, after all? Still, the wards had held, and the wells of power beneath the palace were near depthless.

"Indeed. It gives us a chance—well, maybe not a chance, but it allows us to slow their progress." Arona pointed to the wall above the gates where Bryn patrolled with some of the other defenders, watching the battle. "We can retreat to rest and, as they return to assault the gates, resume attacks with fresh forces."

"True. Yet I can't help feeling they toy with us."

Arona looked at her sharply. "I don't know. We've killed nine of their champions."

"At what cost, Arona?" There wasn't any need to respond; they'd already reviewed the numbers earlier that day. A hundred and seventeen of Kynna's defenders had died to claim those nine kills. Nobody had to do the math for her—the ratio wasn't sustainable. The fights had been raging, on and off, for six days now, and Arona didn't think they'd last much more than another week. The queen sighed heavily. "I suppose it's selfish of me to hold out so long. I should see that champion from Voth. I should tell him I'll accept Bomar Lund's offer."

Arona turned her gaze to the courtyard inside the main gates. The strange champion, Resh A'kel, had moved his tent inside when the assault began. Still, he refused any hospitality and seemed to await Kynna's decision patiently.

"Who's this?" Kynna asked, bringing Arona's attention back to the field. A solitary figure approached from the Khalidaysian encampment. When he stood on the edge of the battlefield, not a hundred yards from where the furious fight played out, he lifted his head to the sky and *roared*. It was a sound that woke the primal fears lurking in the depths of Arona's mind—like thunder and a viper's hiss combined.

"The dragon," Arona murmured, relieved to find her voice didn't quaver.

The battle calmed as the combatants looked toward the sound, and then the lone figure shouted something that didn't reach Arona's ears. The Khalidaysian attackers broke off, forming a tight formation as they retreated from the much larger cluster of Kynna's defenders. Slowly, they fell back, and it seemed the defenders would let them—no doubt happy for the reprieve. Arona counted a dozen bodies on the grass, and she knew most or all of them would be Kynna's people.

The dragon—tall and shaped much like a handsome Fae—stepped forward and deposited a large white box on the grass before him. Then, he straightened and shouted something at Kynna's defenders before turning and following his troops back to the Khalidaysian encampment.

One of Kynna's champions, a woman from a city called Rone, ran forward to collect the box. Arona watched as she gingerly pried the lid open, peered inside, and then closed it again. She said a few words to the other defenders before stretching out her magnificent crimson wings and launching herself into the air, soaring toward the tower where the queen and Arona stood. The wards wouldn't bother her; they could discern between friend and foe, thanks to a simple drop of blood deposited into a brazier at the heart of the palace.

When the woman landed, bloody and heaving for breath, she gasped, "My Queen, the man left this for you. Forgive me for looking inside, but I had to ensure it wasn't trickery."

Kynna nodded, frowning. "Thank you, T'vajja. Give it here."

"My Queen—" The woman looked around the rooftop from Kynna to Arona to the many Queen's Guard standing at their ready positions. "I fear it's something terrible. Forgive me for bearing this to you. I—"

"T'vajja! This isn't your fault. Hand it to me."

The woman stepped forward. She was a tall, powerfully built woman, and beneath the dirt and blood, her armor gleamed like burnished platinum. She narrowed her feathery crimson eyebrows and said, "Better I should hold it. Just take the lid off, Your Majesty."

Kynna's scowl deepened, but she didn't argue. She reached forward and removed the stained white lid of the box. Of course, Arona was too short to see inside, but the queen didn't leave the contents a mystery. "That's Bomar Lund, if I'm not mistaken. So, then. They seek to break our spirit before they kill us."

Arona's small hand shot out and gripped the edge of the box, pulling down so she could see within. Sure enough, a perfectly preserved head sat on a yellow silk cushion. Bomar had been a handsome man, it seemed, with a well-defined jaw and cheekbones and a sharp, regal nose. "You're certain?"

Kynna nodded. "I am, but take it to that champion below to confirm. Perhaps it will persuade him to join our cause."

Arona shook her head. "Better I escort him out of the palace first. It might persuade him to join the other side if he learns his master is dead and still considers our cause doomed."

Kynna shook her head in dismay. "Ancient gods, Arona. I wouldn't have thought that. I wasn't made for this sort of thing."

The feathered warrior's eyes sprang wide, and she hissed, "Nonsense, my Queen! It's what we love about you—you're kind and good, not conniving and vile like the dogs who attack us! They're spitting on thousands of years of tradition by attacking you! Surely, the Veil Walker Council will come to your aid soon!"

Kynna smiled and stretched out her pale gray-hued fingers to touch the woman's blood-smeared brow. "Your love is well received, T'vajja. Thank you. Now, give that box to Lady Arona and go tell our defenders to rest while they can."

Arona took the box, sending it straight into a storage device, then watched as the woman bowed to the queen before leaping off the tower to glide down to the battlefield. "You're sure you want me to tell him? We could still offer your hand in marriage. He doesn't know the king's dead. Maybe he'll fight beside us while we send a false messenger."

Kynna smiled almost sadly as she replied, "No, dear Arona. Take him outside the gate and show him the head of his king. We'll see what his honor demands of him."

When Victor opened his eyes on the spirit plane, he found himself sitting on the grass a hundred paces from the enormous, pulsing void construct that had earlier defeated him. He stood, glowering at the thing invading his spirit. It hadn't noticed him yet, or, if it had, it didn't care. It was busily taking bits of the spirit realm and hauling them into itself, very slowly but surely digging itself deeper into the fabric of the place. Was that metaphorical? Was that a symbol of its attacks on Victor's spirit?

He knew it *was* assaulting his spirit, but he wasn't so sure he should take the thing literally anymore—it *looked* like a monster, and it certainly seemed to be physically attacking the spirit plane—and him if he let it—but Victor knew there was more to it; this place wasn't meant to be taken literally. He could alter his own appearance, could he not? He could walk ten steps and travel a thousand miles. No, the thing was a representation of the void Energy that was working its way into him, and Victor knew what to do with Energy.

He strode forward. Allowing his spirit-self to manifest the nature of his physical body, he expanded his size until his head was well above the great bulk of the void infestation. As he neared the thing, more inky tendrils sprouted from its quivering bulk, lashing out toward him. Victor ignored them as they wrapped around his mighty legs. They were just strands of void-attuned Energy, and he knew he could resist them. The curse was struggling to mar his flesh in the real world, was it not? Why should his spirit manifestation fear the Energy? This was but a thorn he had to pluck out and flick aside.

Victor looked inward, to his brilliant Core space and the impossibly dense layers of his aura gathered around it. Looking at it, his titanic pride bristled. He'd built it up through labors and trials, treasures and boons. It was loaded with the dreadful fear that used to weigh on his heart, the rage he cultivated to keep his fear at bay, and the countless victories and deeds he'd accumulated along the way. He knew that his mythic class and the primordial essence of his bloodline were like multipliers applied to the aura he'd built—that it was a match for most veil walkers' auras already.

Victor's aura was further strengthened by his will, and, moreover, it was the vehicle that could deliver the commands of his will, imposing it on the world. With that understanding, Victor unleashed it, letting it ripple out of him like a tsunami of determination, fury, and dread, like a kaleidoscopic tidal wave of conquered foes and killing intent.

The tendrils of the void infestation recoiled, releasing his trunk-like legs and withdrawing, but Victor wasn't simply trying to defend himself. He sent his aura out, *willing* it to surround the enormous, building-sized blob. It washed over the pulsating, quivering thing, and everywhere it went, the thing's tentacles snapped home until it was just a smooth, quivering mass of gelatinous Energy that strained against the pressure of Victor's aura.

As he applied pressure, dragging against the gigantic thing, pulling it toward him out of the hole it had dug in the spirit realm, it erupted in a frenetic attack, battling against the grip of his aura. Ten thousand tentacles smashed outward, stretching his aura thin, trying to punch through. Victor stumbled back, his mental grasp slipping as his will began to unravel. Growling, Victor straightened up and poured his hope-attuned Energy into his pathways.

The very nature of his hope, a near polar opposite to his fear, born out of his need to resist the empty void in his heart, bolstered him, and Victor stood straight again. With the crushing force of his will, he pressed his aura back down, smashing the tentacles into nothingness as he regained his firm grasp on the infestation. "Come on, you *pinché* fucker!"

Focusing everything he had on the effort, he held the infestation tightly, dragging it back, step by step, ripping it from the hole it had dug into the spirit plane. It struggled and thrashed, but Victor was relentless. He brought it, quivering and pulsing, out of the ground and dragged it onto the grass. With the thing ripped free and at his mercy, he pulled it farther and farther from the hole, ensuring there was no chance it could pull itself back in if it broke free from his grasp.

There was no need for his caution, however. As the infestation was excised, Victor felt his will surge. His aura grew harder and denser, and he roared as he squeezed it down, crushing the void Energy into a globe half its original size. As he toiled, growling and grimacing, smashing harder and harder, he saw the top layer of the inky void-attuned Energy begin to shimmer and shift toward gray. He was breaking it of its affinity, but was that what he wanted?

Victor had a Spirit Core—the void Energy was useless to it. If he crushed it into unattuned Energy, he could cultivate it. Something made him pause, though; *something* in him hungered for that dark, hungry Energy. Victor took a minute to look inward, to contemplate the hunger, and then he realized what it was: his elder Breath Core was pulsing, throbbing, eager to take it in. Could that be? His current affinities were for magma and blue ice—elements. Was his Breath Core not elementally aligned? He'd assumed so, but perhaps that wasn't how Breath Cores worked, at least not *elder* ones.

"Okay, then," Victor growled, using the crushing force of his will, his utter dominance over the void infestation, to draw it out, crushing down, while he pulled a long streamer of it toward him. He felt it thrashing and panicking, and he grinned, some of his rage slipping into his pathways as he savored the struggle. When the tendril of void was close enough, he emptied his lungs and then inhaled, drawing the thread of void into him.

When the void entered his mouth and throat, he could feel it struggling against his aura, but he'd made himself a fortress with his will, as Chantico had once advised him to do. The Energy slid off his flesh and into his lungs, and there, Victor's Breath Core drew it in. With his inner eye, Victor watched as his two orbs of Energy—smoldering magma and steaming, crackling blue ice—flared brightly. They *wanted* it! That was when he saw the flickering, sparkling, difficult-to-define Energy motes lingering on the outer edges of his Breath Core space—remnants of the *potential* from the royal jelly.

He'd thought he'd be forming a new orb in his Breath Core, one composed of the void, but that wasn't the case; his hunger—some latent instinct awakened by the jelly—was guiding him, and he knew what to do. Victor split the tendril of void-attuned Energy into twin threads and let his other Energies draw them in—one to his magma and one to his blue ice. It seemed incongruous to him; shouldn't the void consume the other Energies? Was he being foolish by listening to the hunger in his chest?

As he watched, though, the magma and blue ice didn't fade, consumed by the inky black void. Instead, their nature began to shift as more and more of the void flowed into him. The magma, always glowering and angry, stayed so, but it took on a darker aspect—a depthless quality that made it seem like a smoldering window into an endless abyss. Meanwhile, the blue ice lost its shimmering, brilliant luster, becoming pale and flat, with strange fractals beneath the surface that reminded Victor of things lurking beneath the ice on a frozen lake, half seen and waiting.

Seeing that he wasn't destroying his Breath Core with the impulsive decision to cultivate the void, Victor redoubled his efforts. He stepped closer to the infestation, still crushing it down with his will, but widening the tendril he was pulling toward himself. He inhaled deeply, again and again, drawing torrent after torrent of the stuff into his Breath Core. He did so dozens of times, and then, much like he'd experienced with his Spirit Core, he felt his Breath Core break through a plateau, and the orbs of potent Energy within grew denser, heavy with the weight of what he'd cultivated.

More than that, his breath pathway widened and grew sturdier, and when he drew his next torrent of void-attuned Energy, it was more than double the amount he'd drawn before. His Breath Core had been at the ninth stage of "advanced," so he assumed he'd just broken through to epic. Meanwhile, his grasp on the infestation grew firmer and firmer as it shrank and Victor drained it of its essential Energy.

Victor worked on that vast collection of void Energy for a long time, swelling the orbs of Energy in his Core to the point where they broke through three more times, and then, with a final inhalation, he drew the last of it. Victor stepped over the grass toward the tiny ball of shimmering light that he held fast with his aura.

He picked it up, releasing the force of his will, and watched as the tiny, flickering shard of Loss Chenasta's spirit—a manifestation of his will—evaporated into wisps of steam that faded into nothingness. He'd done it. He'd destroyed the curse. Relief washed over him as a weight of worry, one he'd grown so accustomed to that he'd forgotten it existed, melted away. Standing tall, he turned, scanning the landscape until his eyes fell on Lifedrinker's haft standing proudly in the air.

Victor jogged over to her and grabbed hold of her, lifting her out. She was cold at first, but then the wonderous material of her haft warmed under his touch, and her voice came to him, clear but dreamy. *"Is that you, heart-mate? Have you come for me, at last? Your touch is familiar but not . . ."*

"It's me, *chica*. God, I'm so sorry I let you get hurt. Are you okay?"

"I've slept long and deep, dreaming bloody dreams. I was hurt, but no longer. Now that you hold me again, with such mighty hands, can we bring terror to your foes? Can we drive them, bloody and broken, from your lands? Can we punish them for the insolence of thinking they could stand before you?"

"There she is," Victor said gently, stroking her haft as he lifted her enormously heavy head to his shoulder. "What foes, though, *chica*?"

"The ones I dreamed of. The ones who threaten your home and make your women fearful."

"What?"

"I think they spoke near my body. Many times, I heard them as they lamented your absence. My spirit dreamed of them; I saw their long faces, their fear-filled eyes. Long have I watched as your enemies tormented them with their presence. Come, battle-king, let us save your women!"

Victor's heart was pounding as he listened, and he had no arguments for her. "Let's go." Even as he spoke, he cut the thread of his Spirit Walk spell, and his eyes flew open on the material plane. As he stood, he read through several new System messages:

*****Congratulations! Your Elder Class Breath Core has evolved to: Primordial Class.*****

*****Your Magma affinity has been mutated to: Abyssal Magma.*****

*****Your Blue Ice affinity has been mutated to: Nullfrost.*****

***** Congratulations! Your Breath Core has advanced: Epic 4.*****

*****Congratulations! You have earned a new feat: Void-Forged.*****

*****Void-Forged: You have been reforged and tempered by the void itself. Rather than be destroyed by the void, you have conquered it and made it a part of you. As the void is now a part of you, you will have a natural resistance to void-type attacks. Moreover, when you channel your breath weapons, nearby enemies will feel the weight of the end. Their morale will suffer, and they may flee or freeze.*****

Despite his urgency and worry at Lifedrinker's words, Victor's lips split into a grin, and he quickly glanced at the Breath Core values on his status sheet:

Breath Core:	Primordial Class: Epic 4		
Breath Core Affinity:	Abyssal Magma: 9; Nullfrost: 9	Breath Core Energy:	67000/67000

Seeing the new value for his Energy, Victor's chest rumbled with a low chuckle. "All that fucker managed to do was make me stronger." Slamming a fist into his palm, Victor stepped forward and twisted the key to his vault—it was time to pick up Lifedrinker and see how bad things were. As a torrent of hot, steamy air hissed out, he pushed the door wide and, for the first time in months, felt the touch of the sun on his face.

45

DIRE CIRCUMSTANCES

Resh A'kel sat before his tent, watching the commotion at the gates as those of Kynna's champions who couldn't fly came inside. Arona studied his expression, wondering what went through his mind as Kynna's people fought and died daily while he sat there playing at being neutral. Unfortunately, his face gave her no clues to his thoughts; as always, his demeanor remained calm, his expression almost disinterested.

Arona looked over her shoulder to the Queen's Guard who'd accompanied her. "Stand here, prepare your ranged attacks, but do nothing unless I activate my shield. If he leaves peacefully, follow us to the gate, and ensure the passage is secured."

The guardians—all Tier Nine—saluted, and she descended the rampart steps to the courtyard. The beleaguered defenders were still clustered near the gates, talking as soldiers did after a battle—all bluster and relief. Not all, she supposed; she saw a few despairing faces—those who'd lost friends on the field, no doubt. She was spared having to confront her distaste for public speaking and platitudes when Bryn arrived, storming down another set of stairs with a dozen other defenders. She'd see those brave men and women into the palace and ensure they felt appreciated.

Arona hurried across the courtyard to the strange champion and his tent. When she drew near, he stood and bowed. "Lady Arona."

"Resh A'kel, I would ask that you accompany me without. I have word from the queen, and it would be best if you prepared to depart."

The man's sharp, angled brow narrowed over his singular eye. "Has something occurred? I note the fighting ended earlier than usual today." He gestured to the loose procession of defenders moving toward the palace and the awaiting staff and family, many of whom bore tokens of their love and appreciation—flowered wreaths, scarves, baked treats. The customs varied from kingdom to kingdom, and Kynna's burgeoning empire spanned many cultures.

"Please, sir. Accompany me, and I will answer all of your questions." Arona didn't give him a chance to question her further, turning on her heel and striding toward the gates. She hoped he'd follow and that there wouldn't be any violence. She'd left a spot of light-attuned Energy back on the stairway beside the Queen's Guard. It was a window she could peer through, a simple spell that allowed her to know without turning her head if Resh would comply.

To her relief, he turned, touched something on his tent, sending it into storage, and then glided gracefully after her. The four portcullises inside the gate tunnel were still open, thanks to the defenders' recent withdrawal, but the gate was closed. When Arona reached it, the soldier on duty had to pull the chain to signal to the crew above in the gatehouse that she desired to pass through. While they waited for the enormous amber ore gates to part enough to slip through, Arona looked at Resh.

As always, his face betrayed no emotion, but he nodded when he saw her looking. "I'm not a fool. If you had good news for me, you wouldn't make me leave the palace to hear it. I don't know what hidden strategies your queen means to employ, but I wish she'd taken King Lund's offer. I've wanted to fight against the Khalidaysians since this thing started."

Arona nodded, gesturing to the opening between the gates, indicating he should precede her. As he stepped through, dwarfed by the eight-foot-thick metal gates, she followed, saying, "You may yet have a chance. We'll see."

Outside, on the blasted, scarred battlefield where the great fighters of Ruhn had been going at each other for nearly a week, Resh stopped and pointed to the figure standing two hundred yards distant. "What's he doing?"

Arona frowned, surprised to see the dragon hadn't moved since delivering Kynna's "gift." "I think he's waiting to see your reaction."

"My reaction?" Resh's eye narrowed, and Arona, for the hundredth time, wondered how he'd lost the other one. She supposed it might not be missing—the platinum band made it impossible to know. "They've done something to King Lund."

Arona nodded, smiling sadly. "I'm sorry, Resh. He delivered your king's head a few minutes ago, when the fighting ceased."

He looked past her to the partially open gate. "I heard the portcullis glide down behind us, and I began to wonder why your queen might suddenly fear me. She's unsure where my loyalties will lie now that Bomar Lund doesn't hold my leash."

"She doesn't know you."

He nodded. His arm twitched, and with a flicker of silvery light, his long, liquid-looking sword was in his hand. "No, she doesn't." He turned toward the dragon champion, Dro Vah. "He knows me well enough, though. He stands there because he expects me to challenge him."

"Will you?" Arona licked her lips and then hastily added, "*Can* you?"

"I've never fought him. I sat with him a time or two when Bomar attempted to parlay with the empress. Yes, I spent some weeks at Khaliday while he was there, and I saw Dro Vah bullying the local champions. I've never seen him play all of his cards, however. Still, he knows me. He knows I was in service to Bomar when he took the man's head. Honor has its demands." He stalked away from her, straight toward the shirtless, smirking champion from Khaliday.

Arona wanted to say something—to wish him luck or apologize—but her mouth was dry and she couldn't find her voice. Of course, she *wanted* him to kill Dro Vah, but *could* he? Had she just aided in whatever greater manipulations were at play here? Was the man, calm and stoic, striding toward his doom?

To her surprise, Dro Vah summoned a pair of swords, short and curved. It surprised her because of his roar earlier; she'd half expected him to transform into a gigantic reptilian monster and swallow Resh A'kel whole. That didn't happen, nor did the two exchange insults. In fact, neither said a word before, in a flash of silvery light, Resh flickered through the air and engaged. His longsword rippled through the air, difficult to track, but Dro Vah was ready; a strange, chime-like ring echoed over the field as he blocked the blow.

Arona had to channel solar Energy into her pathways and cast a spell to boost her speed to observe the battle properly. Resh was grace incarnate, moving with such speed that his sword seemed to draw long, silvery lines through the air that persisted as it was rebuffed by Droh Vah, only to loop around and try again from another angle. They fought that way—frenzied and fast—longer than she could maintain her speed-enhancing spell, and she had to pause to let her Energy recover as the ringing chimes of their swords clashing continued to echo through the air.

To her unaided eyes, they were a blur, and occasionally flashes of silver, purple, green, and red punctuated their battle. No doubt they were carefully throwing spells, attempting to break the stalemate of their blades. She refused to be left devoid of Energy, so she was still struggling to see what was happening when it suddenly stopped, and Resh A'kel fell back, his platinum battle gi torn and bloody. Arona saw then that he'd left a hand behind, and he seemed to struggle to put weight on his left leg.

Even so, he clutched his silvery longsword, one-handed, watching as Dro Vah, seemingly unscathed, strode after him. "Well fought, little one." The dragon's voice rumbled over the battlefield, and Arona unwittingly took two steps back into the narrow gap of the open gate.

Suddenly, the small swords were gone from Dro Vah's hands, and an enormous black-bladed great sword appeared there. He held it high, chuckling darkly. "Soulreaper is hungry, and you'll feed him well."

To his credit, Resh A'kel didn't cringe or shrink away, though even nearly two hundred yards distant, Arona could feel the baleful, hateful Energy pouring out of that dark weapon. The champion held his head high, and as blood drizzled out of the sleeve of his gi, he held his silvery longsword high as well, ready to parry. Dro Vah had changed, though, and now he towered over the smaller man, and Arona couldn't imagine Resh could parry that massive blade. Grinning maliciously, he heaved it back and down, carving a black streak through the air as he moved to execute the last fighter who might have stood a chance against him.

Something happened before that dark blade could smash through Resh's guard and cleave him in half. A jagged, purple-edged rip in the fabric of reality appeared behind the smaller champion, and Dro Vah froze mid-swing. As Arona watched, spellbound, three enormous ebony claws slipped through the rip in the universe and curled around Resh A'kel, tugging him toward the dark void beyond. As he disappeared, a voice that turned Arona's bones to water shattered the silence: "*NOT YET.*"

Arona fell, her mind reeling from the psionic blast that accompanied those words. When she recovered, she hastily looked up, only to see Dro Vah striding away, back toward the Khalidaysian encampment. Some *thing* had saved Resh A'kel's life. Or had it? Was whatever had taken him better or *worse* than what Dro Vah had intended? She pulled herself to her feet and looked to the guard station. She had to clear her dry throat and swallow before she could bark, in her usual raspy voice, "Close it!"

Victor was in his elevator, halfway down from his tower, when he felt the presence of *something* and heard the echo of its voice in his mind. He couldn't make out the words, but they had the feel of a warning or a threat. Then the feeling was gone, and his elevator came to a halt. Whatever it had been had been weighty—something like Azforath or the ivid queen. He was sure the message hadn't been for him. It felt more like he'd overheard something meant for someone else, so he just added it to the list of things he needed to ask Kynna about.

He'd been a little surprised to find his quarters empty and unguarded. Not even Feist had been present at his door. A small voice in the back of his mind had begun to wonder if he was too late. Had everyone been killed or dragged away to prison? He didn't think so, though. If Khaliday conquered Iron Mountain, they'd install a new puppet immediately; the duchy was too wealthy to leave ungoverned.

When he stepped out of the elevator into the marble-floored hall that made up its ground level, his thoughts were confirmed—people were *living* there. The space was reminiscent of a refugee camp. Beds and cots were set up in rows, some separated by dividers, but others entirely in the open. People sat around chatting. Children played games on the floor, and overall, despite the fact that they were there to avoid being slaughtered by House Khaliday, the mood was almost festive.

As Victor walked through, quite a few people looked his way, and though they appeared to be interested in his presence, none seemed to recognize him. He'd stopped to look in the mirror, and he hadn't changed all *that* much. His eyes were more golden than before, and his skin a bit more bronzed with an underlying luster that he imagined would have made most of Hollywood seethe with jealousy. His hair, soft to the touch, had a metallic sheen, and his teeth— his teeth were the most changed. They were sharp, and his canines were those of a predator.

While he'd been in the vault, he'd made himself smaller than before, though, and perhaps that was why no one reacted to him. He was a handsome, striking fellow, but he didn't look like a titan. Maybe it was more than that; perhaps people had lost hope of him ever emerging. Perhaps they didn't recognize him because they'd already mentally accepted that he was gone.

Whatever the case, as he made his way through the palace, it wasn't until he came to the central hall, where many of his palace staff were busily trying to manage the overloaded populace, that a familiar voice said, "Your Grace?"

Victor turned to see Draj Haveshi, hollow-eyed and exhausted, standing at the head of a procession of pages and clerks, all of whom seemed equally overworked. "Draj! It's good to see a familiar face. I see Kynna brought many guests."

"Your Grace! You've returned!" He dropped the heavy book he'd been carrying, and it struck the marble with a resounding thud. At his outburst, people began to take notice of the scene and gather around. Victor heard their hushed exclamations—"It's the duke!" "Victor—the champion!" "He's back!" "I thought he was dead!" and a hundred others.

"Where's Kynna?" Victor asked, eager to get moving before he was mobbed.

"Atop the Mountwatch Spire, Your Grace. Come, I'll escort you!"

Victor looked down the crowded corridors, knowing he'd have to walk through a thousand people to get to the right set of stairs, and shook his head. "I'll make my own way." With that, he turned and strode down the immense central hall toward the front doors of the palace. People lined the hall—another camp for Kynna's people. Tents and cots crowded the aisle, and people who were now aware of his presence crowded the way, stretching out hands, calling out greetings, and asking all manner of questions; chief among them was whether he was going to stop the attackers.

Victor reached into his aura and released his hold on his body's *potential* a little, swelling in size so he stood head and shoulders above the tallest of those

Ruhnic people. It made it easier to proceed, though he didn't shove people aside. He let them lay their hands on him as he went by. He even held his palms out, accepting their touch, knowing they'd been bereft of hope for too long.

When he reached the wide-open doors, he turned his back to the courtyard and faced the throng behind him. As a hush settled over the crowd, he raised his voice and shouted, "I am back, and yes, I'm going to *fight!*" The words had the desired effect. The crowd erupted in cheers as he turned and continued outside. Standing in the courtyard, he focused on the highest point in the perimeter wall and cast Tactical Reposition, instantly traversing the space between.

Standing on the wall, he turned to run his eyes over the many spires towering above his palace. The tallest was his, but there, near the front, was Mountwatch Spire. Victor glanced left and right, ensuring no one was standing too close, though some guards had noticed him and were hurrying his way, wide-eyed. He channeled Energy into his wings, launching himself into the air. As he soared, trailing billows of black smoke, he watched as the small figures atop the tower grew larger.

He saw Kynna immediately, her crystalline crown flickering with the sun's light. Beside her was Arona, pale and beautiful, her sharp blue-eyed gaze already tracking his movement. The rest of the people were all Queen's Guard, staring at him, mouths agape. Victor soared higher than the tower, then streaked toward it, canceling his wings as he grew near and landing, catlike, beside Kynna. "My Queen," he said, smiling at her shocked expression.

He was expecting her to be happy to see him. He wasn't expecting her to burst into tears and fling herself into his arms. He was wearing a simple, if finely made shirt, and when she pressed into him, he almost recoiled, worried she'd touch the void in his chest. He remembered, though, with a soft chuckle, that it was gone, and then he folded his arms around her and pulled her close. "I'm sorry I'm so late, Kynna. It took me time to process the treasure I consumed."

He made eye contact with Arona and saw the relief on her face as she smiled at him. Still, he saw worry in her eyes, but before he could say anything, Kynna pulled back, straightening her crown and sniffing. "I'm just glad you've made it, Victor. We face dire circumstances."

"Yeah?"

Arona cleared her throat, nodding. "They've amassed an army of steel seekers. They have around forty—"

"It *used* to be fifty!" Kynna interjected.

Arona nodded, reaching out to grasp the queen's wrist. "That's right. The queen's defenders have battled valiantly every day for nearly a week, yet we've lost more than a hundred to claim those ten lives. Our champions grow weary, and morale is low."

Kynna quickly added, "Worse, Matessa's champion, the dragon, hasn't even been helping them. None of our people can stand against him, Victor. He just slew Resh A'kel, one of the strongest of the champions employed by the great houses."

"Well," Arona said, stepping closer to the queen, "he didn't quite slay him. Something pulled him through a rip in the universe."

Victor's eyebrows shot up. "Just now?"

Kynna nodded. "Yes, a few minutes before you arrived."

"I think I felt it." Victor rubbed his chin. "Why was Resh A'kel fighting for you?"

Arona shrugged. "I don't think he was. He was fighting for his honor. It seems the dragon, Dro Vah, had a hand in the death of Bomar Lund, who was flirting with the idea of joining Kynna's side in the war."

Victor folded his arms, peering out over the blasted landscape of the battlefield. "Well, you've done an amazing job of holding them off. Everyone should be commended. It sounds like I've got around forty assholes and one dragon to defeat, huh?"

"Victor! No one—" Kynna began to say, but when Victor looked at her, something in his eyes stopped her words. "You're different."

He smiled, nodding. "I had a productive nap."

Arona released the queen's wrist and grasped Victor's shoulder. "I can *feel* a difference in you. Will you tell us what—"

"My Queen!" one of the Queen's Guard said sharply, pointing toward the battlefield. Victor turned to watch as dozens of figures approached from the Khalidaysian encampment.

"They're launching another assault," Kynna said with a sigh. She raised her voice, commanding, "Alert Baroness Bryn to prepare the defenders!"

As one of the Queen's Guard hurried toward the stairwell, Victor called out, putting a little command into his voice, "Stop!" The woman practically slid on the stones as she hurried to comply. Victor turned to Kynna. "Let your defenders rest. I'll meet these *champions* myself."

"I'll join you—" Arona started to say.

At the same time, Kynna protested, "You can't go alone!"

Victor waved them both to silence. "I'll handle this." He turned to observe the motley force approaching. They were all shapes and sizes—tall, squat, humanoid, and monstrous. He could barely get a feel for their power from such a distance, but their equipment and demeanor spoke volumes. These were powerful people, accustomed to victory. Some were gigantic, some were winged, some wore armor that made their features impossible to discern, and some were hardly clothed. He saw axes, swords, bows, and even companion animals—great wolves, birds of prey, and a creature that looked as if a bear and rhino had borne a child.

He gestured toward the attackers. "They'll assault the gate?"

"Yes, and destroy it handily if we don't fight them!"

Victor nodded, smiling, as he began to don his armor. He summoned his impossibly heavy Aegis of Charyssor, chuckling as he easily lifted it, sliding his arms through the seam before sealing it around his torso. Next, he put on the crown of the Dark Colossus, and, stepping away to give himself a little more room, he pulled the Umbral Greaves of the Hollow over his light linen pants. That done, he took off his comfortable leather slippers and donned his Terror-Scale Boots.

Finally, as Kynna and Arona watched, he stuffed his hands into his Gauntlets of the Mountain's Might and summoned Lifedrinker. Immediately, she hissed into his mind, *"Is it time, heart-mate? Will we slay your foes?"*

Victor grinned savagely, watching the cluster of enemy champions approach, now only fifty yards or so from the gates. "It's time, *chica.*" He looked at Arona and Kynna and winked. "Don't worry, ladies. I've been dreaming about this kind of fight for a long time. This is the shit I live for." With that, he bunched his legs and activated Titanic Leap, launching himself into the air.

He'd angled himself perfectly, and, as he began his descent, streaking toward the ground, he released his hold on his body's potential and surged in size, expanding to his natural, nearly thirty-foot height. His body swelled with power, and he roared, holding Lifedrinker one-handed as he plummeted downward—tens of thousands of pounds of enchanted metal and titanic muscle and bone. As the Khalidaysian champions took note of him and blazed to life with magical shields and potent attacks, he laughed and screamed, "Ancestors! Watch me fight!"

46

TO BREAK THEIR WILL

As Victor fell, he channeled Sovereign Will into his strength and vitality, bringing them to 1559 and 1541, respectively. He didn't look at his status sheet to confirm the numbers, but he could *feel* the difference in himself. He'd broken through some kind of threshold in his cocoon-like state within his vault. Most of his attributes were significantly higher, but with his Sovereign Will boosting his strength and vitality, he felt he'd transcended some sort of limit—and he wasn't even berserk. Was this what it felt like to be a steel seeker? A veil walker?

It wasn't that he was deluding himself into thinking he *was* one of those. He knew he was still, technically, an iron ranker. He also knew that he'd been fighting—and beating—steel seekers since he'd become Tier Six. Looking back at himself, as he was then, he knew he was something different now. He was a true titan, freshly forged and just coming into his power, yes, but a titan nonetheless. Why else would he have the audacity to leap into battle with not one or two, but twenty-six steel seekers?

The thought made him laugh as he plummeted toward incoming fireballs, arrows, spears, and a dozen other attacks. When he was fifty yards from the ground, the first spell hit him—a lance of pure, red, destructive force. It slid off his aegis, leaving a trail of sparks but otherwise doing no harm. He batted aside a massive five-hundred-pound lance of dark metal—Lifedrinker was unimpressed. He shrugged off a dozen fire attacks, shards of razored ice, a storm of arrows and knives, and then smashed into the ground, right at the center of the pack of champions.

Several champions attempted to create distance between themselves and Victor, likely because they excelled at ranged attacks rather than direct melee. Many leaped to attack, smashing into one another in their frenzy to get to him. Victor saw axes, spears, knives, swords—even claws and spiked gauntlets. None of them seemed to have counted on the effect his impact with the earth would have.

Even expanded to his full size of nearly thirty feet, Victor was far denser than a normal creature. His titanic flesh and bones were hundreds of times more resilient than a natural human's. Add to that the colossal weight of his armor and Lifedrinker, and the impact was more like dropping a battle tank from a skyscraper than that of a man jumping off a building. For good measure, as he hit the ground, Victor stomped, casting Wake the Earth.

The concussion was like a bomb going off. The ground erupted in outward-flowing ripples of earth ten feet high. A great cloud of dust exploded into the air, riding the shockwave as the world shook and split, and fiery magma geysered forth from a dozen different fissures. The champions charging to intercept Victor where he would land were thrown back, one and all. Those running to make distance were smashed down by the shockwave, as if a giant—one bigger than even Victor—had slapped them on the back.

Victor stood at the epicenter of his destructive landing, lifted Lifedrinker high, and *roared*, casting Voice of the Angry Earth. The spell was designed to be amplified by the strength of the caster's aura, and Victor's aura was *strong*, fully off its leash. He remembered when he'd stood up to Ronkerz's aura, how it had required all of his effort, but he'd done it. Comparatively, he felt as though his aura had reached those levels—no, it had surpassed them. As the thought flitted across his mind, part of him wanted to leave that very second and hunt Ronkerz down for a rematch—he wanted to make *him* bend to *his* aura.

The thought was just a fraction of a millisecond of distraction, though, and he pressed on with his planned attack. Voice of the Angry Earth served a purpose beyond announcing his might: It was meant to brutalize the senses of his foes and drive them to their knees. Its purpose was to begin softening their will. As his voice broke like thunder, a roar that shook the walls of the palace behind him, his foes, already struggling to find their footing, already channeling Energy into abilities that would right their balance, were smashed with the weight of Victor's will.

The effect was profound. Many of the champions around him had their immediate thoughts dashed from their minds as they struggled to combat the weight of Victor's aura. Those few who'd kept or regained their feet succumbed, falling to a knee or collapsing entirely. Those already down were hit even harder, their struggles to stand or move making their defenses sluggish.

Victor wasn't done, though—he'd only just begun. Standing at the center of the crater he'd created, he cast Core Domain, fueling the hungry spell with a thick ribbon of fear-attuned Energy. Shadows burst outward from him, cloaking the blackness of moonless midnight. The ground, already treacherous due to his landing and Wake the Earth, became a shifting landscape of nightmares tailored to each beholder's personal fears.

Some of the champions found themselves struggling in thick, soupy water. Others were no longer struggling to stand on dirt and rock, but amid moldering corpses. Still others saw the soil teeming with rats or insects, snakes or maggots. Grasping, decayed hands sprang from the earth, and the air echoed with the chorus of individual nightmares. Many of the champions had already been panicking, but this new scenario, this nightmare incarnate, broke them further.

Standing at the center of his nightmare domain, Victor laughed as he watched these champions struggle. It was a cruel laugh, but it was rooted in righteous fury—these were not men and women to be pitied. These "champions" had come together to bully and massacre those weaker than themselves. They were here to break into Victor's *home* and slaughter men, women, and children. They would show no mercy, and neither would Victor.

The nightmare had more effects than to terrorize his foes. It was Victor's *domain*, and he was aware of the beings within it. It helped him recognize who was suffering the most and who was resisting his will. He could tell that more than half of the champions arrayed against him were broken, ready to flee, but that wasn't enough. Gathering his Energy, Victor cast Dread Imperative.

The spell called for rage- or fear-attuned Energy, and Victor was unsure if it would make a difference which one he used. Since he'd already created a domain rooted in fear, he channeled rage into it. A wave of malignant red light rolled outward with him at the epicenter, and where it passed over the foreign champions, he could see how it invaded their minds. Their eyes widened, their faces twisted into visages of terrorized madness, and many of them ceased their futile attempts to flee his domain, falling to writhe on the ground, convulsing with screams and howls.

Victor, face grim despite his carnal grin, scanned his domain, surveying his foes. Were they ready? He could feel some of them fighting to regain control, struggling to turn the tables on him with a well-placed, well-timed spell. He wasn't surprised—these were champions, after all. With a great inhalation, Victor focused his gaze on those with the strongest wills, those who were, inch by inch, fighting to claw their way out of his terrorizing spells. Then he breathed abyssal magma on them.

On some instinctive level, Victor knew the magma, laced with the emptiness of the void, would further break them. His eyes blazed with hungry crimson flames as the torrent of fiery lava, rippling with waves of impossible black, poured forth, engulfing his struggling foes. They burned and screamed. Some died outright, but those who didn't were broken in other ways. Victor felt their wills shatter, and his nightmare domain swooped in, taking their minds away from their tortured bodies.

Satisfied with his efforts, Victor finished his planned attack. Gathering a tremendous surge of Energy, he cast Maw of the Broken Will. He felt his rage-attuned Energy gather around him, slipping its furious tendrils into the fabric of the universe, and, with a sharp punctuation of his will, he *pulled*, ripping open a rift, a jagged chasm into a realm of nightmares, devoid of any other Energy or any hope of salvation for those drawn within.

All of his efforts up to that point had been made to soften his foes, break their wills, and prepare them for the maw. As long, shadowy, grasping claws stretched out of the rift, grabbing hold of his enemies, few even struggled. Those who did could not resist the strength of Victor's will as he commanded his terrible spell to pull them in. By twos and threes, they succumbed and slipped into that gaping, awful fissure until only Victor stood on the battlefield, several burned, twisted corpses arrayed around him.

He still held Lifedrinker on his shoulder, and he could feel her disappointment, her urgent need to fight. "Not yet, *chica*. These aren't worth your efforts. We'll water the soil with their blood, but your fight is yet to come." As he spoke, Victor looked inward, saw that he'd burned more than a hundred thousand Energy, and allowed his fear domain to fall away; he wouldn't need it.

When the darkness lifted, he could feel the eyes of thousands on him and knew the walls and tower tops were covered with people. He looked toward the Khalidaysian encampment and saw that an audience had gathered there, too. The other champions, and their leader, no doubt. He hoped the dragon was among them. He hoped he'd see what he was doing and come down to face him. If not, Victor would have to take the fight to him. This assault on Kynna—on the veil walkers—couldn't go unpunished.

As he had the thought, his knuckles tightening on Lifedrinker's haft, the first of his enemies was thrown from the maw. The champion was more of a beast than a man—a great bear with vaguely bipedal features. He writhed on the ground, coughing in deep, chuffing gasps, struggling to crawl. Victor knew the man's Energy was gone, his will utterly annihilated by his nightmarish pocket realm. He took two strides and cleaved Lifedrinker through his neck, sending his head rolling.

There began a great slaughter, as one after another, his Maw of the Broken Will ejected his foes, broken and ruined, and he put them down. It was dark, bloody work, the kind of thing that no man would take pride in, but Victor knew it had to be done. He had to make it clear that continuing this siege, that confronting him, meant death. As before, he hardened his heart by reminding himself what these men and women would do to the people—the children!— taking shelter within his palace. He reminded himself that they'd happily slayed Kynna's defenders for days.

When he finished, Lifedrinker bloody on his shoulder, he stood and faced the enemy encampment, defiant. The foreign champions shrank back from his gaze, distant as they were, and they and Victor knew it was over. None of them had come forward to aid their broken comrades. Their best chance had been when Victor's Energy had been partially depleted—that time was already past.

He contemplated shouting threats or challenges. He contemplated charging into their ranks. This wouldn't be over until the imperial family was broken. Shouldn't he find the commander of this assault? Was one of those distant observers the empress? He was just about to step forward, to kill or send those remnants fleeing, when a figure stepped out of the crowd, a tall man, devoid of armor, but wielding a massive black two-handed sword that rippled with waves of malignant red Energy.

Victor knew immediately that this was the dragon. This was the man Tes had warned him about. He took one step toward Victor, but then a torrent of Energy so thick that it looked like a volcanic geyser erupting exploded out of the torn battlefield around Victor and lifted him a hundred feet into the air. Apparently, the System had decided his current battle was over, and it was paying him his due.

"Go, you coward!" Troyssas bellowed, watching the giant, transfixed by a veritable *river* of rich, translucent Energy, soar into the sky.

"So you aren't just fond of your own voice, eh?" Dro Vah chuckled, forcing a yawn to highlight his boredom. "You really *are* stupid. You've never heard of a System rebuke?"

Troyssas frowned. It sounded familiar, but, in all honesty, he couldn't recall what it meant. "Enlighten me."

"If I try to strike him while the System has him like that, I'll be struck with a bolt of tribulation Energy and left stunned. The rebuke would be commensurate with the amount of Energy it's currently doling out to that bastard."

Troyssas groaned, reaching up to tug on his hair—he'd grown it out and had his man plait it for him. "Wonderful. Then he'll be even stronger when you face him."

"Face him?" Dro Vah chuckled again. "What makes you think I'll face him?"

Grand Prince Troyssas felt his face purpling with fury as the horror he'd just gone through rapidly converted to rage. "I just watched that man slaughter more than half the champions we brought to bear here!" He waved an arm, indicating the ranks of fighters standing to either side of his pavilion. Even as he did so, he realized their numbers had thinned—where had they all gone? Were they fleeing? "Do you think these *champions* can stop him?"

Dro Vah chuckled, waving a placating hand. "I only wanted to see your reaction. Of course I'll slay that man. A giant, or *titan* as he calls himself, is no match for a dragon. I've killed bigger than he. Besides, those little fear tricks won't work on a dragon—I'm immune." He sat down in the grass, laying his long, evil blade across his knees. Lifting a hand, waving it lazily, he added, "Relax. When the time is right, you'll finally see what your sister has been paying for."

The battlements were a frenzy of celebration as the soldiers watched Victor absorb the Energy from his slaughter. Arona, small in stature compared to the people of Ruhn, struggled to keep from being jostled by their hysteria. It reached the point where she cast Solar Shell and let the blazing shield of golden Energy keep people at bay as she climbed atop a crenellation to better see the field below.

"Hard to believe, isn't it?" Bryn shouted, trying to be heard over the mayhem.

Arona glanced at her. "That he won?"

"That he slaughtered more than twenty steel seekers in a matter of minutes! Did he advance somehow? Is he a veil walker?"

Arona shook her head—not because she thought the answer was no, but because she simply didn't know. "I'm at a loss. That spell—he trapped them all. How? Did you *feel* the Energy surge? It reminded me of some of Vesavo's great workings. Maybe he did . . . maybe he's a steel seeker, at least."

"I'm so glad we weren't down there. I'm so glad we weren't inside that field he created. Even from a distance, it shook me. I had to look away." Bryn's voice was nearly lost in the clamor as she spoke more softly, but Arona had good ears. She heard her.

"I understand what you mean. I almost felt sorry for them, but then I remembered those they've killed. I remembered *why* they wanted to break our gates. Besides, I've seen worse. At least Victor killed them quickly." She shielded her eyes as she watched the stream of brilliant Energy pouring into Victor. Had anyone ever received so much at once? Twenty-six steel seekers—it seemed impossible. How many levels would that give her? Even in Tier Nine, she had to think that two or three steel seekers would amount to a level. "Twenty-six . . ."

"What?" Bryn shouted.

Arona shook her head. "Nothing."

Despite the intensity of it, the enormous *amount* of it, the Energy didn't make Victor senseless as it had done so often in the past. He was aware of every second as he floated into the air, and the Energy poured into him. He was like a bird on a high-voltage line, but rather than being electrocuted, he was being flooded with power, and his body was awash with endorphins, dopamine, and every other pleasant chemical the Energy could squeeze out of his glands.

As his Core absorbed the Energy and his body was instilled with it, he felt each level it granted, and, in a new twist, was given System messages *while* he was under the influence of the Energy infusion:

*****Congratulations! You have achieved Level 96 Doomforged Tyrant and gained 24 will, 24 strength, and 5 vitality.*****

*****Congratulations! You have achieved Level 97 Doomforged Tyrant and gained 24 will, 24 strength, and 5 vitality.*****

*****Congratulations! You have achieved Level 98 Doomforged Tyrant and gained 24 will, 24 strength, and 5 vitality.*****

*****Congratulations! You have achieved Level 99 Doomforged Tyrant and gained 24 will, 24 strength, and 5 vitality.*****

*****Congratulations! You have collected enough Energy to transcend the mortal ranks and begin the synthesis of your learning. Do you wish to be guided through this process? Yes/No.*****

Still floating above the ground, still in the System's grasp, Victor tried to remember the advice he'd been given. Dar wasn't against using the System, but hadn't his ancestors told him to eschew its help when it came to . . . *whatever* happened after Level One Hundred? Should he let the System help him get started, or should he walk his own path and figure it out alone? He remembered Azforath's words, *"You must simply find a way to make the Other leave you be—to stay out of your way as you progress as you should, without the . . . limitations it imposes."*

That was the word Victor had been looking for—*limitation*s. He didn't want the System to limit him. "No," he said.

*****Warning! You have selected to forge your own Mantle without System guidance. This choice is irreversible. By rejecting guidance, you will be foregoing System optimization and Mantle stability safeguards. Are you certain? Yes/No.*****

"Yes."

*****Congratulations! You have reached Level 100. Your excess accumulated Energy has been deposited into an Energy well that resides in your spirit space. You can use this Energy to help refine your Mantle. In the future, all collected Energy will be deposited in your Energy well.*****

Victor felt the remainder of the Energy surge into him, and then he fell to the ground, as gently as a feather drifting on a breeze. He could feel the Energy in him; he could feel the power of his new ranks. He lifted Lifedrinker to his shoulder, grinning as he faced the enemy camp. He was ready for a good fight—*he* was a *steel seeker*!

47

A TITANIC CLASH

As Victor watched the dragon approach, an enormous black sword resting on his bare shoulder, his mind was split—half paying attention to his foe, and half contemplating the momentous milestone he'd just reached. It wasn't just the attribute points he'd gained from earning four levels in his Doomforged Tyrant class, but the fact that he no longer seemed to have a class at all. He'd taken a quick peek at his status sheet and seen the "class" line had been replaced to read:

Mantle:	Unforged

Was "mantle" a different word for class? Was that what the System called the custom class he had to design and perfect in order to ascend to the status of veil walker? If so, why had no one ever mentioned that word to him? Dar had specifically used the word "class," Victor was almost positive. Tes had never mentioned the word "mantle," but then, she didn't operate within the System at all. As much as he might like to say he'd stepped away from the System by refusing its aid, the status sheet and terminology on it were all part of it.

Could the System use different terms for different people? Different species? Was the fact that he'd awakened his primordial titan bloodline responsible for the fact that he was building a "mantle" and not a "class"? Was it better or worse? More likely, he decided, it was just another word for the same thing.

Beyond the strange terminology, Victor was fascinated by the idea that all of the extra Energy he'd received was being stored in an Energy well in his "spirit space." How was he meant to access that place? Should he cast Spirit Walk? What about steel seekers who couldn't spirit walk? Surely they had access to their spirit spaces. He supposed he might have had some guidance on the matter from the System if he hadn't chosen to go his own way. At least the System hadn't condemned or threatened him . . .

Combating for space in his already crowded mind were thoughts about the war, and the effect his slaughter of the Khalidaysian champions would have. Obviously, the dragon—Dro Vah, he thought his name was—still intended to do battle. What then? Would the rebelling veil walkers concede if he slew this preeminent champion of the empire? Would they come and try to kill him?

Dro Vah wasn't far now—only twenty or so paces for a titan. As he approached, he'd steadily grown larger, confirming for Victor that he was more than he seemed. When he stopped, ten easy strides away, he stood nearly eye to eye with Victor, and as he watched, the man's flesh morphed from smooth, tan flesh into gleaming black scales. His face changed, too, becoming decidedly draconic—angular yellow eyes, a long, tooth-filled snout, and a bristling crown of ivory horns.

Victor grinned, shifting Lifedrinker off his shoulder, holding her cross-ways before himself. She wasn't huge in his titanic hands, but she wasn't small either—a perfect battle-axe he could swing with one or two hands. After they stared at each other for several seconds, Victor spoke first. "I hear you slew Bomar Lund and his champion."

"The king, yes. The champion was saved—some great being wasn't ready to let him die. I think, perhaps, he would have rather had the quick death." As he replied, Dro Vah stepped sideways with his long, well-muscled, scaled legs, elegantly moving toward Victor's flank.

Victor matched his movement, sidestepping in the other direction. "He made a bargain for power, perhaps."

The dragon shrugged. "Perhaps. I care not, though I would have enjoyed his Energy."

As they continued to circle one another, Victor formed the pattern for Velocity Mantle in his pathways. "I've never fought a true dragon. You are one, yes? Or are you simply some dragonling with an advanced bloodline?" Victor expected the words to get a rise out of the other champion; if he were a dragon, he'd hate to be called something lesser, and if he were some sort of dragonkin like Lesh, the implied insult would infuriate him. If he'd angered the man, though, he hid it well.

Dro Vah snorted and shrugged. "We'll see. Just as we'll see how much of a *titan* you truly are." He snarled, and a puff of greenish-black vapor escaped his nostrils as he lifted his sword and took a step closer, closing the distance between them. "Now, enough chatter—Soulreaper hungers." Victor saw the muscles in his legs tense just in time to cast Velocity Mantle. As his mind and body surged with Energy and the resultant speed, he barely managed to bring Lifedrinker up in time to block that malevolent blade from piercing his throat.

Lifedrinker screamed in fury as she clanged against the sword, knocking the blade aside. Victor didn't let her momentum carry her far. He stepped forward and returned the attack, choking up his grip and chopping her down toward the dragon's shoulder. Dro Vah pivoted smoothly, avoiding the blow and hacking his black great sword at Victor's exposed hip. Victor let go of Lifedrinker with one hand and slapped the sword away with his Gauntlet of the Mountain's Might.

The impact stung—some hot, destructive Energy pulsed out of the sword, bypassing his armor and entering his flesh. It was short-lived, though, and he had a split second to wonder how badly it would have hurt a lesser being—one without the resilient, dense flesh and bones of a titan. From there, the fight grew more and more intense, as the two gigantic combatants hacked, parried, dodged, stabbed, kicked, punched, and otherwise tried to slaughter one another.

Their furious battle carried them down from the smooth, grassy field onto the blasted wasteland outside the palace gates. The ground was treacherous—fissures, boulders, even pools of cooling magma—but Victor moved around them as if he'd been born to it. Dro Vah, too, was unusually graceful. They fought over boulders, down into massive fissures and out, straddling craters, sharpened spears of stone, and pits that seemed bottomless. All the while, the music of Lifedrinker's clash with Soulreaper rang out, each impact carrying the resounding, concussive force of a massive bell being struck.

Victor was aware of his Energy use—Velocity Mantle wasn't a cheap spell. Still, he'd changed much since he'd last used it. With nearly 220,000 Energy in his pool, even a hungry spell could only drain it so fast. Moreover, with his will now topping one thousand, his passive regeneration was incredible. He could keep fighting using just that spell for a very long time. Apparently, Dro Vah enjoyed a similar abundance—that, or whatever magic made him so fast didn't cost him much Energy.

As their violent dance continued, Victor began to fall into a rhythm. He noticed Dro Vah's favored reactions to his attacks and began to recognize the other man's patterns. As his mind slipped into the trance of battle, and he started capitalizing on the dragon's limitations, he realized he was the better fighter. Dro Vah might also have an epic-tier melee skill, but it wasn't as advanced as Victor's. How that could be—how he could have more skill than a dragon who'd ostensibly lived for hundreds of years—he couldn't understand. It didn't matter, though, as the Paragon of the Axe showed its ghostly edge, and his foe began to bleed.

Before that point, Victor had scored hits with Lifedrinker, but every one had been grazing—the dragon was too fast, too smooth, to let her edge bite. Instead, she slid off his scales as he shifted, his movements perfect in their economy. The same could be said of Dro Vah's dark blade; it hit Victor's armor a dozen times, but barely managed to scratch the dense metal of his aegis or slide along the scales of his greaves. The sword, again and again, tried to impart its hot, wracking Energy through Victor's armor, but he shrugged it off, unfazed.

Now that he'd coaxed out the paragon, though, Lifedrinker's edge took on a ghostly gleam that extended her reach by a third. When she clashed with Soulreaper, the sword recoiled, and Victor saw chips in that dark blade. When she touched Dro Vah's scales, the ghostly extension of the paragon bit deep, and dark blood sprayed forth. The dragon growled and roared, his fury apparent, but he was too engrossed in his efforts for words.

Victor carved a deep cut in his opponent's shoulder, another on the dragon's ribs, and then, when he nearly cut through Dro Vah's left leg, the man screamed his fury and belched a cloud of green noxious gas that stung Victor's eyes and forced him to retreat. When he exited the cloud, his armor ticked and hissed, clearly taxed by the caustic nature of Dro Vah's breath weapon. His flesh itched and stung, but he was otherwise unbothered. Again, he wondered if Dro Vah was used to a greater effect.

The thought was fleeting; Victor's attention was instantly taken by the tremendous roar that erupted from the gas cloud, and then Dro Vah leaped at him, much changed. He was still bipedal, but he'd nearly doubled in mass. The dragon's shoulders were like enormous boulders topped with razor-sharp black spines. His head was much larger, and so was his maw and the massive yard-long fangs that protruded from his gums. His arms were long, and the black sword looked small in his enormous fist. Moreover, his scales had grown thick and glassy, like thousands of plate-sized, perfectly interwoven shields of dark crystal.

When he laid into Victor, his movements had slowed considerably, but the force behind those blows had its own way of multiplying the velocity. Victor parried the first blow of the sword, only to be battered by a tremendous clawed swipe. The blow knocked him reeling, and then Dro Vah whirled, and a short, thick, spike-covered tail blasted into Victor's chest, lifting him off his feet and sending him soaring straight into the amber ore gates of his palace.

His impact was reminiscent of a train crash. Metal ground against metal. Bolts the size of small trees shrieked as they bent and scraped against the magically reinforced marble of the walls. Even so, the gates held—bowed in the middle, but whole. Victor was briefly stunned, long enough for Dro Vah to approach and belch another cloud of caustic gas at him. As his exposed flesh began to sting and his eyes burned and grew bloody, he felt his ire awaken. The rage in his Core seeped into his pathways as he pushed himself away from the damaged gates, and he decided to use it. He cast Iron Berserk.

It was the first time he'd gone berserk since he'd emerged from his vault, a primordial titan. As the power of his rage flowed through him, he felt his muscles expand, his tendons, ligaments, and bones swelling to accommodate his much increased strength, and as his vision tinted toward red, he found the caustic gas nothing but a minor irritation; his already prodigious regeneration had accelerated to the point where the acid couldn't gain purchase.

As he stepped through the cloud, scanning for his foe, the ground shook with the density of his mass. He hadn't grown much vertically—a few feet or so—but he'd grown in power, massively. The synergy of his Sovereign Will, Titanic Rage, and Berserk meant that his strength, enhanced by his crown, had gone from 1196 to more than 5100. As he strode out of the gas cloud, Dro Vah was waiting, and again, he whirled, swinging his massive tail at him.

This time, Victor braced himself and caught his tail against his ribs, pinching it under his arm as the massive, titanium-hard spikes ground and bent against his aegis. Dro Vah looked startled, but not as much as when Victor took his gauntlet-covered hand and gripped that stubby, scaly appendage. He squeezed with all his might and felt the scales crack and grind into the flesh beneath.

Dro Vah screamed, but Victor wasn't done. He took a step back and to the side and whipped his arm out and back, flinging the dragon against the palace walls. The impact shattered the air like thunder. The great enchantments that made the palace walls nearly impervious to assault strained under the force of the crash. Stone cracked, but so did scales and bones. Victor faced his stunned, bleeding foe, and with fury heating his blood, unleashed a torrent of abyssal magma on him.

He roared as he breathed the black-streaked red lava, his eyes crimson in their glee for the destruction he wrought. The lava covered the dragon, splashing against the walls, cracking the stone further, and Dro Vah convulsed in a paroxysm of pain and panic. Victor took two strides toward his thrashing foe, lifting Lifedrinker high, intent on hacking the dragon's thick, spine-covered neck until his head came off. Then, in an eruption of green-tinted Energy, Dro Vah expanded, revealing his true form.

A roar that shook the ground like a rocket launch echoed over the battle-field, and then a dragon, easily eighty feet from tail to snout, launched itself at Victor. He managed to get one armored elbow up, catching it in Dro Vah's enormous maw, stopping him from snapping those jaws shut around his head. Despite the monstrous beast's size, Victor maintained his feet. He was close to forty feet tall, and his weight was sufficient to hold his ground. Still, as Dro Vah snapped down on his arm, grinding those adamant teeth into his armor, worrying it apart as it thrashed its great neck left and right, he felt his flesh and bone begin to part.

Victor roared and hacked Lifedrinker at the dragon's neck, only to have his other arm caught up in a massive, taloned claw. He fought, jerking his arm left and right, but the dragon's strength was a close match for his own. Worse, Dro Vah used the leverage of his grip to pull Victor against the straining, gnashing work of his jaws, further splitting his flesh. Finally, with a horrific ripping, snapping sound, he bit Victor's arm off and, with nothing resisting the pull of his claw, flung him to the side, sending him sliding over the charred battlefield to fall into a chasm.

Victor's mind was a haze of fury and pain. The pain was minor, though—it began to fade immediately as his regeneration took effect, mending the torn tendons, bones, vessels, and flesh, building upon their torn ends, and replacing his lost limb in seconds. His regeneration couldn't replace his lost gauntlet, but his aegis regenerated inch by inch, coating his arm in its impossibly dense carapace.

He could hear the dragon approaching. He could *feel* it. The ground shook with its approach. His initial rage had cooled, and he smiled as he lay there, cradling Lifedrinker. "Well, *chica*, at least we know he's a real dragon. I wonder if he's shown us all his cards now?" She didn't answer with words—her fury and hunger for his enemy's blood were too intense. He felt *that*, though, and his smile grew broader.

He'd just begun to stand, gripping the edge of the fissure, when a wash of green boiling liquid poured over him, accompanied by another dragon roar. The burning of the acid was intense, worse than the gas by a hundredfold. Victor held Lifedrinker clear, but his armor suffered greatly. Still, the artifacts held up to their claims of being "nearly indestructible." He bent his legs, alight with the pain of having his flesh dissolved, and used Titanic Leap to get clear.

Soaring through the air, his flesh reformed near instantly, and he watched as the dragon snapped enormous black wings and launched after him. Victor grinned and channeled Energy into his magma wings. When they sprouted from his back, he poured Energy into them, streaking away from the palace toward the stretch of grassland beyond the blasted battlefield. He could feel Dro Vah gaining on him, and something about being chased brought a laugh out of him as he tore through the air, leaving a cloud of black smoke in his wake.

He could *feel* his pursuer and knew Dro Vah would be on him in seconds, so he angled toward the ground and landed, sliding through the grassy soil, digging a great trench with his boots. He turned and saw the dragon pump its wings and bring its massive rear talons to bear, aiming to impale him. Victor's grin was feral as he ended his Iron Berserk and cast two other spells: Glacial Wrath and Roots of the Angry Mountain.

As the colors bled from the world, and things turned cold and dismal, Victor stretched his enormous hand toward the incoming talon. He carried out his plan, but most of his mind was distant, preoccupied with the many itching, nagging slights and insults he'd borne. He thought of the empress and her kin, and how they dared to assault his home and his people. He thought of the undead fiends his ancestor, Chantico, had told him about. How could the fool, Xelhuan, turn his back on his kin? How could he torment and defile the people of his world?

Distantly, he felt the talons impact his hand, and he closed his mighty fist, crushing the dragon's dense, scaled bones in his grip. How fast the dragon had been flying, he didn't know, but when Dro Vah struck Victor, he was halted instantly, and the earth under the dragon exploded in a jet of magma that would put many volcanoes to shame. The angry earth had spoken, and the sudden, unyielding impact snapped the bones in the dragon's leg, and its momentum carried it forward to impact Victor with tremendous force. Victor was a pillar of unmoving metal and titan flesh, though, and the dragon's scales and flesh bent and stretched against him, and its bones broke as lava bathed it.

With the inexorable strength of a glacier, Victor thrust Lifedrinker forward against Dro Vah's girth, pressing the top edge of her crescent blade into his scaled flesh until she slid between two great scales and punched through his thick hide. As Dro Vah screamed, his bones breaking, his scales burning, his belly punctured and invaded by Lifedrinker's edge, Victor smiled the cold smile of death's messenger.

The collision was over, and Victor threw the dragon to the side, pulling his blood-soaked fist out of the hole he'd made—Lifedrinker was still inside Dro Vah's belly. He watched, detached, as the dragon writhed. It was a mighty being. Its flesh and bones were strong—perhaps if the creature had improved its bloodline, it might have been as sturdy as he. It wasn't, though. Victor was unbroken, and he could see the creature couldn't heal as rapidly as he could.

Its rear leg was still twisted—a sack of shattered bones. Its scales, where they'd been bathed in lava, were cracked and dark, their glossy sheen ruined. Dro Vah's chest was distended where broken ribs tried to pierce their way out. The great hole in his guts, where Victor had stuffed Lifedrinker, smoked and smoldered as the dragon's caustic blood gurgled forth, steaming as it sizzled the grass.

Victor contemplated his foe. Had he not threatened his people? Had he not tried to kill Victor? Here was a being who deserved his ire. With cold, patient anger, he strode toward the dragon, noting a significant surge of Energy coalescing at Dro Vah's Core, only to be drained away as Lifedrinker drank her fill. His fury cold but unyielding, Victor inhaled deeply and bathed the dragon in a cone of nullfrost.

The near-liquid ice was so pale as to hurt the eyes of those who gazed upon it. As it coated his foe, Victor could see the strange shifting *things* beneath its surface and, once again, Dro Vah convulsed with panicked death throes. This time, however, he had no greater form to assume. He couldn't expand his way out of Victor's breath weapon. Worse, what Energy he might call on to resist the horrible icy embrace was being consumed by Lifedrinker as she wormed her way deeper and deeper into his chest.

Victor, standing more than forty feet high, massive of shoulder, steaming with the glacier's cold, glowering with the fury of an eon, stepped forward and, once again, exhaled a stream of nullfrost, this time directing it into the gasping dragon's face, into its eyes and mouth. With great satisfaction, he watched the creature convulse again. As Dro Vah writhed, jerking his head away from Victor's breath attack, the frozen flesh and muscles of his neck cracked and broke, and it fell with a massive, ground-shaking thud. Victor stepped forward and stomped on his skull, shattering the frozen bones.

His foe vanquished, Victor turned his cold, furious gaze upon the Khalidaysian encampment and roared. He drove his fist through the frozen scales and flesh of Dro Vah's broken carcass and gripped Lifedrinker's haft. Ripping her free in a shower of glistening, crystalized gobbets of flesh and blood, he stalked toward the enemy camp, intent on delivering the full weight of his wrath.

He'd only taken two steps, though, before a shaft of brilliant light burst from the sky, and then a woman stood before him. She was tiny in comparison, standing a mere ten feet tall, typical of the people on Ruhn, but she stared haughtily at Victor as she focused her aura on him. He felt it gather around him, probing, working to pierce his pathways and sever the connection to his Glacial Wrath spell. He resisted, pushing back with his own aura. The effort and the invasion focused his cold, inexorable wrath on the woman, and, as he glowered at her, her face shifted from angry to surprised to concerned.

"Stand down!" she shrieked, and again that aura pressed against him. Victor's scowl deepened, his cold, calculating rage glancing inward, assessing the strength of his Core. His Energy was more than half depleted, but his well was deep. He wouldn't bend to this woman.

"No," he rumbled, taking another lumbering step toward her, despite the pressure of her aura.

The air flickered around her, and then she stood another twenty paces farther from him. "Then you will die!" she screamed, and in her outspread hands, a ball of silvery Energy began to form, its brightness rivaling that of a star.

48

CONFLICT'S END

Victor focused on the woman before him, his slow, contemplative rage quickening as he recognized her attempt to thwart him. He took a lumbering stride forward, and then the blazing star she'd built in her hands erupted into a beam, lancing out and striking him full in the chest.

The white-hot Energy instantly heated the faintly iridescent, blue-black material of his aegis to a malleable near-liquid, then a fraction of a second later, it burst through, boring a six-inch hole through Victor's chest and exploding out his back in a shower of orange and red sparks. The pain was immense, and if Victor hadn't been forty feet tall and capable of ungodly regeneration, it might have been a fatal wound. As the beam faded, though, all it had accomplished was to slow his stride and further fuel his ire.

"I said *stop!*" the woman screamed, flickering with light, instantly shifting her position to Victor's right flank, where, again, she began gathering a brilliant orb of Energy.

If nothing else, she'd succeeded in turning Victor's mind away from the Khalidaysian encampment. He turned toward her, considered the best way to deliver his wrath, and then cast Tactical Reposition. He appeared behind the woman, and though his instinct was to simply stomp her into the ground, he lifted Lifedrinker's blood-slick edge and brought her down toward the much smaller being's skull.

She was fast, though, and her aura, unable to dominate Victor, was still thick around her. She was immediately aware of his presence, and she erupted in a white fire so intense that it annihilated the grass and melted a crater in the earth, transforming the rocks and dirt to slag. Victor was thrown back, his exposed flesh scorched black, and his armor strained to the limits of its durability. He crashed to the ground with an earth-shaking impact, momentarily stunned. The eruption of fiery Energy had scorched his eyes, and his vision briefly faded to yellow-gray before his regeneration returned his sight.

Rage flooded Victor's pathways further, but the nature of his transformation made it impossible for his blood to boil. Instead, his mind fragmented, chasing down a hundred different avenues for revenge in the mere seconds it took him to climb to his feet. If he'd cast Volcanic Fury instead of Glacial Wrath, he might have teleported to her again, cast Core Domain, and then followed with Velocity Mantle to try to overwhelm her with brutality. He hadn't, though, and his glacial fury was too cunning to squander most of his remaining Energy on an uncertain tactic.

Instead, Victor's calculating mind considered the possibility that this woman, whom he now recognized as the veil walker who'd been mediating the terms between Kynna and Livessa—the meeting where Victor had first seen Drok the Skull—might have enough Energy to outlast him. After all, a veil walker's well of Energy could run very deep, indeed. If he tried to kill her quickly, he might find his wrath unsatisfied. A glacier didn't think in terms of seconds or minutes or days, however. He could bide his time. He could bury this grudge and let it grow, nurturing it into—

Victor's contemplation of a slow, grinding vengeance against the veil walker was cut short by an ear-shattering explosion of thunder and the brilliant crimson arc of an enormous lightning bolt. It split from the heavens, arcing down and poleaxing the veil walker. She gyrated with the electric current, her arms thrown wide, her hair standing on end as her eyes flew open, glowing crimson like the electricity arcing through her.

A second later, as Victor stood surprised, wondering what twist of fate had befallen his foe, Lohanse appeared, gliding out of the sky on his shimmering crystal disc. He circled the stunned woman, and Victor watched as he held forth a huge ruby-shaded crystalline staff. "Submit, Wesper. Your rebellion is done. Two of your kin have already fled, and with your distraction here, my allies have subdued the rest."

Wesper had fallen to her knees as the lightning finished coursing through her, but now she slowly struggled to her feet, shaking her head so bits of broken platinum hair showered down around her, trailing smoke as the impossibly fine strands smoldered. "You *fool*, Lohanse!" she hissed, her voice quivering with pain and fury. "Are you so content to let this upstart destroy the peace that has lasted millennia?"

Lohanse clicked his tongue, bringing his disc around to land between Victor and Wesper. "You and your allies upset the peace. You're the ones trampling on tradition. Submit now and be judged. Banishment is still a hope for you." He pointed upward. "Our brothers and sisters watch, waiting to see if you will refuse. Will today be the end of your great climb?"

As their conversation continued, Victor shifted his gaze toward the encampment he'd meant to destroy before the woman arrived. He could see it was empty. His foes had fled. Slowly, inexorably, he exerted his will and pushed his cold, grinding rage down, reaching into his pathways to sever the connection to his Glacial Wrath. As his anger faded and the colors returned to the world, he sighed, releasing a mountain's worth of tension from his shoulders and inhaling the ozone-scented air.

". . . go now. Comply, and your judgment will be fair," Lohanse was saying. The woman nodded, then looked up at Victor, still the size of a titan, towering over both veil walkers.

"You surprised us, steel seeker. You surprised *me*. I harbor great dread in my heart for what will befall Ruhn, but I bear you no grudge."

Victor stared at her for a long moment, contemplating the complexity of his emotions. Seconds ago, he would have said his grudge was enough for both of them and that he'd have his vengeance even if it took a thousand years. The aspect of his Glacial Wrath had faded, though, and he held more hope in his heart than rage. Still, the rage was there, and the fear that drove it. He couldn't silence those parts of himself. "You've done great harm here. You've caused hundreds of deaths. At least the customs of this world have prevented that number from climbing into the thousands or millions. I hope Lohanse and the other veil walkers remember those lost lives when they render judgment."

Wesper's face, oval with sharp features, was soot-stained, and her glinting silvery eyes red-rimmed and bloodshot from her ordeal with Lohanse's lightning. She looked sad and a little pathetic as she nodded. Then, to Victor's surprise, she knelt before Lohanse so that he could easily snap a crystalline collar around her neck. Without another word, she stood, gathered a surge of hot Energy, then shimmered and disappeared.

Victor snorted. "She gave in easily enough."

Lohanse held up his crystal staff. "Another blast like the one I gave her would have broken her, and she knew it. Besides, she stood no chance against the two of us, let alone my allies who truly *are* watching."

Victor folded his arms, contemplating the words. Was Lohanse that much stronger than another veil walker? Could he defeat her with just two spells? He supposed there was probably a wide array of strength when it came to veil walkers, just as there was with steel seekers and iron rankers.

Lohanse approached and clapped Victor on the shoulder, smiling broadly. "Well *done*, Victor! When I came to warn you those months ago, I didn't dare to believe you could actually stand up to Khaliday! I'd hoped, but . . ." He trailed off, pointing behind him. "You're about to receive some Energy from the System."

Victor turned and, sure enough, a broad flow of shimmering ghostly Energy was pouring out of Dro Vah's corpse toward him. He braced himself, expecting the usual euphoria and loss of control as it infused him. It didn't happen that way, however. The Energy entered his pathways, but he felt it course toward his Core space and then through it, into what he had to guess was his spirit space. It happened quickly, and he didn't feel much other than the heady rush as the Energy passed through his pathways. He didn't even receive a message from the System.

He turned back to Lohanse, frowning in puzzlement. He struggled to find words for a moment, torn between asking the man for advice about what had just happened and confronting him about his interrupted vengeance. However, Lohanse capitalized on the silence and spoke instead. "I see you've made great strides. I can feel the weight of your aura; it's much changed since last we spoke."

Victor frowned, irritated because he *wanted* to be friendly with the man. He *wanted* to tell him about what he'd experienced, but he didn't like Lohanse driving the conversation. Almost petulantly, he changed the subject. "What will become of House Khaliday? I trust this"—Victor gestured toward the battle-field outside his palace—"will suffice for a duel of conquest. By that right, Kynna should be empress."

"As soon as we've put these rebelling veil walkers under lock and key, the Council will round up House Khaliday and exact judgment. We'll allow Queen Kynna to have a voice in the proceedings. I anticipate that the ruling members of the family, especially Matessa and Troyssas, will face death, while the others will be banished."

"I guess that'll have to do." Victor stretched his neck, pleased with himself for being so calm after the battles he'd just fought.

"Tell me, Victor, how did you make such gains? The man you were, the one I delivered my warning to, was mighty for an iron ranker, but this display was obscene. When you slew that throng of champions, we in the aerie, holding our little stand-off, were beyond stunned. It crushed the morale of the rebel veil walkers."

Victor shrugged, happy enough to feed Lohanse some half-truths. "I had some tricks up my sleeve—natural treasures and a high-tier dungeon I had access to. As your little friend noted, I'm a steel seeker now."

"My little friend . . ." Lohanse sighed, shaking his head, and Victor saw genuine sorrow in his eyes. "You don't know how true your teasing words are. Wesper once professed her love for me. I was caught out like a fool by this rebellion."

Victor concentrated, harnessing his body's potential, drawing it in, and reducing his size to better match Lohanse's. When they stood nearly eye to eye, he asked, "Can you tell me something, Lohanse? When you were a steel seeker, did you have to create a mantle or a class?"

"Ah, the System's terminology is new to you? You didn't have a master to spoil the ascension message? Many treat the terms as interchangeable, although my master taught me that they are philosophically distinct. A class is something rigid, meant to sit atop your spirit and alter how you interact with the world. A mantle is formed by you, *for* you, meant to mold perfectly to your spirit—" He paused, shaking his head. "I'm about to overstep. I'm assuming you eschewed the System's guidance?"

Victor couldn't see a reason to lie, so he just nodded.

"The journey of a steel seeker is best accomplished alone. What works for me, what makes sense to me, might not for you. Without the System's guidance, you'll have to do a lot of experimenting, but I admire your spirit. If I ever thought such a choice was right for someone, I'd say it was you. You've done nothing but shatter expectations since you arrived on our world. Do you intend to stay?"

Victor sighed, turning to look back at his palace and the throngs of people gathered atop the walls and flooding out of the gates. "I'd like to stay a while, but I have obligations. I'll come back from time to time, I'm sure. I've grown fond of this place."

"I owe you a debt of gratitude. If Khaliday had won, I would have lost my leadership role among the veil walkers, but things would have returned to normal for Ruhn, save for the fact that everyone would have known our rules and laws are a farce—a fiction maintained for appearance's sake. A free people cannot exist when they know there are different rules for the elite than for everyone else." He nodded toward the palace. "Your queen's victory is good for the world. The masses need to know that the mighty can fall. I hope the reign of House Dar will be just and that Kynna won't fall into the same trap as Matessa Khaliday."

"I think you'll find Kynna a very different type of ruler." Once again, Victor turned toward his palace, watching as a formation of Queen's Guard pushed through the crowd at the gates.

"Go, Victor. Be with your people. Tell your queen she is victorious, and I'll soon meet with her. The barrier preventing travel to and from this world will be lifted by tomorrow."

"All right." Victor held out his hand, and Lohanse clasped it. "It was nice to get to know you a little, Grand Judicator."

"Likewise, Champion."

Victor released his hand, then turned and marched back toward his palace. As he approached, the roar of the crowd was almost deafening. He was eager to rest and talk with his close friends. He was eager to pull out his Far Scribe books and reconnect with all his loved ones, who must have been worried sick. Even so, he stopped along the way and, swinging Lifedrinker in a few well-placed blows, carved the heart out of Dro Vah's chest, and put it into his storage ring. He wasn't going to pass up his first dragon heart.

* * *

Later, after he'd basked in the adulation of the crowd and had Kynna publicly honor him with one accolade after another, gifting him enough lands and titles to make him a king in his own right, Victor finally managed to pull away from the public and make his way back to his tower, but only after promising to dine with Kynna in a few hours. He wasn't *really* tired, not after the Energy he'd received from his battles. More than that, he enjoyed the people's attention; he loved seeing the joy on their faces, especially the children who'd been suffering in ignorance, aware that something was wrong, but not how dire things truly were.

Nevertheless, he felt a need to take stock and correspond with his loved ones and other people he owed updates to—Ranish Dar, for instance. He also had a feeling in his gut that Chantico was waiting to speak with him on the spirit plane, and closer at hand, he knew he owed a visit to Khul Bach. He hadn't spoken to the spirit since before he'd been cursed, and there was much news the old Degh spirit deserved to hear.

The palace was relatively quiet as he made his way through it; most people were still in the courtyard, on the walls, or outside the gate watching the Queen's Guard collect the corpses of the steel seekers Victor had slain. They'd promised, of course, to save the valuables for Victor to pick through. So, when he was halfway to his tower, it was easy enough to hear the rapid footsteps behind him, and he turned to see Arona and Bryn running toward him down the wide marble corridor.

He chuckled. Of course, he wouldn't be left alone for more than a few minutes. He didn't mind, though. He was pleased to have their company; they were a good deal different than an exuberant crowd of thousands, and they'd be happy to entertain themselves while he went through his correspondence. "Hey," he said as they closed the distance.

"The queen wants us to tell you dinner will be brought to your quarters, and Arona and I will be attending!" Bryn announced.

Victor laughed. "You don't need an excuse to chase me down." He smiled and held up his arm, inviting her to come close. When she did, he wrapped his arm over her shoulder, then lifted his other arm, arching his eyebrows at Arona.

She chuckled and shook her head. "Your arms are too large."

Victor growled. "Get over here!"

She relented and came close, and he draped one big arm over her shoulder, pressing her tight to his side for a minute while he squeezed Bryn. When they'd had enough, squealing for him to let up, he turned and pulled them along with him as he continued walking. "Thank you both. I'm sorry for all the worry I put you through."

Bryn was quick to object. "It wasn't your fault!"

"Even if it were, I'm your friend," Arona added, as though that were enough to explain everything. The words made Victor warm inside, and he was content to walk without speaking for a while.

When they reached his tower and stepped into the elevator, Bryn said, "I can't *believe* how you thrashed that dragon! When we saw what he did to Resh A'kel . . ."

"Pity I missed that guy. Sounds like he made an impression on you."

Arona responded before Bryn could, "He was very handsome. I think he liked Bryn—"

"You *witch*!" Bryn shoved Arona's shoulder. "I saw how you looked at him!"

Arona laughed, and though her voice still had that characteristic scratchy quality, it was a joyous, high-pitched sound that Victor couldn't remember hearing before. It made him realize just how vital his victory had been for her. Her post–Death Caster existence had centered on his time at Iron Mountain. To her, Kynna and Gloria represented a new life—one that wasn't rooted in death and the many macabre things she'd done in Vesavo's service. As Victor had languished from his curse, she'd had to keep open the possibility that this new existence would be over shortly after it had begun.

"What are you going to do with yourself now, Arona?" he asked, interrupting their playful banter as the elevator door opened.

"What do you mean?"

"I mean, you have a whole new life ahead of you. Are you going to seek out the Fae? I bet you could get a meeting with that Fae consul back on Sojourn. What was her name?"

"Consul Rexa. But, Victor, I don't want to do that. I want to stay with you! I want to help you with whatever *you're* doing next."

Victor looked from her earnest expression to Bryn's, noting how she'd gotten very quiet, too. After a second's pause, he shrugged. "We can talk about that. I'm not exactly eager to be alone." He pulled open his suite's door and added, "Now, come on! I need to have a stiff drink before I start reading these Far Scribe books."

49

CHECKING IN

While Arona and Bryn drank and celebrated the release of months of tension, Victor sipped his drink and read through his Far Scribe books. Surprisingly, the mead Arona had poured him was strong enough to affect him; she said it was from Sojourn—stuff made with ingredients chosen for their potency, designed for steel seekers and veil walkers.

She'd purchased it on the same trip she'd taken to buy his will-enhancement potions, apparently sure that they'd have something to celebrate . . . *eventually.* So he had a pleasant buzz and some warmth in his chest and face as he perused the many messages he'd missed while he'd been incapacitated in one way or another.

Luckily, it seemed Dar had been in communication with Kynna; his messages to Victor were short and straightforward, basically wishing him luck and letting him know that he'd seek vengeance if the imperial coup was successful. Victor grimaced at the idea, wondering what it would look like if Dar brought an army of veil walker allies from Sojourn to Ruhn, intent on making war with the veil walkers there. What would his punishment for the empire look like? He was glad to have helped avoid such an eventuality.

He wrote him a quick reply, letting him know of his victory. He also took the opportunity to push against the boundaries of the service he'd promised to the Spirit Master. He told him he'd picked up a new karmic debt and may need to confront it before returning to Sojourn. If he knew Dar, he had a feeling the master would see his promise to Chantico as both important to resolve and a good learning opportunity. It wasn't that Victor was certain Chantico would want his help immediately, but he wanted to be prepared for that possibility. He could *feel* his promise to her, just as he could feel she was waiting to speak to him, lingering nearby on the spirit plane.

He had updates from Rellia, Edeya, and Efanie. Rellia had made her first foray into Du's dungeon and gained two levels. She was understandably ecstatic, and it seemed the dungeon and its management had become a new obsession for her, surmounting even her drive to civilize the Free Marches. Edeya wrote him several lengthy notes about everyone on Sojourn and what they were doing. Victor found himself smiling along as he read them, and his desire to return grew stronger with each message.

She said everyone was gaining levels and enjoying life at the lake house immensely. It was almost funny how often she brought up the lake house and their fear that Dar would grow weary of their presence, but apparently, the Spirit Master hadn't been around at all. In fact, the staff hinted at rumors that the man was off-world doing research, something Dar hadn't mentioned to Victor in his messages.

Apparently, Olivia, his cousin of sorts, had been running dungeons with the three of them, and they'd all been studying weapon skills, with Lesh acting as their instructor. Victor grinned, taking a big swig of his drink, imagining the dragonkin turning Dar's lake house into a dojo for melee fighters in Sojourn. He wrote back, gushing to Edeya about how proud he was of her and letting her know, in loose terms, about his success on Ruhn. He signed off with, *"Be sure to give Lam a hug for me, tell my cousin I'll write to her soon, and make sure Lesh and Darren know that I'll have gifts for you all when I next come to Sojourn."*

Efanie, the Fae-blooded governess he'd brought from Sojourn to watch over Cora, indicated that she'd heard rumors of his condition. How that could be, Victor wasn't sure, but he had to assume Rellia had let something slip to his governor, who had then spilled the news to Efanie. "Something like that," he grunted. She was concerned about him, but he had a feeling it had a lot more to do with his duty to Cora than anything else. She wrote at length about the girls—Cora, Deyni, Chala, and others Victor didn't know—elaborating on their continued studies.

Cora was showing promise in fencing and was learning styles from both Kethelket and Efanie. Deyni, while still fascinated with taming the animals of the wilds, had been carrying her egg—the one Tes had given her—everywhere, and though it hadn't shown any outward signs of life, the little girl was certain she could feel something inside. Efanie thought perhaps she was already building a connection to the nascent drake.

More than lessons in hunting and fighting, the girls were learning academics thanks to Olivia. It seemed she was earnest about her plans for creating a school and higher education system in the Free Marches. She'd returned to the human colony, First Landing, more than once for visits and used the newly established portal to the Free Marches to visit with Rellia on the subject. Thanks to Victor's encouraging letters, it seemed the women had leveraged his governor, Gorro ap'Dommic, into building the first schoolhouse. Victor smiled at the idea, imagining the Shadeni and Naghelli children sitting in a classroom with Cora and the other kids from his village.

After he wrote back to her, letting her know how pleased he was and assuring her that he was well, he put the book aside and picked up the one he shared with Valla. He had just turned it to a new message when Bryn, stumbling drunk, tripped over the coffee table and crashed onto the couch beside him. "Oof!" she grunted, while Arona giggled.

"Arona, you didn't give her this mead, did you?" Victor held up his nearly empty glass.

She shrugged, affecting an innocent pout. "Just a sip of mine."

Victor sighed and helped Bryn sit up. "Are you all right?"

"Fine," she mumbled, but her eyes were narrowed to slits and the word sounded more like "*Frie.*" Victor chuckled and gave her shoulder a gentle shove, watching as she collapsed in slow motion onto the pillows. He pulled her feet onto the couch so she lay there, curled in a fetal position, already mostly asleep. He glared at Arona. "There goes your company, and dinner hasn't even started!"

"She'll come around; her vitality is good." Arona gestured to the book on his lap. "You have much more to read?"

"Just Valla's."

She nodded and walked toward the balcony. "I'll watch the sunset."

Victor watched her go and lean on the railing, looking toward the mountain, then off over the town where the sun was turning the sky shades of orange and red. Bryn shifted and grumbled something inarticulate, and Victor, smiling and shaking his head, read Valla's note:

Victor,

I've heard from Rellia that you've been to the dungeon you set up in the mountain a few times, but it's been weeks since then. I know things must be hectic for you, but knowing you had that curse to deal with and then being faced with months of silence again, I can't help but worry. Of course, when I feel that way, I wonder if I'm being unreasonable.

Wasn't it I who decided we needed time apart? Do I have any right to expect you to write? After our last conversation at my mother's house, I felt good about us. I felt we'd reached an understanding and that your love for me, while strained by my choices, remained. That makes this silence all the more worrisome. I don't think you would intentionally leave me to wonder your fate, and so, my mind has begun to drift down dark paths. Did that curse get the better of you, Victor? Am I writing to a ghost?

I feel powerless, as you might guess. I know you're on Ruhn, but I'm so distant from that world! I'd need to beg leave of my mentors here and then travel to Sojourn to seek passage from there. I have the funds, but . . . oh, why am I writing this? I should strike it out, but then you'd wonder what I had written. The point is, I'm feeling desperate, and I'll do what I must to learn your fate. I hope I hear from you soon. I know some patience is in order—didn't you tell me you slept for nearly six months from the last natural treasure you consumed? Perhaps you've done something similar.

I pray, to whom or what, I don't know, that I'll hear from you soon.

I love you, Victor.

Valla

Victor sighed and looked up, glancing first at Bryn, snoring away, and then at Arona, who was still leaning on the balcony, watching the clouds drift through the colorful sky. They looked like hunks of cotton candy to Victor. Shaking his head, he picked up his pen and wrote a reply:

Valla,

I'm sorry to keep you waiting. You were right; I was out of it, having consumed a potent treasure. The good news is that I beat the curse, and I've finished my work here on Ruhn. I want you to know that I'll never begrudge you the right to know what I'm doing or how I am. You know I love you, too. There's nothing that will change that. I consider you family, whether we're together or not.

There's a lot going on here at the moment, so I don't feel like I can really focus on writing you a proper letter. I wanted you to know that I'm safe and your love isn't unappreciated. I'll make time to write you a lengthier update soon. I'm sure you might be interested in the details of what happened with my curse and how things ended up here on Ruhn. All in all, it's a happy ending, though many good people lost their lives.

Stay safe, and regardless of my upcoming, lengthier letter to you, let's make plans to get together again soon. We can meet on Fanwath.

Love,

Victor

He closed the book, sent it into storage with the others, then stood, approaching the balcony doors. "Hey, Arona?"

She turned, cheeks flushed from alcohol, the glow of the sunset behind her. She looked ethereal and beautiful, and Victor wondered how he might feel about her if his heart weren't so damn busy with Valla and Tes. "Yes?"

"Um, can you give me a few minutes to commune with a, uh, spirit mentor of mine? I've got time before dinner still, yeah?"

"Yes. Kynna said she'd be along an hour or two after sunset."

Victor nodded. "Perfect. I'll be in the workshop with my vault."

"You won't lock yourself inside and disappear for half a year, will you?" she asked, her raspy voice light and teasing.

Victor laughed. "Nah, not this time."

She smiled, pointing toward Bryn. "We'll be fine, but don't miss dinner."

"I won't." Victor left her, still looking out over the balcony, and walked through his chambers to his workshop, where he'd left his vault. As he went, he thought about Valla's letter and his response. It didn't seem that long ago when they'd been living together in Sojourn, unsure about what Dar would ask of him or the future in general. It didn't seem long, yet at the same time, it felt like a hundred years. He'd been through a hell of a lot since then, and the gravity of the things he'd accomplished made them seem all the more prominent in his mind, overshadowing his past. If a year could make such a difference, what would ten or a hundred do?

He unlocked his vault, stepped inside, and found the crystal containing Khul Bach's spirit. He sat down and channeled a little Energy into it. As always, the world changed instantly, shifting onto a flat plane with angular shades of white and gray, making it feel as if he were inside a house of broken, jumbled glass shards. As usual, Khul Bach sat before him, though for a change, he didn't speak right away. His face looked almost troubled as he gazed upon Victor.

After a while, Victor cleared his throat. "Are you all right, Khul Bach?"

"You've changed so much. Has it been so long? Will my people still be there when you return to Zaafor?"

Victor chuckled, shaking his head. "It hasn't even been a year since I last spoke to you. I'm still on Ruhn, though I've just finished my task here. That's why I'm speaking to you. I wanted to give you an update on my plans."

"Only a year? And here you sit with a spirit that outweighs my own! You've grown beyond my tutelage, Victor."

"Well, that's all right. You've still lived a lot longer than I have; your experience makes you a valuable advisor, Khul Bach. That's another reason I'm here."

"Oh? Do you intend to return to Zaafor now? Will you conquer the Warlord and free my people?"

Victor smiled. "I want to, and I will, but there's another I owe a favor to, and her need may be more pressing. I don't *know* that, but I feel it"—Victor slapped his stomach—"in here."

"*Another* with a need more pressing than mine?"

Victor sighed. "As I said, I don't know. She's an ancestor of mine, and she helped me to achieve the growth you've noticed. Without her help, I might have drifted for centuries trying to figure out how to make use of a potent treasure I consumed. All the people I cared about would have died or moved on. Your people would have languished longer. Do you see why I might feel the burden of my debt to her?"

"I do. Meanwhile, it is I who bears a debt to you, not the other way around. I promised to guide and mentor you, but I did very little—certainly not worth asking you to go to war for an entire species."

"I made that promise to you regardless of any help you offered me, Khul Bach. I intend to keep it. Still, allow me to talk to my ancestor and determine the order of events. I promise you, the Warlord will feel my wrath; it just might have to wait a little longer."

Khul Bach nodded, lifting his eyebrows as his usually stern expression lightened and his lips curled into a smile. "Already, I feel you could stand against him. If he still stagnates, if he's the same . . ." He shook his head and chuckled. "I have true hope for my people again, Victor. Thank you for remembering your promise to me."

Victor assured the old spirit that he was only doing what was right, and then the two of them spent a little while catching up. Victor told him about his struggle against the curse and some of his duels, but as the conversation dragged on, he worried that he'd miss his dinner appointment with Kynna and the others. He made his excuses, promised to visit again soon, and then cut the flow of Energy to the shard, snapping himself back into reality.

As he blinked his eyes and saw the diffuse amber sunlight coming in through his open vault door, he remembered the shard's uncanny effect on time—he'd only spent an instant of real time speaking to Khul Bach. "Huh," he chuckled, suddenly a couple of hours richer.

He figured he could spend the extra time with Arona and try to get Bryn to sober up, but that pressing urgency in his gut told him he had a more productive way to spend the next hour or so. For the first time in a long while, he summoned his coyotes and as they came into the world, yipping and snarling at each other, he said, "Wake me up if anything happens." They gathered around him, lying on the vault floor or sitting just inside the door. Feeling very secure with Arona out in the parlor and his coyotes watching him more closely, Victor cast Spirit Walk.

"There you are, little brother!" Chantico said, immediately.

Victor stood up, inhaling deeply as he looked around the spirit plane. Iron Mountain soared into the cosmos not far away, and it was hard to stop staring, but he forced himself to turn his attention to Chantico. She stood not far away, her skin faintly luminescent as she regarded him with a broad smile. "Hello, Chantico."

"I've waited for you, as promised. You'll need my help to find Dark Ember—they've yet to open any of the stones your *System* has provided."

"I could feel you," Victor said. "It was like an itching in my gut, an urgency. Were you doing that on purpose?"

"No, not on purpose, though we're closely tied and my impatience might have bled through while I lingered this close to you on the spirit plane. I sensed your victory and was eager to congratulate you. Did you crush a mighty foe?"

Victor nodded. "I think so, but with what you helped me accomplish, I didn't find it that difficult."

"Good! You'll need every ounce of strength when you visit my son's world." She frowned, her red, bow-shaped lips turning downward and her eyes unfocusing as she battled some inner turmoil. "I feel so cowardly sending you off to deal with Xelhuan, but I simply can't do it. Do you understand? I feel fate connected us for this reason. You're my chance at redemption. By aiding you and convincing you to take on this burden, I can lift this weight from my spirit."

Victor nodded. "I've never had a child, though I can imagine what it's like. I don't think I could harm Deyni, for instance, even if . . . if she'd done something terrible." Victor couldn't even wrap his head around the idea. Deyni *wouldn't*.

"Thank you for trying to understand, Victor. Are you ready, then?"

Victor laughed. "No! Can't you wait a while? I have other obligations—people who want to see me, people I promised aid to before you helped—"

"Victor! I can wait a *while*, but you must understand something: My body is a universe away! It is quite difficult to linger here! My mind was adrift, lost in a millennia-long meditation, but now that you've focused me, now that you've awakened my spirit and reminded me what it is to be alive, I yearn to move on! If my cause is not urgent enough, think of the millions suffering on Dark Ember. I promise you, there is no need that is more urgent than theirs! Think of the thralls you freed during the invasion of your lands. Think of the stories they told you! Millions are suffering worse on Dark Ember even as you and I speak!"

Victor chuckled, shaking his head. "You don't have to do that. I had a feeling your request would be urgent, and I'll be ready to help you soon. I just want a little time—a few days at most." He suddenly remembered Arona's desire to come with him. "Will I be able to bring allies?"

"If they are well-versed in spirit walking, aye."

"And if they aren't?"

She frowned. "If I were present in the flesh, I could help transport your allies. As it is, if you want them to come, you'll need to open a proper gateway. You can use the *System* that holds sway in this part of the universe. Conquer one of the cities on Dark Ember and take control of the *System's* stone."

"I mean, I think I can do better than that. I have a portable teleportation array . . ."

"I think you fail to grasp the distance between Dark Ember and this part of the universe. Even a Void Master would struggle to open such a gateway. I don't mean to say it's impossible, but I think your chances of using the *System* would be much better. Still, try your array when you get there—perhaps I'm underestimating it."

"All right. So give me a few days, and I'll return to the spirit plane here. Agreed?"

"Go, then! The sooner you handle your business, the sooner we can depart!"

Victor smiled at her impatience, watching as she clenched her fists. He had to remind himself that she was a being on par with Azforath and that he owed her almost everything. That reminder helped to keep his face respectful as he nodded and again promised, "I'll be back soon." Then he cut the Energy to his Spirit Walk.

His coyotes were quick to crowd around, licking his face, and he laughed, giving them all a good pet before sending them back to the spirit plane. He still had a lot to do, and he wasn't quite sure how he was supposed to conquer a bunch of old-school veil walkers, but his outlook was good as he exited his vault and turned the key, reducing it down to a bauble he could hang around his neck.

He'd faced so many threats on his life, yet managed to come out stronger every time, that the idea of tackling some enemies whose power seemed almost unfathomable just didn't daunt him the way it might once have. Hanging the chain over his head, he clenched and unclenched his fists, nodding to himself. Then, as he stared at his heavy, powerful fist, he remembered his fight with Dro Vah. "Hey! I need to find my gauntlet!"

50

❧

THE ENEMY YOU IGNORE

Itold Draj to handle it personally. You should have all of their belongings, including Dro Vah's sword and your gauntlet, delivered tomorrow morning. Luckily, one of my Queen's Guard spotted your dismembered arm near the gates!" Empress Kynna Dar said. She was sitting close to Victor, near the head of the table, and was talking about the armor, weapons, and magical gear of the champions he'd slain outside the palace. He supposed he'd probably inadvertently destroyed some of their belongings, but what was there would be his.

"It must be a great fortune's worth of magical artifacts," Bryn said, still a little tipsy from the alcohol Arona had given her.

"Well deserved, wouldn't you say, Baroness?" Kynna asked, arching one of her perfect eyebrows.

"Um, of course! I didn't mean to imply—"

"Oh, hush." Victor chuckled. "You're fine. As for the equipment being delivered here, thank you, Kynna."

"You're most welcome. I knew you didn't want to be out there, surrounded by a throng of adoring citizens while you sifted through all those remains. I appreciate you spending the time with us that you did—you've attained folk hero status among our people. Even so, I'd love to invite you to a state dinner at the capital. I intend to invite representatives from every nation. I think it will—"

Victor held up a hand. "I can't promise that's going to happen, Kynna. I have much on my plate"—he shoved the near-empty plate in front of him back a few inches, chuckling—"that I need to see to. There are people I need to meet with and pressing matters I need to attend." They'd been eating for a while, and thus far everyone had avoided the specter looming over the conversation: What would Victor do now that his quest to deliver Kynna the empire was done?

"Can you tell me about any of that? I'd so hoped that you'd fall in love with this world—that you'd want to spend more of your life here." Her words were so candid and sincere that Victor found himself wanting to comfort her. She leaned closer as she spoke, and he had the distinct impression that she'd utterly blocked out the fact that Bryn and Arona were sitting across the table from her.

He smiled and in a softer, less firm voice, said, "I *do* love things about this world. I've grown very fond of Iron Mountain, in particular, and the people here." He glanced at Bryn, smiling as he caught her eye and saw the glimmer of moisture gathering there. "I'll most definitely want to spend time here now and then, perhaps months or years, but there are other places and people I care about, too. There are other *worlds* I want to visit, worlds I want to *discover*. I'm not ready to settle down in one place. I'm not sure I ever will be."

Kynna nodded, pressing her lips together as she cleared her throat and looked down briefly. Was she tearing up, too? Victor hastily tried to move the conversation forward. "When I nearly lost the battle with my curse—I mean, when I locked myself in my vault, I spent time communing with one of my living ancestors."

Kynna looked up, eyes wide, suddenly very interested. He could understand why; she'd been spending time corresponding with her own living ancestor, Ranish Dar. "You did? Have you done so before?"

"Yeah, through visions of one sort or another, but I'd always thought she'd moved on. I thought she was one of my ancestors who'd passed through the veil. It turns out, she's not. She's still in this universe, though very distant from here. She's been trying to do something—ascend, cross the veil, I don't know exactly what—but there's something here holding her back. She has a karmic debt, a weight on her spirit, and she's asked me to help her resolve it."

"Do you owe her a debt?" Arona asked, suddenly more interested in the conversation.

Victor nodded. "She guided me through my struggles. More than that, she's my ancestor, and she's gifted me power in the past—saved my life."

"Well, as I know you, Victor," Bryn said and, emboldened by her tipsiness, leaned forward to grasp Victor's hand in hers, "you'd help her without any sort of debt."

Victor grinned and squeezed her hand. "You're probably right." He looked into her brown eyes, still glistening from unshed tears. "Remember how grouchy you were when we first met?" She snorted and, embarrassed, pulled her hand back, hiding her face in her napkin as she pretended to wipe her nose.

"What must you do for this ancestor of yours?" Kynna asked. "How can I help?"

Victor shook his head, idly fidgeting with his fork, tapping it on the side of his plate. "You can't help. I mean, at least not right away. The world where I must go is very distant—beyond the reach of most who can create gateways, and sealed off from the System's teleportation network. My ancestor will guide me there through the spirit plane."

"But Victor—" Arona started to say, but he held up a hand.

"Once I'm there, I'll find a way to connect to this part of the universe. My ancestor suggested conquering one of the cities and taking control of the System Stone. I think that should be doable." He locked eyes with Arona. "I don't think it will take too long, and I promise I won't forget about you. We'll be able to communicate via Far Scribe books." He said the last to the whole table, including Bryn and Kynna.

"If I were still a Death Caster, I could likely follow you through the spirit plane. As I am now . . ." Arona shook her head, trailing off.

"Your Energy isn't right for it. I know. Don't worry, because your Energy is perfect for what we must accomplish there—it's an entire world ruled by Death Casters."

Kynna clicked her tongue. "You're so sure you can conquer a city alone?"

Victor shrugged. "Maybe I could, but I don't intend to. I'll build an army there. Dark Ember is inhabited by human thralls, enslaved by their undead masters. I know this because I've fought some of their armies on Fanwath when the System allowed them to invade."

"As you slay their masters, you think they'll come to fight for you?" Arona asked.

"Yeah, I'm pretty sure they will."

She didn't argue. Instead, she turned to Kynna. "I'd be happy to stay here with you while Victor secures a foothold on this undead world. I could help you vet and train some proper advisors."

Kynna's smile returned, and she leaned across the table to take Arona's much smaller hand in hers. "Would you, truly? It goes without saying that your presence and assistance would be most welcome—*cherished*!"

Victor sat back and inhaled deeply, breathing out slowly, sending the tension he'd felt building since his discussion with Chantico out with his breath. He'd wondered how Kynna would take his departure. He'd feared Arona would be hurt or feel lost if he left without her. She wasn't ready to go back to Sojourn yet, after all. It was apparent, however, that he should have given her more credit. She'd lived a long life already and had a resourceful outlook. She'd be good for Kynna, too. No doubt there were many snakes lying in the grass, waiting for the opportunity to take advantage of her kindness.

He figured he'd spend a day more on Ruhn, sorting out his business, then he'd visit Sojourn and shower some gifts upon his friends there. Why not? He had the artifacts and magical equipment of nearly thirty steel seekers coming his way. Maybe he'd ask Dar for a bit of advice about his "mantle" while he was there. After that, he'd take a quick trip to Fanwath to check in, and then it would be back to Ruhn to meet with Chantico and travel to Dark Ember. It meant a lot of traveling in just a few days, but it would be easily done with his teleportation array.

Nodding, listening to the three women at the table speaking about near-term plans, he felt very content and lucky. He'd made some good friends on Ruhn and had many more waiting on other worlds. More importantly, he had the means to visit and support them all. He didn't know how long Chantico's quest would take, but it was good to know the people he cared about would be all right while he was gone.

Of course, he still had his promise to Khul Bach to fulfill, but that shouldn't be a big deal. He was already, in his estimation, on par with the Warlord. Surely, conquering some Death Caster veil walkers would only make his eventual run-in with the man all the easier. He still had a dragon heart to eat once he had a little time to spare. Despite the large meal he'd just eaten, his stomach rumbled at the thought. Chuckling, and as if to confirm his confidence was well-placed, Victor sipped his wine and read through his status sheet again:

Status			
Name:	Victor Sandoval		
Race:	Nascent Primordial Titan: Legendary 5		
Mantle:	Unforged		
Level:	100		
Breath Core:	Primordial Class: Epic 4		
Core:	Spirit Class: Legendary 5		
Breath Core Affinity:	Abyssal Magma: 9; Nullfrost: 9	Breath Core Energy:	67000/67000
Energy Affinity:	Hope 9.4, Fear 9.4, Rage 9.1, Unattuned 3.1	Energy:	218056/218056
Strength:	1096 (1196)	Vitality:	1102
Dexterity:	380 (585)	Agility:	403 (608)
Intelligence:	512	Will:	1015
Points Available:	0		

Titles & Feats:	Titanic Rage, Ancestral Bond, Flame-Touched, Greater Titanic Constitution, Titanic Presence, Desperate Grace, Unyielding Challenger, Elder Magic, Born of Terror, Battlefield Awareness, Battlefield Presence, Aura of Command, Legendary Titan, Mountain's Resilience, Primordial Behemoth's Regeneration, Blood Supremacy, Primordial Wyrm's Fervor, Peerless Warborn Mind, Flight of the Lava King, Presence of the Tyrant, Void-Forged

Skills:	
System Language Integration	Not Upgradeable
Spirit Core Cultivation Drill	Epic
Breath Core Cultivation Drill	Advanced
Cooking	Basic
Animal Taming	Basic
Unarmed Combat	Basic
Knife Mastery	Basic
Spear Mastery	Advanced
Bludgeon Mastery	Improved
Axe Mastery	Epic
Breath Weapon Mastery	Improved
Tactical Mastery	Basic
Grappling	Advanced
Sovereign Will	Epic
Titanic Leap	Improved
Aura Veil	Epic
Spells:	
Iron Berserk	Epic
Channel Spirit	Improved
Prismatic Illumination	Epic
Project Spirit	Improved

Spirit Walk	Advanced
Tether Spirit	Basic
Abyssal Tyrant	Epic
Imbue Spirit	Improved
Honor the Spirits	Improved
Alter Self	Improved
Velocity Mantle	Epic
Wild Totem	Advanced
Impart Nightmare	Improved
Guardian's Rescue	Epic
Volcanic Fury	Improved
Wake the Earth	Basic
Roots of the Angry Mountain	Advanced
Greater Spirit Binding	Advanced
Voice of the Angry Earth	Basic
Locate Ally	Basic
Core Domain	Epic
Glacial Wrath	Epic
Tactical Reposition	Basic
Standard of the Last Light	Epic
Dread Imperative	Epic
Maw of the Broken Will	Legendary

Thoargh, Warlord of Zaafor, slid out of bed, careful to keep his pearlescent white-feathered wings from brushing the naked flesh of the woman lying there. She was lovely, he thought, running his eye over her crimson flesh, to the downy black feathers of her own wings. A *Ridonne*, she called herself, and one of the mightiest from her world—his agents had assured him. He padded over to the window and peered out at the glorious, starlit city.

"*Sojourn*," he whispered, tracing the crystalline towers with his gaze, admiring how the lights within gave each one an iridescent sheen in the darkness. What a place! He supposed he owed that dragon witch some thanks. The way she'd humiliated him, the way she'd effortlessly tossed his strongest men aside— it had opened his eyes to the possibilities beyond his singular backwater world.

Without her interference, he wouldn't have learned of "steel seekers" and "veil walkers." He wouldn't have discovered that he was "steel bound" and had been for centuries. Coming to Sojourn, though, finding a mentor in that powerful, if foolish, man, Consul Yon, had opened new doors for his advancement. Thoargh had finally moved beyond the stagnation that had driven him mad with vexation.

Zaafor was still there, awaiting his return, but the more he learned, the more power he grasped, the less he cared. No, with the things Yon taught him, he'd truly unlocked the potential of the many bloodlines he'd stolen. He'd built a mantle that not only incorporated what he'd mastered as a warlord, but so much more besides! Again, he glanced at the sleeping woman on his bed.

He concentrated for a moment, trying to remember her name. "*Vessa-dak,*" he whispered, letting his mouth get a feel for the consonants and vowels. What had she said? A world, peerless in its beauty, kept innocent and ripe? Her people held power there, though their control was waning; the citizens, in her words, needed to be reminded why the Ridonne ruled over them. Naturally, Thoargh found the concept intriguing. Was it not similar to what he'd done with Zaafor? It wasn't why he'd seduced her, however.

No, he'd taken an interest in her and her people when he'd learned that the world she called home was home to another. Thoargh felt his ire stirring and pushed it down lest his aura disturb his guest. "*Victor,*" he hissed. That bastard had used his hospitality. He'd killed his people. He'd *stolen* from him and fled, leaving his dragon guardian to cover his tracks. Well, his pet bitch couldn't protect an entire world, could she? No, if Victor wanted to hide from his wrath, then those he cared for would have to pay the price.

Thoargh smiled, looking out over the city again. He felt a deep well of satisfaction in his gut. When it came to his vengeance, it was no longer a matter of *how,* but simply of *when.* Was he ready yet? Could he still learn more here? If that dragon *did* happen to come calling, wouldn't it feel good to taste her blood? If he couldn't face her alone, perhaps some of his new allies would like to join the fun. He chuckled, thinking of the many unsavory yet disturbingly powerful people he'd made acquaintances with on Sojourn. How many of them might profit from the destruction of a mighty dragon?

He'd bide his time. He'd finish his mantle and gather his allies. He'd use his budding connections to the Ridonne to facilitate the invasion, and then deliver his vengeance. Smiling, he shifted his vision, accessing one of his bloodlines, the *Kythana,* which enhanced the colors of the night, tinting things toward violet and pulling out the details from the otherwise muted palette. The city went from beautiful to garish, and he grinned, exposing his fangs, pleased by his corruption of it.

ABOUT THE AUTHOR

Plum Parrot is the pen name of author Miles Gallup, who grew up in Southern Arizona and spent much of his youth wandering around the Sonoran Desert, hunting imaginary monsters and building forts. He studied creative writing at the University of Arizona and, for a number of years, attempted to teach middle schoolers to love literature and write their own stories. If he's not spending time with his dog, you can find Gallup writing, reading his favorite authors, or playing *D&D* with friends and family.

RESPAWN YOUR CURIOSITY

follow us on our socials

podiumentertainment.com

@podiumentertainment

/podiumentertainment

@podium_ent

@podiumentertainment